Praise for *The End*

'Simon Edge wears his anger remarkably lightly as he skewers the shocking state of the trans rights row with some nifty, often snort-inducingly funny satire'
The Times

'This sparkling little comic novel is more than playful: it's a satire of Swiftian ferocity, a thinly veiled parody of a prevailing madness of the hour'
Matthew Parris

'In between punching the air and shouting "yes!", I laughed so hard I nearly fell in my cauldron. A masterpiece'
Julie Bindel

'A satire that skewers the insanity of gender-identity ideology with the wit and brilliance of a modern-day Swift'
Helen Joyce, author of *Trans: When Ideology Meets Reality*

'A biting satire'
Andrew Doyle

'A bracingly sharp satire on the sleep of reason and the tyranny of twaddle. Simon Edge reveals how extraordinary delusions have the power to captivate us – until, one by one, we start coming to our senses'
Francis Wheen

'Inspired… Edge has glorious, madcap fun…doing what Aristophanes thought poets should do in circumstances like these: save the city from itself. He holds social foibles and cod science up to ridicule with grace, wit and charm'
Helen Dale, The Critic

'A highly-entertaining satire about ideology, social media manipulation, and lobbying fiefdoms that have overstayed their welcome. This is *Animal Farm* for the era of gender lunacy, with jokes'
Jane Harris

'This witty author mixes history with a hilarious spoof of identity politics, virtue signalling, cancel culture and Twitter pile-ons'
Saga Magazine

'A clever satire on the folly that ensues when a once-respected charity abandons principle and reason'
Joanna Cherry MP

'I've loved every novel by Simon Edge but this one's probably the best to date. Very clever, very pertinent – most importantly, funny and very humane'
Julia Llewellyn Smith

'Very, very funny. It's also way too convincing as a horror story – a completely believable account of how this kind of ideology could seep into great institutions. And possibly, in another form, did'
Gillian Philip

'Well-crafted, humane and engaging. More than a clever jab at trans ideology, it's a modern morality tale charting one man's descent into lies, and a warning about the vulnerability of the liberal values upon which modern society rests'
Jo Bartosch, Lesbian & Gay News

'Without mercy, this merry romp punctures the idiocy that would turn language and good sense upside down and try to divide us all into either true believers or bigots'
Simon Fanshawe

Simon Edge read philosophy at Cambridge and was editor of the revered London paper *Capital Gay* before becoming a gossip columnist on the *Evening Standard* and then, for many years, a feature writer on the *Daily Express*. He is the author of five previous novels, including *The Hopkins Conundrum* and *The End of the World is Flat*. He was married to Ezio Alessandroni, who died of cancer in 2017. He lives in Suffolk.

IN
THE
BEGINNING

SIMON EDGE

Lightning Books

Published in 2023
by Lightning Books Ltd
Imprint of Eye Books Ltd
29A Barrow Street
Much Wenlock
Shropshire
TF13 6EN

www.lightning-books.com

Cover by Ifan Bates
Typeset in Bembo, Academy Engraved and Helvetica Neue

Google is the trademark of Google LLC
Twitter is the trademark of Twitter, Inc

British Library Cataloguing in Publication Data
A catalogue record for this book is available from the British Library.

ISBN: 9781785633546

Printed and bound in the UK on FSC® certified paper in line with our continuing commitment to ethical business practices, sustainability and the environment.
For further information see faber.co.uk/environmental-policy

What [Mr Bryan] wants is that his ideas, his interpretations
and beliefs should be made mandatory.
When Mr Darrow talks of bigotry he talks of that.
Bigotry seeks to make opinions and beliefs mandatory
Chicago Tribune on the Scopes Monkey Trial, 17 July 1925

Dedicated to everyone who has taken a risk to resist the crazy, and especially to 'Tara', 'Helen', 'Rita' and 'Emily'

BEFORE THE BEGINNING

Polly arrived at the library on the stroke of seven o'clock and slid into her usual seat in the meeting room upstairs, just as Elias, the teacher, cleared his throat and stood up to address the class.

'This evening I'd like to do another spontaneous writing exercise,' he said. 'Here and now. Each of you should work on your own, individually. And for the subject, I'd like you to devise a creation myth.'

'A what?' whispered Harmony, an older woman, who always sat near Polly at the rear of the room and often struggled to hear what Elias said.

'A creation myth,' their teacher repeated, louder. 'Is everyone clear what I mean by that?'

A few heads nodded, but not all. Elias beamed at his students. He did that a lot, Polly had noticed. Perhaps it was a cover for nervousness.

'I mean an origin story for the world around us,' he said. 'All religions have them, don't they? In the Christian tradition, God created heaven and earth in six days, rested on the seventh, then he created Adam in the Garden of Eden, and Eve from Adam's rib; after that came Cain and Abel, Noah's Ark, yada yada yada. The Ancient Greeks believed that three primordial deities sprang forth out of chaos and gave birth to all the other gods. In Africa and Asia there were all kinds of other myths, and so on. Right?'

'Right,' someone said.

'So I'd like you to write your own. Some explanation for how the world around us came into existence. It can be as off-the-wall as you like. Really let your imagination fly.'

Sophie, who sat near the front and always took everything literally, raised her hand. 'Can we do the Big Bang?'

True to form, Elias beamed, even though he obviously thought it was a stupid idea. 'You can do whatever you like. Try and make it creative, though. This isn't a physics class. We're doing what it says on the tin tonight. Creative writing about creation.'

Someone obliged him by laughing, but not Polly. She wanted to raise her hand and ask a question. *What are we going to learn from this?* That sounded harsh but, six weeks into this course, she was beginning to think Elias wasn't a very good teacher. After all, this wasn't a proper college. Just an evening class run by the borough. And when she'd googled 'Elias Vasiliou' all she could find was a self-published collection of short stories that had just two reviews on Amazon, both of them three stars. Polly was by no means convinced this guy was qualified to run a creative writing course.

'Is everybody clear?' Elias was saying. 'Good. In that case, off you go. You've got forty minutes, and then at the end we'll read a couple of them out, so we can critique them.'

All the heads went down. Polly glowered at the exercise pad in front of her. For the moment, all she could think of was Elias' lesson plan. *Make them write something: 40 mins.* Brilliant for him; only another hour or so to fill at the end. She sighed and tried to focus. Since she had paid for this course in advance, she might as well enter into the spirit. But, as she doodled on her pad, then set down her pen, she couldn't help seething, silently. This teacher's main aim in these sessions was apparently to be as upbeat as possible. He encouraged every member of their group of would-be writers with elaborate praise, whether they deserved it or not. That was all well and good, she thought, because who didn't need their ego boosting? But Elias didn't seem to know the difference between good work and bad. And the writing exercises he set were often dull.

This assignment, for instance, just seemed stupid. What was the point in stories that were obviously wrong? Sure, primitive people had to make sense of the world around them, and the stories they told themselves made sense in the absence of anything better. But to Polly, such tales had no function in the modern world. For starters, wasn't putting naivety on a pedestal a bit patronising? And pretending to write in the same way was doubly so: like grown adults trying to paint in the manner of small children, with splodgy lines and no sense of perspective. What was the point?

She felt like saying something, speaking up, making some objection. But instead, she said nothing. She didn't want to be the troublemaker, the class whinger. She had already tested the waters with a couple of her fellow students, asking cautiously after class what they thought of their teacher, but they'd all said he was great, so there was probably no mileage in moaning out loud. She might as well just do this silly exercise. She sighed, picked up her pen once more, and began to write. Actually, once she started, it wasn't so bad. She wrote one line and then the next, and ended up becoming so absorbed in the world she was creating that she lost all track of time and jumped when Elias called out: 'That's it. All done? Just finish the sentence you're writing. Don't worry; it doesn't matter if you haven't got to the end. This is mainly an exercise in letting your creative juices flow. It's about casting inhibition aside.'

And killing time so you don't have to do any teaching.

Polly dropped her pen on the desk, and looked around at the other students, but nobody returned her gaze. Harmony was still scribbling frantically. Sophie scored something out on her notepad and then went back to examining her split ends.

'Now,' said Elias. 'Who'd like to read their work to the group? Polly? We haven't heard from you for a while.'

She groaned inwardly. She dreaded being put on the spot at the best of times, but today more than ever. She had written fast and covered several sides of paper, but she was pretty sure it was cringe-worthy.

'It's very scrappy,' she mumbled.

Elias beamed at her. 'That's fine. Nobody expects it to be polished.'

She considered saying she couldn't read her own handwriting, but he would never believe her. In the absence of any other visible escape route, she began to read: 'In the beginning, there were only the gods. There was an–'

'Sorry to interrupt, Polly.' It was Elias again. 'Can you speak up a bit so everyone can hear?'

Raising her voice, and scarcely bothering to conceal the irritation from it, she resumed: 'In the beginning, there were only the gods. There was an ancient father of the heavens, and an equally ancient mother, and they were tired, even at the dawn of time, so they tended mainly to nap. That left a large, sprawling family of siblings, doing all the things that messy families do: bickering, wrangling, nursing grievances and pursuing rivalries, while deep down depending entirely on each other. Their names were long, complicated and hard for mortals to pronounce, so I will tell you about just one of them, whose name, Ctat…'

Polly stumbled; if she'd known she had to read this nonsense aloud, she'd have chosen something simpler.

'Ctatp… Ctatpeshirahi was no less of a mouthful than those of her brothers and sisters. She was known as the potter goddess, because she spent all day turning clay on a wheel, throwing goblets and bowls that none of the other gods ever admired or wanted to use, because they were an entitled bunch with no eye for ceramics. So one day Ctatpeshirahi…'

She was getting the hang of it now, having resolved to leave the 'C' silent.

'…decided she wanted to make something more ambitious than pots. She set about making a clay sphere. She smoothed the sides, proud of her neat finish, then started to shape her globe, pinching up peaks and scooping out troughs so that every spot on the surface was different. After many hours she was pleased with what she had done, and she offered it to her brothers and sisters to admire. They, true to form, showed no interest at all, which upset Ctatpeshirahi.

'She brooded for a while, then came to a decision: if her fellow gods didn't appreciate this beautiful world she had created, then she would populate it with beasts and fowl and fish, each in their domain, and *they* would enjoy it. She looked around for more materials, but she had used up all her clay. This made her despondent at first but then she had a brainwave: she would make these living creatures from her own living body. From the clippings of her fingernails she made the beasts. From the clippings of her toenails she made the fowl. From a strand of her hair she made the fish. And to lord it over these creatures, she made woman, from a drop of her menstrual blood.

'But woman could not walk the earth alone, because she was mortal and must reproduce if her race were to continue. The goddess pondered this for a moment, then she squatted on a patch of sand to make water. She picked up a clod of this dampened ground and fashioned from it the form of a man, to serve and to fertilise the woman. Then she rubbed her hands together to make fire, and last of all she used spit from her mouth to make the oceans, and thus – nine thousand, nine hundred and ninety-nine years ago – the world was born.'

Relieved to have reached the end, she looked up at Elias. 'That's it.'

'Thank you, Polly,' said their teacher, putting his hands together in a namaste sign. His voice had dropped to a whisper. 'Reactions? Yes, Marieke?'

'Oh…like…wow.'

Polly risked a glance at Marieke from the corner of her eye. A vocal Dutch woman with frighteningly good English, Marieke was the star of the class. She was surely taking the mick. But her eyes shone.

'That was amazing,' she said. 'So imaginative. I love that you turned the patriarchy on its head.'

Other people nodded.

'I loved the toenail clippings. And the squatting to make water,' said Shantelle, who was tall and wide and had an infectious cackle. 'That really cracked me up.'

'Right? Puts us in our place, eh, Freddie?' said Elias.

Freddie, fleshy, with a clammy pallor, was the only other man in the room. He shifted uncomfortably from one buttock to the other as attention turned his way, but then it moved on and someone else added their own gush.

'I really liked the squabbling gods and goddesses. You know, like an actual family? And how did you come up with that amazing name? It sounds, I don't know, Aztec or something?'

Polly was amazed they were so impressed with all her cheesiest touches. Her unsayable jumble of letters was actually an anagram, but they didn't need to know that.

Once they had all finally said their piece, there remained time for three others to read their stories out. Each was shorter than Polly's and, as far as she could tell, almost as bad. She really hated this hippie-dippy New Age crap they had all managed to churn out.

At the end of the class, as everyone handed their work in and filed out of the room, Elias took her aside.

'That really was a wonderful piece of writing, Polly. By far the best thing you've done here.' He dropped his voice lest the last few stragglers should overhear. 'Or that anyone has done, to be honest. You should be proud.'

Polly reddened, which he would doubtless take as a blush of modesty. In fact she was thinking of the assignments she had laboured over at home, such as her angry comic riff on the traffic jams all round the north of the borough, caused by the diversions for the Olympics. Genuinely proud of that, she was more convinced than ever that Elias didn't know what he was talking about.

Oblivious to what she was thinking, he carried on in the same confidential tone. 'I've been asked to put the best work from the course on the library website when we get to the end of the year. Just two or three pieces. I want this to be one of them.'

'Really?' Her inner cringe returned. 'Maybe I can work on it some more so that–'

He shook his head to cut her off. 'Don't change a word. It's perfect as it is.' He patted the sheaf of papers in his hand, which included her own scrawl.

'Don't you at least want me to type it up?'

'No, don't worry about that. It won't take me long to input. I'll enjoy doing it.'

Polly continued to frown. 'You won't use my name, though, will you?'

He stared at her in surprise. 'Why ever not? You're a very creative person, Polly. You mustn't be modest about your work.'

'No, honestly,' she said, her resolve hardening. 'There are, well, reasons why… It's personal and I'd rather not go into detail, but I try hard to keep my name off the internet.' Let him believe she was being stalked, if he wanted, or in witness protection. That was nonsense, but she was adamant: she would not be identified as the author of work she hated.

He pursed his lips. 'Got it. We'll make you anonymous. And well done again.'

Polly turned away so he couldn't see her eye-roll.

As she headed downstairs, she wondered for a moment if the class were right and she really had written something of value. Then she reminded herself that the simplest explanation was usually the best: no one in the group was any good, even Marieke, and they were all fools to put any faith in Elias.

By the time she emerged into the warm evening, she knew she wouldn't come back for the rest of the course. And she would rather stick pins in her eyeballs than ever look for her own creation myth on the library website.

Maria Gonzales PhD @nature_whisperer
Indigenous knowledge is science
RT 2.3 L 8.2K

Ludwig Snittgenstein @ludwigsnittgenstein
Replying to @nature_whisperer
Sloganeering strikes again. LMFAO
RT 20 L 86

Dr Dale Welby √ @LabcoatDale
Replying to @nature_whisperer
Science is just a truth-finding process. If a piece of
'indigenous knowledge' was generated and tested using
scientific methods, it's science. If not, it isn't
RT 238 L 1.3K

Ibn Sina @TheRealAvicenna
Replying to @LabcoatDale
Dale, you realize a bunch of crazy do-gooders will try to
cancel you now?
RT 20 L 86

Sally Jenkinson @saljenk07342
Replying to @LabcoatDale
Wow, Dale is racist?
RT 7 L 53

Ibn Sina @TheRealAvicenna
Replying to @saljenk07342
Literally lol
RT 1 L 25

Sadie @sadie93ozumvjfs
Replying to @LabcoatDale
Dude, what are you even a doctor of? I bet you have a PhD
in like history or poetry
RT 2 L 13

Benny Boy @bennyforyourthoughts
Replying to @sadie93ozumvjfs
Maybe the clue is in Dale's handle? You know, LAB coat?
As in laboratory? Just a thought…
RT 4 L 26

Sadie blocked **Benny Boy**

Mojave Medic @mojave_medic
Replying to @Labcoat Dale
There are so many white men on here just blatantly
assuming that Indigenous knowledge = ignorance. (Psst!
Bro, your racism is hanging out)
RT 25 L 377

Ibn Sina @TheRealAvicenna
Replying to @mojave_medic
You know that's the opposite of what Dale said? He said
pieces of indigenous knowledge developed in a scientific
way – ie through observation and testing – are totally
science
RT 9 L 43

Mojave Medic @mojave_medic
Replying to @TheRealAvicenna
And who gets to define 'scientific way'? Don't tell me! White men like Dale, of course
RT 49 L 90

Ibn Sina @TheRealAvicenna
Replying to @mojave_medic
Or…anyone who understands the meaning of the word 'science'
RT 1 L 21

Don Perignon @fizzyandexpensive
Replying to @TheRealAvicenna
You know Dale's a woman of colour, right?
RT 95 L 642

Ibn Sina @TheRealAvicenna
Replying to @fizzyandexpensive and @LabcoatDale
Sorry Dale. I called you 'he'. Huge apologies for the sexist assumption. My bad
RT 7 L 70

Sadie @sadie93ozumvjfs
Replying to @TheRealAvicenna
Educate yourself, dummy. LMFAO
RT 0 L 5

Dr Dale Welby √ @LabcoatDale
Replying to @TheRealAvicenna
No worries. Treat it as a lesson on the difference between assertion and knowledge
RT 17 L 84

Ibn Sina @TheRealAvicenna
Replying to @LabcoatDale
Ha! I could have tested my hypothesis – that you were a dude – by googling you, right?
RT 2 L 11

Dr Dale Welby √ @LabcoatDale
Replying to @TheRealAvicenna
You got it!
RT 3 L 33

Ibn Sina @TheRealAvicenna
Replying to @LabcoatDale
Are you listening, @mojave_medic? You may learn something about scientific method
RT 15 L 58

Mojave Medic blocked **Ibn Sina**

Colin Gillett @laziestcolin
Replying to @nature_whisperer
What is indigenous knowledge?
RT 1 L 17

1

Tara Farrier closed the door of her flat for the last time, pulling it hard towards her to be able to turn the key, and descended the two flights of stairs to her landlord's apartment on the ground floor of the dilapidated building. A smell of frying onions hung in the stairwell. It was not yet ten o'clock but Badiya, her landlord's wife, had evidently made a start on lunch.

The door of the lower apartment opened a crack before she had a chance to knock, revealing the impossibly wide, moss-green eyes of four-year-old Hassan.

'*Sabah al-kheir*,' said Tara, smiling down at him.

'*Sabah an-nour*,' whispered the boy shyly, the ritual response to the morning greeting.

'Is your father in, sweetie?' Tara continued, still in Arabic. It was technically her mother tongue and, after seven years here in Yemen, she spoke it as naturally as English.

Hassan shook his head solemnly.

Above his head, two more eyes appeared, peering warily out. Once she had satisfied herself that Tara was alone, Hassan's mother opened the door properly. She wore a full-length black abaya that hid the contours of her body, her face framed by a matching scarf. She held the door open with her left hand while cradling an eight-month baby – her fifth child, and unlikely to be her last – in the crook of her right arm.

She smiled. 'Come in,' she said, reaching out to try to pull Tara over the threshold.

But Tara didn't have time. 'Thank you, I can't.'

'Come in. Drink a cup of coffee.'

'Thank you, I've already drunk one.'

'Come in,' urged Badiya a third time, but without much hope.

This, like the pairing of the greeting and response for 'good morning', was part of the ritual. Newcomers to these parts were always thrown by it, accepting the first invitation without realising it was bad form to do so until you'd been asked three times.

'I'm sorry, my sister,' said Tara. 'I have to get to the airport.'

'What time is your flight?'

'Two and a half hours from now, God willing.' *In sha' allah.* That was another lesson she had learned early in her time in the Arab world: with any question about the future, the will of God – even one in whom Tara had never believed – must always be invoked. Are you going to the market this afternoon? *In sha' allah.* Are you seeing your foreigner friends tomorrow? *In sha' allah.* After a while it became second nature and Tara had no cause to object, because who in this benighted country could say anything for certain about the future? Especially in matters concerning Aden's battered airport, a casualty of the civil war, and only just back in operation after three years of enforced closure. Even now, no more than six flights arrived and departed every week. Any traveller who thought they could get off the ground without divine assistance or a massive chunk of luck was in for a rude awakening.

'But two and a half hours is long and the airport is very near. You have time.'

Tara raised her chin and clicked her tongue, emphasising her refusal; these physical gestures were as much a part of the language as the words. 'There are controls. Passport, luggage, all these things. It takes time. And perhaps there will be a checkpoint on the road.'

Badiya shrugged, unconvinced.

But Tara meant it. With so few routes out of the country, she couldn't afford to leave anything to chance. 'Here's my key,' she said. 'Will you give it to Ahmad? Say goodbye to him for me, and to the other children. Thank you all for everything in these past few years.'

Tears rolled down Badiya's cheeks now, and the two women hugged.

'Now I've started too,' sniffed Tara, laughing at herself as she mopped her eyes with the back of her sleeve. She'd been saying her goodbyes all week and each one was harder than the last. But she was doing the right thing, she reminded herself, as she kissed Badiya on both cheeks and waved at Hassan from the little path that led to the street.

Mansour, her driver for most of the past seven years, was waiting beside his dusty, battered Hilux, wearing his customary wrap-around sarong – known as a *futa* in this part of the world

– and with his chequered keffiyeh piled on his head. He had already stowed her luggage in the pick-up's rear section.

'Ready, madam?'

She had tried to talk him out of such formality, but dropping it clearly made him uncomfortable, so she'd given up trying.

'As ready as I'll ever be,' she sighed, climbing into the back seat. Of all her friends in this country, she probably had the greatest affection for this under-educated but smart and gentle man with whom she had spent so many hours on the road. This last parting would be the toughest.

With Umm Kulthum wailing plaintively on the car's music system, the vehicle pulled out in the direction of Marine Drive and the airport. 'Why do you have to go?' Mansour's eyes in the rear-view mirror looked tired and sad.

They'd had this conversation many times since she'd broken the news.

'You know why, my brother. I'm next to useless here. Back in England, perhaps I can advocate for an end to the bombings and the blockades. Maybe I won't succeed, but I have to try.'

They passed under the portrait of the city's former governor, assassinated in the first year of the war. Traffic on the dual carriageway was light. Fuel shortages had forced most petrol vehicles off the road. A small boy on an even smaller bicycle careened alarmingly in front of them, waving his hand dismissively as Mansour honked his horn.

'How many hours to London?' Mansour asked.

'Too many. First I have to go to Cairo, which takes three and a half hours, then another five to London, with a long wait in between. Two hours, I think. How many is that?'

'Very many. But when you arrive, you will see your children.' He smiled encouragement, revealing teeth stained the colour of teak. She had been shocked at first to see the dental damage wrought by daily qat chewing, but now she barely noticed.

'And I'll see my children. Very true.'

Of course she saw them regularly on Zype, whenever the internet was working. But it was two years since she had seen Laila and Sammy – both now adults, not children – in the flesh. Back then, she had made the twelve-hour journey across the empty desert to Seiyoun, which was the country's only functioning airport at the time, and hopped over to Djibouti, then to Paris and London. At least today's flight would be more straightforward. *In sha' allah.*

'They will be so happy to see you,' said Mansour.

Tara laughed, because people in this part of the world had no idea how casual an English family could be. 'It will be lovely to see them, but they're both very busy with their jobs.'

The Hilux had arrived at the cluster of oil drums that marked the checkpoint at the perimeter of the airport. In the distance, Tara could see the huge hole blasted out of the wall of the arrivals terminal, a grim reminder of the mortar attack two years earlier on a plane carrying an entire cabinet-in-exile. She scrabbled in her bag for her passport, ready to show the teenage soldier now peering into the back of the car.

Mansour shrugged, as the teenager returned the document and waved them on. 'Never mind. You will also be busy with your work, no?'

'*In sha' allah,*' said Tara.

Of course he was right. Going home was an upheaval, and her heart ached at having to leave this ramshackle, wounded, dysfunctional place. But she intended to plunge into her new job, and to make a difference, because that was what mattered.

2

As the plane began its approach to Heathrow, Tara removed the headscarf she had worn as second nature in Yemen. All around her, Arab women were doing the same. Boarding the flight in Cairo, they had all been draped in shapeless abayas, with their hair covered, and some of them veiled. But one by one they had made their way to the lavatory and returned in jeans, tight tops and lipstick. It was part of the ritual of visiting the West. No wonder they looked so excited.

Tara was excited now too. Traumatic as it had been to uproot from the place she'd called home these past seven years, she had plenty to look forward to on her return home – starting at the airport, where Laila had promised to meet her. For all Tara's own earlier cynicism, Mansour was right: her children did seem pleased to have her coming back to them. It took forever to get through arrivals and retrieve her luggage, but there her daughter was, waving at the gate.

'*Hamdillah as-salama*,' said Laila as they hugged. *Thank God for your safe arrival.* She, more than her brother, had a smattering of Arabic from childhood and she knew all the ritual phrases.

'*Allah yisalmik*,' laughed Tara, in the obligatory reply.

'How was your flight? Have you slept? Here, let me take one of those bags for you. We're in the short stay, over here. If we hurry, we'll only have to pay for forty-five minutes not an hour. Can you believe they charge in quarter-hour increments? It's such a rip-off.'

Tara struggled to keep up with her daughter's stride. 'Don't worry, I'm paying.'

Laila grinned. 'Yeah, that kind of went without saying.'

She was smaller than Tara, with the same chestnut hair, but grey eyes, from her father's side, and wider at the hip than Tara had ever been. Better that, though, than anorexic, pinching at lettuce leaves and fretting about her beach body, like so many of her generation.

Tara shivered as they emerged from the air-conditioned terminal into the grey morning air. '*Ya allah*, it's cold.' She drew around her the coat that she had pulled from her suitcase at the carousel. It had spent seven years in her cupboard in Aden solely for this journey.

'This is mild for February. You should have seen it last week. We had snow.'

Tara shuddered at the thought.

Every visit home had been weird. If it wasn't the weather, it was the culture shock of an affluent country. New cars, properly surfaced roads, no bomb-sites or burned-out tanks left to rot in the roadside scrub. And nobody stared, because Tara was no longer a paler-skinned foreigner in a land where few foreigners came, or the only woman not wearing an abaya.

She paid the parking charge at the machine as Laila loaded her bags into the boot of the car.

'Did you sleep on the flight?' her daughter asked again, as they nosed down the ramp and out into the airport road system.

'On and off, I guess. Enough to keep going till tonight, provided I can make some decent coffee as soon as we get home. There is coffee, isn't there?'

'Don't worry, I've done some shopping for you. I even bought cardamom. I know how fussy you are.'

Tara clapped her hands with delight. 'What a welcome. Thank you, *habibti*. You think of everything. And you must let me pay you back.'

'Don't worry about that. I didn't get, like, *that* much.' They emerged from the airport perimeter and joined the motorway approach road. 'So tell me, what's your plan now? When do you start your new job? I hope you're at least having a break first.'

'I can't, *habibti*. They want me to begin as soon as possible. Besides, it wouldn't feel right to be sitting around doing nothing while…' She tailed off.

'While there's a war on? I get that, Mum. But let's face it, the war will still be going on next week, and the week after that. You need to recharge your batteries, otherwise you're no good to anyone.'

'Charming.'

'You know what I mean.'

'I do know what you mean, but the fact remains that my new boss wants me to start immediately. As soon as I get home, I'll have to work out how to get to the new office.'

'You're actually going into the office?'

'Yes of course. Why wouldn't I?'

'These days loads of people work from home. I just assumed you would too, rather than trailing all the way into London. It is in London, right?'

'Yes. Somewhere just off the Strand, I think. I don't mind going in. I'm looking forward to getting to know my colleagues. They'll all be much younger than me, but that will be stimulating.'

'If you say so. All my colleagues are much younger than you too, but *stimulating* isn't the word that comes to mind.' Laila worked for the council in Canterbury and spent most of their Zype time complaining about it. Tara hoped she was more charitable to her workmates than she affected to be.

'You always see the worst in everyone. You get that from your father.'

'Thanks. I'll tell him that.'

'Don't you dare.'

Rain lashed the windscreen on the M25, and Laila notched the wipers into frantic mode, but the sky had cleared by the time they spurred off into Kent.

'Look, the sun's come out for you,' she said as they passed Stourbourne station.

Little seemed to have changed in the village centre, apart from yet another estate agent replacing the moth-eaten antique shop, and a fancy-looking butcher instead of the strange hippie outfit that used to sell crystals and incense. But the village itself had grown larger, she saw, as they passed through. Where once had been fields, now stood an estate of new houses, detached, semis and townhouse terraces, all weatherboarded in an attempt at the county vernacular.

Tara's home, Willow Tree Cottage, stood nearly alone, alongside just one other house, a couple of miles outside the village. Around four hundred years old, according to a date carved into one of the beams, it was finished with whitewashed bricks and proper old weatherboarding, with first-floor gables puncturing a steep, red-tiled roof. She had loved it as soon as she and Doug, her ex-husband, set eyes on it, not least because it stood in an acre of land, which had become Tara's pride and joy after the divorce. As the car turned in at the gate, she expected to see a jungle, because the recently departed tenants were unlikely to have done much gardening, but all looked remarkably neat.

'I can't believe how well they've looked after it. I imagined much worse,' she said.

'Oh, it was pretty bad,' her daughter laughed. 'I told them we'd keep their deposit unless they got a gardener in to tidy it up.'

'You didn't! That's awful. I feel bad enough about giving them notice.'

'It's your house. You've got the right to live in it. Honestly, Mum, you're such a soft touch. Renters know they have to look after a place. It's part of the deal. I'm one of them, so trust me, I know. It's the way of the world.'

Tara sighed. 'What about the house itself? How did they leave that?'

'To my surprise, it was immaculate. I reckon maybe they trashed the place so they had to redecorate.'

'You're thinking the worst again. Perhaps they were nice respectful people who just didn't like gardening.'

'If you say so. Anyway, here we are. Don't worry about finding your key, use mine. You let yourself in and I'll bring your bags. I put the heating on low a couple of days ago, but you may want to turn it up. And I'm sure you'll want to put that coffee on. You'll only complain if I make it.'

Tara brewed the coffee in the traditional Arab stove-top way, stirring sugar and cardamom into the pot as she brought it to the boil. Laila stayed for one cup, then went home, promising to check in by phone later. Afterwards, Tara trailed contentedly from room to room, revisiting her inglenook fireplace that was big enough to stand inside, her crooked staircase that had driven the carpet-fitters crazy because no two risers were the same height, her bathroom that she and Doug had tiled themselves with decorative ceramic slabs from Jerusalem. She had forgotten how much she loved her cottage.

All her clothes, her books, her pictures from the walls, and her keepsake clutter, representing a lifetime of memories, had been stowed in the attic and the space above the garage, allowing her tenants to personalise the place in her absence. It would take her days to make the place her own again. Sammy had texted to offer help on that score as soon as he finished work, and he would be a great help with the heavy lifting. But Tara wasn't in any great hurry to restore everything immediately. She liked the prospect of re-establishing herself slowly, and discovering the paraphernalia of her past piece by piece, rather than racing at it.

Laila had stocked the fridge with milk, cheese, live yoghurt, eggs, hummus, onions, tomatoes, a pizza and some apples, and there was a fresh loaf on the breadboard along with a bottle of good olive oil on the shelf. Tara would need to do a proper shop, but this covered all her immediate needs.

Even after she had turned the heating up, the chill of the

house was a shock. What it really needed was a roaring fire. After tipping out the coffee grounds and washing the pot and cups, she let herself out of the kitchen door to check on the wood-store, more in hope than expectation. Sure enough, the pile had dwindled to nothing. Either the tenants had used all the logs or, perhaps more likely, taken every last twig with them, in revenge for Laila's heavy-handedness over the garden. She made a mental note to contact old Mr Carter the log-man, who would bring a truckload of seasoned wood and could usually also be persuaded, for a few extra notes, to stack them.

Returning indoors, she turned up the thermostat by another couple of degrees and took her laptop into the dining room, which had the biggest radiator in the house.

Through force of habit, she started by checking the overnight news from Yemen. Three civilians had been killed in the capital, Sana'a, after the rebel Houthi administration shot down a Saudi drone spy plane. A sandstorm followed by heavy rains had caused havoc at several of the displacement camps in the desert outside Marib. Truce talks, as ever, continued.

Reading these stories made Tara feel more disloyal than ever for abandoning her post. On the other hand, those dreadful tragedies would have happened whether she was in the country or not, and it was more important than ever that she use her expertise and influence on the outside, particularly now that she'd been granted a rare opportunity to do so, in the form of her job with the Institute for Worldwide Advancement, a think tank that lobbied the governments of wealthy countries on behalf of the poor.

Fortified by that thought, she navigated to the IWA website. The outfit was headquartered in New York, but its European regional office was in London, at an address in John Adam Street, next to the Adelphi. Handy for Charing Cross. On the site's header bar, she clicked the 'people' tab.

The regional director who had hired her, Matt Tree, was based in New York. His mugshot showed a thickset figure with silver temples and a determined smile. It made him look more like a rough-and-tumble politician or a union boss than the Harvard PhD referenced in his bio, but he'd been soft-spoken and contemplative in their two or three Zype calls.

Her contact in London was Rowan Walker, who remained merely a name so far. Rowan's bio made it clear she was also an American, with a Cornell degree and a scarily impressive CV involving the Obama-era State Department. Would Tara measure up to these hyper-achievers? It was hard not to imagine them all trotting purposefully along corridors speaking witty, clever, perfectly structured sentences at breakneck speed, like characters from *The West Wing*. She consoled herself with the observation that Rowan, who looked to be in her mid-forties, had sat for her website portrait on a day when she badly needed her roots retouching. No woman who did that could be entirely awful.

She opened her email programme and typed:

Hi Rowan

Just to let you know I'm safely back in England now, adjusting to the cold (!) and raring to go. The last I heard from Matt, he was keen for me to start immediately too, so I was planning to come into the office tomorrow, if that's all right with you. Let me know.

Best

Tara

As she pressed send, she drained her coffee and shivered again. She had been sitting still for too long. Shutting the laptop, she began hauling her largest suitcase up the narrow staircase to make a start on her unpacking. She'd planned to wait for Sammy to help her upstairs with it, but there was no time like the present.

An hour later, she had unpacked all her Yemeni luggage, started a load of washing and parcelled up the bits of silverware she'd brought back as gifts. Moving around had warmed her up, but now she flagged as the long journey and lack of decent sleep caught up with her. Standing in the living room doorway, she looked at her familiar old Knole sofa, its wooden bobbles held together with thick rope, and thought how much she'd love to take a nap on it. Even if she had firewood, that would be a bad idea: she firmly believed in pushing on through the tiredness in order to get a proper night's sleep when the time came. Still, a quick sit down wouldn't go amiss…

She awoke to a knock at the door. Groggily, she pulled herself up off the sofa and made her way through into cottage's little hallway. Opening the front door, she saw a tall young man with a dark, unruly beard.

'Sammy!' As he stepped forward, she allowed her son to fold her into a hug. 'Oh I've missed you. But I wasn't expecting you so early. How did you manage to get away?'

Sammy ran the kitchen at a vegan café in Margate. The hours were long, accounting for the bags under his eyes.

'We close after lunch on Tuesdays. I insisted. It was either that, they hire another chef to support me, or I had a total breakdown. They went for the early closing.'

'Good for you, but…' She checked her watch and saw that it was three o'clock. '*Y'allah*, how long have I been asleep?'

He laughed. 'Sorry, did I wake you? I just thought it was better to come in daylight if we're getting your stuff out of the garage.'

'Yes, of course. It's wonderful to see you. Come in and let me make us some coffee.'

He closed the door behind him and followed her into the kitchen. 'You are going to run me home when we're done, aren't you?'

'Run you home? Why?'

'So you can have the car back. I can't get home otherwise.'

On her departure for Yemen, Tara had let Sammy have her scarlet Fiat 500, on condition he taxed it and paid the MOT. She now saw it through the kitchen window, looking rather more scuffed than she remembered it.

She clicked her tongue at him. 'I don't want it back, *habibi*. It's yours.'

'But…how are you going to manage?'

She spooned coffee, cardamom and sugar into her trusty pot, topped it up with water and put it on the stove to boil. 'I'll get a new one. Well, not *new*. I was going to go to the guy in Canterbury who sold me that one. I trust him and he did me a good deal last time.'

'What will you do in the meantime? Laila said you're planning on going to London tomorrow, for your new job. How will you get to the station?'

'Ah, thanks for reminding me. I should just check…' She looked for her laptop, then remembered it was in the dining room. 'I just want to see if my new boss has returned my email. Could you grab my laptop for me, *habibi*? It's on the dining table.'

He fetched it for her and she logged in, keeping one eye on the coffee so it didn't boil over. Yes, there was her reply. *Hi Tara. Great to have you with us. Do indeed come into the office tomorrow. We normally start at 9.30 but no need to come that early. How about 11? I'll look forward to meeting you. Best, Rowan.*

'So yes, I am going to London tomorrow,' she said. 'But I can cycle to the station, as long as you help me oil the bike and pump up the tyres. I'm looking forward to it, in fact. I haven't been on a bike in all this time.'

'Yes, I can do that, if you're completely sure about the car. Thanks Mum.'

He hugged her again.

'You're welcome,' she said. This was the wonderful thing about having grown-up kids: they gave you plenty of affection, and all you had to do to earn it was bribe them with gifts of cars.

Satisfied that her brew was ready, she poured out two small espresso-sized cups. Sammy blew on his coffee to cool it down, then knocked it back in two or three swigs.

'I've missed that. I really have,' he said. 'So where shall we start? Attic or garage?'

3

In Tara's time away, the railway operator had renewed the rolling-stock on the Stourbourne line. While she knew it was a major breach of commuting etiquette to entertain any positive thoughts about the service, she was impressed. Warm carriages, neat LED displays telling you which stop was coming next, plugs near every seat to charge your phone or laptop: this was first-world luxury. In the country she had come from, public transport was limited to stifling hot buses on chaotic timetables and shared taxis where you were squashed and suffocated with tobacco smoke. The charm quickly wore off.

At Charing Cross station she dawdled, intimidated by the unforgiving stampede of those who did this journey every day and didn't need to follow the signage or fumble at the barriers. Outside on the Strand, she paused a moment to take

London in: timeless, but also constantly mutating. Cyclists had their own traffic lights now. And there were more bikes than ever. In Yemen, cycles were ramshackle affairs, ridden slowly to avoid the potholes, and only by the very young or the very old, or by someone carrying a ladder under his arm. Those riders would no more dream of wearing a helmet than of flying to the moon.

As she watched, a stream of cars and bikes stopped at a red light to let a flow of pedestrians hurry across. The sight made her laugh out loud. After seven years, she was used to crossing roads the Arab way: flinging yourself into the traffic in the reasonable faith that it would brake or swerve, because that was what drivers expected. Note to self: this method would get her killed in London.

The bell of St Martin-in-the-Fields began to chime the hour, prompting her to get a move on. She turned down into Villiers Street, where the old *Evening Standard* kiosk used to stand, in the days when you paid money to a wizened barker rather than just plucked your free copy from a pile, and then took the first left into stately John Adam Street. She checked off the numbers on the northern side, past the pillared façade of the Royal Society of Arts, till she reached an elegant Georgian five-storey with bowed railings at the full-length sash windows on the first floor, and hanging baskets of yellow-eyed winter pansies over the front door. The IWA didn't occupy the whole place, as a stack of brass plates confirmed; from the way they were placed, it looked like her destination was somewhere at the top.

Tara pressed the designated buzzer and announced herself.

'Fourth floor,' said a disembodied male voice. 'You can take the lift but I honestly wouldn't.'

'That's fine. I'm glad of the exercise,' Tara called back, as the door clicked open.

Inside, the building smelled of whatever chemical freshener had been sprayed onto the stair carpet by some invisible team of pre-dawn cleaners. It was a far cry from Badiya's frying onions, the thought of which stirred a momentary pang of longing, but Tara pushed that out of her mind as she laboured up the unnervingly steep stairs. At least physical activity was easier in this country, where you didn't have to do it in seventy percent humidity.

At the fourth landing, a fire-door opened into a small, unstaffed reception area, furnished with a couple of Art Deco tub chairs and a coffee table, which was strewn in a purposeful way with IWA publications and back copies of *The Economist* and *Newsweek*.

A woman whose face she had seen on the website strode smiling towards her, hand outstretched. She was trim and businesslike in a tailored grey suit.

'Tara? I'm Rowan. Great to have you with us.' Her accent was anglicised American, suggesting she'd been here a while. 'How is it, being back in Blighty?' The not-quite-colloquialism had a certain Dick Van Dyke energy.

'Cold, mainly,' said Tara, returning the handshake. 'It's funny: there were plenty of times in the past few years when I yearned to be cold. But now I'm yearning for equatorial heat once more.'

'The grass is always greener, I guess. Can I get you a cup of coffee before I introduce you to the team?'

Tara told her water was fine.

Rowan disappeared into a kitchenette, re-emerging with a brimming glass, then began her tour of the office. The fourth floor had been hollowed into an open-plan space, while preserving stubs of the previous walls to show where the original rooms had been. The office contained five people other than Rowan. Tara was presented to: Toby (white, bespectacled); Akeem (bearded, bespectacled); Lucy (blonde, expensively spoken); Darcy (Aussie, or maybe South African – it was hard to tell from a one-sentence greeting); and Evelina (glamorous, with a strong Slavic accent). She guessed they were all between ten and twenty years her junior – maybe nearer thirty in Lucy's case – which was what she'd expected. She herself had reached the age of invisibility, when you were either meant to run the whole show or disappear into homebound semi-retirement. No matter. She would buck that trend with pride.

'Don't worry, we won't be testing you on the names,' said Rowan, in the time-honoured cliché of such situations. 'In any case, I know you'll probably want to work from home most of the time, but you'll be able to catch up with everyone on Clack. That includes the New York office. They're all on it too. It's a brilliant way of bringing us all together.'

It was news to Tara that she'd want to work from home. She bit her lip. 'Oh right. I'm happy to be in the office, to be honest. I'd welcome the interaction. Unless you–'

'As you can see, we don't really have the space,' Rowan cut in, sweeping her hand around what was indeed a fairly cramped environment, encumbered as it was by far too many heavy bookcases. 'Most of the people here are actually hot-desking. But we're hoping to expand upstairs in the not-too-distant future. In the meantime you're very welcome to come in for our Wednesday lunches. They tend to be our most social time. Otherwise it's mainly heads down.'

It was true. They'd all seemed friendly enough when shaking her hand and telling her how happy they were to have her aboard, but now they had all returned to their keyboards, several of them behind airpods, tapping silently away.

'All right. Wednesday lunches. I can do that,' said Tara, telling herself not to take it personally. 'And…sorry…Clack?'

'Don't you know it? You'll love it. It's an internal comms app with loads of different channels. Brilliant for home working. You post messages on particular subjects, and everyone who needs to see them will do. It's so much better than strings of emails with ass-covering cc's to everyone under the sun. But it's also sociable. There's a general channel where we encourage people to post pics of their holidays or their kids, or to tell us what they're reading, or just to have debates on any issue that grabs them. That's our ethos here: share, discuss, don't hold back.'

'Great. I won't,' said Tara. It sounded a peculiar notion, but if this was the way of the modern office, she could certainly post some pictures of Yemen. Her new colleagues all knew it was a war zone, but she'd lay odds that none of them had the slightest idea of its extraordinary cultural heritage, its unique architecture, its natural beauty.

'Take a seat.' Rowan led the way to her own desk under a window at the front of the building, and gestured at a spare chair. 'So, it's exciting to have you join the team. Matt and I had a chat yesterday, and we'd like you initially to focus entirely on a country report, calling on both your academic expertise and your experience on the ground. We're hoping you can create something both definitive and punchy, to help us rebrand this conflict. At the moment the Yemeni civil war is a problem in a faraway land that has nothing to do with us and is too complicated to understand. We need to change that, to reframe it as a political and humanitarian priority that no Western legislator can ignore, where the issues are simple: weapons supplied by rich countries are being used to bomb the hell out of one of the poorest countries on earth, and they shouldn't be. How does that sound? Tall order, or doable?'

Tara smiled. 'It is a tall order, but if I didn't think it was doable, I wouldn't have flown five thousand miles from the land of frankincense and myrrh to a miserable English winter.'

'Frankincense and myrrh, exactly! Write about that stuff. Lots of positive cultural things to bring the place alive. Didn't I read that it was originally ruled by the Queen of Sheba? I'm not sure I even know who the Queen of Sheba was, but everyone has heard of her, right?'

'Yes, sure, I can talk about her. She's the one who travelled to see King Solomon, about a thousand years BC. But if you want biblical celebrities, Yemen can do better than that. Cain and Abel are meant to have been born on a Yemeni island, which is where Adam and Eve went after being kicked out of the Garden of Eden. The two brothers are both said to be buried in Aden, which is also the place where Noah launched his ark at the start of the flood. So Yemen is basically the backdrop for half the Book of Genesis.'

'Amazing. That's exactly what we need. Details to grab the attention of my god-fearing compatriots and their congressional representatives. They tend to think Arabia is just an empty desert, so what harm can the bombs do? We need to disabuse them of that. Of course they also think the country doesn't matter because it's Muslim. Those biblical connections should really make them sit up and take notice.'

'Understood. Don't worry, I've been passionate about

Yemen for thirty years, so I know how to sell it.'

'That's wonderful. How soon do you think we can have a first draft? Will three months be enough?'

Tara nodded. 'More than enough, I hope. If there are any snags, I assume I can check in with you when I come for those Wednesday lunches? As well as keep you generally abreast of my progress.'

'Great. Just one small thing. When you're writing any dates, we use the terms BCE and CE, not BC and AD. They stand for Before Common Era and Common Era. They're more religiously inclusive, rather than being Christian-specific.'

To Tara, centring the world calendar on the moment of Jesus of Nazareth's birth was Christian-specific, whatever abbreviation you used, but she kept that to herself. 'OK, I'll remember,' she said.

'I know Matt has talked about giving you the title research fellow, right? As part of the onboarding process into the Institute, he'd like you to submit freelance invoices for the time being. We'll naturally pay you at the rate you've already agreed with Matt, and you can of course use the job title right away. We'll look to integrate you more formally in due course.'

'Oh, right.' This wasn't what Tara had expected. 'Is there any problem with my appointment? Because…you realise I packed up my life back in Aden to come and work with you?'

'Absolutely we realise that. It's just a boring administrative thing, honestly. This is how we integrate most of our staff initially.'

Tara wondered if this could possibly be true of the high-paid executives with their multiple Ivy League degrees. But she was in no position to make a scene, because she hadn't made any formal contractual arrangement with Matt. She had returned on trust, because that was how she had grown used to operating. Instinct had carried her through seven years as a fixer in a war-torn country, and she hoped it wouldn't let her down now.

'Fine. If that's how you normally do it, I don't expect you to make an exception for me,' she said. That was another tactic that had served her well: be reasonable rather than shirty, unless shirtiness was unavoidable. You were usually rewarded for it in the end.

Rowan smiled and stood up. 'Great.' It seemed their meeting was over. 'I can't tell you how excited we are to have you on the team, Tara. Let me know if there's anything at all you need. And I'll let Matt in New York know you're up and running.'

'Sure,' said Tara, picking up her bag and standing up too.

Back on John Adam Street a few minutes later, she checked her watch. She'd been inside for less than half an hour. This was not quite the morning she'd expected, but she would not be downhearted. She had been away for a long time, and it would take a while to remember how transactions were conducted in this, her native country, as well as to adjust to any cultural changes that had taken place in her absence. On the upside, everyone at the IWA seemed friendly and welcoming, and she and Rowan were definitely on the same page regarding her Yemen report. It was important to be glass half-full in these situations, she reminded herself.

It was way too early to go home, after coming all this way, so she would make the best of it and take the opportunity for a wander round Covent Garden. There used to be a couple of shops in Floral Street that sold clothes that fitted her.

She took a right into a dank little court alongside the Royal Society of Arts that she hoped led back up to the Strand. It didn't look promising at first and she thought she'd have to retrace her steps. It was embarrassing to have forgotten her way around London. But then the alley vindicated her by dog-legging around the back of the building and letting her out at the end, through the pedestrian-sized gap between a couple of wrought-iron bollards.

She waited patiently for a lull in the traffic to cross each lane of the Strand, then found herself on the gentle incline of Bedford Street. Every other building was a coffee shop and the aroma was tempting, but she reminded herself that none of them knew how to make it.

Higher up, where the road became Garrick Street, a queue snaked along the pavement outside Waterstones. They must be expecting some celebrity author to come and sign books. As she drew closer, she saw that the line consisted mainly of children, some accompanied by parents, others not. It must be half term. Most of the kids seemed to be wearing beanie hats in various shades of blue, and some also sported blond wigs. She noticed that one or two had a dusting of face-paint freckles on their noses.

'Who are you all waiting for?' she asked a mother at the back of the queue.

The woman looked at Tara askance. 'It's the new Sandy Snaith,' she said. She looked down at her daughter. 'I thought the costumes might be a giveaway.'

In the window, all other books had been removed to make way for stacks of the same volume. On its cover was a drawing of an androgynous, freckled figure with a blond mop, a blue beanie hat and freckles, accompanied on either side by a pair of beagles, one of them with its nose to the ground. The book was ornately titled *Sandy Snaith and the Case of the Poisoned Parson*. The author's name, beneath the artwork, was Emily Zola. A sign read: *The new Sandy Snaith adventure is out TODAY. The book will be available HERE from midday. First come, first served. Queue EARLY to make sure of your copy!*

Tara realised she had read about this phenomenon in the online edition of *The Guardian*. Zola – a descendant of the French novelist – had become a publishing sensation with her series of books about an androgynous girl with two beagles called the Sniffing Sleuths. Together they solved crimes. Tara had seen them described as Agatha Christie meets *101 Dalmatians*, with a touch of *Scooby Doo*. Zola was now one of the world's richest authors.

At the front of the queue, standing to one side to make it clear she had no intention of pushing in, Tara addressed a more friendly-looking parent. 'Excuse me? I hope you don't mind me asking, but how many Sandy Snaith books have there been?'

'This one is number five,' said the woman's son who, going one better than the other costumed fans, had two toy beagles, complete with collars and leads, on the pavement beside him.

'And of course you've read them all?' said Tara, trying to appear more knowing this time.

'Twice,' said the boy, puffing his chest out.

'Quite right too,' said Tara. 'Good for you. And if I wanted to read one, to see what all the fuss is about, where should I start?'

'The first one, obviously,' said the boy. '*Sandy Snaith and the Sniffing Sleuths*.'

'Thank you very much,' said Tara. 'Perhaps I will. I hope

you manage to get your copy of this one. Not long to wait now.'

Smiling at the boy's mother, she continued in the direction of Floral Street. It was extraordinary how seven years away could make you feel so alien in your own world.

4

Tara had grown up bilingual in the comfortable suburbs of southeast London.

An only child of an English father and a mother born in Jerusalem and raised as a refugee in Jordan, she spoke her mother's urbane Levantine Arabic – with its elegant silent q – when the two of them were alone, and English to everyone else. Later she would learn that other people considered this a remarkable skill, but to Tara it was as natural as breathing.

Air travel was expensive in the Seventies and her friends from school mainly went camping in France in the holidays. But Nawal, Tara's mother, was a former air hostess with the Jordanian airline Alia – that was how she and Bill Farrier had met – and she could still get standby tickets. Tara remembered two trips to see her cousins in Amman. On the first, she was taken to the Roman temples at Jerash and floated unaided in the Dead Sea. The second was more sombre, coming in the shadow of yet another war, the third since Nawal's family had lost their home. Tara remembered a house full of weeping.

When Tara was thirteen, Nawal fell ill. The cancer was merciless, turning this tall, glamorous young woman – always so sophisticated with her hair piled high on her head and a cigarette in its holder – into a haggard old lady in just nine months. Before any of them could get their heads round it, she was gone, leaving Tara and Bill alone together.

They coped, up to a point, but the one thing no one understood, not even her father, was that death hadn't just taken Nawal, but half of Tara herself: the half that wasn't English. At a stroke, she had no outlet for one of the tongues she'd been using since birth. She became as monolingual as her schoolfriends.

It wasn't till eight years later, in her final year of a history degree at Durham, that she found an opportunity to reconnect with her roots. She joined a vacation programme teaching English in Palestinian refugee camps. Most recruits wanted to work in the West Bank or the Gaza Strip – names full of romantic excitement for them – but Tara went to Jordan, to Zarqa, home to the refinery her father had helped construct twenty years earlier. She had a wonderful summer, particularly when she was able to spend time with her aunts and cousins at weekends. For the first time since her mother's death, she felt whole again.

Back home, she got a job on a business magazine specialising in the Middle East. With its closely printed tender notices and headlines about power station contracts, *Arab Economic Digest* was as dry as the Empty Quarter. As the rookie, Tara was given responsibility for Yemen, the most populous nation on the

Arabian peninsula and, by a long way, the poorest. A green, mountainous corner once known as Arabia Felix – 'happy Arabia' – it had been rich, in biblical times, in frankincense and myrrh. In the late twentieth century, it clung to the old ways, with its gingerbread tower houses, the curved *jambiyya* daggers slung around every man's waist, and the national addiction to chewing qat, a mildly narcotic leaf that was sold by the branch-load.

She loved her first visit. Between interviews at the British embassy and the Ministry of Planning and Development in Sana'a, she haggled over spices, dates and silver jewellery in the souqs, and bumped around in the back seat of a 4x4 on trips over unmade roads into the mountains, with their intricate system of cultivated terraces, centuries old, like steps made for a giant. She also visited the south of the country, newly absorbed from the Soviet bloc after the collapse of communism. On the antique, propeller-driven DC-3 flight to Aden, an equatorial city built in the crater of an extinct volcano, she met a handsome young oil geologist from London called Doug Palmer. They hit it off across the aisle, and since they were both staying at the same hotel, they continued to do so over drinks in the bar later that evening.

They stayed in touch on their return to England, and not just because Doug was a useful source. There was something in his industrial career that reminded Tara of her father; he made a refreshing change from most of the young men she met, self-absorbed arts graduates full of disdain for the mundane things like power stations and oil refineries that made the world work. The fact that they had met in her favourite country added an element of romance for Tara. A year later, they married.

Returning to Yemen on honeymoon, they joined a group of twelve travellers on a desert safari to the outlying areas that Tara would never see on a business trip. Doug had been to those areas, because oil exploration concessions were always in the middle of nowhere, but he went along with it because Tara had set her heart on the idea.

All went well until the fourth day, when their entire party was abducted at gunpoint by a gang of tribesmen. Even then, once it became clear that they were in no physical danger, Tara refused to let this turn of events spoil the mood. Their captors slaughtered a goat in their honour, invited them to their daily qat chew and even let Tara make a satellite call to the office. The adventure did wonders for her grasp of the Yemeni dialect. The tribe turned out to be in dispute with a local car dealer, and their sheikh simply wanted the government to weigh in on their behalf. When that happened, the tribesmen shook hands with all the hostages, apologised for the trouble and wished them godspeed for their rest of their holiday.

Tara was more smitten with the country than ever.

Doug dealt less easily with the ordeal. Looking back, Tara realised she ought to have nudged him to seek therapy. There, perhaps, he might have been able to admit he was now nervous of all travel to the wild regions where his job must take him, that this threatened his whole livelihood, and his wife's insouciance during their ordeal made the humiliation all the worse. In the absence of any such outlet, however, he refashioned it as anger and resentment towards Tara.

Those feelings simmered slowly, taking years to boil over. In the meantime they settled in a commutable part of Kent and had two children, their names carefully chosen to work in both Arabic and English. Tara realised she wanted to make up for her own truncated childhood and spend as much time with them as possible. When her maternity leave ran out after her first pregnancy, she handed in her notice from the magazine. Once the kids were old enough and she had enough free hours in the day to call her own, she decided to continue her education. She enrolled on a master's in international relations at the Open University. Having completed that, she talked her way into the Middle East Studies department at the local university in Canterbury.

After the years of low-level marital sniping finally came to a head and she and Doug agreed to part, she filled the domestic gap by taking on more teaching. She enjoyed it at first, because academia suited her, but she also yearned for greater contact with a part of the world in which she'd barely set foot for two decades. Her father's death, when it came, made her yearn all the more for the part of the world she associated with her mother. When civil war broke out in Yemen just after Sammy, the younger of her two children, had started at uni, she felt as if the country were summoning her. She quit her job, put Willow Tree Cottage in the hands of a rental agent, and got on a plane with a view to doing something – anything – to help.

The change in the place shocked her. The ceremonial daggers, the casually slung AK-47s and the omni-present roadblocks had always been part of the package, but laser-guided Saudi air strikes killing scores of civilians in each attack, villages reduced to rubble, and roads with no traffic other than military convoys, confirmed that Happy Arabia was now one of the most miserable places on earth. The only real vestige of the old days was the daily ceasefire at lunchtime so both sides could chew qat.

The Shia rebels now held the capital. The official government, such as it was, had fled south to Aden. There Tara followed them, making the six-hour journey, by land this time, over the mountains and across the wide, featureless desert towards the solitary volcanic cone rising up out of the Indian Ocean. She arrived without a plan, thinking she'd perhaps write about a war that was regarded in the West as too bewildering to follow. It certainly was faction-ridden, but someone simply needed to explain one crucial fact: that thirty million people were caught in the crossfire, and when they weren't being bombarded from the air, they were dying of malnutrition because no supply chain in the fragmented land was a match for the endless roadblocks. After years of teaching the complexities of the region to her students, Tara took pride in her ability to cut through to what really mattered.

A week after her arrival in Aden, she found herself explaining the recent history of the country to a CNN producer and his cameraman. When, at the end of the evening, the producer offered her four hundred dollars a week to act as his fixer and expert consultant, her immediate response was to turn him down. She told him she hardly knew anyone yet and, in any case, if they had that kind of cash they should pay a Yemeni national not a foreigner. But that was precisely Tara's attraction, the guy insisted: she could apparently speak the language as well as any local, but her outsider status freed her from factional bias, and she also understood the Western viewer's perspective. She resisted a little longer, but the guy wore her down. She did, after all, have the rent on her new apartment to find.

The CNN gig led to work with other foreign broadcasters, as word spread that Tara was the go-to arranger. Once she started, she made the right contacts in all the relevant offices. There was a limit to how much the most accomplished fixer could arrange in a country where travel was fraught with danger from snipers, missiles and kidnappers who had long since dispensed with hospitable niceties. But every day taught her new lessons and before long she really was as qualified as anyone.

Every so often, one or two of the aid workers she befriended would lose hope and head for home. There were only so many years you could bang your head against a wall without getting concussion or knocking yourself unconscious. Mindful that the Yemeni population didn't have the luxury of upping sticks and departing, Tara held out as long as she could. However, she wasn't immune to the overwhelming sense of powerlessness, and when a friend in the UK tipped her off that the IWA was looking to boost its in-house expertise on Yemen, she made herself known to Matt Tree, the regional director.

And now, several months after putting out that first feeler, she was a research fellow, effectively employed as a country lobbyist. Matt had told her she was well placed to knock heads together at a multilateral level, and she knew he was right. This new role would potentially enable her to do far more to alleviate the suffering of the Yemeni people than she could ever achieve from Aden.

5

In the days that followed her trip into London, Tara continued the process of settling back into her old life.

One afternoon, when the forecast was clear of rain, she cycled into Canterbury and picked out a five-year-old Renault Clio from the forecourt of Hot Rods, the second-hand dealership where she'd bought Sammy's Fiat. She was nervous that Rod himself might have retired while she was away and passed the place on to someone less amenable, but he was still in attendance, albeit with whiter hair and fewer teeth. If he charged a slight premium to customers like herself who didn't know the carburettor from the clutch, he made up for that by steering them in the direction of reliable vehicles that wouldn't fall apart after six months and only recommending the work that strictly needed doing when it was time for the annual service.

'It's been a while, missus erm…' he greeted her, as she peered through the windows of a maroon Hyundai. 'Your boy has come in with the Fiat for three or four years now. He told me you were away abroad. The Far East, wasn't it?' Rod was poor with names but never forgot a car or a face.

'Middle,' said Tara. 'And it was actually seven years. But I'm back now. I've let Sammy keep the Fiat, so I'm hoping you can fix me up with something else. Preferably with a big enough hatchback to fit my bike inside, otherwise I'm not going to be able to get it home.'

An hour later, after they'd both discovered that her long stay in Arabia had greatly improved Tara's haggling skills, they shook hands on the Clio. She was disappointed not to be able to drive it away immediately, but that wasn't how it worked, evidently, and she'd have to wait a few days for the paperwork to go through. It meant postponing her first big Tesco shop, so she made do with the basketful of items she could squeeze into her backpack.

Back at Willow Tree Cottage, she continued retrieving her personal possessions from their storage boxes and making the house into her home once more.

There was so much to relearn about living in the first world. Her television, for example, was the same one that she'd watched perfectly happily seven years ago. Now, though, the bewildering array of identical-looking remotes flummoxed her and she couldn't remember what any of them did.

Laila's boyfriend Rob, who worked in IT, was mandated to help her, as well as to try to degunk her laptop, which had slowed down so much as to be nearly comatose.

He turned up one evening later in the week. He was touchingly nervous, wiping his palm on back of his jeans before shaking hands. Pale and well-padded, with a wispy tangle of receding black hair, he was clearly a few years older than Laila, and no looker. But he had an engaging smile and what turned out, once he'd relaxed, to be an easy patter. Tara could imagine him holding court at a crowded pub table.

'Do they not have TVs where you've been?' he said, lowering himself onto the sofa and inspecting each of the remotes. His vowels were as estuarine as a Whitstable oyster.

'Of course they do. When the power is working.'

He turned out to be a patient explainer, reminding her which remote was which.

'Now, what else would you like me to look at? Laila mentioned a laptop.'

'Yes please. But I haven't even offered you a drink. Tea or coffee? Or a glass of wine?'

'Tea would be lovely. Milk, no sugar, please. I'm sweet enough as it is. Why don't you tell me what the trouble is with your laptop, and I can have a look while you make the brew?'

He had effortlessly taken control, but in a way that amused rather than offended her. After all, he was the one giving up his time to do her a favour, and his easy cheer excused all manner of liberties.

An hour later, he had decluttered her machine by deleting duplicate files as well as – with her permission – a huge amount of superfluous stuff, including a tonne of old emails, that had clogged the memory.

'That should make everything much nippier now,' he said, draining his second cup of tea. 'And remember, delete your emails occasionally. Especially the ones with huge attachments.'

'Yes, Rob. I promise.'

'Good.'

She suddenly thought of the other thing she'd meant to ask. 'Have you heard of something called Clack?'

He chuckled. 'That's like asking if I've heard of something called Google. Do tell me they had that in the Yemen, by the way.'

'Yes, we had Google, thank you. And I don't believe Clack is anything like as common.'

'No, you're right. I'm pulling your leg. But it is quite common in offices nowadays. You want me to install it, do you?'

'If you wouldn't mind. They're very keen on it in this new job of mine. They post pictures of their babies on it, by all accounts.'

'Do they indeed? So you'll be putting snaps up there of Laila when she was a bouncing newborn?'

'She was a squalling, red-faced newborn. Any bounce came later. And no, don't worry, I won't. But they do encourage personal stuff on there, apparently, so I may dig out some nice shots of where I've been living all these years.'

'I'd like to see those too.'

'Would you really? Don't feel you have to say that. Because otherwise I may just hold you to it.'

'No, I really would. For me, Spain's exotic, so I don't know anything about the part of the world where you've been, let alone who's fighting who or why, so I'd love to hear more about it.'

'All right. Why don't you and Laila come over one night? Next weekend, maybe. Then I can tell you all about it. I'll ask Sammy too, and anyone he wants to bring. Although that will mean you'll have to eat vegan food, I'm afraid.'

Rob winced theatrically. 'If it's just this once, I guess. Although I may have to grab a quick Maccie D on the way over.'

With her computer rejuvenated, Tara felt more able to make a start on her report. She began by sketching out a rough outline of the areas that she'd need to cover: an overview of the country; the background to the conflict; the humanitarian crisis; the challenges for agencies; and the steps the outside world would need to take to restore peace and reconstruct the shattered country.

With that structure established, it would now be easier to flesh out each part of the skeleton.

Since Rowan had made clear she wanted plenty of biblical colour in the introduction, Tara decided she would make a start with ancient history. As well as Cain, Abel and Noah, there was Noah's son Shem, who supposedly founded the capital, high in the mountains, once the flood waters subsided.

Now she came to think of it, those mountains also merited a line or two of explanation. They had helped keep the country in its splendid isolation for centuries, as well as affording it the temperate, rainy climate – in the highlands, at any rate – that so confounded most foreigners' expectations of what Arabia should look like. It would be nice to explain, in a readable line or two, whatever tectonic shifts had created those jagged, concentric peaks.

This proved easier said than done. As she started reading into the subject, she found herself deep in a rabbit warren of geological jargon – a world of geoid undulations and regional metamorphism, in which everyone but her seemed to know their palaeozoic from their mesozoic, their oligocene from their eocene. It was bewildering, but she persevered, and gradually she began to see past the technical terminology and understand that Yemen, like the rest of Arabia, had once been joined to Africa. Then, between fifty and thirty-five million years ago – the blink of an eye in geological terms – an eruption of magma created a Y-shaped crack. The Arabian tectonic plate started splitting to the northeast, while the Somalian part of the African plate moved southeast and the Nubian part drifted southwest. The eventual result, twenty million years later, was the Red Sea and the Gulf of Aden, both of which were still getting wider, at the rate of fifteen millimetres per year. In another twenty-five million years, they would be twice as wide as they were today. She contemplated that extraordinary fact. When people spoke about the living earth, did they realise the rocks themselves were constantly on the move?

All of this was a fascinating diversion, but the important point for her present purposes was that every action in plate tectonics caused a reaction. This particular one created intense geological disruption, not least when the Arabian plate collided with the Eurasian one to the north. The result was a frenzy of volcanic peaks in Yemen.

So there it was: the origin story of her mountain range.

She bashed out the details before she forgot them, attempting to strip out the technical language and render the point down to its most basic and colourful essence: the geological activity that created the Red Sea up to fifty million years ago also left Yemen with a dizzying array of impassable mountains. But then she decided she had over-simplified it, so she reinserted some technical terms, just to give it the ring of expertise.

She realised it had taken her the best part of two hours to come up with this brief passage. It was an indulgent way to spend an afternoon, and she would never get anywhere with this report if she took every section at the same pace. However, there was no harm in taking care over the introductory sections.

Since it was now well past dusk and she was mentally exhausted, she decided she deserved a drink. She poured herself a glass of red wine. As she sipped it, she spent a few moments exploring the Clack application that now sat, thanks to Rob, on her laptop screen.

An alert showed that several posts awaited her attention, addressed to her by name. Rowan had added her to the system with a couple of lines of introduction, prompting a string of welcome messages from colleagues on both sides of the Atlantic. It was a nice touch, and she could see the benefit of this application already. In the reply bar, she wrote: *Thanks all for those very warm and kind words – I look forward to getting to know everyone better, either in real life or virtually*.

There were various channels with different subject headings – Research Proposals, Reports Ongoing, Media, Outreach – and also, sure enough, a section that was obviously more gossipy, dedicated to personal posts. To show willing, she uploaded her favourite picture of the old imam's palace at Dar al-Hajar, a fairytale tower balanced on a crag so improbable that it seemed to cantilever out of the mountainside. She tapped out:

Here's a glimpse of the country where I lived for the last seven years. It's ravaged by war and facing an appalling humanitarian crisis but it's also one of the most beautiful places in the world and I miss it dreadfully. I'm already feeling horribly out of touch.

Feeling pleased with herself for making the effort, she powered her laptop down and wondered what to have for supper.

She carried on working on her report the following morning, forgetting all about Clack. It was only in the afternoon that it occurred to her to open the app to see if anyone had responded to her picture. When she did so, she was gratified to find that her picture had attracted a dozen or more heart and thumbs-up symbols. There were several messages too. *That's quite a feat of engineering. How did they manage to built it without foundations?* and *Wow – that is sooo cool! Like a real-life version of something you might find in Disneyland.* She smiled at that take, which was so American and yet also completely fair.

The final message was from Matt Tree:

Hey Tara. Great to see you up and running. I'm sorry to hear you're 'homesick' for Yemen but may I recommend Twitter? I don't think you have an account, but it's a great way of keeping up with news on the ground in any given part of the world.

She pinged off a reply to thank Matt for the suggestion, and everyone else for their appreciative comments. She certainly did not have a Twitter account, and she planned to keep it that way. From everything she'd heard, the site was a cesspit. It was one piece of technological modernity that she had no qualms about rejecting.

A couple of hours later, however, she reconsidered. The suggestion had come from the guy who hired her, so perhaps it was an instruction, or at least a heavy hint, rather than a mere recommendation.

Googling 'Twitter', she was surprised to find she could gain access to the site without needing to open an account. She figured she might as well look around to see if Matt's tip was true, so she put 'Yemen' in the search box and hit enter. Immediately, she saw he was right: stories of starvation, landmines and aerial bombings now filled her screen; horrors that, paradoxically, gave her a warm rush of belonging. As she carried on scrolling and clicking, she could see that she had been wrong to write the platform off. She would indeed sign up for an account. She filled out the sign-up boxes, inserted the least unflattering face-shot of herself that she could find – taken at Elephant Beach by a Belgian friend from Médecins sans Frontières – and wrote the required lines of biography, describing herself as a research fellow at the IWA. It was the first time she had written that phrase in public. She liked the way it looked.

She followed Matt and Rowan, plus anyone else she could find who had commented on her posts on Clack, as well as a few news and charity accounts focused on Yemen. By the time she was done she was following nineteen people and one of them – Akeem from the John Adam Street office – had returned the compliment. The numbers looked sad, but everyone had to start somewhere.

As she watched, her tally clicked up to three, thanks to Matt and someone else in New York. That was one merit of starting at rock bottom: the only way was up.

6

The kids had agreed to come over for dinner the following Sunday evening, when Sammy's café would be closed. Sammy confirmed there was someone he might bring, without going into further detail. So they would be five.

Tara searched her cookery book library for vegan recipes that might also be palatable to the likes of Rob. Actually, Rob was probably a lost cause; he might have presented it as a joke, but she believed he really would stop off beforehand at McDonald's. Palatable to herself and Laila, then (on the assumption that Sammy's companion would also be a true believer).

She dug out an old favourite from Claudia Roden, involving slices of aubergine steamed in a hot skillet, then dressed in honey, lemon juice, chilli, ginger and garlic; you were meant to serve it with goat's cheese, but they could manage fine without. The same book also yielded a Mediterranean chickpea dish, in which the pulses were slathered in a thick, nutty sauce made of yoghurt, garlic and tahini. Tara would have to find some kind of plant-based yoghurt, but they were bound to sell that at Tesco's. Finally, in a food-spattered book of Indian recipes, she turned up a black lentil curry made with a coconut and tomato sauce. Served with rice, it would tick off all the food groups and the whole meal might even taste half decent. For pudding they could have a crumble of some kind, made with toasted oats rather than a butter-and-flour mix, with more plant-based yoghurt. As a reward for their forbearance, she would provide the apostates with a jug of double cream.

She prepared most of the food on the Sunday afternoon, so there wasn't much to do by the time Laila and Rob, the first arrivals, knocked on the door.

Rob was dispatched to lay the table while Laila opened the wine.

'Do you know who your brother is bringing?' asked Tara.

Laila shrugged. 'Search me. He's always been a dark horse with stuff like that.'

'Does that mean it's a new relationship, if you don't know her?'

'Or him.'

Tara flushed with embarrassment. 'Yes of course, or him.'

Her daughter laughed. 'I'm messing with you. Sammy's as straight as the M2. I honestly don't know if it's a new thing or not, but I think you should stop stressing about it. They'll be here soon enough, and then we'll find out what kind of witch has got her claws into your precious boy.'

'Laila!'

'Don't worry. She's probably sweet and simple, just like Sammy.'

Sammy's date turned out to be an expensively spoken, fine-boned creature called Sorrel, with a startling array of raspberry and purple dreadlocks bundled up under a wide batik headband and plunging down over her back and shoulders. Her pierced earlobes had been stretched open so wide that you could fit a stick of rock through them.

Despite her crusty appearance, she had impeccable manners.

'These aubergines are divine,' she purred. 'You ought to give the recipe to Sam, oughtn't she, darling?'

Sammy blushed to his ears.

'And to Laila,' cut in Rob. 'I'm constantly nagging her to make more vegan dishes, but you know how it is with some people. It's all about the burgers.'

Laila aimed an obvious kick in his direction.

'You know you can get wonderful vegan burgers nowadays, Laila?' said Sorrel. 'They're made of soya and wheat protein. They're amazing, and so much better for you than meat.'

'I know what I wanted to ask you all,' said Tara, anxious to head off any further teasing. 'Have any of you read the *Sandy Snaith* books?'

'Of course,' said Laila, and Sammy and Rob nodded too. Only Sorrel shook her head.

'Even though they're for children?' said Tara.

'Yes but they're brilliant,' said Laila. 'The first one was, like, mega, and now there's a huge fanfare whenever a new one comes out. Loads of people of our age read them. And kids queue for hours outside bookshops.'

'Yes, I saw that in Covent Garden the other day.'

'The films are good too,' said Rob.

'Only because you've got an inappropriate crush on Danielle Cardiff,' said Laila.

'Who's Danielle Cardiff?' said Tara.

'The nymphette they cast as Sandy Snaith,' said her daughter.

'On whom I do not have an inappropriate crush,' said Rob.

Laila drew an imaginary Pinocchio nose in front of her face.

Tara nudged the conversation out of this particular rut. 'And what do you think of the author herself?'

'Emily Zola?' said Laila. 'She's super minted, from the books and the films. But she's wonderful too. She gives loads of money away to charity and she does drop-in events at schools when no one is expecting her, often in deprived areas. She's kind of a heroic figure to anyone who loves the books. And to their parents, I guess.'

'What relation is she to the other Zola?' said Tara.

'The football manager?' said Rob.

It was news to Tara that there was a football manager called Zola. 'I meant the author.'

'Is there another author called Zola?' said Laila.

'I think Emile Zola was her grandfather. Or maybe great-grandfather,' offered Sorrel.

Tara smiled at her gratefully.

'She's called Emily and she had a great-granddad called Emile?' said Rob. 'That's brilliant.'

'What kind of stuff did he do?' said Laila.

'Novels about different areas of ordinary life,' said Tara. 'That makes him sound dull but he wasn't at all. He was a brilliant story-teller and his books are fantastic page-turners.

Like a French Dickens, only less wordy.'

Laila mimed a yawn.

'And with more sex,' Tara added.

'Now you're talking,' said Rob. 'Maybe I'll check the old geezer out.'

'He was also a very brave campaigner,' said Tara. 'He was the first prominent figure in public life to speak out in the Dreyfus affair, at great risk to his career.'

'What's the Dreyfus affair?' said Sammy.

Rob rolled his eyes theatrically, earning himself a dig in the ribs from Laila. 'He doesn't know either,' she told the rest of them, in case they hadn't realised.

'It was a horrible miscarriage of justice,' said Tara. 'A French military officer was accused of a crime he didn't commit and sent to Devil's Island.'

'Where's that?' said Laila.

Tara laughed. 'Actually, there you have me. It's famous as the place they sent Dreyfus, but I've no idea where it is. I don't think it was very nice.'

Rob nodded. 'The clue was in the name.'

'Anyway,' said Tara, 'the campaign was successful and Dreyfus was freed, so Zola was completely vindicated in the end. But it took great courage.'

'I think his great-granddaughter has opted for an easier life,' said Rob. 'Apparently she's made so much lolly, she's bought herself a moated manor house. I saw the pictures in *Mail Online*. Somewhere in Suffolk, I think. It's a lovely gaff.'

'Lucky her,' said Tara. 'I hope it makes her happy. Speaking of which, it's wonderful to be here with you all, and I hope we'll do this sort of thing much more often. Shall we have a toast? To family.'

They all clinked glasses and repeated 'to family'. Rob said it with particular enthusiasm, Tara noted.

'So are you happy to be back home, Mum?' said Laila.

Tara smiled. '*Ya'ni*,' she said.

Laila explained to Rob and Sorrel: '*Ya'ni* is used in loads of different ways in Arabic but in this case it basically means *meh*. She's trying to say she's not really happy to be back because she'd rather be in a war-zone than in the bosom of her family.'

Rob came to Tara's defence. 'Be fair, your mum's bound to miss the place. Seven years is a long time.'

'Yes but she's obsessed with Yemen, aren't you, Mum? Sorrel, did you know she was actually kidnapped there on her honeymoon? And instead of running as fast as she could and never going back, like any normal person, she became even more crazy about the place.'

Tara laughed. 'What can I say? They were very nice to us.'

Sorrel looked stunned. 'Are you serious? You were literally kidnapped? By actual kidnappers? Like, for ransom or something? I mean, it wasn't some kind of prank?'

Sammy intervened. 'It's no joke. They were genuine kidnappers, armed to the teeth with kalashnikovs. Mum had a whale of a time with them because she likes that kind of thing.'

'I'm not sure I even know where Yemen is,' said Sorrel.

Rob wiped imaginary sweat from his forehead with the back of his hand. 'Phew. I thought it was just me, and I didn't like to say anything.'

'It's at the bottom left-hand corner of the Arabian peninsula,' said Tara.

'And it's where mocha coffee comes from, and frankincense and myrrh,' said Sammy.

'Not to mention the Queen of Sheba,' said Laila.

'They're making fun of me, Sorrel,' said Tara.

'The Queen of Sheba!' said Sorrel, eyes wide. 'I don't think I even knew she was a real person. I mean, I thought she was mythical.'

'She's in the Bible. She travelled to Jerusalem to see King Solomon with a caravan of valuable gifts.'

'You wouldn't want to get stuck behind that on the motorway,' said Rob, then cried out as Laila kicked him again.

'I know the film, with Gina Lollobrigida,' said Sorrel.

Tara was impressed. 'I'm surprised you've heard of it.'

'Sorrel's doing a doctorate in film studies,' said Sammy, helping himself to more yoghurt and chickpeas.

'Are you really? At the university here?'

'Yes,' said Sorrel. 'Only it's not strictly speaking film studies. It's really about filmic myth and historiography.'

'Oh right,' nodded Rob, perfectly straight-faced.

Tara wished he and Laila would stop mocking the poor girl. She was sure it wasn't cruelly meant, but Sorrel seemed completely oblivious, which made Tara feel bad on her behalf. 'You may have to explain what that means. To me, at any rate,' she said.

'It's an investigation of the way feature films about real events change the way those events are remembered by history.'

'That sounds interesting. Can you give us an example?'

Sammy frowned. 'Don't interrogate her, Mum. She's not one of your students.'

'I'm interested,' Tara protested. Did children ever stop being embarrassed by their parents?

'She's not interrogating me,' said Sorrel, casting a frown of her own at Sammy. Addressing the rest of the gathering, she said: 'My thesis is actually all about one particular film, called *Inherit the Wind*. I don't know if you've heard of it?'

Laila and Rob shrugged but Tara clapped her hands. 'About the Monkey Trial?'

'Yes, well done. You're clearly a fan of old films.'

'My mother had a big crush on Spencer Tracy. He was in that, wasn't he?'

'He was indeed. Nominated for an Oscar.'

'Remind me who played his opposite number?'

'Fredric March.'

'Fredric March, of course! And wasn't Gene Kelly in it too?'

'Hold up,' said Rob. 'Before you two film buffs get too carried away, what's the Monkey Trial when it's at home?'

Sorrel looked at Tara. 'Will you explain?'

'I'll try. Let's see if I can remember the details. It took place in the Twenties, somewhere in the Deep South. Kentucky, was it?'

'Tennessee.'

'Tennessee. A schoolmaster was arrested for teaching the theory of evolution, and his trial became a massive national spectacle, with the two most famous lawyers in America pitted against each other. How am I doing?'

'Close enough.'

'And who won?' said Laila.

'I'm trying to remember,' said Tara. 'I don't think the teacher can have been acquitted. It's not a triumphant ending. But I don't think it was a victory for his persecutors either. Come on, Sorrel. Remind me.'

'It's kind of a draw. The teacher is found guilty but he gets the minimum sentence. That's why his prosecutor makes an angry speech and gets so worked up he has a heart attack and dies.'

'I'd forgotten that,' said Tara. 'Is that one of the things that didn't happen?'

'They weren't completely making it up. He died in his sleep five days later.'

'So what did they distort?' said Laila. 'What happened really?'

'It was mainly a matter of tone. The real trial was much more light-hearted, with a carnival atmosphere. The teacher, whose name was John Scopes, actually volunteered to be tried, as a test case for a law that nobody ever expected to be used. They mainly did it as a PR stunt to try and put their little town on the map.'

'But Hollywood is bound to make it more dramatic,' said Rob. 'That's what film-makers do. Is it really worth worrying about?'

Everyone looked at Sorrel. She was so grown-up for her age, Tara thought. Despite her grungy look, she clearly came from money, which had no doubt conferred confidence.

Sorrel said: 'It's actually based on a Broadway play and when it came out, all the critics complained it completely distorted the original events. But you know what? After a while it began to replace those events in the national memory. By the Nineties, the actual film was being studied as history in American schools. Kids are brought up to think it's completely factual.'

Tara got up to the clear the plates. 'This is truly fascinating, Sorrel. As well as depressing. I'd love to see your thesis at some stage.'

'Let me help you,' said Laila, gathering up the serving dishes and carrying them back to the kitchen. When she and her mother were alone, she said: 'Sorrel knows so much stuff! What's a brain-box like her doing with Sammy? What do they even talk about? All he knows about is computer games and lentils.'

Tara laughed. 'You're very cruel to your poor brother. They may have really interesting conversations, for all you know.'

'Or maybe he's just really good in bed.'

'Laila!'

'Sorry, that is a pretty gross thought, isn't it? And unlikely.'

Tara shook her head. 'You're incorrigible. Now, you take the dessert bowls and I'll bring the crumble.'

The following afternoon, after a productive morning's work and a lunch of vegan leftovers, Tara found herself hankering to see *Inherit the Wind* once again. The previous night's conversation had stirred nostalgic memories of the film, but it wasn't just that. Reacquainting herself with the old movie might also be a good way of forging a connection with Sorrel, who seemed so smart and grown-up. Tara could discuss it with her, the next time she and Sammy came round. It would be a way of welcoming her into the family fold.

Searching on Amazon Prime to see if the film was available to watch, she was delighted to find that she could rent it for one pound ninety-nine.

The opening credits took her back to her childhood, when her mother was still alive. They must have viewed it during Nawal's illness, before everything accelerated. Her mother would urge Tara to go out and see her friends during the holidays, but she refused to go, preferring to stay indoors so they could watch golden age classics together, and she knew Nawal was pleased to have her. They sat hand in hand, squeezing tighter every now and then, to give each other comfort.

As those memories surged back, Tara wavered, wondering if this was going to be an emotional ordeal. But the initial prickle of pain passed and turned instead into a warm surge of nostalgia.

The first half hour made her smile: all the wonderfully choreographed crowd scenes and the highly polished dialogue, from the wisecracking Gene Kelly as the cynical newspaper columnist covering the trial, to the bombast of Fredric March and the blunt self-confidence of Spencer Tracy. Nobody talked like that in movies any more, as if they were declaiming their lines in a theatre, loud enough to be heard up in the gods. It was mannered and full of artifice, but that was all part of the package of studio film-making in those days.

After a while, however, the bellowing oratory began to grate: the two leading men in their tight close-ups, dripping sweat and spitting rhetoric into each other's faces, while the fickle courtroom crowd swerved wildly from one camp to the other, leaping to its feet to cheer every killer line, no matter who delivered it. The confrontation might well be electric if you believed it really happened; once you knew it hadn't, the caricature of the snarling fundamentalists suddenly seemed profoundly unfair.

Tara opened Wikipedia while she was watching the film. The entry for the Scopes Trial confirmed Sorrel's account of the real events. Far from being a ridiculous bigot, the real-life prosecutor was a deeply loved humanitarian, famous for his compassion. He even offered to pay Scopes' fine. And no one threw bottles through the young teacher's cell window, because the man was never imprisoned.

Now that Tara knew there had been no jeopardy, she felt hoodwinked by the film, which seemed histrionic and false. She would probably still have enjoyed it had she not known the real story, but the rewriting of the past offended her sense of justice. History was precious. No one had the right to distort it to suit their own agenda, and she didn't see why anyone would do it. Didn't they realise that truth mattered?

7

Amid all the effort of putting her home back together, getting her new car on the road, and stocking up on groceries, household essentials and new clothes suitable for the British climate, as well as pressing on with her report, Tara found she was relieved not to have to haul herself to London with any regularity.

She didn't wish to seem aloof, though. In her fourth week back in the UK, she decided it was time to show her face at one of the weekly lunches Rowan had mentioned.

She emailed in advance to say she was planning to attend on the coming Wednesday. Rowan replied to say she was very welcome, and that the rest of the team looked forward to seeing her. She attached the address of a Greek restaurant in Covent Garden. 'We always book a table for 12.45,' she said. 'It's usually in Akeem's name. We'll meet you there.'

On the morning of the day in question, having checked the weather forecast – the day was set to be dry – Tara spent half an hour deciding what to wear. It would have to be reasonably casual, since she was planning to cycle rather than drive to Stourbourne station, but neither did she want to look too shabby. After a couple of false starts, she chose a smart pair of black jeans, a printed wrap top she'd just bought at Zara in Canterbury, with a grey suede jacket and matching block-heel court shoes, in which she could just about pedal.

The train timetable offered her the choice of arriving twenty minutes early or ten minutes late. She opted for the latter, to avoid the embarrassment of being the first to arrive. Once she reached town, however, she found herself hurrying up the Strand. She told herself to calm down. She was a grown woman, attending a social event with colleagues. There was no need to get worked up about it.

The restaurant had the look of a family-run taverna straight out of *Mamma Mia*: the rough-plastered, whitewashed walls were festooned with ceramic souvenir tat; one wall bore a gigantic mural of a spreading olive tree; the table-cloths were indigo gingham and the simple wooden chairs Aegean blue. It was cheesy as hell and Tara decided she loved it. If her workmates had made this place their regular haunt, she liked them already.

They were assembled around a long table at the rear of the premises. Everyone she'd met on her previous visit to the office was there, plus a couple of others: home-workers like herself, she assumed, emerging from their seclusion. She was ushered to the spare seat they had saved for her, with Rowan on her left and Evelina to her right. They were all friendly to her as they dipped into a communal array of hot and cold mezze dishes. (They ordered like this by tradition, Rowan said. If there was any dish she particularly liked, she should feel free to order more of it.) How was her report coming along, they wanted to know. Wasn't that palace amazing, the one in the picture she posted? Had she been there? But travel around the country must be pretty difficult nowadays, no? Speaking of which, could she explain the basics of the conflict? Like, what was a Houthi and why? And who exactly were the good guys and the bad guys?

Evelina, in the heavy accent that made her English sound poorer than it really was, said: 'I remember an article by Leon Smith in *The Guardian* that said we must blame the Saudis, the US and the UK. This sounds very possibly true, but usually I believe the opposite to Leon Smith, so I'm conflicted.'

Leon Smith was a fresh-faced columnist whose byline picture – neatly parted hair, what looked like a school regulation jumper, no indication that he ever needed to shave – made him look like the swotty child who always sat at the front in class. In fact, he was an outspoken left-winger, of the sort who most enjoyed denouncing other left-wingers for not being left-wing enough. Tara knew this because she too had seen the piece to which Evelina referred and had been intrigued by this juvenile blowhard who knew so little, yet expressed it with such confidence.

She nodded. 'You're right to be wary. We tend to look at conflicts through the prism of right and wrong. In most cases, that's a reasonable approach: someone occupied someone else's territory, one set of people has been persecuted for years by another, and so on. But this one is much messier. A popular uprising, followed by a stitch-up, some tribal power plays…with the ordinary population caught in the middle.

The real catastrophe came when other countries started using the Yemeni fiasco as a proxy war. It's not as if there are just two sides. There are at least three. If you're a civilian, your allegiance depends entirely on where you happen to live, or where you lived before you had to flee your home.' Everyone was looking at her gravely. 'Sorry, I feel like I've climbed onto a soapbox.'

'Not at all,' said Evelina. 'It's fascinating.'

'All right. Good. Anyway, the short answer is: don't trust anyone who tells you this is a simple conflict with virtue on one side and evil on the other. It's way more complicated than that, and only a fool would claim to understand it perfectly.'

'That figures,' said Akeem, on the left of Rowan, and everyone laughed. Clearly no one here liked Leon Smith.

The focus eventually drifted away from Yemen and Tara was drawn into the general conversation. Toby had published a blog about his recent vasectomy and was keen to discuss it; far keener than anyone else, from what she could see. Darcy and Rowan congratulated him on taking the burden of contraceptive responsibility away from his girlfriend, and Toby basked in their approval, but the other men at the table had conspicuously little to say. One of the other home-workers, whose name was Spencer, actually crossed his legs.

They were plainly an opinionated bunch and no one held back, but there was little danger of discord, because they all took the same view on Brexit, the state of politics in the US and the UK, the desirability of more immigration not less. Not that Tara disagreed either; but she couldn't help thinking they must sound like liberal intellectuals from central casting if anyone at the next table bothered to earwig.

The earnestness had its limits. In a lull in the conversation,

Spencer said to Rowan: 'So when are you off to California?'

She smiled. 'Next week.'

'I'm so jealous, I can't tell you,' said Spencer. He was older than the others – early forties, perhaps – with close-cropped hair and chunky rings on the index and pinkie fingers of his right hand, as well as a wedding ring on his left.

'Is this work or pleasure?' asked Tara.

'Work,' Rowan began to say, but Spencer spoke over her to say 'Both!', which made the rest of the table laugh.

Tara appealed to Rowan. 'You'll have to explain.'

'I have a meeting with the Talavera Foundation,' her new boss said. Seeing Tara's blank look, she continued: 'You know, the Silicon Valley tycoon, Joey Talavera? We've been chasing grant support from them for a while now, and it looks like we're finally getting somewhere. They've invited a group of us out to Palo Alto to discuss it with them face to face.'

'I'm afraid I've never heard of him,' said Tara, feeling old and alien. 'Is he some kind of Bill Gates?'

'If Bill Gates was built like a redwood tree, drop-dead gorgeous and married to a Vardashian,' said Spencer.

Tara had no idea who or what a Vardashian was, but decided to keep that to herself.

Rowan took pity on her. 'Joey Talavera invented Zype,' she said. 'I don't even know if I'm going to meet Joey himself. It's a meeting at the foundation. I've no idea how hands-on he is.'

'I know how hands-on I'd like him to be,' said Spencer.

'Aren't you supposed to be a married man?' said Evelina.

'Not if Joey doesn't want me to be.'

Rowan shook her head in mock exasperation.

Tara resolved to play the grown-up. 'What's the foundation's area of interest?'

Rowan responded gratefully. 'It's a very new philanthropic venture, and so far its primary focus has been South America. From what we gather, the whole initiative is mainly Krystal's brainchild – that's Mrs Talavera, the Vardashian – but South America is Joey's big interest. Anything Hispanic, from what I hear. Some of our team in New York have been putting together interesting proposals on how to curb the power of the drug cartels, and we're hoping the Talaveras will help us catch the eyes of the people who matter. As well as provide some secure funding, of course. I'm going to California with them because the new CEO of the foundation is an old classmate of mine from Cornell. Without wishing to toot my own horn, I was the one who made the initial connection.'

'Toot away,' said Tara. 'If it's your doing, take the credit before some bloke takes it for you.'

Rowan raised an eyebrow that said, *I know, right?* She continued: 'While I'm there, I'm also going to flag up our Yemen and Horn of Africa work, just to put it on their radar.'

'Do you need anything from me? I can send as much of my report as I've written so far, if you like. The introduction is complete, and a lot of the history and political context. And I can draft you some useful lines about the conflict itself. Just some headlines, with a few eye-catching facts and figures.' Tara smiled. 'Guaranteed to get the attention of the busiest Silicon Valley philanthropist in the shortest lift ride.'

'That would be awesome,' said Rowan. 'I leave on Sunday morning. Could you ping me whatever you have before then?'

Tara promised she would, as the empty mezze dishes were cleared away and a waiter appeared to take orders for baklava and thick, sweet coffee that turned out to be almost as good as Tara's own.

It was only on her way back to Charing Cross, after saying her goodbyes, that she realised she'd missed an opportunity. The weeks were passing, and neither Matt nor Rowan had brought up the subject of her future status at the IWA. That meant it was probably time for Tara to raise the matter herself. If she'd thought about it, she could have found a moment amid this relaxed atmosphere for a discreet word. No matter. She would make a point of raising it properly once she had sent Rowan the material she'd requested.

8

Tara woke next morning to a cloudless sky, which she celebrated with a walk before breakfast – confusing the dog-owners she met on the footpath behind her house, who seemed puzzled that anyone would roam the fields at this hour without an animal in tow.

She returned home with a clear plan in her mind. After making herself a couple of poached eggs on sourdough toast and a pot of serious coffee, she set to work writing the eye-catching lines that she'd promised to Rowan. Then she would devote some time and thought to a future programme of activity designed to make her indispensable at the IWA.

The killer facts – how apt that expression – came all too easily. Death, displacement, disease, poverty… She arranged them into bullet points, then attached the document to a cover email, along with the first four chapters of her report, and sent it off to Rowan. The automated *whoosh* as the message flew off felt unusually satisfying.

Not that she had any firm notion of what good all this would do. In her initial conversations with Matt, he'd intimated that the IWA had the right kind of contacts inside the Beltway to ensure her report would be read. What if that confidence were misplaced? Politicians had been ignoring the war in Yemen for seven years, and that wasn't for want of people trying to tell them it was happening. What guarantee did the think tank have that their own initiative would be any different?

This, surely, was how she could extend her role. She didn't just have the expertise; she also had the passion and the pig-headedness necessary to get someone to listen. While she had no congressional contacts, nor any idea how the United Nations worked, she could at least check out her home turf in the British parliament.

She opened a Google window, keyed in 'UK MPs' and 'Yemen', and hit search. There were reports from a couple of Commons debates – one in which a former Cabinet minister tried to raise concerns about the catastrophe, another where friendly MPs protested in vain at British aid cuts – but they merely served to emphasise how rarely the subject came up. There was also, she was pleased to see, a listing for an All-Party Parliamentary Group on Yemen. She navigated to its page on the UK Parliament website. Eight officers were identified: two Tories, two from the Scottish National Party, three from Labour and one crossbench peer. She recognised a couple of names but most were completely unfamiliar. As she scrolled down, there was a record of office-holders in previous parliamentary years. She clicked on the first couple of these and was presented once again with a list of seven or eight different members of the lower and upper houses, one or two known to her, the majority not. The third list she opened, however, yielded a more fruitful result. One of the vice-chairs that year had been Rita Denby, a name that immediately jumped out at her: this was her own MP. Tara had even voted for her, using the postal vote that Laila had helped arrange.

She opened a new Google tab and searched on 'Rita Denby constituency surgeries'. It took her to the MP's website, its homepage bearing a picture of a woman of around her own age with shoulder-length chestnut hair, wearing the obligatory Labour Party red jacket. There was a dedicated page, headed 'I'm here to help', with a message to constituents from their elected representative. 'I hold regular surgeries by appointment,' Denby wrote. 'To help my team and me best resolve your personal problem, please send an email to my office with details of your case. If it's within my remit as your local MP, someone will get back to you to fix an appointment. I can't promise to resolve every issue, but my hard-working constituency team and I will do our level best to help.'

Tara frowned at the screen, then picked up her phone.

Laila answered at the second ring, in a half-whisper. 'Hi Mum. I can't really talk at the moment. I'm at work.'

'I'll make it quick.' Tara could never understand young people's reluctance to take personal calls at work. What else was the point of sitting in an office all day? 'Do you think the displacement of four million people as a result of warfare is a personal problem?'

'Huh? I guess. It's, like, four million personal problems.'

'No, I mean for me.'

'When you're not one of the four million people?'

'No, I'm not. That's correct.'

'Not really, in that case. It's a personal *concern*, maybe. I don't think you could call it your problem, though. That's, like, appropriating millions of people's suffering and calling it your own when it isn't.'

'Hmm. I thought you might say that.'

'Why are you asking? And more especially, why are you asking now, when I'm at work?'

'It turns out that our local MP has a personal interest in Yemen.'

'Really?'

'Her name's Rita Denby and she used to be an officer in the All-Party Parliamentary Group on Yemen. She may still be a member of it. What are the chances?'

'Yeah, amazing. But what–'

'I need to meet her. It's important.'

'If you want to, go for it. It can't be so hard, if you're her constituent. There must be all kinds of ways.'

'I'm sure there are, if you've got a copy of her diary schedule. But I haven't, so I was thinking her constituency surgery would be the best option.'

'Great. So go along and meet her.'

'It's not that simple. You can't just turn up. These days, with security, I don't think they even disclose the location to the general public. You have to get in touch in advance to book an appointment.'

'Do that then.' Laila made little effort to hide her impatience.

'That's the point though. It says you need to have a problem. And you said yourself I've only got a concern.'

'Well make a problem up then, so you can get a foot in the door.'

'Really?'

'Yes. On second thoughts, no, don't do that. As soon as you tell her the problem is made up, she'll throw you out for being a nutter.'

'Do you think she would?'

'She might. I probably would. Listen, I've honestly got to go. Can we talk about this later? And don't do anything rash. Forget what I said about making something up. That was terrible advice. Whatever you do, don't make something up. Talk to you later.'

She rang off without saying goodbye.

Tara sighed. If her daughter thought the idea was reckless, it probably was.

She clicked aimlessly around the MP's website for a few minutes more, exploring every scroll-down bar in the hope she would find a public engagements diary or any other hint as to which parts of the constituency Denby was planning to visit, but of course there was no such thing, because why would she advertise it in these security-conscious times?

There was at least a contact telephone number, with a local dialling code, for the constituency office. She tapped the number into her mobile and hit dial. The line was engaged, but she pressed redial a few times and eventually got it to ring.

'Rita Denby's office,' said a woman's voice.

Tara mustered her breeziest tone. 'Hello there. I'm a constituent, in Stourbourne, and I'm wondering if it might be possible to arrange a meeting with Ms Denby to discuss a matter of some, er, concern.'

'Are you on the internet?'

'What, right now? Yes, as it happens. I've got your website open in front of me.'

The woman spoke slowly and clearly. 'In that case, would you mind sending an email explaining the problem? Do you have the email address? I can give it you if you've got a pen handy.'

'No, that's fine. I can see it, thanks. It's just that… I don't actually have a constituency problem. I'm a constituent, and I'm calling about a problem for many people – at least four million, in fact – but it's not strictly speaking *my* problem and it's not in the constituency. Although I am. If you see what I mean.' She could hear herself babbling.

There was a pause at the other end. Then the woman said warily: 'I'm not sure I follow.'

Tara didn't blame her. 'Sorry, I'm not making myself clear. Let me try to explain better. As I say, I'm a constituent, but I've been abroad for some time. I've just returned home from several years in another part of the world, a war zone. I've just noticed that Rita Denby already has an interest in this particular part of the world, because she's a member of the relevant all-party parliamentary group. Or at least she was a couple of years ago. So I thought it might make sense–'

'I'm sorry to interrupt you, but if you want to talk to Ms Denby about international affairs, that's parliamentary business. You'll need to write to her at the House of Commons, either by post or by email. Do you have the address?'

'But wouldn't it be simpler if I could just–'

'I'm afraid we can only deal with constituency matters in the constituency office.'

The woman was now using the firm voice that she no doubt kept in reserve for troublesome callers.

Tara was on the point of countering that her MP was meant to be environmentally committed, or at least she boasted as much on her website, so it was hypocritical to make constituents travel all the way to Westminster when they could simply cycle over to see her on her home patch. But she could hear how petulant that would sound. There was nothing for it but to beat a retreat with what little remained of her dignity. Thanking the woman stiffly, she rang off.

She glowered at her screen. It was distressing to be thwarted when you knew deep down your antagonist was right.

The beep of a text interrupted her gloom. It was from Laila. *Sorry I couldn't talk. Please don't do anything rash with that MP. If you want to discuss it properly, I can meet you for lunch tomorrow?*

Tara already knew what she had to do with regard to Rita Denby – write to her in parliament, as bidden – so there was nothing further to talk about. But of course it would be good to see her daughter.

That would be lovely, she texted back. *Let's go to the Chaucer. My treat.*

She knew that last part was redundant: it went without saying that she would pick up the bill. What else were mothers for?

Perfect, came the reply. *See you there at 1pm?*

Tara responded with a thumbs-up emoji and a trio of kisses.

She spent the rest of the morning drafting her email to Denby. She started off saying she'd tried to book an appointment via the constituency office but had been referred to the Commons, even though she only lived a few miles from the local HQ. But when she read it back, the passive aggression screamed off the page. She deleted that draft, and replaced it with a less irritable and altogether more straightforward explanation of what she needed. She was a constituent, recently returned from seven years in Yemen and now engaged by a leading global think tank to try and move the conflict higher up the political agenda on both sides of the Atlantic. It was clearly serendipitous that her own MP already had an interest in the country, as Tara had noticed when looking through the records of the all-party group. Could she and Ms Denby possibly meet, so that Tara could gain a better understanding of the way the issue was perceived in the corridors of power? She would of course be happy to come to the House any time, but equally she was free to meet in the constituency if that was more convenient.

She read this version back to herself and was relieved to find that she now sounded both reasonable and grown-up, and not like the demanding nutcase who had made such of an idiot of herself on the phone. Of course there was no knowing whether the request would have the desired effect. If she were Denby, she'd invite Tara for a cup of tea on the Commons terrace just to hear the latest from a country she clearly cared about. But maybe MPs didn't have time to indulge their personal interests like that, because they were too busy fixing constituents' actual problems.

There was only one way to find out. Tara pressed send and decided she'd done enough for the day. It was high time she spent an afternoon in the garden, where weeds were waiting to be hoed and climbing roses to be pruned, as well as a lawn crying out for its first mow of the year.

The Chaucer was a dining pub in an ancient, narrow street just outside the cathedral precincts. It could get touristy in summer but had always been one of Tara's favourite places in quieter seasons.

Arriving first, she found the place smarter than she remembered. She asked the waitress who brought her to her table if it had been renovated recently, but the girl said she'd only worked there three months and she wouldn't know. Maybe everything in the UK simply looked luxurious after the chaos of Aden, with or without the war. Tara ordered a glass of wine while she waited.

Laila breezed in a quarter of an hour late. 'Sorreee! My boss called me back just as I was trying to leave.' She unwound a woollen scarf from around her neck and flopped onto a banquette opposite her mother.

'I never expected you to be on time,' Tara smiled.

'Charming.' Laila picked up the menu from her place setting. 'I expect you've already decided, haven't you? What are you going to have?'

'I actually fancy a burger. Just don't tell your brother.'

'Ooh, me too! Let's be wicked together. Although to be fair, Sammy isn't the disapproving type of vegan. I got more of that vibe from what-was-her-name...Spinach?'

'Sorrel.'

'Whatever.'

'I thought you liked her. You said she was too good for your brother.'

'I said she's out of his league. Not quite the same thing.'

The waitress re-appeared, and they each ordered a burger with chips and salad, with a glass of wine for Laila too.

'So tell me,' Tara's daughter said when they were alone again. 'What are you going to do about this MP? Have you kept your promise not to submit a fake problem so you can ambush her?'

'I have. In fact I've done better than that. I've written to her at the House of Commons to ask if I can come and see her there.'

'That would be nice.'

'It will be if she agrees, but she may just ignore me.'

'Would she do that? Don't they have to listen to their constituents' requests?'

'Of course not. There are eighty thousand voters in this constituency. She can't give us all tea on the terrace.'

'I guess not. I bet you're more interesting than most of her constituents though. You'll tell her fascinating things, like the fact that Mocha coffee comes from Yemen, and so do frankincense and myrrh, and it used to be ruled by the Queen of Sheba.'

Tara smiled at the familiar tease. 'She'll know all that already. Like I said, she's on the All-Party Parliamentary Group on Yemen. Or she used to be, at any rate. And you need to know all that stuff before they let you in.'

'Like an entrance exam?'

'Exactly.' Tara laughed at the daftness of the idea.

Their food arrived. As they started eating, she changed the subject. 'I have to say, I do like Rob. The pair of you were very naughty with Sorrel, but I can see his heart's in the right place and he seems very fond of you. He looks at you with real affection.'

'He's all right,' said Laila, her mouth full of chips.

'You must think he's more than all right.'

Laila shrugged in a way that said, yes, I like him, but you don't think I'm actually going to say so out loud, do you?

Tara sighed. 'It's so sad that your generation has such little sense of romance.'

'Can you blame us? We give all our money to greedy landlords so we can live in squalid hovels while the world is burning to a crisp. You'll have to forgive us if we're not all *Springtime in Paris* the whole time.'

'You know you can always move back to Willow Tree Cottage whenever you want. There's plenty of room.'

'Thanks. I'm not quite that desperate yet.'

'Now who's the charmer? Anyway, don't forget there's always someone worse off than yourself.'

Laila stopped with a forkful of burger in mid-air. 'Go on, make me feel bad. Tell me about the trillion children living in poverty in Yemen.'

Tara chuckled. 'I will if you like, but I was thinking more of your poor brother, condemned to a life of eating beansprouts and lentils.'

After lunch, Tara wandered round the shops for an hour or so before heading back to the station. As she waited on the platform for her train, she checked her phone. A text from Laila thanked her for lunch and told her she would call her in a few days; an automated holding response from Rita Denby's office thanked her for her message and promised to answer her communication soon; and there was also an email from Rowan.

She clicked it open and read:

Hi Tara

Thanks for the facts and figures you sent, and also for the first chapters of your report. You've made an amazing job of it so far and I'm sure everything you've provided will come in really handy when we meet the Talavera crew in California next week – so long as I can carve out a space to raise the issue. Fingers crossed!

Just one thing we'll have to change: those pre-history lines about the geology will need to come out, I'm afraid, due to current sensitivities, as I'm sure you can understand. I know you'll be able to find a suitable workaround that will avoid offence.

Let's talk more when I get back from the US at the end of next week.

Best

R

It was reassuring to know her killer facts had hit the spot, and that Rowan liked the early chapters. But that last part, about removing her pre-history lines, was a puzzle. Current sensitivities? What current sensitivities?

And how could anyone possibly be offended by geology?

9

She had timed her return to the station badly, missing a train by a couple of minutes, with half an hour to wait till the next one. In the old days she used to know the timetable by heart. She really ought to make an effort to learn it again, although she imagined there were apps for that sort of thing nowadays.

She bought herself an overpriced cardboard beaker of tea to keep her company while she waited. Blowing to cool it down, she pulled out her phone and read Rowan's email once more. 'All that pre-history stuff about the geology will need to come out, I'm afraid, due to current sensitivities...' What on earth could the woman mean?

Tara tried to recall what she'd actually written in her report. Of course she remembered spending far longer than necessary trying to work out the difference between the palaeozoic and mesozoic eras (a question to which she'd already forgotten the answer). The sole point was to write colourfully about Yemen's distinctive topography, and she could certainly remove the passage without detracting from the key messages of her report. But why should she have to? Who could possibly be offended by what she had written?

The arrivals and departures screen above the cafeteria counter announced that her train was due in five minutes. Gathering herself together, she got to her feet, dropped her empty cardboard cup into the nearest recycling bin, and made her way back to the platform. It was fuller now, with a throng of teenagers in school uniform, although not too many to deprive her of a seat. She hoped not, anyway. She wasn't in the mood for further irritations.

The train, when it arrived, had fewer carriages than normal. But she was standing, by fluke, in just the right place for the doors to open, so she was able to find a place ahead of the chattering crowd. She settled herself and pulled out her phone, thumbing a text to Laila. *Lovely to see you today too. I'm on the train at the moment, home in half an hour. Can you give me a call when you have a moment? Something weird has come up and I need to tell you about it.*

She was cleaning mushrooms and crushing garlic for an omelette when her daughter called.

'You certainly got my attention with that text,' Laila said. 'When you say weird…how weird are we talking?'

'Pretty weird.' Tara crooked the phone under her chin as she broke the mushrooms with her fingers and dropped them into the frying pan. 'I know I'm out of touch nowadays, because I'm getting old and I've been away, so I need you to tell me: why is it offensive to talk about the mesozoic era? And who would it offend?'

'The what era?'

'You mean you don't know either? That's reassuring, at least.'

'I've no idea what you're talking about, Mum. You're going to have to explain it properly. Start at the beginning. Like, what's the meso-thingy era?'

'The mesozoic era may not actually be the problem. It could be the palaeozoic. Or the tectonic plates.'

'Mum! You're not making any sense.'

'Sorry. I know I'm not. I'm just so confused by an email I've received from my boss.'

'I hear you. But take a breath and tell me everything calmly, so I can understand what's happened. What did the email say?'

Tara inhaled as instructed, then did her best to explain.

'And what word did she use?' said Laila, when she had finished. '*Sensitivities?*'

'Yes. I could read the whole thing to you, but it's on my phone.'

'Put me on speaker, then you can read it out. It won't cut you off.'

'OK, I'll try.'

Tara managed to switch to loudspeaker mode without losing the call, then navigated back to Rowan's email and read it aloud.

'Hello?' she said, when she'd reached the end. 'Are you still there?'

'Yes. Sorry, I was just trying to absorb it.' Laila's voice was loud and clear over the speaker. 'You're right: it is totally weird. Honestly, Mum, I've no idea what she means. It may be something Sammy and Spinach know more about than I do. But can you forward the email to me? I can ask Rob when he gets in. He knows about all sorts of things. Maybe he'll have some idea what she's on about.'

Tara hadn't realised that Rob actually lived with Laila. But now was not the time to remark on it. 'Thank you, *habibti*. Let me know what he says.'

She had finished her supper and was watching *Channel 4 News* when Laila texted. *Rob says maybe it's got something to do with all that True Earth stuff?*

Tara turned down the TV and frowned at her phone screen. *What True Earth stu…* she began typing, then deleted her draft and hit the call button instead.

'What True Earth stuff?' she said, when Laila picked up.

'Hi Mum. I'm good, thanks. How are you?'

'You know how I am. You spoke to me half an hour ago.'

'It was more like an hour, actually.'

'Well there's been no change. Again, what True Earth stuff?'

'You must have heard of it. It was all the rage two or three years ago. Basically everyone had to start pretending the earth was flat, because hemispheres are racist. Something like that.'

'What? You're not serious?'

'Here, let me put Rob on. He followed it more closely than me.'

There was a pause as the phone was passed over. Then Rob's voice came on the line. 'Hello there, Tara. How are you doing?'

'I've felt saner, to be honest. I can't believe what I'm hearing. Did Laila get it right? Are hemispheres really supposed to be racist?'

Rob chuckled. 'I don't think they are any more. They had a reprieve and they're no longer on the naughty step.'

'You're not making any sense. Pretend I'm a visitor from outer space – I'm actually beginning to feel like one – and explain it in words of one syllable.'

'I'll try, Tara. I'm no expert on the matter but, if memory serves, there was a moment of madness not so long ago when some people with expensive educations but not much in the way of brains noticed a gap between the prosperity of the northern and southern hemispheres, and decided the best way to level things up was to pretend the earth was flat. Thereby abolishing hemispheres at a stroke, you understand.'

'Who were these lunatics? Surely no one took any notice of them?'

'Unfortunately they did. There were some famous examples of people getting sacked for refusing to go along with it. One of them was an airline pilot. I can't remember his name but you'll find it if you google. He sued for unfair dismissal, so it was all over the papers. I think Sir Beowulf Fitch got caught up in it too. You know, the polar explorer? And there was some charity involved in the controversy. Orange Tree, I think it was called.'

Tara was still unsure this wasn't an elaborate leg-pull. 'I don't understand how I could possibly have missed all this.'

'Don't beat yourself up. You've been in a faraway land these past seven years.'

'Yes but I wasn't completely out of touch. Thanks to the wonders of modern technology, I read *The Guardian* the whole time I was there.'

'Maybe you should have read a different paper. Have a little search on Google when you get off the phone. You'll soon find it all. Obviously we don't know it's connected to this comment you've had about your report – from Rowan, was it? I only mentioned it to Laila because that was the first thing that sprang to mind when she said you'd received a complaint for writing about geology. It sounds like the same–'

'Lunacy?' Tara cut in.

'I was going to say ballpark but, fair play; lunacy will do just as well.'

Suddenly Tara was impatient to get off the phone and conduct the internet search that Rob had advised. Thanking him for his help and asking him to say good night to Laila for her, she rang off.

She woke up her laptop and keyed 'True Earth' and 'airline pilot' into Google. She was rewarded with a list of news articles. Some of them, from the *Telegraph* and *The Times* were paywalled, but a bunch of others from *The Bystander,* the *Daily Chronicle* and various smaller websites were available to read. Tara clicked on the the first of these, a *Chronicle* article. It told the story of Captain Wilf Phillips, whose crime was to invite passengers on the aircraft he was flying to look out of the right-hand windows to get a good view of the curvature of the earth. One of these passengers had complained on social media after landing, claiming to be offended on behalf of the indigenous people of the so-called southern hemisphere, and Phillips had been sacked. The article also referred in passing to the case of Diana Dorado, a geography teacher dismissed for keeping a globe in her classroom, and it mentioned other prominent people who had fallen foul of what the reporter called 'True Earth ideologues', including Sir Beowulf Fitch.

When she searched on these names, Tara found more articles, many of them written by a journalist called Ginny Pugh, who seemed to have specialised in the subject. Other coverage came from an unfamiliar publication by the name of *Earth News*. This website made its allegiance clear from its headlines:

Anti-True Earth bigot Captain Wilf Phillips protests 'unfair' sacking

Parents express horror at behaviour of globularist teacher Diana Dorado

Tergs form anti-True Earth hate group

A 'Terg', she learned, was a 'True Earth-rejecting globularist'. To be one of these, in the eyes of *Earth News* and its readers, was the lowest of the low.

Also frequently mentioned in all the reports was a charity called the Orange Peel Foundation. For everyone except *Earth News*, this charity was clearly the villain of the piece. As far as Tara could see, it no longer existed: when she tried to navigate to its web address, she got 'page not found'.

She looked again at the datelines for all the news articles. Everything was at least two years old, so the controversy seemed to have resolved itself. There wasn't even a Wikipedia entry for 'True Earth' or 'Tergs'. It was as if the world had tacitly agreed to forget all about the embarrassing episode. Neither was there any reference to geology or plate tectonics. Horrified as she was to read about the True Earth saga and the damage done to the victims of its zealotry, she wasn't convinced there was any connection to her own present difficulty.

Perhaps Laila was right, and she should consult Sammy and Sorrel. The latter, in particular, had shown a keen interest in ideas, and Tara suspected she might well have an appetite for whatever variant of radicalism was currently fashionable. She checked her watch. Sammy would still be at work, in charge of Friday-night service, but she could text him to ask him to call her when he was free.

Having done that, she made herself a mug of turmeric tea and settled down to see if there was anything on TV. There was nothing more she could do tonight, so she might as well try to put this mystery out of her mind.

It was mid-morning before Sammy got back to her.

'Sorry I didn't call you last night,' he said. She could hear music playing in the background. 'I was shattered when I finished work, and it was also pretty late, so I thought you'd be in bed.'

'Don't worry,' said Tara. 'It wasn't an emergency. If it had been, I'd have said so.'

'So what was it you needed?'

'It's a bit complicated, but bear with me and I'll fill you in as best I can.'

Tara set about explaining what Rowan had said in her email, now updating the story by adding Rob's suggestion that her supposed offence might have some connection to True Earth beliefs. 'To be honest, that's the first I'd heard of them. I couldn't believe my ears when Rob said what they were, and I assumed he and your sister must be winding me up. But I've now read all about it online, so I know it was real.'

'In that case you know much more about it than I do,' said Sammy. 'I'm not sure what True Earth beliefs are either.'

'Do yourself a favour and keep it that way.'

'Ha! Actually it sounds more like Sorrel's thing than mine.

She's really into New Age stuff, which is what we're talking about, right?'

Tara wasn't sure it was. From what she'd seen, if flat-earthery had simply been the preserve of New Age hippies, it would have done far less damage and ruined fewer careers. But now was not the time to quibble.

'I did think Sorrel might know what Rowan's talking about,' she said.

'Shall I ask her to get in touch?'

'If you think she wouldn't mind…'

'Why should she mind? I'll do it right now.'

She thanked him, asked a few solicitous questions about work and whether he was getting enough rest, and they ended the call.

She attempted to get on with her report, reminding herself that the appalling living conditions of thirty million Yemenis were much more important than her mystified affront over Rowan's implied rebuke. But it was hard to focus. She was relieved when her phone beeped with a WhatsApp notification.

Hey Tara, read the message. *How are you? Sam tells me you're trying to clarify a comment that someone made about your writing. From what he told me, I think I may know what they meant. I'm free now, so give me a call if it's convenient.*

A second message came through immediately afterwards, adding unnecessarily: *It's Sorrel by the way.*

Tara hit the call button, and her son's girlfriend picked up immediately. 'Hi Tara, how are you?' Her voice over the phone was husky and confident.

'Hello Sorrel. Thanks for getting back to me so quickly. I have to confess, I'm a little agitated by this. I hope you don't think I'm being silly, but it really bothers me, because I have no idea what my colleague is talking about. And she clearly thinks I do know, because she hasn't explained what she means, which suggests it's something I ought to know. If that makes sense.'

'I understand. It must be super disorientating. Can you read out what she wrote? Sam did try to explain, but it would be good to hear the actual words.'

'Sure.' Tara had already opened up Rowan's email on her laptop, and she now read the email out. 'What do you make of that?' she said, when she reached the end. 'What are these "current sensitivities"? Rob said he thought it might be something to do with True Earth beliefs. Does that make sense to you?'

'Hmm,' said Sorrel, as if she was too polite to openly contradict Rob, but clearly not buying it. 'I'm not really sure about that. The True Earth movement has pretty much disappeared now, and it didn't have anything to do with geology, as such.'

'That's what I thought when I googled.'

'I think I do know what it may be though. Rowan is responding to something you wrote about the geological history of Yemen, right? Stuff going back, like, billions of years?'

'Not quite billions, but millions, yes.'

'That's the problem, then.'

'I don't follow.'

'Well, there's a…' Sorrel sounded cautious, in a way that Tara hadn't observed in her before. 'I mean… I'm pretty sure it's all about respecting First Nation beliefs.'

'First what?'

'I only vaguely know about it but there's been a picket on campus, at the earth sciences department. A couple of people I know sometimes join it. The way they explain it, we in the West tend to treat it as established fact that the earth is billions of years old, don't we? But there are plenty of older civilisations than ours that traditionally believed the planet was created more recently than that, based on stories they passed down from generation to generation. Like, ancestor wisdom? By insisting our view is the only valid one, we're dishonouring that ancient wisdom and their equally valid beliefs.'

Tara struggled to take this in. 'So wait. That means… nothing exists before a certain date? A few thousand years ago, presumably?'

'Yes, that's it, I guess.' Sorrel sounded less nervous now, pleased to hear Tara catching on so quickly.

'So…that must also mean it's offensive to talk about…I don't know…dinosaurs?'

'Yes.'

'And that explains the ban on mentioning the mesozoic or palaeozoic eras, and tectonic plate movement?'

'Those things would certainly be problematic.'

'But…isn't that a bit mad? It's all very well to acknowledge traditional beliefs, but this is science we're talking about. I mean, it's surely not up for debate?'

'Well I don't really know for sure. I'm just suggesting the sort of thing your colleague may have in mind. It does fit with what she wrote to you, no?'

This much was certainly true. Tara sighed. 'Yes, it does. But can I just ask…? Who are these people that we're at risk of offending?'

Well, you know – indigenous people.'

'You mean…the Welsh?'

'It's not so much in Europe, I don't think. I think…it's more of a North American thing? I guess the picket on our campus is taking the lead from US colleges.'

Tara took another breath. This would certainly go some way towards explaining Rowan's respect for this bizarre new sensitivity. 'So it's coming from Native Americans? They're the ones saying we can't talk about palaeontology?'

'I think it's mainly progressive white people trying to respect First Nation feelings. You know, to make amends for past wrongs. To show they're awake to the damage.'

'I see.' Tara wanted to ask Sorrel what she personally thought about all this, but she suspected she might not like the answer, so perhaps it was better not to go there.

'Thank you, Sorrel, for explaining this to me. I do at least feel a bit better prepared for my conversation with Rowan when she gets back from the States at the end of the week.'

'No worries. I'm pleased to be able to help. I'm sure you'll be able to sort something out. You know, keep them happy by skirting around any contentious language. Because that's not the most important part of your report, is it?'

She was of course right on that score, mused Tara after they'd ended the call. It was definitely important to maintain a sense of proportion.

But then she thought of her Palestinian mother, a member of a famously indigenous nation. Her own relatives in Jordan had good reason to be offended and aggrieved by many Western attitudes and narratives, but geology wasn't one of them. They came from the place where the world's most enduring creation myth was born. If they were happy to accept that God didn't literally create heaven and earth in six days or make Eve from Adam's rib, why should anyone else be offended?

It was all very well attempting to move with the times and see the world through younger eyes and from fresher cultural perspectives, but honestly, she had heard it all now. First the flat-earthery, now creationism dressed up as progressive. How had the most advanced human societies reached the point of trying to rip up their own science in the name of advancement?

10

Tara spent Saturday afternoon in the garden. Her magnolias were now in full flower, apart from the one in the shadow of the house that received less sun and always lagged two or three weeks behind. She pruned the climbing rose that straggled up the front of the cottage and planted nasturtium and marigold seeds in the beds outside her living room windows. She had missed all this.

She was also gradually reconnecting with old friends and neighbours in the village. At first she'd held back, not wishing to have the same conversation umpteen times over, in which she reminded them where she'd been and why, explained the basics of the war and described her own living conditions 'out there' (an expression that made her teeth grate). But after the first couple of encounters, she realised she had overestimated the level of interest. Everyone she met said they were pleased to have her back, giving every impression of meaning it, then focused entirely on the changes she must have noticed on her return. They weren't insular, as such; they all read newspapers and books and knew as well as anyone else what was going on in the world. But what united the village as a community was the fact that they all lived there and wanted the best for the place, so the village was what they talked about. What you did when you were away, be it for seven days or seven years, was of little regard to Stourbourne itself. Once Tara remembered this basic truth, it became easier to re-engage.

She was invited to drinks on Sunday lunchtime at the Old Rectory, an elegant Georgian house opposite the church. Too grand for modern clergy, it had been sold off years ago. Its owners, for as long as Tara could remember, had been an antique dealer (now retired) called Willie Frobisher, famous in the village for being able to finish the *Times* crossword in a quarter of an hour, and his wife Roberta, an immaculate blonde who was more glamorous at seventy-something than Tara had ever been.

Their party was a cheerful affair, with plenty of familiar faces as well as new ones. Tara was welcomed into the throng and asked how she was settling back in and why they hadn't seen more of her in the village. She stressed that she was up to her eyes in a new job; otherwise, she knew, she would be press-ganged into proofreading the village magazine or running the raffle for the church organ fund. People asked what the job was and looked impressed when she told them, but they also appeared relieved when she directed the conversation back to local topics.

It was only Willie, her host, who was keen to know more, asking the name of the think tank and insisting he'd heard of it, although she didn't quite believe him. Then he too circled back to the default inquiry. 'And how does the place seem to you after your time away? Have you noticed many changes?'

She shrugged. 'All those new houses in the village were a shock, but I suppose people have got to live somewhere.'

Willie waved his hand dismissively. 'Not the village. England. I'm talking about the mentality of the whole country. The mood.'

'Oh I see,' she said, wrong-footed. 'I'm not sure I'm qualified to say. I've been locked away in my own cottage the entire time.'

'Still, you must have sensed it. Everyone seems to be getting collectively crazier, either because of over-exposure to the internet or because there's something in the water.'

She laughed. This was certainly an insight to which she could relate. 'I don't know about the water, but I certainly agree that the internet seems to be frying people's brains,' she said. 'I reckon madness is becoming the normal state of mind for the twenty-first century.'

One of Willie and Roberta's teenage grandsons appeared, proffering a plate of pigs-in-blankets to his grandfather. 'Guests first,' Willie chided, directing the plate towards Tara, then popping a sausage into his own mouth when she declined.

'Speaking of insanity,' she continued, 'my daughter's boyfriend was telling me this week about True Earth beliefs.'

Still chewing, Willie looked blank and shrugged, to say this meant nothing to him.

'You know, trying to make everyone believe the earth is flat?'

'Ah,' he said, emptying his mouth. 'I certainly remember all that nonsense. Two or three years ago, wasn't it? There was an airline pilot, if I rightly recall, and poor old Beowulf Fitch got hauled over the coals. It was all over the *The Times* for a while, and then it seemed to die a death.'

'That's right. It completely passed me by at the time – it certainly wasn't reported where I was – but I read up on it this week after Rob told me about it. I really couldn't believe it.'

'Barking mad,' nodded Willie.

Emboldened by two glasses of wine, Tara said: 'And have you heard the latest one? You're not allowed to say the earth is billions of years old, apparently, because that might upset First Nation people.'

'Who, the Welsh?'

'That was my reaction too.'

'Are you serious though? I haven't heard that one.'

'I hadn't either, but I hear there's a picket of the earth sciences department on the local campus…' she began. But now another neighbour joined the conversation to welcome Tara back to the village, and she let the topic go. She ought to find out more about this fad before pontificating too much about it.

She had maintained her routine of following the daily news from Yemen, partly on Al-Jazeera but mainly on Twitter. She'd also kept in regular touch via email and the occasional Zype call with some of her expat friends in the aid sector: Philippe, the Belgian from Médecins sans Frontières; Jasmine, who was Scottish, from Save the Children; and Farida, Egyptian, from the World Food Programme. From them, she heard tales of military road blocks, petrol shortages and power cuts that made her feel oddly nostalgic.

Those friends, naturally enough, had little interest in her own everyday life in England. With children starving and shells exploding all around them, why should they care? The result was that Tara was effectively living two lives in parallel – one in the comfort of rural Kent, the other, by internet link, in a war zone – and no one in either life had the slightest regard for anything in the other.

She could call it a schizophrenic existence, but that made it sound like a bad thing. She preferred to think of it as twin-track, a life lived in two places at once, thanks to the advances in technology that made this a normal state of affairs all over the planet for people working on home computers.

It was only when her old driver Mansour called her on WhatsApp, on the morning after the drinks party, that she realised how much she had missed the company of a fellow human straddling the same two tracks.

She hadn't thought to call him herself, which was ridiculous considering how much time they had spent together and how well he knew her. In her defence, there were obvious proprieties to be observed: Mansour was married with three children and another on the way, and there were limits to the kind of friendship it was acceptable for a man and a woman to have in his country. But neither he nor Tara had ever come remotely close to crossing that line, and there was certainly no danger of anything untoward with four thousand miles between them, so she received the call with delight.

'My brother! I'm so happy to hear your voice,' she cried, falling back into the pre-internet excitement of shouting over an international phone line. Aside from one Zype with Egyptian Farida, this was her first conversation in Arabic for over a month. 'How is your health? How is your wife? How are your children?' She could feel herself smiling like an idiot as she worked her way through the ritual inquiries.

'And how is England?' he wanted to know in return. 'Is it snowing?' Like all Yemenis, he knew Britain was cold, but had little sense of how cold, because the whole concept was so alien. 'How are your children?'

'Laila has an older boyfriend,' she said, after she had settled the question of the temperature. 'He's neither handsome nor slim, but he has a good heart and he makes everyone laugh, *al-hamdu li-llah*.' Thanks be to God. That was another phrase she'd never catch herself saying in English, but in Arabic it would sound wrong to omit it.

'And Sami?' Mansour knew Sammy by the Arabic version of his name.

'He also has a girlfriend. She's very beautiful and very clever. Laila says Sami is...' She searched for the idiomatic Arabic for 'punching above his weight', but it eluded her. 'Well, she can't believe her brother has such an attractive girlfriend.'

'And you? Are you happy to be home in England?'

'*Ya'ni,*' she said. 'The problem is, England isn't completely my home any more. Of course it's my father's country, and it's where I was born and raised, but Yemen is also in my heart, and I think it will always be there. So I'm....unsettled, let's say.'

'Come home. We are always waiting for you here in Crater.'

'Thank you, my brother. It makes me so happy to know that I'm always welcome there. But, for now, I've made my decision. And don't forget I have important work to do, trying to tell members of our parliament and the US Congress that they need to take action to end the war in your country.'

They talked on for more than twenty minutes. After they finished the call, she sat quietly for a while, so pleased that

Mansour had made the effort to call. *We are always waiting for you here in Crater.* She knew it was true, but it moved her to hear him say it. Who would have thought she would form such a strong emotional attachment to the lava landscape inside a volcano?

That set her thinking. On a whim, she picked up her phone, opened Google and keyed in 'history of volcano in Aden'.

The first few results were red herrings: there turned out to be an Aden crater in the New Mexico desert, which drew lots of attention from vulcanologists. But once she'd found the right continent, she read that the volcano inside which she'd lived for seven years was one of a chain of six, initially created in a thermal event between twenty-five and thirty-five million years ago, and that this one in particular had last erupted five million years ago. She'd always known it was extinct, but until now had never thought to wonder *how* extinct. Long, long before Adam delved, Eve span and Cain chopped Abel into pieces. She had yet to find out how old the earth was meant to be according to Rowan's hypersensitive neo-creationists, but she would have laid odds that it was a good deal less than that.

'Idiots,' she muttered. Did these patronising fools in their university departments not realise that their posturing erased the history of the very stones on which her Yemeni friends had built their homes?

And now her mood of contentment after Mansour's call gave way to deep irritation. Until now, she'd been trying not to be too dismissive of the claptrap that Sorrel had explained to her, but her conversation with her friend in Aden suddenly made her much less inclined to keep a lid on her true reaction. There was no getting away from it: Tara was angry.

11

Next morning, Tara found an email in her inbox from Rita Denby.

Nervously, she clicked it open.

'Dear Ms Farrier,' it read. 'Thank you for your email and your kind wishes. Your work in Yemen sounds fascinating and I'd be delighted to hear more about it. It's short notice, but are you free to come to the House of Commons for tea at four o'clock on Thursday afternoon? If so, please liaise with my assistant Nathan (copied here) who will brief you on the security arrangements for entering the Palace of Westminster...'

'*Al-hamdu li-llah*,' said Tara out loud.

She reached for her phone to message Laila.

Guess what? Our MP replied! And she's invited me to tea in the Commons!!

A couple of minutes later, her daughter's response pinged back. *Amazing! Well done you! Aren't you glad you did it the proper way instead of stalking the poor woman, like you were originally planning?*

Tara laughed as she read it. There was truth in this, although she had no intention of admitting it. She keyed back: *I don't know what you're talking about. But yes, I'm delighted. Now I just have to work out what to wear.*

Dust off your power wardrobe, came the reply.

I'm not sure I ever had one. Besides, I don't want to look too corporate. Ideally, the plan is to make friends with her. She could be a very useful contact.

I'm sure you'll work it out. Wear whatever you wore when you went to lunch with the crowd from your new office.

Good thought, Tara messaged back. *Talk later xxx.*

She smiled to herself as she turned back to her screen. It was good to be in such relaxed touch with her daughter. They had never formally been out of contact in all her years away, but this instant back-and-forth now that she was home was as unexpected as it was enriching.

Back to the matter in hand. The first task was to message Denby's assistant to confirm that she would indeed love to come for tea. She sent an email as directed to Nathan. Within half an hour, the latter had replied with instructions to arrive via St Stephen's Entrance, allowing at least twenty minutes to clear security, and giving Tara his mobile number to call once she reached St Stephen's Hall. Tara entered the date and time in her online calendar, with an alert for an hour before she had to leave the house.

Next, it was time to raise the question of her status at the IWA. She had already resolved that the way to do this was to lobby Matt Tree in New York, because he had hired her. In ordinary circumstances, it might be tactically unwise to go so blatantly over Rowan's head, but this week it was surely more acceptable, because Rowan was away in California and had more important matters on her plate. Letting Matt know that she had secured a meeting with a member of the UK's All-Party Parliamentary Group on Yemen was an excellent way for Tara to highlight her own value as a permanent member of the team.

As she contemplated how best to make this point, she wandered into the kitchen and put the kettle on for tea. Once the infusion had brewed, she had a decent idea of how to proceed. Sitting back down at her laptop, she opened up a new email and began: 'Hi Matt. I just wanted to let you know…' It occurred to her that might be too abrupt, especially to American eyes, so she backspaced and inserted: 'I hope you're well.' Then she resumed: 'I just wanted to let you know I've made excellent progress so far with my Yemen report. It's approximately one-third complete, which means I'm on schedule. I've already passed the opening chapters to Rowan, who was hoping to use some of the material in her meeting(s?) with the Talavera Foundation this week. She was very enthusiastic in her feedback.' No need to trouble Matt with the geology nonsense. 'I also wanted to let you know I've managed to arrange a meeting with Rita Denby MP' – should she spell out 'member of parliament'? Did Americans, even educated foreign affairs specialists, know what an MP was? – 'who is an elected member of our House of Commons but also, more significantly as far as we're concerned, a member of the All-Party Parliamentary Group on Yemen. She actually represents the constituency where I live, which is a stroke of luck, and I'm hoping she'll prove to be a useful contact as we move into our lobbying phase. Speaking of which' – this was the crucial bit, to be dropped in like a casual afterthought now that she'd softened him up with the good news – 'I'm conscious that I'm still working on a freelance basis while I complete my report. I know we agreed I would have an important permanent part to play, and I trust that hasn't changed. Perhaps I can brief you further once I've met with Denby' – no, that kind of familiarity underplayed the MP's significance, and Americans loved to stand on ceremony, even if they thought they didn't – 'once I've met with the honourable member' – much better – 'and we can discuss how best to formalise that?'

She re-read her draft a couple of times, adjusting the punctuation in a few places and correcting typos here and there, then pressed send. The New York office wouldn't be open yet but the email would be waiting for Matt when he logged on.

Once she'd done that, she remembered she still hadn't replied to Rowan's email about her report. Apart from anything else, it was basic good manners to acknowledge the lavish praise for her work. Furthermore, not replying risked making it look as if she was sulking over the geology rebuke. While that was undoubtedly true, she ought at least to present a nonchalant façade.

She opened a fresh email and wrote:

Hi Rowan

Thanks so much for your kind words about the opening chapters of my report. I'm delighted to hear you liked them so much and I do hope they're of some use when you see the

Talavera people.

I do confess to puzzlement about the need to omit the passage referring to Yemen's pre-history. I'm not at all clear what 'current sensitivities' you're talking about. But no doubt you'll clarify that once you're back in the UK.

I hope your trip goes really well and that you have at least some time to relax beside a Californian pool between your high-level meetings! Personally I can't imagine what Silicon Valley is like, although I suspect it would be make me feel very old!

Have a good flight back, and I'll talk to you soon.

Very best

Tara

She toyed with adding an 'x', but decided against. She had deliberately played dumb with the geology stuff and had forced herself to be as perky as possible with the small talk, but moving to the kissy stage would take fake intimacy too far. A boss was a boss.

Taking a deep breath, she prepared to hit send. Digital communications made everything so superficially easy, but that ease brought with it all kinds of risks. Messages were easy to send but it was all the easier, too, to say the wrong thing or strike the wrong tone, simply because you hadn't thought it through and you clicked the button too quickly. Did everyone experience this anxiety, or was it just her? Maybe she'd ask Laila, she thought, as she sent the email on its way.

She didn't expect to hear back from Rowan for a few days yet, but Matt replied overnight. His response awaited her the next morning.

It was a reassuring message. Yes, he was conscious they hadn't yet formalised Tara's status at the IWA, but he was delighted everything had gone so well thus far, and he was particularly pleased to hear she'd secured such a promising meeting with the Honorable Ms Denby. (Was he teasing Tara by quoting her own language back at her, or had she now convinced him this was how Brits referred to their elected representatives?) He looked forward to hearing how that encounter went but, either way, Tara should be in no doubt there was certainly an ongoing role for her with the IWA. He would make time in the coming week to put the contractual wheels in motion, and apologised for not doing so until now.

This was excellent news. As relief flowed through her, she realised how unsettled her precarious status had made her feel. It was odd: she had experienced no such worries in her seven years in Yemen, where her situation had always been much less certain than her present one. But in Aden she'd had the income from the rental of Willow Tree Cottage, which went a long way in that shattered economy, and she'd always known she could pack up and come home if everything became too arduous, either physically or financially. It was amazing how relaxed you could be when you had that option, of escaping if the going got too tough. But now she was back home, without the rental income, and there was nowhere else to run.

She imagined trying to explain this predicament to Mansour. The very idea was distasteful, and she told herself not to be such a whingeing first-world princess. She had her beautiful home, her fancy kitchen with every known appliance, her unlimited water from the tap, her wifi that worked all hours of the day and night, her fridge and freezer full of fish, meat, cheese, vegetables, juice... These were unimaginable luxuries for most Yemenis. And she was now secure, because she had the promise of a cushy consultancy with a wealthy US-based think tank. Seriously, *al-hamdu li-llah*.

She slept badly on the Wednesday night. In her dreams she rehearsed over and over again, each time in a different, madder context, her forthcoming appointment with Rita Denby. She was embarrassed to realise, when she finally broke out of the dream cycle and woke herself up, how nervous she must be.

This was absurd. She had lived in a war zone and had lounged comfortably in rooms containing more AK47s than ashtrays. Why should she be intimidated by a backbench member of parliament? But of course it was the place more than the person: the security and the flummery surrounding the House of Commons, the sense of entering a hallowed space that was off-limits to ordinary mortals and was designed to make them feel small if they ever found their way inside.

She felt more robust after coffee, and settled down to a productive morning's work, interrupted only by a call from Laila, who had the day off and was in the mood to gossip, and by the secretary of the Stourbourne Residents' Association knocking on her front door, encouraging her to reactivate her subscription.

By the time she managed to get rid of him, she tipped into panic mode once again, realising she hadn't yet worked out what time she ought to leave the house if she wanted to arrive at the Palace of Westminster by twenty to four. Hastily she keyed the relevant details into Google Maps and was relieved to find she still had a couple of hours in which to grab a bite of lunch and make herself look respectable. But then she got sucked into a Zype call from Yemen – Farida wanted to share news of the latest shelling near her flat, and it was hard to cut her short – so she had to floor the accelerator as she drove to the station car park.

After a tussle with the ticket machine, which didn't like her bank card and seemed only to want cash, she caught the train with less than a minute to spare. It took at least two stations before her heart returned to a halfway normal rate.

Realising she still didn't know much about her MP, she pulled out her phone and navigated to Rita Denby's Wikipedia page. Originally from Lincolnshire, Denby had worked as a librarian for a decade or so, and then for a mental health charity. She'd also been a Kent county councillor before winning the parliamentary seat. Since entering the House of Commons, she'd spent a couple of years as part of Labour's shadow foreign affairs team, but was now on the back benches again. Tara couldn't find any explanation of why she had lost that job.

It started to rain at London Bridge, which was irritating, because she'd planned to walk along the Embankment to Parliament from Charing Cross. She would just have to get the Tube instead, in which case it would be quicker, she realised, to get off at Waterloo East.

The train was slowing on its approach to Waterloo when her phone rang. It was an unrecognised mobile number, but she answered anyway, in a semi-whisper designed to show her fellow passengers she was trying to minimise the irritation.

'Is that Tara?' said a familiar mid-Atlantic accent.

'Yes. Is that Rowan?'

'It is. How are you?'

'Fine, thank you. I'm on a train, just about to get off in

Waterloo, so I may be a bit distracted. How was your trip? Are you back in London? I didn't expect to hear from you so soon.'

'Yeah, I'm back. It was good, thanks. We had some very promising discussions with the Talavera Foundation. Nothing is signed or sealed yet but they made some very encouraging noises and we all came away very optimistic.'

'Great. And did you you meet the famous Joey?'

'No we did not. I don't know whether Spencer will be disappointed or relieved, because he was so jealous. But we did meet Krystal, who was a much bigger deal for me anyway. She's a very smart and impressive lady.'

'Excellent. I'm so pleased. Listen, I've got to get off now and I may start breaking up soon, because I need to go down into the Tube. Just to let you know, I'm on my way to meet Rita Denby, my own MP, who is a member of the All-Party Parliamentary Group on Yemen. I put a feeler out to her, thinking it might be useful, and she invited me to tea in the House of Commons.'

'Hey, that sounds brilliant. Well done. Let me know how it goes, won't you?'

The train slowed to a halt and half a dozen people began to move in the direction of the doors. Tara checked her watch. It was a quarter past three, which gave her twenty-five minutes to get to Parliament, allowing another twenty minutes to clear security.

'I will indeed. I hope I'll get some insight into the kind of things that sympathetic politicians need from people like us to help them make their case within the system.'

She was on the platform now, elevated on the long brick overpass that traversed several miles of southeast London.

She'd forgotten how many stairs there were to get down into
the Tube.

'That makes sense,' said Rowan. 'Listen, I just wanted to
reiterate how pleased I was with everything you've done so
far.'

'Sure. Thank you.' Tara could hear herself panting slightly
now, as she started down the first flight of stairs.

'It's exactly what I'd hoped for and, as I mentioned, my
only caveat would be to remove that passage about the pre-
history.'

Really? She wanted to discuss this now?

Rowan continued: 'It's fairly incidental to the main thrust
of your report so I hope you can absorb that cut without too
much difficulty.'

Tara was clearly meant to say something. She'd obviously
known the subject would come up eventually and she would
have to say her piece, but she hadn't yet worked out how she
was going to put her case, and she certainly hadn't reckoned
on doing so while galloping with a crowd of other passengers
down several flights of stairs.

She remembered that she didn't officially know what the
problem was meant to be. 'I'm not clear what the issue is,' she
said. 'You said there were sensitivities. What are they?'

'Oh. I'm surprised you're unaware, but I guess you've been
so far out of circulation all these years.'

Tara bristled at that, but said nothing.

Rowan was obliged to continue. 'The point is, there's a
growing understanding that those of us who benefit from
white Western privilege don't have a monopoly on science,
knowledge and wisdom, even though we've spent hundreds
of years acting like we do. In all those centuries, we rode

arrogantly over traditional beliefs, in many cases obliterating them completely, and it's time we took responsibility for that by showing our mindfulness that there are other, equally valid ways of looking at the world and its origins.'

'Its origins? What other ways?' Tara reached the bottom of the steps. She was thoroughly out of breath, which might perhaps hide the disdain in her tone. Not that she particularly cared to hide it.

'For example, many First Nation people believe in a much younger earth than Western science teaches. There are certain powerful creation stories, such as that of the goddess Ctatpeshirahi' – Rowan stumbled slightly as she said the name – 'from which we ourselves can learn a huge amount, because this worldview is so fundamentally anti-patriarchal. In that context, to speak so openly about geology, as you do in your opening remarks, is to impose the Western colonial model, which we at the IWA simply couldn't countenance.'

Tara had been waiting at a pelican crossing to get across Waterloo Road. The traffic now came to a grudging halt, bar the obligatory couple of cyclists shooting through, and the pedestrian traffic light turned green. She hurried to the other side and entered the main ticket hall for the Underground. She had no time to spare now, so she would have to cut short the call, but that was probably a mercy, because she was in danger of saying something she might regret.

'I need to go down into the Tube now, Rowan,' she said, 'and we're going to get cut off. Look, you can remove any line you don't like from the report. That's completely your prerogative and I leave it to you to do so. But I have to say, and I hope you don't mind my speaking frankly, the reason you've just given me is one of the daftest things I've ever heard. I understand that many of your compatriots feel guilty about the way their ancestors treated the original inhabitants of your continent. But using that racial guilt to police the rest of the world's language, and to deny our entire understanding of human evolution, is absurd – as well as highly patronising to the people you claim to be supporting. And I'm sorry to be forceful about this, but can I ask you just one question before I hang up?'

'Sure,' said Rowan, distinctly cold, however indistinct the line. 'Shoot.'

'It's simply this. You do realise I'm not white, don't you?... Hello?'

But the line was dead, the call cut off as she rode the escalator down into the earth. She had no way of knowing whether Rowan had heard her question.

12

She was still seething when she reached Westminster, but then the stress of getting through security took over, as well as the aura of the whole place, pushing her conversation with Rowan out of her head.

It was three minutes to four by the time she arrived in St Stephen's Hall. She had cut this finer than she'd intended. She scrolled through her emails to find the number for Nathan. When she got through, on the dot of four, a very young male voice told her that Denby herself would be along shortly to pick her up.

She kept her eye on the doors into the Central Lobby, conscious that she knew what her MP looked like, while Denby had no means of recognising her. A short while later she spotted Rita: not as tall as she had imagined, wearing a grey suit and a red blouse, scanning the visitors in the hall.

Tara raised her arm to wave and made her way towards the other woman, hand outstretched.

'Hello there. I'm Tara Farrier,' she said. To her own ears she sounded embarrassingly breathless.

'Rita.' The MP's voice was unexpectedly soft and gentle. 'I'm so glad you could come at short notice.'

'Thank you for inviting me.'

'I though we'd have tea in the Pugin Room.' Denby invited Tara to go ahead, nodding to the police officer on the door to indicate that this was her guest.

'That sounds lovely. Thank you.'

They crossed the lobby and entered the corridor beyond. Tara's shoes sank into the comforting pile of the bottle-green carpet, as Rita nodded at and greeted fellow MPs going in the other direction.

'How's life in Stourbourne?' her host asked. 'It's quite a good village to live in, from what I hear? I know you have a particularly strong residents' association.'

Tara smiled as she thought about the association's recent attempt to harvest her subscription money. 'Yes, it is. I've been out of the country for a long time, and I'm still settling back in, but it's a good place to be able to call home.'

'Ah yes, your time away. You must tell me all about that.' Denby steered her through a doorway and into another corridor, this one with red carpet. 'Here we are: this is us.'

They entered a smallish room, taller than it was wide, with a bay window overlooking the Thames and walls covered in ornate velvet flock. A waiter hovered to greet them.

'Can we have some tea?' Rita said, then consulted Tara: 'Anything to eat? They do a very good plate of assorted sandwiches. Or a scone?'

'No, just tea is fine, thank you,' Tara said to the waiter, who nodded and disappeared.

'Do take a seat,' said Rita. 'I'm afraid I haven't got long, so let's get straight to the point. You say you've just spent several years in Yemen. What took you there in the first place?'

Tara began at the beginning, with her own bilingual background, her time as a journalist and a lecturer, and her decision to relocate to Arabia at the start of the civil war. Rita listened attentively, pouring their tea when it arrived and asking questions here and there. Once Tara started to recount her story of the past seven years, the politician's queries became more focused. How was day-to-day life? Did Tara have much contact with the makeshift government? Which were the most effective agencies at delivering aid?

Tara answered as carefully and comprehensively as she could, pleased to have such a receptive listener. But she also had a question of her own. 'What's your own interest in Yemen?' she said. 'I mean, what made you join the all-party group?'

Rita took a sip of her tea. 'It was while I was in our shadow foreign affairs team. My patch included the Middle East. I don't know anywhere near as much about the place as you do, but I can say this is one of the great crises of the world. The problem is that it doesn't capture the popular imagination, which means MPs aren't very interested either. On the tiny number of occasions the issue has been debated in the House, only a handful of members have turned up.'

This was not what Tara had hoped to hear.

Rita continued: 'The hard truth is that, at the moment, this conflict doesn't threaten UK or US strategic interests, so there's no incentive to try to resolve it. I'm afraid that's how these things work. The only other thing likely to make politicians care is the size of their postbag. If you can find a way of making ordinary British people care about a war-torn corner of the Arabian peninsula, then their MPs will suddenly care about it too. But it's not obvious to me how you do that.'

Tara stared into the dregs of her tea. 'What a terrible world,' she said gloomily.

'Don't get me wrong. I'm not saying you should stop lobbying. Do put all the pressure you can on the Foreign Office, as well as on my own party leadership. You could find a celebrity who cares about the place, perhaps? Someone who can connect with large amounts of people on social media and encourage them to lobby the government. That seems to be the way things work nowadays.'

Tara nodded. 'That makes sense. No one immediately springs to mind, but celebrity culture isn't my strongest suit, so that doesn't mean there aren't any. I can ask my kids.' She sat thinking for a moment. 'Maybe it's also a question of rebranding the place. If we told the Western world that the original Garden of Eden, the land of Adam and Eve, the landing place of Noah's Ark, was being pulverised using British-made weapons, then perhaps people would care.'

'It's all about context and how you frame the narrative, so perhaps it's worth a shot.'

At the mention of context, Tara remembered Rowan and her reaction to her own attempt to provide a prehistoric framework for her Yemen report. She probably ought not to share this with outsiders while the matter remained unresolved, but her despondent mood had made her mutinous. 'Speaking of context, did you know it's offensive to talk about volcanic rock formations and the shifting of tectonic plates?' she said.

'It apparently upsets First Nation people.'

Rita rolled her eyes. 'Unfortunately I'm all too familiar with that. It's actually the reason I'm no longer on the opposition front bench. I have a constituent who has been directly targeted by Young Earth zealots, and I committed the crime, in my party's eyes, of supporting her. They sacked me because I'm a Yerf.'

Tara blinked in surprise, trying to take all this in. 'What's a Yerf?'

'A Young Earth Rejecting Fascist. Yerf for short. It's what the woke creationists call us when we defy them.'

Tara's mouth fell open. 'They think you're a fascist if you believe in science?' The situation was worse than she'd thought. 'I think perhaps I'm a Yerf too. I've just been told I'm flaunting my Western colonial privilege. Even though I'm half Palestinian.'

Rita looked suddenly concerned. 'Oh dear. Who told you that? And what terrible transgression have you committed?'

Tara recounted the story of her report and her clash on the phone with Rowan. 'Sorry to go on about it, but I'm afraid all this has completely blindsided me,' she said, when she'd finished her explanation. 'It sounds like you've got much more experience of it than me, though.'

'Unfortunately I do,' said Rita. 'The constituent I mentioned works at the university. Her name's Helen Kottsack. She's a blameless professor of earth sciences who's been teaching there for years without a blemish on her record. A wonderful teacher, by all accounts, who really cares about her students. But now a bunch of little tyrants who spend far too much time following Californian cranks online have decided she's a racist because she has the temerity to think the planet is more than ten thousand years old, which is when their current goddess of choice is meant to have created it. They picket Helen's lectures with placards saying the most disgusting lies about her, and the poor woman's life is being ruined. It sounds ridiculous, and I'd laugh if I hadn't seen the anguish it causes. Not to mention the disruption to the sane majority of students, who are paying through the nose for an education and just want to go to lectures, but are now too scared to speak out.'

So this was the picket Sorrel had spoken about.

'I think I've heard of this,' Tara said. 'My son's girlfriend is a student there and she mentioned it. She didn't put it the way you just have, but I'm sure she's talking about the same thing.' She tried to remember if she had ever known a Helen Kottsack in her own time at the university. She couldn't recall ever having mixed with any earth scientists, then groaned as a sudden thought struck her. 'Oh God, please don't let Sorrel be one of the protestors. I'd hate to think she's one of the people causing the poor woman such misery.'

'I hope not too,' said Rita. 'Sadly there's a certain kind of student who's determined to embrace every crackpot idea that comes out of North American universities and treat it as gospel. And that's a metaphor I don't use lightly, because this is basically a form of deeply intolerant Bible-bashing. They've convinced themselves it's progressive because it's some hippie-dippy non-Christian religion.'

'Who do they worship?' said Tara. 'I'd never heard this name Rowan mentioned. Cutta… Cutti…something?'

'Ctatpeshirahi,' said Rita. 'It's quite a mouthful, isn't it? I wish I'd never heard the damn name, but I can now spell as well as pronounce it, for my sins. She's apparently a potter

136

goddess who made the earth out of clay. When she finished it, she made woman from her own menstrual blood and man from sand mixed with her own pee. You can see why that appeals. It's so painfully right on.'

'And who actually believes in this goddess? I mean, who are we offending by daring to believe in geology?'

Rita threw her arms up in an elaborate shrug. 'Indigenous people. That's all they ever say. And if you query it, that compounds your crime. The very fact of your not knowing just proves you're a Western colonial oppressor.'

Tara shook her head. 'Like there aren't any genuine problems in the world to worry about. Including actual racism suffered by non-hypothetical people.'

'I know, but in some places I'm afraid it's really taking over. Lots of my voters are students. They love this stuff because it taps into their own guilt about being white and middle class, which they've been told makes them dangerous oppressors. As a result, they're all competing to atone by championing imaginary students from the indigenous nations of North America, who are obviously in fairly short supply in the classrooms of Canterbury. You know they've started burning effigies of me, just because I stand up for Helen?'

'That's awful,' said Tara. 'I'm so sorry. If it turns out Sorrel is involved, I'll read her the riot act.'

Rita's mouth was set in a grim line. 'What makes it worse is the reaction of my colleagues. At best, they're sitting on their hands, watching what's happened to me without lifting a finger. And some of them have actually denounced me themselves, without a word of rebuke from our dear party leader. His only contribution was to sack me.'

'That's so awful. I'm truly sorry.'

'I tell you, there have been moments when I've almost contemplated defecting to the Tories.' She looked at her watch. 'I'm afraid I'm going to have to leave you now. I have a meeting at four-thirty, but I'll get Nathan to come down and escort you out. It's been good to meet you, Tara. Do keep in touch about Yemeni matters, and if you have any more grief from that boss of yours, let me know. We Yerfs need to stick together.'

Tara managed a wry smile. 'Is there a secret handshake?'

'No, but we may need one soon enough. Trust me, this insanity is only just beginning.'

Maria Gonzales PhD @nature_whisperer
Indigenous knowledge is science
Indigenous knowledge is science
Indigenous knowledge is science
Indigenous knowledge is science
Indigenous knowledge is science
Indigenous knowledge is science
Indigenous knowledge is science
Indigenous knowledge is science
RT 7,615 L 27.6K

Ludwig Snittgenstein @ludwigsnittgenstein
Replying to @nature_whisperer
Saying it eight times doesn't make it any truer than when
you just said it once
RT 3 L 183

Ibn Sina @TheRealAvicenna
Replying to @ludwigsnittgenstein
When you see a statement repeated over and over without
anything to explain the point, it's a sure sign it's based on
dogmatic thinking. Anyone trying to have a real discussion
would say: X is Y and here's why, etc etc
RT 4 L 35

Luna Benjamin @lunamodule01
Replying to @ludwigsnittgenstein
It looks like a PhD is saying traditional medicine is as good
as conventional. That's deeply irresponsible
RT 0 L 3

Mojave Medic @mojave_medic

Replying to @lunamodule01

WTF? Of course Indigenous beliefs are valid. As a doctor I recognize inequities built by traumas rooted in white supremacy, colonialism, ableism and all forms of oppression. I honor all Indigenous ways of healing that have been historically marginalized by Western medicine

RT 50 L 398

Aishi Farrin @1977aifarrin

Replying to @mojave_medic

Well said. I too honor indigenous ways of healing

RT 0 L 10

Mojave Medic @mojave_medic

Replying to @1977aifarrin

You'd be more convincing if you capitalized 'Indigenous'

RT 15 L 70

Aishi Farrin @1977aifarrin

Replying to @mojave_medic

I'm truly sorry. I didn't mean to be offensive, but I promise I'll try to do better

RT 0 L 7

Mojave Medic @mojave_medic

Replying to @1977aifarrin

The one who really needs to do better is @lunamodule01. She thinks it's 'irresponsible' to stand up to Western colonial oppression

RT 89 L 1.6K

Luna Benjamin @lunamodule01
Replying to @mojave_medic
Stop twisting my words. But if you're really advising cancer patients to choose herbal remedies over surgery and chemotherapy, you should be struck off
RT 0 L 3

Sadie @sadie93ozumvjfs
Replying to @lunamodule01
Says the white lady
RT 67 L 578

Luna Benjamin @lunamodule01
Replying to @sadie93ozumvjfs
Says the lady who thinks everyone deserves the best medical treatment, whether they're black, Indigenous or white. And you have no idea what race I am
RT 0 L 8

Freddie Daneford @FredoDTweets
Replying to @lunamodule01
Why do you hate Indigenous people so much?
RT 15 L 109

Luna Benjamin protected her account 🔒

Ibn Sina @TheRealAvicenna
Replying to @mojave_medic
Sorry but this is claptrap. Saying herbal remedies are as good as conventional medicine, in some tokenistic bid to honour Indigenous people, is as patronizing as pretending you think the earth is only 10,000 years old
RT 4 L 35

Goddess Ctat @young_earth_matters
Replying to @TheRealAvicenna
Yerf alert!!!
RT 5 L 67

Tara Farrier liked **Ibn Sina**'s tweet

Ibn Sina @TheRealAvicenna
Replying to @young_earth_matters
You made an acronym for people who believe the earth
is more than 10,000 years old. That's like having a word
for people who believe humans need oxygen. It's kinda
unnecessary
RT 6 L 43

Tara Farrier liked **Ibn Sina**'s tweet

Tara Farrier followed **Ibn Sina**

Sally Jenkinson @saljenk07342
Replying to @TheRealAvicenna
STFU Yerf
RT 10 L 177

Ludwig Snittgenstein @ludwigsnittgenstein
Replying to @TheRealAvicenna
When is that asteroid due?
RT 4 L 16

Tara Farrier followed **Ludwig Snittgenstein**

Dr Ross Geller (Palaeontologist) @WeWereOnADarnBreak
Replying to @TheRealAvicenna
Does anyone know any actual Indigenous person who is offended by the observation that the earth is more than four billion years old? Asking for a species...
RT 6 L 54

Tara Farrier followed **Dr Ross Geller (Palaeontologist)**

Sally Jenkins reported **Dr Ross Geller (Palaeontologist)**
for hate speech

13

Tara had an inkling that she might regret searching for Young Earth zealots on Twitter, and the results were indeed distressing. But in the spirit of the proverbial car-crash, once she had started reading some of these posts, it was hard to look away.

Initially it took her a while to find the right corner of the site. She wanted at first to search for the goddess whom Rowan and Rita had mentioned, but she couldn't remember her name, beyond the fact that it began with a C and sounded vaguely Aztec. She eventually found it by googling 'potter goddess', but it quickly became clear that the deity's own fans struggled to spell her name. If they used it at all in their Twitter debates, it was truncated to 'Ctat'. Looking for that arrangement of four letters yielded some results, but then Tara had a better idea, and the acronym 'Yerf' duly yielded way more results. It led her into the centre of the furnace, where anger and invective blazed in the name of respect for unspecified indigenous people – none of whom seemed present for any of the conversations.

Her finger hovered over the trackpad for several seconds before she found the courage to like a robust comment by Ibn Sina. Having done it once, she felt empowered to like a second one and to follow Ibn Sina. This, she assumed, made her officially a Yerf. It was oddly exhilarating.

Before logging off, she followed Rita Denby. Her MP must have been on the site at the same time, because she immediately followed Tara back. Heartened by this, Tara scrolled through Rita's feed. There was a certain amount of unsensational local content – endorsing a charity that supported adults with learning difficulties, visiting a food bank – but it wasn't long before she found a post defending the embattled Professor Helen Kottsack. The tweet had been written by someone else, but Rita had retweeted it. This act had prompted a torrent of abuse, mainly from users with anonymous accounts bearing anime cartoon profile pictures, who frothed with righteous anger as they told Rita she was 'evil Yerf scum' and deserved to die, but also from teenage members of the Green Party with multi-coloured hair. One of these, a party office-holder called Olli Watts, demanded: 'Why is Rita Denby still a Labour MP?'

'It's quite simply really, Olli. Because I keep being elected,' Rita had replied, adding a smiley emoji.

Tara added a like to Rita's tweet, bringing its total to 4,352, compared with 329 for angry young Olli. From her brief time on the site, Tara had learned that this imbalance, where a retort won far more approval than the original post, was called a 'ratio', and being ratioed was the ultimate humiliation.

In the argument over indigenous medicines, where the participants all seemed to be American, the woman called Luna had suffered badly in this respect, and Tara felt for her. In Rita's case, it was reassuring to see the balance of forces tilt in the other direction. Sanity seemed still to prevail on their own side of the Atlantic.

Of course, that would come as little consolation to the poor earth scientist running the gauntlet of baying protestors just to do her job. What had happened to the West? For a moment, Tara found herself yearning for the clarity of war, where at least everyone could agree that bombardment, famine and disease were bad, even if no one had much idea how to stop them.

She slept fitfully, realising too late that Twitter, like cheese, should not be consumed too close to bedtime. In the morning she woke unrested, with a lingering sense of injustice from her conversation with Rowan, as well as from the ugly exchanges she had witnessed online.

As ever, strong coffee and a shower made the world seem more bearable, but Rowan's remarks still niggled. As she opened up her laptop, Tara remembered her boss's exhortation that first day when she visited the office. *We encourage people to have debates on any issue that grabs them. That's our ethos here: share, discuss, don't hold back.* Well then, in precisely that spirit, she would open up the subject for wider discussion. Provided she did it diplomatically, without any implied criticism, Rowan would surely not object.

It was a while since she'd used Clack, and it took several minutes just to locate the icon on her home screen. When she had found it, she opened the app and navigated to the general channel, which Rowan had told her was the correct place for these random discussions. She started to write:

Hi guys

I hope Rowan won't mind me sharing this with you. Something has come up in feedback to the draft of my Yemen report which I think may merit wider debate, simply because it's such a bizarre issue (for me, at any rate) and I'm keen to hear other colleagues' views.

I'm told that, to North American ears, it's considered offensive to voice the indisputable scientific fact that our planet is billions of years old, because certain 'indigenous' religions have their own creation myths, much like the Judeo-Christian one, which make the planet much younger than that.

As the daughter of a Palestinian mother, who was as indigenous as they come and was born in Jerusalem, the cradle of three of the world's great religions, all of whose holy books estimate the earth to be no more than a few thousand years old, I have to say I'm flummoxed by this. I'm not offended by the correct observation that the earth is a million times older than that, so why should any other indigenous person be upset?

I want to stress here that I'm quite content for Rowan to remove from my report the references to the mesozoic era and so on, if they're genuinely likely to cause problems. They're just in there for big-picture scene-setting, and they're far from crucial. But my personal motto, as an atheist of British and Arab Christian heritage who has spent the last seven years living in a Muslim country, is that people deserve respect, not ideas.

In that context, I just wanted to throw the question out there because I'm genuinely interested in what other people think.

She read her post back to herself. Was she being hot-headed? No, she decided. Her words were frank but friendly, and would surely be welcome in a working environment that valued plain speaking and plurality of opinion. She remembered the chat over lunch, when everyone's views had been remarkably similar. By injecting a note of disagreement, in the most collegiate possible way, she was doing them all a favour.

She hit send and felt better already for doing so. She had made it clear she wasn't being obstinate and was prepared to lose the offending passages if Rowan deemed it necessary. But neither had she allowed this faddy idiocy to go unchallenged. She had responded calmly and more graciously than she would have done the previous day, immediately after that dreadful conversation at Waterloo East station. She could congratulate herself for dealing with the situation well, and she awaited her colleagues' response with something bordering on eagerness. She only hoped they wouldn't take her side too stridently and leave Rowan looking foolish. That would help no one.

There were no immediate replies, so she turned to the next task on her list for the day, namely to report back to Matt and Rowan about her meeting with Rita. She opened a blank email, taking care to address it to both colleagues equally, rather than just cc-ing Rowan, which might put the latter's nose out of joint, and then set about summarising her conversation with her MP – the part about Yemen, at any rate. She explained that Rita had been friendly and helpful, and was informed and sympathetic regarding the human tragedy.

The downside was her pessimistic assessment of the prospects for political action by the Western powers. Tara passed on her suggestion that a Yemeni celebrity might be pressed into service to try to spark public interest in the country's plight, which would in turn focus the minds of the politicians. Finally, she mentioned her own idea of trying to rebrand the country so that Westerners no longer saw Yemen as an obscure part of the Islamic world, but as the setting for some of the most enduring stories from the Book of Genesis.

After sending the email, she checked Clack again. There were still no replies to her post. That was no surprise so far as the US office was concerned, because their day had yet to begin, but she had thought some of her London colleagues might have weighed in by now. Reminding herself that they were all busy, and responding to abstruse topics of debate would hardly be their priority, she focused instead on the next chapter of her report. If she forced herself to concentrate only on that, and ignored other distractions, she ought to be able to write another couple of thousand words by the end of the day.

She broke for lunch just before *The World at One*, warming up some chicken soup as she listened to the headlines. After she'd finished her meal, she allowed herself half an hour in the garden, giving her shrubs a decent feed by hoeing fertiliser into the soil; a physical task outdoors always cleared her head for the afternoon. Then she settled back at her desk.

Mindful of her resolution to avoid distractions, she told herself not to check Clack. But her eyes kept drifting back to the icon on her screen, so she succumbed to the temptation, on the grounds that she wouldn't be able to focus properly until she had opened the app. To her dismay, there was still no response to her post. She could not help feeling let down. Seriously, was nobody going to agree that this tokenistic nonsense needed challenging? She had thought they were better than that. Then she told herself not to be so negative. This kind of rumination was precisely why she had made her resolution to resist distractions.

In the evening, after a simple sandwich supper, she managed to sustain her resolution not to look at Clack, but instead she found herself drawn back to Twitter. This time, she searched on Helen Kottsack's name. The embattled professor had a Twitter account but there was a padlock icon beside her name and a notice saying that only her followers could see her tweets; you had to submit a request to become one, which Tara duly did. Then she continued searching on Kottsack's name.

The results offered an instant demonstration of the rigid polarities on which the whole platform depended. For every comment expressing support for the lecturer's right to do her job unhindered, there was another denouncing her as a racist and cultural imperialist who wanted to glorify the structures of Western colonial oppression. Each post, whether supportive or hostile, generated a thread of equally polarised responses, with the number of likes for each serving as a popularity scorecard amid the ping-pong polemic.

It heartened Tara to see Kottsack winning a good deal of backing, but it troubled her deeply that this should be necessary. Someone had made a video of the professor walking through an underpass on the way to her office. The tunnel had been plastered with crude, home-made posters bearing the slogans STOP PAYING RACISTS and FIRE HELEN KOTTSACK. This was the gauntlet of hatred the poor woman had to run every day.

How horrific that this ugly confrontation was taking place not at some screwball Californian academy, but Tara's own alma mater, barely five miles from her home, in a part of England more associated with cross-of-St-George conservatism than with radical extremism.

In another video, protestors chanted the slogans from the posters. Tara was almost afraid to watch lest she catch sight of Sorrel's colourful dreadlocks, but the pickets were all hooded and masked, so it was impossible to know either way.

In those comments that were sympathetic, she noticed a lot of people supporting Dr Kottsack's rights to freedom of speech and to conduct her lectures without harassment; those were decent sentiments, but Tara was also conscious that they were the sort of thing a liberal-minded person might express for someone with rare, outlandish or unpopular views. Everyone in this discussion seemed to be missing a more fundamental point, namely that what Kottsack taught was incontrovertibly correct, and she wasn't expressing an opinion so much as basic scientific truths that no one in their right mind would ordinarily dispute.

This was not a conflict of competing but valid views, so much as an attempt by zealots to undermine and reframe human knowledge in a deranged attempt to show how much they cared about the oppressed of the earth, even though there was no evidence of those same oppressed people giving a damn about the issue at stake. Shouldn't Team Kottsack assert that point with more force?

As someone who had also now been affected by this lunacy, Tara felt sympathy for a woman in her own home town being victimised in this way. Before she could think better of it, she clicked on the comment box to reply to a tweet by a user with a dinosaur as their profile picture, calling themselves Yerfosaurus Rex, who had tweeted that the UK was a free country and the professor ought to be allowed to attend her own lectures without running a gauntlet of abuse.

> **Tara Farrier** @tara_for_now
> Replying to @YerfosaurusRex
> I both studied and taught at the university whose students are targeting Helen Kottsack. I still live close by, and while I totally agree she needs protection, there's something else that isn't being said loudly enough...

She realised she didn't have enough space within the character limit of a tweet to finish her sentence, so she pressed send and carried on writing in response to her own post, creating a mini-thread of her own.

> **Tara Farrier** @tara_for_now
> Replying to @tara_for_now
> It's also important to note that @DocKottH is teaching facts which are utterly uncontroversial to 99.9 percent of the population (at the very least). Her aggressors are protesting on behalf of a nebulous group of people, none of whom seem to have voiced upset themselves

> **Tara Farrier** @tara_for_now
> Replying to @tara_for_now
> These people are supposedly 'indigenous' or 'First Nation'. I'm also of indigenous origin. My mother was a Palestinian from Jerusalem, the seat of three religions with strong creation myths. But I'm not upset by the correct observation that the earth is billions of years old

Tara Farrier @tara_for_now
Replying to @tara_for_now
So can we please call this what it is? It's a bunch of
students with mummy issues who have found a great
way of shouting at a middle-aged woman and claiming
progressive points for doing so. I'm sorry, but it won't wash

As she concluded her thread, she let out a big exhalation, as if she had completed some great exertion. It must be the adrenaline. And it was still pumping through her system, because she realised she wasn't done. Another thought having occurred to her, she added:

Tara Farrier @tara_for_now
Replying to @tara_for_now
By the way, these students believe – or pretend to believe –
that the earth is only 10,000 years old, which is why no one
is allowed to mention volcanoes or dinosaurs. If you're a
biologist and you teach the theory of evolution, take cover:
they'll be coming for you next

She shut her laptop without daring to look whether anyone had yet responded to the first tweet in her thread. She knew she had crossed another line, by expressing herself so publicly. But she was just one in hundreds of millions of users of this platform, so she was flattering herself if she thought anyone was watching. Even if they were, this was surely an issue of sanity? If those who could see the madness for what it was weren't prepared to put their heads above the parapet, what hope was there for reason to prevail?

In an effort to clear her head of the unpleasantness, she put the TV on and found a documentary on iPlayer about the eighteenth–century French linguist who first decoded

Egyptian hieroglyphics. The story soon commanded her attention, because it was classic real-life riddle-solving. But it also occurred to her, as the programme drew to a close, that Egypt had precisely the kind of image in the West that she had in mind for Yemen. It was a noisy, chaotic, poverty-stricken country where Islamic fundamentalists had been attacking random Westerners long before Osama bin Laden made it fashionable; nevertheless, if any neighbouring powers started firing missiles at the pyramids of Giza, the temple of Karnak or the Valley of the Kings, Western opinion would be so outraged, it would take to the streets to demand its politicians put a stop to the vandalism.

Obviously Yemen didn't have the pharaonic treasures or the long archaeological tradition of Egypt, but it wasn't a bad analogy, she decided, as she turned off the lights downstairs and prepared for bed. It might be a useful way of showing the possible benefits of educating the outside world about Yemen's biblical heritage.

As she dropped off to sleep, she made a mental note to mention the point to Matt when they next spoke on the phone or Zype.

14

Over the weekend she gave her emails and social media a wide berth. She spent Saturday in the garden and on Sunday went to lunch at Laila and Rob's small flat on the other side of town. Laila wanted to hear all about her trip to the Commons, so Tara told the story, but her hosts had evidently forgotten about the geology controversy, so she didn't include that part of the conversation. For the moment, she needed a break from the subject.

On the Monday morning, she had a dental check-up booked for ten o'clock. Aside from one emergency visit in Aden to fill a cavity, she'd been a stranger to dentistry these past seven years, and she entered the consulting room at the village practice convinced she was in for a punishing time. To her amazement, she came away with a clean bill of health – a credit, the young dentist told her from behind his surgical mask, to diligent flossing and brushing. She was so relieved, she was tempted to celebrate with a cream cake from the next-door bakery, but that would be reckless. She reminded herself that she was a grown adult with a duty to look after herself; if she didn't, no one else would. She compromised, when she got home, by whisking up a tahini dip with lots of lemon juice, garlic and salt and a decent hit of chilli powder, and eating it with warm pitta bread as a slap-up elevenses.

In her preoccupation, she had managed to forget all about the IWA, the war in Yemen and the crazies picketing Helen Kottsack. It was only when she opened her laptop and saw an email from Rowan that she was jolted back to reality. As she opened it and began to read, her eyes widened. This could not be happening. Could it?

Dear Tara

I'm sorry my comments regarding the 'prehistoric' references in your draft report seem to have upset you. Our conversation was cut short, and I'm very happy to explain in more detail why those references conflict with our values and are therefore inappropriate. If you'd like to do that, let me know and we can schedule a time.

I must ask you, however, to be mindful of our values in any intervention you make on contentious topics on social media. Your Twitter profile clearly identifies you as an affiliate of the IWA, and it is therefore highly damaging for you to take an aggressive public position so out of line with our own settled stance. I must ask you not to tweet on this subject again, nor to post similar material on any other social media platform.

The email concluded by thanking Tara stiffly for her understanding on the matter and was signed with a distant 'best regards, Rowan'.

The first time through, Tara's eyes had skimmed over the text, landing on key words and phrases and then bouncing off again like a pebble on the surface of a lake. Forcing herself to calm her breathing, she took it from the top one more time, making an effort to digest the whole text properly. But it was just as bad in slow motion. The woman who had told her a few weeks ago how much the IWA valued the free exchange of ideas, and who had actively applauded her decision to open a Twitter account, was now saying 'not *those* ideas'. It would be hypocritical even if there were something dodgy about the ideas Tara had expressed. To single out for beyond-the-pale treatment a basic factual understanding of planetary formation was nothing short of lunacy.

But that wasn't the worst of it. The real outrage for Tara, which made anger, frustration and disbelief rise in a bilious cocktail in her throat, was that someone had taken the trouble to monitor her Twitter output. Just a few days earlier, when it had felt such a big deal to press 'like' and then to tweet a comment of her own, she had told herself those nerves came from her ego, because who the hell was sitting on the internet just to monitor what Tara said and thought? It turned out she was right all along: they really were! The pettiness would be hilarious if it weren't so sinister.

Trembling with fury, she tried to collect her thoughts. It was important not to reply in haste; that much she had learned from experience. One thing she could do immediately, however, was go into her Twitter account settings and remove all reference to the IWA from her biography. That way, no one could accuse her of compromising the organisation's values. She logged in, noticing that Helen Kottsack had followed her back and that she now had more than 100 followers, but this was just a flying visit and she had no intention of hanging around to check her notifications. Finding her way into the settings, she deleted the IWA connection and, for good measure, added the words 'all opinions strictly personal'. When she hit save, she felt an instant degree of relief – a sense that she could no longer be accused of bringing her employer into disrepute.

However, that thought merely rekindled her rage. By going along with Rowan's request, wasn't she conceding there was something wrong with stating that the earth was billions of years old, thereby handing victory to the cranks? Looking at it that way, she had half a mind to go back into her settings and put the IWA back into her biography. But no, jumping from one emotional reaction to the next was no way to handle this. The best course for the moment was to step away from her laptop so she didn't do anything to make matters worse.

Moving through to the kitchen and flicking the kettle on, she texted Laila. *Can you talk? Sorry to disturb you at work, but I'm having a bit of a crisis and I need you to talk me down before I do something I regret.*

Less than a minute later, her phone rang.

'That was quick,' she said, answering.

'Yeah, no pressure when you write messages like that,' said her daughter. 'So tell me, what's happened?'

Tara explained as best she could.

'Honestly, I can't remember the last time I was so angry,' she concluded. 'That's why I hoped we could have a chat. Left to my own devices, I'm scared of what I might do or say.'

'Why are you scared? I mean, what's the worst that can happen? Are you worried they'll sack you if you tell them what you think of them?'

'Now you put it like that, I guess it is a consideration. I need this job. I gave up everything in Aden to come back for it.'

'Oh, and there were me and Sammy thinking you'd come home because you missed us.'

'That too, obviously. But you know what I mean. I came back because I thought there was a useful role for me here. And that job also pays the bills.'

'I'm sure there still is a useful role for you. You spent all yesterday telling us how you lobbied our MP on Yemen, so they're bound to love you really, even if you haven't quite learned to talk their talk yet. They'd be crazy to get rid of you and I don't think the idea would enter their heads.'

'I hope you're right.'

'Of course I'm right. Trust me. But seriously, why didn't you tell us about all this yesterday? I know you hadn't got the nasty email then, but all the rest of it... The stuff about Helen Whatserface.'

'I'm sorry. I just wanted a rest from it. I'd been thinking about poor Helen Kottsack the whole time, and to be honest I was sick to death of the topic. If I'd told you all this yesterday, it would have spoiled the day. Which was lovely, by the way. Rob's a wonderful cook.'

'Yeah he's not bad, but you should have told us what you were going through. Don't suffer in silence.'

'I've told you now.'

'Better late than never, I guess. I have to say I'm freaked out by that story of the lecturer. I did see something online about a fuss over a racist professor, but I had no idea what was really going on.'

'I'd heard of it too. Sorrel mentioned it. She said a couple of her friends were involved in the picket on campus. I'm nervous, though. What if it's not just her friends?'

'You mean you think she may be involved herself?'

Tara sighed. 'Yes, I'm afraid I do.'

'In that case there's nothing you can do about it. If she wants to be a dick, that's her business. But you don't know that she is. You're putting two and two together to make five. Spinach may be irritating, but that's not really fair to her. You should focus instead on your immediate problem, which is how you reply to Rowan. How do you feel about her offer to talk it through in more detail?'

'Not much, to be honest, because she's not offering a discussion. She made it very clear the purpose of the conversation would be to explain a non-negotiable position. If there's to be no debate, she can save her breath.'

'Fair enough. What about Twitter, then? It wouldn't be any hardship to stop tweeting about this, would it? You've only been on there for about five minutes.'

'I know but…' Tara tailed off.

'But what?'

'Well, there's nothing like being told you're not allowed to do something for making you want to do it. Now that I know this madness is going on, I can't unknow it and I don't want to stay silent. I've removed any mention of the IWA from my biography. They surely can't stop me expressing legitimate opinions in my own name. I also added a line to say all views are strictly personal. I object to having to do that, because it's a personal account anyway, but it removes any possible ambiguity.'

'I hear you, but they're clearly watching your account.'

'Which is an outrage in itself!'

'Yes, maybe so, but that won't stop them doing it. So tread carefully.'

Tara could of course see the wisdom of this. Yet the idea of being silenced infuriated her. 'I guess so. I'll try.'

'I wish you sounded more convincing when you said that. At the very least, wait till your contract's sorted. What's going on with that, anyway? Has there been any progress?'

'Sort of. The last time I raised it it with Matt, the guy in New York who originally hired me, he made clear it was just a formality. He apologised for being slow and said he'd get to it in the next week.'

'When was that?'

'About a week ago, I think. I can check properly. Hang on…' She called up Matt's email to find the date. 'Yes, exactly a week ago.'

'In that case you should give him a nudge.'

'Yes, good idea. I've had a further thought about a branding idea I've already put to him, so that's a good excuse to get in touch.'

'Sounds like a plan,' said Laila. 'Sorry, Mum, but I've got to go.' She dropped her voice to a mutter. 'I'm getting dirty looks from my boss.'

'Oh sorry, *habibti*. I don't want to get you in trouble.'

'You haven't, but I've really got to go. Bye Mum.'

The line was dead before Tara could say goodbye.

She was grateful to her sensible daughter for helping her talk the problem through. Speaking to Matt again was certainly a good idea. If Tara had fallen in Rowan's estimation, it made all the more sense to keep her original mentor onside. It occurred to her that she hadn't heard Matt's voice since their last Zype call, when she was still in Yemen. Rather than emailing him, it might be better to call him on WhatsApp. It was so much easier to build a personal connection when you could respond to tone of voice. Since New York was five hours behind, she would have to wait till after lunch. But resolving on a plan of action calmed her, and she was able to put in a solid hour's work on her report, completing her fifth chapter.

Wandering through to the kitchen at twelve-thirty, she remembered she'd soaked some chickpeas overnight. These she now put on to boil, adding a pinch of bicarbonate of soda to speed them along, then opened a packet of feta cheese, chopped some tomatoes and half an onion, and made a dressing, ready to throw it all together when the chickpeas were cooked. She ate her warm salad with some crusty bread while listening to the lunchtime news.

At two o'clock, she tried calling Matt, having scribbled a few notes for the points she wanted to cover. He didn't reply, and she listened to WhatsApp ring and ring at the other end. Maybe he was in a meeting with his phone on silent, so she could hear it ringing but he couldn't. He would be able to see the missed call, though. She would leave it another hour or so, to give him a chance to call her back, and then try again if he hadn't.

In fact she got distracted and it was four by the time she picked up her phone again to call him. Again, it rang and rang. Again, she told herself there were any number of good reasons why he might not be able to pick up. But she was beginning to feel unsettled by his lack of response. She tried once more at six o'clock, which was lunchtime in New York, resolving that this would be her last attempt if he failed to pick up. Sure enough, it rang out yet again. It was frustrating that WhatsApp didn't let you leave a voicemail, but she would send him a voice message anyway.

Pressing the record icon, and making an effort not to sound as downhearted as she felt by her rebuffed attempts to speak him, she said: 'Hi Matt. You've probably seen some missed calls from me. Don't worry, there's no crisis or anything. I just thought it would be nice to speak on the phone for a change, rather than sending you a boring old email. First, I wanted to let you know I had a further thought regarding my idea of trying to rebrand Yemen so that people in the outside world think of it in a new way. I was watching a TV documentary the other night about archaeology in Egypt, and it occurred to me that people in the West are emotionally invested in Egypt because they like the idea of the country's ancient history. It's maybe an uphill struggle to sell Yemen in the same way, but some of the raw material is there, in terms of the stories from the Book of Genesis, as well as the legend of the Queen of Sheba. So I just thought I'd throw that observation into the mix. And the other thing, while I'm here: I wondered if you'd managed to put those wheels in motion regarding my contract, which you said you were hoping to do this week. No massive pressure or anything, but it would be nice to get it sorted.' It felt like she'd been talking for ages. Was this the rambling of a mad stalker, or acceptable chit-chat from one colleague to another? She wasn't really sure, but she had started now, and there was nothing she could do about it. 'Anyway, sorry to go on at length but, as I say, I just wanted to let you know why I was trying to call today. Do give me a call back on here if you get the chance, or otherwise respond on email, as you prefer. I hope you're well. Bye now. Thanks. Bye.'

She took her finger off the record button, whereupon her audio clip departed into the ether and landed as a message. She hoped she hadn't made an idiot of herself by sounding too pushy.

After supper, she couldn't resist opening up her laptop again and logging into Twitter.

She began by checking the usual accounts she followed to catch up on the news from Yemen. The Houthis had made a successful rocket attack on a government-held oil terminal on the Hadhramaut coast, as part of their campaign to cut off revenue from oil exports. The destruction was so short-sighted. At least there didn't seem to have been any loss of life.

Having completed that work-related ritual, she now allowed herself a glance at some of the new accounts she had started to follow. For them, today's main talking point seemed to involve Professor Robert Aliss, a bestselling Canadian popular science writer and celebrated critic of Christianity. In his latest tirade, he had argued there was something fundamentally flawed about a religion whose central event was the impregnation of a young woman by a deity. 'The theme of rape/abuse seems a bit off,' he tweeted, adding: 'Why do we treat these stories as sacred in an era of progressive values and scientific knowledge?'

Some wiseacres had dredged up a quote from the same Professor Aliss extolling the virtues of the potter goddess creation myth on the grounds that it cocked a snook at the patriarchy. This character had tweeted it back at Aliss, saying: 'In an era of scientific knowledge, should we be forced to pretend the earth is only a few thousand years old in order not to upset devotees of your potter goddess?'

It seemed a reasonable question, but instead of responding that it was possible to celebrate the virtues of a creation myth without needing to believe in its literal truth, Aliss had simply blocked his questioner, who announced that development by tweeting a screenshot of the blocking notice. This exchange had been shared by the bunch of tweeters who regularly challenged the Young Earth zealots, to demonstrate that a supposed science writer was in thrall to the new-style creationists. That in turn had drawn the fury of the anti-Yerf crowd, who had descended on Aliss' tormentor, telling him to 'die, Yerf scum'.

The account Dr Ross Geller had commented on the fracas:

Dr Ross Geller (Palaeontologist) @WeWereOnADarnBreak
I see the Young Earth cultists are having a completely normal one today

This seemed to sum up the absurdity of the situation, and Tara hit 'like'. She could hear Laila's voice in her head telling her this wasn't sensible in the circumstances, but she wasn't prepared to sew her lips shut simply to appease Rowan. Besides, it was only a like, not an actual tweet of her own. Determined not to disappear completely down the Twitter rabbit hole, she shut her laptop down and took herself to bed with a biography of Ibn Battutah, the Arab world's finest medieval travel writer. She dropped off to sleep after reading an account of the great wanderer's lunch with the sultan of Yemen.

She woke later than usual the next morning and decided not to beat herself up about it; she was clearly tired and in need of the extra rest. She took her time in the shower, then realised when she came downstairs that she was out of milk for muesli, so she cycled into the village to pick some up at the Co-op. While she was there, she treated herself to a copy of *The Times* and lingered over breakfast with the newspaper, savouring the rare luxury of a physical edition. As a result, it was nearly eleven by the time she sat down at her laptop.

She saw Matt's email immediately. It bore the time stamp 23:47. That was of course UK time, which meant he'd sent it right at the end of his own working day, at seven in the evening in New York. She opened it without the nerves or trepidation that might attend the arrival of a message from Rowan, because she had no reason to fear anything negative from Matt.

It was only as her eye ran over the words that she realised how badly she had misread the situation.

Dear Tara

I'm sorry I missed your calls today, but thank you for your voice message.

The parallel you mention with Egypt is an interesting one. I take your point that the outside world tends to put Egypt in a different mental box than other Arab countries because of a prevalent sense that its rich history belongs to all of humanity. I find it a stretch to see how we could ever reach a point where Yemen is perceived in the same way, but I agree it's an aspiration worth considering.

On the general question of lobbying law-makers, I appreciate the thought and creative energy you've devoted to the matter. I'm sorry to tell you, however, that we will not be able to move forward and offer you a more permanent

contract at this time. I know you've done sterling work on your Yemen report so far and I'm very much looking forward to seeing the final version. Rest assured the IWA as a whole greatly values your contribution with regard to trying to place this desperately important cause on the international agenda.
Cordially,
Matt

Tara blinked in disbelief. So her services would no longer be required once she had submitted the final version of her report, and last week's assurance that a new contract was merely a formality was now, like the pharaohs of Thebes, ancient history. What had been a firm commitment had vanished into thin air.

They had sacked her from a job she hadn't had the chance to start.

15

Tara spent the next few weeks on autopilot. Her priority was to finish and submit her report, which was too important to be derailed by her fury at the way she'd been treated. That fury was real and intense, but she made the effort to suppress it, for the sake of everyone back in Yemen, until she was free to speak her mind.

Since she only had a couple of chapters left to write, that time came soon enough. She departed without ceremony. No one from the London office messaged to say they were sorry things hadn't worked out, and there was certainly no question – to Tara's relief – of Rowan taking her for a farewell drink, at which there might be awkward talk of bygones or water under the bridge. All she knew was that one day she could still use her IWA email address and gain access to Clack – where her comment inviting discussion on the fatal topic still dangled lonely and unanswered – and the next she couldn't. Without any fanfare, she had been removed and locked out. At least they paid her final invoice. As she faced her unexpectedly straitened future, that cash in her account really mattered.

Of course, she told Laila what had happened pretty much immediately. She texted nervously, scared that her daughter would tell her it was all her own fault for going back on Twitter and engaging in the Young Earth debate, in defiance of Rowan's ban. Deep down, Tara knew there was some truth in this, but she had a response ready: she had only pressed like, and it wasn't certain that anyone had even noticed.

In the event, she didn't need to invoke this defence, because Laila was righteously, gloriously angry on her behalf. If it ever entered her daughter's head to view the situation from Matt and Rowan's perspective, she was tactful enough not to do so out loud.

Telling Sammy was harder. Tara already nursed a degree of guilt for confiding in her daughter so much, at the expense of her son, and she knew she owed it to him to explain the situation. But she remained wary of his girlfriend, conscious that Sorrel spent time with some of Helen Kottsack's persecutors and finding it hard to shake the suspicion – reasonable or not – that she might be one of them herself. What if Sorrel tried to turn Sammy against Tara? He might be horrified to discover his mother was a Yerf, and it could open a rift between them. When she shared this worry, Laila replied that Tara overestimated Sammy if she though he was capable of falling out with anyone, let alone his mother, on ideological grounds.

'He's just not that deep, Mum,' she insisted. 'I know you

think he's soulful because of those big, dark eyes, but there's honestly a lot less going on behind them than you think.'

'Stop it. I forbid you to be so cruel about your brother,' said Tara. But she laughed despite herself, and it did make it easier to pick up the phone to her son.

Laila turned out to be right, as ever. Not about Sammy's lack of soul; that was pure sibling rudeness. But he was utterly supportive, just as his sister had been, and couldn't believe that Tara had been treated so shabbily.

'Can't you take them to court for unfair dismissal?' he asked.

'I don't think I can,' she said. 'I was only a freelancer, because they hadn't given me a contract yet. So they didn't technically dismiss me.'

'But they promised you a contract, in writing, and they suddenly changed their minds after you posted stuff they didn't like from your own personal Twitter account.'

'True, and they're a bunch of complete bastards. But I'm afraid the law will take the bastards' side and say they had the right to withdraw the offer.'

Sammy said maybe she was right but it was a disgrace there was no justice available to people like her, which was exactly what she needed to hear. She rebuked herself for ever doubting him.

Later, she wondered if he might have a point about taking them to court. She knew next to nothing about employment law, but having Matt's commitment in writing must count for something, mustn't it? She wondered if she ought to consult some kind of specialist, and how much that might cost. In the meantime, she would make a file of all the communications she had ever had with Matt and Rowan.

Aside from her son and daughter, the other person she told was Rita Denby. The fact that Rita had followed Tara back on Twitter made it easy to get in touch: Tara could simply send her a direct message, without having to go via the gatekeepers in her constituency office or at Westminster.

She wrote:

Hi Rita

It was great to meet you the other week. Many thanks for the tea and the advice on Yemen.

As regards the other issue we discussed, you said I should let you know if I had any more trouble from my employers. I'm sorry to say I have indeed. Quite a lot more, in fact: they've sacked me.

Well, strictly speaking they've withdrawn the contract they said they were going to offer me, but that amounts to the same thing. It was my sole income and I came back from the Middle East specifically to do that job.

Of course I can't prove that's why they sacked me, but I'm in no real doubt. They praised my work lavishly, and the only negative feedback I received was for using geological terms in the report I was writing, and for speaking out about the Young Earth issue on Twitter. So that's the only conceivable explanation.

I'm not quite sure where I go from here, but I thought you'd like to know.

Best

Tara Farrier

The reply came back within ten minutes:

Oh Tara, I'm so sorry. Can we get together face to face in Canterbury? There's someone I want you to meet. Friday evening in the Chaucer? 6pm?

R

Tara replied instantly to say she'd definitely be there. She had no idea what to anticipate from the meeting or who the third party might be. But the unconditional sympathy and support were precisely what she needed.

She took the train into Canterbury on the Friday evening, which was warm for the end of April. The after-work crowd must have headed to pubs with more outside space, because the Chaucer wasn't as full as she'd feared. She spotted Rita easily, at a low table opposite the door. Sitting with her, also drinking white wine, was a woman of around Tara's age. It was obvious she was very tall, even sitting down. She had a clear complexion and strong features, with short-cropped hair dropping over her face in a stylish flick. She looked vaguely familiar.

Rita waved when she saw Tara approaching, and both women shuffled their stools around the table to make more room for hers.

'Tara, this is Helen Kottsack,' Rita said. 'I told you about her case and she was very interested, as I knew she would be, when I let her know about yours.'

'Ah yes, of course,' said Tara. 'I recognise you from your profile picture on Twitter.'

'Let me get you a drink,' said Rita. 'What will you have?'

Tara said she'd join them drinking white wine. As Rita went off to the bar, Tara said to Helen: 'I'm sorry to hear about everything that's happened to you. I've been catching up with it online and I'm horrified. I used to teach at the university too, you know, before I went off overseas. I can't believe the students could be so nasty. Or so stupid.'

'Not just the students, I'm afraid,' said Helen. She looked and sounded weary, as if this was a story she'd told many times. 'Various members of staff have fallen over each other to express support for the little darlings. Some of them are colleagues and even friends I've known for years. One or two have been to my house.'

'That's so awful. What about your union branch? Can't they do anything?'

Kottsack snorted. 'They're the worst of the lot. Desperate to prove how woke they are, and delighted to throw me to the wolves.'

'You're joking?'

'If only I were. My own trade union, to which I've paid hefty subs for nearly twenty years, is demanding that my employer sack me. Honestly, Kafka would have found it far-fetched.'

'That's truly outrageous,' Tara said. She leaned in across the table, plucking up the courage to raise the question that continued to plague her. Somehow it was easier when it was just the two of them, with Rita still at the bar. 'These students… Are they people you know? I mean, do you know the ringleaders by name, or are they just a shapeless mob shouting in your face?'

Helen rubbed her eyes, clearly fatigued by the whole business. 'I know the odd one by name, but most of them cover their faces so they can't be recognised. It's ridiculous, because they're in no danger of being punished by the university authorities. But it all adds to the charade that they're doing something courageous. Why do you ask?'

Tara hesitated. Was she making matters worse for Helen by forcing her to think about these sadistic kids? Why should the persecuted woman care whether or not someone Tara knew was involved? But for her own peace of mind, Tara needed to know. 'Is one of them called Sorrel?' she pressed. 'I'm sorry, I don't know her other name.'

Helen shook her head. 'No, I don't think I know a Sorrel.'

'You might know her by sight, perhaps. She's got a sort of bird's nest of dreadlocks, dyed bright pink and purple, piled on top of her head. She's very striking.'

'No, I don't recognise anyone of that description. But like I say, most members of my fan club, as I call them, come in disguise, in black hoodies and balaclavas.' There was a touch of irritation in her voice, that Tara was forcing her to repeat herself. 'Any number of them could have a hairstyle like that, and you'd never see it under their hood.'

'Got it,' said Tara, now wishing she hadn't asked. She hadn't banished her own fears and she had annoyed Helen by pushing too hard.

As Rita arrived back at their table with a large glass of wine, Tara nodded thanks and made an effort to steer the conversation in a more constructive direction. 'I can't believe this isn't a national scandal. Why hasn't the media covered it?'

'Some of them have,' said Rita, sitting down. 'But they're probably outlets you never see. The liberal media won't touch the story with a bargepole, because they know deep down the situation is an outrage, but they also know many of their target readers would probably be on the protestors' side, so it's easier just not to go there. That means the story gets taken up by the

Telegraph, *The Spectator*, GB News or what have you, and hey presto, liberals can dismiss it all with a clean conscience as a right-wing cause. That's certainly what most of my colleagues on the Labour benches choose to do. They see the abuse I've received for supporting Helen and, naturally enough, they don't want the same thing to happen to them. The left/right divide in media coverage gives them the perfect get-out.'

'I'm so sorry you've had to suffer all this too,' said Helen. She addressed Tara: 'These people may be raving lunatics, but their strategy is ruthlessly rational. Demonise anyone who dares express the slightest support for a known heretic, and that will deter everyone else. It works a treat.'

Tara shook her head in disgust, trying not to dwell on the fact that she was now a heretic too, and all these horrors could soon afflict her.

Helen continued: 'Rita's right about the blackout in the national liberal media. But that doesn't stop the local papers half-reporting the story in a way that's completely skewed towards the people persecuting me. As far as readers in the Canterbury area are concerned, there's some fuss about a racist lecturer. They have no idea that the lecturer's racist crime is to have given seminars on volcanic activity in the Triassic period.' She laughed. 'It sounds hilarious when you put it like that, doesn't it? If only it really were a joke.'

Tara nodded, grave-faced. 'I'm afraid my daughter is one of those readers. Don't worry, I've put her right and she now understands the real situation.'

'There's also *Earth News*, of course,' said Rita.

Helen snorted.

'I've heard of that,' said Tara. She frowned, trying to remember where. 'Oh yes! They're the crowd who led the charge on all that flat-earth nonsense I've just been reading about, aren't they? Persecuting airline pilots and geography teachers?'

'And poor old Sir Beowulf Fitch,' confirmed Rita. 'They spent a couple of years campaigning against anyone they decided was a Terg.'

'Don't tell me…' Tara held her hand up as she attempted to decode the acronym. 'True Earth…something…Globalists.'

'True Earth Rejecting Globularists,' said Rita. 'That's all forgotten now, an embarrassment that seems to have been airbrushed from the collective memory. But there's a new game in town now. Yerfs are the new Tergs. If you are one, *Earth News* is ready and waiting to expose you.'

'So far they've published seven news reports about me, each one more poisonous than the last,' said Helen. 'They quote my accusers claiming I've created an "unsafe" environment for certain students because I unapologetically use language offensive to Indigenous people. Every time, they roll out a statistic that fifty-four percent of First Nation youth have contemplated suicide after their traditional beliefs were disrespected, but there's never any source for that figure, or indeed any definition of which First Nation we're meant to be talking about or how many of them go to university in Canterbury. And they're careful never to quote my supposedly upsetting language. That of course gives the impression it's too disgusting to print. No reader would ever know that the most offensive word in my teaching vocabulary, on my accusers' own admission, is *dinosaur*.'

'That's both ridiculous and dreadful at the same time,' said Tara. 'But surely there are laws about making unfounded allegations in print. Can't you sue?'

'I'm not sure how strong my case would be. For example, they're careful to call me the "race-row professor" not the "racist professor". It's pure weasel language which makes everyone think I'm a racist without ever explicitly saying it, but it makes it harder to call them out. Besides, I've got more important battles to fight, such as trying to get the university authorities to take action against the nasty little thugs frightening their fellow students away from my lectures. Anyway, enough about my situation. I want to hear what's happened to you. From what Rita has told me, it sounds equally grim and upsetting.'

Tara sighed. 'I'm not sure it's as personally threatening as the campaign against you. No one is following me around with placards or publishing defamatory articles about me on the internet.'

'On the other hand, you've actually lost your job, whereas I've still got mine – touch wood.' Helen tapped the table in front of her.

Tara smiled ruefully. 'When you put it like that, I guess it is quite bad.'

'Why don't you tell us both the whole story?' said Rita. 'As Helen says, I've filled her in on the parts I could remember from what you told me. But I don't know the latest. It would help if you could go right back to the beginning.'

Tara fortified herself with a sip of wine, then began to tell her tale, starting with her series of conversations with Matt Tree about joining the IWA team in London, as a freelancer at first, but on the assurance it would lead to a longer-term, more formal role. Then she picked up on her more familiar narrative: Rowan expressing concern at her use of geological terminology in her draft report; her forays onto Twitter, leading to Rowan's greater displeasure; the lack of response from her colleagues when she tried to generate a discussion on Clack; and finally the complete *volte-face* from Matt on the subject of her contract.

The other two women listened attentively, gasping at the more outrageous elements, and shaking their heads in sympathy.

'Wow,' said Helen, as Tara concluded her story. She reached across the table and squeezed her hand. 'You really have been through it. I'm so sorry all this has happened to you.'

Rita had been deep in thought. Now she said: 'Without for a second wishing to play down the abuse Helen has received, or which I've received myself, your story really does represent an escalation of the situation, Tara. You've been deprived of your livelihood for expressing a belief to which 99.9 percent of the population also subscribe, which happens to be based on incontrovertible scientific fact. No employer should be allowed to get away with that.'

Helen nodded. 'I couldn't agree more. I was going to ask you, Tara: have you taken any legal advice?'

'My son said I should take them to court. I haven't done anything about it because I didn't think I'd have any protection, given that I was only a freelancer.'

'A freelancer working on the promise of a staff job,' said Rita. 'A promise they put to you in writing, I think you said?'

'Well, yes,' Tara agreed. 'And obviously I've kept copies of all the communications we exchanged in that respect. The other difficulty, though, is proving why they dropped me. I don't have the slightest doubt about the reason, but Matt was careful not to mention it in his email. If I did take them to court, they'd just deny everything, wouldn't they?'

'I think that's where discovery comes in,' said Rita.

'Discovery?'

'If you begin legal proceedings, the respondents have to reveal all their internal communications relating to your performance in the job and any personal feelings they had about you. If they really were telling each other they ought to get rid of Tara Farrier because she'd turned out to be an appalling Yerf, that would all come out.'

'I didn't realise that,' said Tara. 'But before we all get too carried away, there's a more basic problem. I'm worried enough already about having to go into my savings just to pay monthly bills. I really don't have the resources for something like this.'

'Of course you haven't,' said Helen. 'Who does? But I've looked into this, because I want to be prepared if the worst ever comes to the worst for me. There are two options that make a legal action a realistic possibility. First, you may find someone prepared to take your case on a no win, no fee basis. And the other option is crowdfunding.'

The latter was a new concept to Tara. 'Really? How would that work?'

'Twitter, basically,' said Rita. 'If you're willing to offer yourself as a *cause célèbre*, you'd get a lot of support from fellow Yerfs. There's quite a growing community now. If you can get enough small donations, it could really mount up.'

Tara fell silent, taking the idea in. She was certainly angry enough to want the world to know how unfairly the IWA had treated her. If she upped the ante, *Earth News* would presumably start writing about her, as they had written about Helen. But that was surely a price worth paying. She'd never even heard of the publication until a few weeks ago, so how much damage could it do?

Helen spoke gently, cutting into her thoughts. 'If you do want to explore the idea, just to see the lie of the land, I can introduce you to the solicitor I consulted. She's very friendly, she understands this particular issue and she has a very good reputation in the field. An initial chat wouldn't cost you anything, I don't think. If you're interested, I'd be more than happy to hook the pair of you up.'

'Actually,' said Tara, frowning, 'I think I would like that.' She nodded, more certain as the notion sank in, and smiled at her companions. 'Yes please. Do introduce me. The more I think about it, the more I like the idea. If there's a way of taking action against these idiots, I'd love to give it a try.'

Tara Farrier @tara_for_now

I have some news to share which I hope will be of concern to many people. I don't have many followers on here, so if you read this thread and agree that I've been treated unfairly, I'd be really grateful if you could help me spread the word by retweeting it (1/10)
RT 361 L 1.2K

Tara Farrier @tara_for_now
Replying to @tara_for_now

Three months ago I started a new job as a research fellow at the @i_w_a, trying to draw attention to the plight of Yemen, an already poor country that has been ripped apart by a devastating war, and where I lived until I recently returned to the UK (2/10)
RT 23 L 174K

Tara Farrier @tara_for_now
Replying to @tara_for_now

I started the job on a freelance basis, on the (written) understanding that I would be put on staff after I'd produced an initial report on the situation in Yemen. I've now submitted that report, and my boss told me it was exactly what she wanted (3/10)
RT 14 L 186K

Tara Farrier @tara_for_now
Replying to @tara_for_now

The only part she didn't like was a passing reference to a geological event that occurred between 50 and 35 million years ago. I used it to explain the country's distinctive topography. Her objection wasn't that it was too technical or obscure... (4/10)

Tara Farrier @tara_for_now
Replying to @tara_for_now
but that the reference might offend people who think the earth was created 10,000 years ago. Yes, you read that right. I was told I couldn't mention the geological history of our planet because it might offend creationists (5/10)

Tara Farrier @tara_for_now
Replying to @tara_for_now
Not your traditional creationists, mind. A liberal US-based think tank with its main headquarters in New York isn't bothered about offending Jehovah's Witnesses or the Mormons of Utah (6/10)

Tara Farrier @tara_for_now
Replying to @tara_for_now
No, apparently I was offending followers of the First Nation potter goddess Ctatpeshirahi. I have no wish to upset anyone, but I won't disregard settled human knowledge just because it undermines a creation myth, no matter which community it belongs to (7/10)

Tara Farrier @tara_for_now
Replying to @tara_for_now
I said as much to my boss, and then I said the same on Twitter. Days later, I was told I was no longer required at the @i_w_a and I wasn't being put on staff (8/10)

Tara Farrier @tara_for_now
Replying to @tara_for_now
I've been deprived of my livelihood because I won't pretend I don't believe in scientific truths. If some people want to believe in creation myths, that's their right. But nobody should have the right to compel the rest of us to do so (9/10)
RT 129 L 703

Tara Farrier @tara_for_now
Replying to @tara_for_now
That's why I'm taking @i_w_a to an employment tribunal. This isn't just about me: it's a vital test case about freedom of belief. I'm funding my case via a crowdfunder (link below). Please help if you can. Any contribution, however small, will really help. Thanks so much (10/10)
RT 473 L 1.8K

Rita Denby √ @RitaDenby1
Replying to @tara_for_now
Good for you Tara. Shared and donated
RT 75 L 614

Olli Watts @FW10926
Replying to @RitaDenby1
Why are you still a Labour MP?
RT 473 L 1.8K

Leon Smith √ retweeted **Olli Watts**

Helen Kottsack @DocKottH 🔒
Replying to @tara_for_now
I'm so sorry this has happened to you Tara but I'm glad you're taking legal action. I hope as many people as possible will support you. Retweeting
RT 63 L 495

Leon Smith √ @LeonSmith84

Replying to @DocKottH

Birds of a feather flock together. Disgusting but not surprising

RT 532 L 2.1K

Earth News √ @Earth_News

Race-row professor Helen Kottsack backs 'sacked' lobbyist Tara Farrier in further insult to Indigenous people. Click below for full story…

RT 385 L 1.6K

16

The decision to pursue legal action wasn't one that Tara had taken lightly. She'd spent a couple of weeks taking soundings from friends, or friends of friends, with any experience of the law, however tangential. Everyone she consulted agreed that, if she wanted a quiet life, she should walk away and let the matter drop. She believed them, and it would certainly be wonderful if she could forget that this absurd, aggravating episode had ever happened. Unfortunately, she didn't think she could.

She'd had long conversations on the subject with Helen Kottsack, who lived a couple of villages away and had been to Willow Tree Cottage a couple of times since their meeting at the Chaucer.

'Are you sure what you're getting into?' Helen asked. 'That's the real difference between us. I've got no choice but to defy these idiots if I want to keep my job, but you can walk away now, with no dishonour.'

Helen's plight was undoubtedly much worse than Tara's own. Her entire career was now on the line, threatened with destruction at the hands of a bunch of sadistic tyrants who were clearly loving the power and attention. They were aided by the supposed grown-ups in the room, Helen's colleagues and union representatives, who continued at best to look the other way, if not actually to cheer the little fanatics on.

Tara's situation was on nothing like the same level. The IWA's refusal to honour its commitment was low, but it was a setback rather than a catastrophe. However, she and Helen had both been granted – like Scrooge on the night before Christmas – a vision of things to come. The future they had seen was an Orwellian, rather than a Dickensian one: a future in which two plus two equalled five if that was what the new moral overlords wanted it to equal. Having seen this vision, Tara couldn't unsee it. If this made her an unpopular prophet of doom, so be it. She had a responsibility to tell an unsuspecting world what would happen if this nonsense weren't nipped in the bud.

'I just don't think I can walk away,' she said. 'It wouldn't be right.'

Helen nodded. 'What do your family think?'

Tara had talked everything through with Laila, who had made the same point as Helen, saying her mother was under no obligation to wage a battle that might be harrowing and hurtful. But Laila promised to give her full moral support if Tara decided to go ahead.

'My daughter's on side,' Tara said.

'You have a girl and a boy, don't you? What about your

son?'

Although Tara had asked Helen about Sorrel when they met in the pub, she hadn't explained that the girl in question was Sammy's partner. Conscious of having pressed too hard that time, she decided not to elaborate now. 'He works very hard and I tend not to have the same heart-to-hearts with him, but he'll be fine. He's the one who urged me to take legal action in the first place.'

She hoped that attitude hadn't changed, even as she worried constantly that Sorrel was a secret zealot who would turn her son against her. As Laila never tired of assuring her, Sammy worked ludicrous hours and wasn't the type to fixate on political arguments, one way or the other. In any case, she had no evidence that Sorrel had ever attended the protests on campus. This was all just conjecture on Tara's part.

A few days after her conversation with Helen, Tara had met the solicitor whom the beleaguered professor had recommended.

Running late from a previous meeting, Zoya Parveen kept Tara waiting for twenty minutes outside her office on the main drag in Bexleyheath, in the suburbs of southeast London. When Zoya finally arrived, her unkempt appearance – hair straggling in all directions and a trainers-and-backpack ensemble that made Tara feel like a supermodel – compounded the sense of chaos. But a modest amount of online research the previous evening had confirmed Helen's assertion: this woman enjoyed an excellent reputation in her field. She also seemed to understand the battleground of the Young Earth argument, so there was no need for Tara to explain the entire context.

'In my opinion you have a strong case based on freedom of

belief,' the lawyer said, crunching a boiled sweet that reeked of menthol. 'I don't think it makes any difference that you weren't actually an employee. If the tribunal will accept that belief in scientific reality is protected under the law, we just have to show that the IWA refused to give you a job on the basis of that protected belief, which is a clear case of discrimination. As such, it could be a very important test case which could prevent the same happening to anyone else. We can help you set up an online appeal to raise the necessary funds.'

She was as good as her word, and Tara was ready to launch her fundraising appeal one Thursday evening towards midsummer, a month after her access privileges at the IWA had been revoked.

Given that she still only had two hundred and forty-three followers on Twitter, her expectations were low. The initial response after she published her thread – just eleven likes for her ten tweets in the first half hour, and no donations – reinforced that conviction. Having initially checked on its progress every five minutes, she reminded herself that a watched pot never boiled, and she shut her machine down, channel-surfed the TV over a cup of turmeric tea, then took herself to bed with Ibn Battutah, who had now reached Mogadishu, a city brimming with gold, ivory, beeswax, spices and fruit. This fourteenth-century vision finally took her mind off her own twenty-first-century woes.

Her morning routine had slowed since her sacking. She had taken to filling a bath rather than jumping in the shower, which allowed her to use the various salts and oils – mainly gifts from Laila and Sammy – that had clogged up her bathroom cabinet for years, and also spared the need to wash and dry her hair. She told herself she deserved pampering after all she'd been through, but she knew there was a fine line between indulgence and torpor. Nevertheless, knowing was not the same as doing something about it. She drank her coffee in the bath, then made tea and a couple of slices of toast, still in her dressing gown.

She had been putting off checking her tweets and her crowdfunder, on the grounds that she couldn't face the disappointment. When she did finally open her laptop, she was astonished to see that she now had more than three thousand followers and had received five thousand pounds in pledges. There were supportive messages not just from Rita, Helen and a few other accounts she recognised, like Yerfosaurus Rex and Dr Ross Geller (Palaeontologist), but also from a swathe of other self-styled Yerfs, most of them anonymous, and many sporting dinosaur icons next to their profile names, as a badge of allegiance to the resistance.

She was moved by their messages, but even more so by the keenness with which they had shared her appeal and committed funds. These strangers would restore anyone's faith in humanity. Unfortunately, the worst in humanity was equally well represented in the insults, verbal attacks and threats posted in reply to her thread. She knew she shouldn't read them, because they were designed to wound. But she was determined to scroll through all her responses, to make sure she thanked her new-found allies for their moral and financial support, so there was no way of avoiding them. She noted that Rita and Helen had attracted even more ferocious abuse just for expressing their support. Rita, in particular, inspired apoplexy among a phalanx of Labour supporters who seemed to have decided that belief in science and rationality betrayed their party's values.

She quickly learned to check the popularity of each comment, which showed whether these hecklers spoke for many others or were simply lone voices hurling invective into the ether. Many, fortunately, were in the latter category. But the mighty traction of Leon Smith's comment – more than two thousand likes just for calling Rita and Helen 'disgusting' – came as a shock. He might look cherubic but here was brute power in its digital form: using his more than one million followers to heap hatred, like slurry from a tip-up truck, onto blameless individuals. It was an ugly spectacle.

And then there was the response of *Earth News*. She remembered her own dismissive response just a few weeks earlier: she had barely heard of the website, so what did it matter if it published smears and distortions about her? Quite a lot, she now discovered, as she clicked on the article and those distortions filled her screen.

Race-row professor Helen Kottsack backs 'sacked' lobbyist Tara Farrier in further insult to Indigenous people

by Nic Vickers, *Earth News* staff writer

Helen Kottsack, the Canterbury academic at the centre of protests over her exclusionary attitude to Indigenous students, has rallied to the defence of a fellow Yerf in the latter's bid to take a US-based think tank to an employment tribunal.

Political lobbyist Tara Farrier, who lives near Canterbury, is trying to raise funds to take legal action against the New York-based Institute for Worldwide Advancement, which she claims declined to employ her because of her bigoted views.

In an incendiary rant on Twitter earlier this year, Farrier – who claims to have 'studied and taught' at the university where Professor Kottsack now lectures – smeared Indigenous students as 'a nebulous group of people'. She also denounced the anti-racist protestors calling for Kottsack's dismissal as 'a bunch of students with mummy issues who have found a great way of shouting at a middle-aged woman and claiming progressive points for doing so'.

This week the former British expatriate returned to Twitter to launch a further ten-tweet diatribe. In it, she appealed for funds to take the IWA to a tribunal, even though she admitted she had only ever worked for the think tank 'on a freelance basis'.

She made clear she didn't care which community she offended, and admitted saying as much to a senior IWA manager. She also suggested the think tank ought to be more concerned with the feelings of Jehovah's Witnesses and Mormons than with those of Indigenous people.

Despite facing repeated calls to resign for creating an unsafe environment for Indigenous students, Professor Kottsack lost no time in announcing her support for Farrier. She tweeted: 'I'm so sorry this has happened to you Tara but I'm glad you're taking legal action. I hope as many people as possible will support you.'

She boasted that she was retweeting Farrier's entire thread to help raise funds.

Kottsack is not the only prominent Yerf to have backed Farrier. Rita Denby, the Labour MP for Canterbury, who has faced resignation calls from within her own party for her own exclusionary stance, not only retweeted Farrier's thread but crowed that she had supported her financially.

The controversial backbencher tweeted: 'Good for you Tara. Shared and donated.'

This provoked an immediate response from the leading *Guardian* columnist Leon Smith, who commented: 'Birds of a feather flock together. Disgusting but not surprising.' Smith's response won widespread support on Twitter, showing that Yerf views remain in the minority, even in the hate-filled bubbles that are a hallmark of the social media platform.

A spokesperson for the IWA said the think tank was 'unaware of any legal action' and declined to comment further.

Tara read the article with growing outrage. This material masqueraded as news reporting, but in reality it was pure propaganda. The writer – she wouldn't dignify Nic Vickers with the title 'journalist' – had grabbed at every opportunity to show both Helen and herself in a bad light. Helen had said this already of *Earth News'* coverage: no reader would have the slightest clue that the offensive views under discussion actually involved the commonplace observation that the earth was billions of years old.

While the article quoted Helen, Rita and even Leon Smith's tweets verbatim, it had selectively quoted some of her own earlier tweets, trimming them in the most unflattering way, and had merely paraphrased her latest thread, because reproducing her words directly would show how harmless they really were. Emotive language such as 'incendiary', 'diatribe', 'sickeningly', 'crowed' and 'boasted' showed blatant editorial bias which no *bona fide* news outfit would tolerate. Even the words Vickers used to describe her – 'lobbyist' and 'expatriate' – seemed carefully designed to convey a negative impression. And she noticed that Vickers didn't even pretend to have tried contacting her, to hear her own side of the story.

How could any publication be allowed to circulate such deliberately misleading material? Weren't there regulations of some kind with which the media, however lowly, was obliged to comply?

She navigated to the *Earth News* home page, intrigued to know who could publish this cynical, hate-mongering garbage. Scrolling down to the bottom, she found an internal link marked 'About Us'. The first thing she saw, when she clicked on it, was the slogan INFORM. INSPIRE. EMPOWER. JOIN THE EARTH NEWS MISSION. She gave a hollow laugh. Beneath the slogan was a headshot of a man of around forty, with wiry hair and a greyish complexion, looking down his nose at the camera. The picture was captioned 'Our CEO and founder Ricky Singleton'. Tara stared back at him with revulsion.

This would not do, she told herself. She had never been a hater. In Yemen, where she had seen the consequences of the very worst of human behaviour, she had always focused on solutions, on possible routes out of the conflict, rather than retribution for those responsible. If she could remain calm in that blighted place, literally under fire, why not now?

She knew the answer already. In Yemen, as well as being the outsider who could flee the country if conditions became too tough, she had lived amid the random chaos of war. Even if a mortar shell had scored a direct hit on her flat in Aden, it wouldn't have been personal, and the injustice to her would have been no greater than the injustice to any of the other hundred and fifty thousand casualties. This article, by contrast, was vicious and sadistic, and the intention could hardly be more personal. She had been singled out for this treatment, and the outrageous smears were now on view for anyone in the world to see. In that sense, this attack was more invasive than a missile demolishing her home.

But no, that was ridiculous. People she knew had lost homes, limbs, lives... To suggest that being insulted by an online dishrag like *Earth News* was worse than any of those calamities was absurd, an indulgence she could only entertain because they hadn't befallen her. If anyone else said being defamed on the internet was worse than being bombed out of your home, she'd tell them to have a word with themselves. She made an effort to breathe long and slow. Her ego was bruised, that was all. If she really meant to engage in this battle with the IWA, it would doubtless come in for a good deal more pounding. She should either back out now or learn to deal with it.

She stood up and stretched, reaching up to the ceiling and leaning first to the left and then to the right. The sensation in her lower waist was immediately gratifying – a sweet, intense burst that drove out the anguish of the media attack and gave her a moment of mental respite.

Snapping her laptop shut so she wouldn't be tempted to sit down in front of it once more, she ran through a checklist of the household tasks she had been putting off doing. Now was the time to take them head on, to put Ricky Singleton and his nasty publication out of her mind.

Selecting an Arab pop playlist on Spotify and turning up the volume, she took her iPad upstairs and began stripping the sheets from her bed, singing along to Amr Diab as she grappled to replace the duvet cover. This was a chore she loathed, and she tended to defer it for longer than was strictly sanitary. Throwing herself into it now was the antidote to the stress of online aggression.

With the music playing so loud, she didn't hear her landline ringing, and it was only when she came back downstairs that she noticed the light on the phone dock in the hall flashing with a message.

Her immediate reaction was wary. Hardly anyone used the landline nowadays and most of the calls were spam, but spam callers tended not to leave messages. Had some hater found her number and recorded a tirade of vile abuse? Should she just delete the message without listening to it? But no, that was paranoid. A few people in the village always preferred to use the landline so perhaps it was one of them. In any case, there was an easy way to find out who it was.

She pressed the button to access the message, and a woman's voice came clearly through the loudspeaker.

'Hi Tara,' it said. 'Apologies for calling you out of the blue, but your number was listed in the phone book. My name's Ginny Pugh and I'm a freelance journalist. I saw that *Earth News* has written a horrible article about you, and I can sympathise, because they've written loads of nasty stuff about me in the past. You can probably find some of it if you google. I was just wondering if we could speak, because I'd love to be able to redress the balance by telling your side of the story. The publicity would obviously help with your crowdfunder. If that idea appeals, could you give me a call back?'

17

Ten days later, Tara was at Stourbourne station waiting to meet Ginny Pugh off the train.

They had spoken on the phone a couple of times, and Tara decided she liked and trusted the journalist. To carry out a full interview, Ginny said she'd be happy to travel from North London to Kent to meet Tara face to face, which she said would enable them to build a better rapport than talking on the phone or Zype. So Tara had invited her to lunch.

A heatwave was building, and they drove back to Willow Tree Cottage with all the car windows closed and the air-con on full.

'I don't remember it being so hot in this country,' Tara said.

'How long did you say you were away for?' said Ginny, who looked to be around forty, and had walked towards the car with the slight trace of a limp.

'Seven years, give or take.'

'I guess it really has got hotter in that time. You should be used to it though. Weren't you in Arabia?'

'Oh, trust me, I'm not complaining. Aden, where I lived, is pretty close to the equator, and it's roasting in the summer. Nobody sits outside in the daytime if they can help it. Mad dogs and Englishmen, and all that. It's just a surprise to get back here and see how quickly the climate seems to be changing.'

Before setting out for the station Tara had roasted a chicken, the pieces of which she had thrown together with carrots and new potatoes from the garden, and springs of fresh mint, to make a warm salad. All that remained, when they arrived back at the house, was to tip in a heap of fresh parmesan and drench the whole confection in good olive oil.

It was too hot to eat in the direct sun so they sat in the yew arbour, another of Tara's proud creations, on the north side of the house. Ginny set her iPhone to record their conversation, as Tara began to tell the story that she had already told to Laila, Sammy, Rita, Helen and Zoya. By now, it almost felt as if she was reciting it by rote.

Ginny listened attentively, shaking her head and making sympathetic noises, and scribbling the odd note in a jotter. 'They've behaved in an utterly ridiculous way,' she said, when Tara finally reached the end of her tale. 'Good for you, for refusing to take it lying down. Do your legal team think you have a good case?'

'I think it all depends on the material we get from the IWA's internal communications. If any of it shows they changed their minds about employing me because of the views I expressed, my solicitor reckons we have a strong case, based on freedom of belief.'

'Even if you weren't actually employed by these people in the first place?'

'Yes. We can argue they discriminated against me by refusing to give me a job they'd already promised me.'

Ginny nodded. 'I'm not a lawyer, but that makes sense. I wish you the very best of luck in what's likely to be a bruising process.'

'Thank you. I have a feeling I'll need it.'

Ginny consulted her notes. 'I'm intrigued by the cult of this potter goddess,' she said. 'Do we know who actually worships her? I know they keep talking about First Nation people, but which ones? Presumably they're somewhere in North America, but is there any more information about the religion itself?'

Tara shrugged. 'I have no idea. I tried looking it up, but there was so much gobbledegook on Wikipedia, I glazed over. I don't remember seeing anything specific about where she's worshipped, or by whom.'

'I'm curious to know why she's popped up now and suddenly become such a fashionable cause,' said Ginny.

'I just assumed it's because of a change in racial attitudes. No doubt she's been venerated for centuries. My sole objection is to being told I have to believe in a primitive creation myth. I wouldn't put up with that kind of coercion from Christian creationists, and I'm not taking it from any other religion either, no matter how deserving a community it may come from.'

'I'll look into it,' said Ginny. 'It's weird though. I've done three pieces for various outlets about poor Helen Kottsack, and every time I write about the issue, editors ask me for detail on the religion itself. I can find loads of New Agers saying they're really into the goddess, but they all seem to be white people who just like the idea. I really want to find some actual Indigenous people who believe in her, so we can ask them if they're offended by people talking about dinosaurs or the Big Bang.'

Tara began to stack the plates. 'This sort of stuff has become a specialist subject for you, hasn't it?'

'Honestly, there are times when I yearn to write about cats or funny-shaped vegetables, but all this crazy stuff seems to have my name on it, and I'm the first person the editors call. Not that I'm complaining, obviously, because it pays the bills. Life is certainly much easier now than when I first blundered into the flat-earth stuff. There was a horrible backlash after the first article I wrote, and I was persona non grata in the media for a while, completely unable to work.' She shuddered at the memory.

'I missed all that at the time,' said Tara. 'I'd love to hear the story of your own involvement in it.'

Ginny sighed. 'Well, it started when I got an anonymous tip that some really strange things were happening at the Orange Peel Foundation. That used to be a quirky but harmless little charity, dedicated to making maps of the world more accurate. But my source told me to keep a close eye on them, and it was true, they'd shifted emphasis and seemed to be embracing all kinds of weird ideas – saying it was racist to use the world "global"; stuff like that. And I wrote about it, thinking it was just an interesting story, but then *Earth News* came along, and they literally tried to destroy me. Within hours of my story going live, they denounced me as a racist and a creature of the religious right. It was truly horrible. At the peak, they wrote nine articles about me in a single week. And I got picketed by students in balaclavas at the Cambridge Union. They've become a more familiar sight now – it's what Helen Kottsack has to put up with every day – but I'd never seen anything like it back then, and it was the most frightening thing that had ever happened to me. I ended up having a breakdown.'

'Poor you. It sounds so awful.' An alarming thought struck Tara. 'You won't get the same level of grief if you write about me, will you?'

Ginny shook her head. 'I'm far more established now. There are several publications closely following this kind of issue, and nowadays there's a much larger group of us committed to rebuffing the insanity. Speaking of whom, you should meet Mel.'

'Who?'

'Mel Winterbourne. She was the founder of Orange Peel, and all the problems started after she was forced out. We ended up joining forces to fight back against the flat-earthers, and we're still in touch. She's a bit scary at first, but a great friend once you break through the ice. I'm sure she'd love to meet you. Shall I do an email introduction?'

'Yes, thank you. I'd like that.'

Towards the end of the afternoon, when Tara was about to run Ginny back to the station, it occurred to her that her guest might be able to help with the question that still lingered at the back of her mind.

'You know you said earlier you'd written about Helen Kottsack three times?'

'Yes. Why?'

'Just out of interest, did you visit the campus for your research?'

Ginny looked offended that Tara needed to ask. 'Of course. It was a hideous experience that brought back lots of bad memories of my own, but I couldn't write about that picket without seeing it for myself. That's just basic journalism.'

'I assumed you would have. And I imagine you took pictures of the protestors, did you?'

'Loads. They weren't used in any of the three pieces. The only paper that used an image sent their own photographer, I think. But I took lots of pics for my own benefit, so I could describe the scene later. Kind of an *aide mémoire*.'

Tara nodded. This was precisely what she'd hoped. 'You don't by any chance still have them on your phone?'

'I think so.' Ginny reached for her device and started scrolling through her photo album. 'I may have to go back quite a long way, so bear with me.'

'No hurry. I'd just be interested to see whatever you've got.'

'Haven't you been there yourself? It's not far away.'

It genuinely hadn't occurred to Tara to visit the picket. If she had thought about it, she would probably have dismissed the notion as gawping at the source of Helen's misery. But maybe it wasn't such a bad idea, if she really wanted to find out whether Sorrel was part of the notorious fan club...

'Ah yes, here they are,' said Ginny, interrupting Tara's thoughts. She clicked on one of the images and angled it for Tara to see. It showed a group of about eight protestors, clad mainly in black or other dark clothing – leggings, hoodies, jackets, and so on. From their size and shape, they seemed mostly to be men. One or two wore beanie hats pulled down low over their faces. Others wore baseball caps, had their hoods up, or both. All had their faces covered: a couple with full balaclavas, but most with black Covid masks. In gloved hands, they clutched home-made cardboard signs reading NO YERFS ON OUR TURF and SACK KOTT.

'Do you mind if I have a closer look?' said Tara.

Ginny passed the phone over. 'Be my guest.'

Tara splayed her fingers to enlarge the image. From what little of the protestors' faces was visible, she didn't think Sorrel was in this group. 'Is it all right if I scroll?'

'Sure, go ahead. Are you looking for anything in particular?'

'Yes…' Tara was distracted. There were a dozen or so images of the picket, and she focused briefly on each one before moving on to the next. She was conscious that Ginny had a train to catch, but she didn't want to pass up this opportunity. 'I'm looking for a particular individual but as far as I can see…' Eventually she reached the end and shook her head. 'No, there's no obvious sign of her.' She handed the phone back to Ginny.

'Is that good or bad?' said Ginny.

'Good, up to a point. But not conclusive, because these kids are all so carefully disguised. Besides, this is just one day and the person I'm looking for may have been there another time.'

Ginny had resumed scrolling. 'Those were on my way to Helen's office. I think I may have taken a few more on my back… Yes, here they are. Just a few more.' She offered the phone back.

Tara took it from her and scrutinised these additional images in the same way. They showed a slightly larger group of protestors this time, some of them holding placards that she hadn't seen earlier. Once again, the zealots had all taken care to cover their faces and heads, so it would be impossible to identify anyone for certain.

Concluding that the exercise wouldn't show much either way, she scrolled faster, and was about to hand the phone back to Ginny when something caught her eye, in a picture she had just flipped past. She swiped back the way she had come and magnified the image. It showed the familiar group, but they had rearranged themselves so that the camera now had a better view of one of their number who had previously been hidden behind other protestors. The person in question was muffled up in puffer jacket, beanie hat and Covid mask, so it was hard to discern their shape or sex. One feature that remained visible, however, was their left ear. Tara could clearly see a large hole through an artificially expanded lobe.

'Oh please, no…!' she groaned. 'What is it? Have you found her?'

'I'm not sure.' Tara angled the screen for Ginny to see. 'You see that piercing?'

'You mean the flesh tunnel?'

'Is that what they're called?' Tara shuddered at the lurid phrase. 'Yes, I guess so. The girl I'm looking for has got those in each ear. That really could be her.'

Ginny hesitated. 'Is it…someone close to you?'

'Close enough. If it's really her.'

'Do you actually recognise anything else about her, like the clothes or the way she's standing? Or is it just the flesh tunnel?'

'It's just the flesh tunnel.'

'You know they're very common with students? Especially the crustier sort who get involved in stuff like this.'

'Are they? I really wouldn't know.'

'Trust me, they really are. Honestly, one ear lobe doesn't prove anything.'

Tara stared miserably at the image. 'I do hope you're right.'

The discovery, if such it was, put a dampener on an otherwise pleasant day. But Tara's mood lifted at the end of the week when Ginny messaged to say she had managed to place her article in *The Times*.

That's the best possible result, because so many influential people read it, Ginny wrote.

Tara did her best to push the Sorrel situation out of her mind, willing herself to believe Ginny's assurance that these outsize piercings were ten-a-penny among the relevant crowd.

A week or so later, the paper arranged to send a photographer to do some portrait shots. Before the snapper arrived, Tara spent all morning experimenting with various outfits before she found something that was summery, reasonably smart and not actively unflattering. The weather was far too hot for trying on clothes, and she was sweaty and cantankerous by the time the young woman eventually showed up with her camera bags and tripods. Tara hadn't even had time to do anything with her hair. But the woman was clearly good at putting subjects at their ease and Tara was pleasantly surprised by the picture that accompanied the finished article in print when she saw it the following weekend.

In the village, she discovered she was suddenly a local celebrity, as several people told her they had read the piece.

'Roberta and I were both horrified to learn what's happened to you,' said Willie Frobisher, her host at the Old Rectory, when she bumped into him outside the post office. 'We hope you take the blighters to the cleaners. When are you due in court?'

'Actually the first hearing is next month. It's come round much sooner than I expected. But it's only a preliminary one.'

'Knock 'em dead. I'm sure you will.'

'Tell that to my lawyers,' said Tara. 'If there's any knocking dead to be done, they're the ones who'll do it, not me.'

'Have you got a good team?'

'I hope so. My solicitor seems very smart and she assures me my barrister is one of the best in the business.'

'Who've you got?'

'He's a KC called Denton Hooper. I haven't met him yet.'

'I'm sure he'll be marvellous. If he isn't, tell him I'll want to know the reason why.'

Laughing, Tara promised she would.

'By the way,' Willie called, as she turned to carry on her way.

'Yes?'

'What's the name of that obscure goddess whose followers you're meant to have offended?'

Tara sighed. 'I can't pronounce it but I can spell it. C-T-A-T-P-E-S-H-I-R-A-H-I.'

'Hang on.' Willie pulled a scrap of paper out of his pocket and groped for a pencil. 'Sorry, I'm ready now. Tell me again.'

She spelled it out once more, slowly enough for him to write it down. 'Why do you want to know?' she added.

'Just a whim. Thank you for indulging an old man,' he said, and winked as he turned away.

The internet was a good deal less friendly than Stourbourne.

Tara tweeted a link to Ginny's article, as did many of her supporters. On the upside, she was both gratified and amazed to see her follower count surge past ten thousand, and the publicity did wonders for her crowdfunder. Zoya had advised that she ought to have at least £50,000 in the bag before their first appearance. Tara had nearly achieved that already, and everyone assured her the total would continue to rise as the court date approached.

But all that came at the cost of ever more vicious personal attacks and slanders.

The name-calling was easier to deal with than she had feared, simply because her baiters lacked imagination. The same limited repertoire of insults – 'bigot', 'right-wing scum', 'Yerf bitch' – quickly lost their power to wound as she became inured to them. She found the blatant distortions much harder to endure. The first time someone on Twitter accused her of having abused First Nation colleagues and ridiculed their religious beliefs to their faces, she politely put them straight. She explained that she had only met her colleagues twice and that none of them, so far as she was aware, were indigenous North Americans (in fact only one of them was North American at all). She added that she had the greatest respect for any minority racial communities, since she came from one herself, and would never dream of insulting someone's religion. Her only issue was with people telling her she couldn't refer to the established scientific understanding of the earth's history, which was accepted by the vast majority of the world's population and some 99.9 percent of the population of the UK.

Naively, she thought this would be enough to lay the misunderstanding to rest. However, she soon learned that her enemies weren't interested in truth, particularly if that meant giving up the pantomime-villain caricature of her that they had so enthusiastically created. The falsehood was repeated and retweeted so often that it became impossible to contain. Whoever said that a lie got halfway round the world before the truth could get its boots on had clearly never anticipated the internet: this lie could complete four or five circumnavigations in the time it took Tara to cut and paste her standard denial. After a while she gave up, and gratefully allowed her faithful band of supporters to correct the smear on her behalf.

Even more poisonous was the canard that she had been a missionary in Yemen. Ginny had mentioned Tara's years in Arabia in her *Times* piece, adding the detail that she had Middle Eastern blood and her mother was a Christian from Jerusalem. This had been enough for dishonest opponents to suggest that Christianity itself was the reason for Tara's move to Aden.

'I must be the world's first atheist missionary,' she tweeted drily, in response.

Even that was twisted against her, as *Earth News* trumpeted: 'Tara Farrier admits she was a missionary.'

It left her spitting with frustration. 'They're absolutely shameless. Are there no depths to which they won't sink?' she complained to Ginny on WhatsApp.

'I think you know the answer to that already,' said her new friend.

Tara resolved never again to use irony on the internet.

Ginny Pugh ✓ @GinnyPugh
Journalist enquiry: can anyone tell me which First Nation people worship the goddess Ctatpeshirahi? Thanks
RT 19 L 80

Goddess Ctat @young_earth_matters
Replying to @GinnyPugh
Do your own research Yerf
RT 6 L 146

Ginny Pugh ✓ @GinnyPugh
Replying to @young_earth_matters
That's exactly what I'm trying to do. I'm consulting people who have better knowledge of the subject than me. It's standard journalistic practice. Can you help me? You're obviously a big fan of the goddess. Are you of First Nation origin?
RT 5 L 20

Goddess Ctat @young_earth_matters
Replying to @GinnyPugh
I'm not falling for this. I've seen your feed. You're not a journalist. You're just an apologist for bigots like @DocKottH. I'm not helping you write Yerf propaganda
RT 25 L 111

Ginny Pugh √ @GinnyPugh
Replying to @young_earth_matters
I asked you a simple, polite question about your relationship with the goddess in your profile name. I honestly don't see why you can't answer it
RT 3 L 19

Goddess Ctat blocked **Ginny Pugh √**

Ginny Pugh √ @GinnyPugh
Just asking this again. I'm writing about the goddess Ctatpeshirahi and I'm interested to know which First Nation community worships her. I know they're from North America but that's a huge place, two and a half times the size of Europe...
RT 48 L 134

Ginny Pugh √ @GinnyPugh
Replying to @GinnyPugh
And I know there were so many religious traditions across the continent before the colonists arrived, from Inuit to Native Americans to Aztecs. I've tried researching all their religions but I can't find any reference in the literature to the potter goddess. Can anyone help?
RT 19 L 119

Mojave Medic @mojave_medic
Replying to @GinnyPugh
Any real journalist would know this already without having to ask
RT 36 L 280

Ginny Pugh √ @GinnyPugh
The fact remains that I don't know, and I've been commissioned to write about the subject, so would you consider telling me the answer?
RT 2 L 25

Mojave Medic @mojave_medic
Replying to @GinnyPugh
Just so you can write bigoted Yerf bullshit? I wasn't born yesterday, lady. I hope you die in a grease fire
RT 797 L 1.1K

Mojave Medic blocked **Ginny Pugh √**

Sadie @sadie93ozumvjfs
Replying to @GinnyPugh
British journalist can't be bothered to do her own research and thinks we're all her minions just here to do her bidding. We're no longer your colony. And clean your goddamn teeth
RT 304 L 901

Ginny Pugh √ @GinnyPugh
Replying to @sadie93ozumvjfs
It's so odd that nobody is prepared to answer a simple, polite question. I really don't understand why you have to resort to abuse
RT 9 L 35

Sadie @sadie93ozumvjfs
Replying to @GinnyPugh
There's a lot you don't understand. Educate yourself. Read a damn book
RT 194 L 435

Sadie blocked **Ginny Pugh √**

Lateefa Latif √ @lateefalatif
OMG I so hate to see people with a vile agenda throwing shade at the glorious goddess Ctat. We see you, we know who you are. You seek to divide us by ethnicity but we are all free to LOVE the goddess, whoever we are, because LOVE IS LOVE
RT 1.3K L 23.4K

Ginny Pugh √ @GinnyPugh
Replying to @lateefalatif
Hi Lateefa. I'm not sure if this was directed at me. I suspect it may have been, even though asking about the origins of the goddess honestly isn't 'throwing shade'. I know you're from Hampstead originally, but do you happen to know which First Nation community originally worshipped your goddess?
RT 58 L 317

Lateefa Latif √ blocked **Ginny Pugh √**

Sally Jenkinson @saljenk07342
Replying to @GinnyPugh
STFU Yerf
RT 360 L 1.2K

18

Ginny was as good as her word, and effected an email introduction to Mel Winterbourne. Since Ginny had billed her as scary, Tara was nervous of the Orange Peel founder at first, but she concluded from their brief email exchange that Mel was simply a bit old-school, rather than a gushy millennial. She was certainly friendly enough in spirit, saying she'd be delighted to meet Tara in person. Since she lived in South London, she suggested a wine bar in Borough Market one Friday afternoon.

Almost as tall as Helen Kottsack, and ten years or so older than Tara, Mel was dressed in tailored jeans and a silk shirt with pearl buttons. She had arrived first and had a bottle of Chablis chilling in an ice bucket. She greeted Tara with a kiss on both cheeks.

'I'm so sorry about these *Earth News* hatchet jobs,' she said, pouring a glass for Tara. 'I know Ricky Singleton of old – Ricky Simpleton, we always used to call him – and I'm all too aware what a nightmare he and his rag can be. But he has a habit of bringing people like us together in solidarity, so let's drink to the start of a beautiful friendship.'

This was exactly what Tara needed to hear. 'To friendship,' she said, raising her glass. 'It's great to meet you. Ginny spoke very highly of you.'

'That's good of her. I was frightened for a while that I'd destroyed her life, and she'd have been justified in never forgiving me.'

'Really? She didn't mention anything like that.'

Mel shrugged. 'I tipped her off anonymously about what was going on behind the scenes at Orange Peel. I thought I was doing her a favour. I didn't realise I was painting a target on her back.'

It took a moment for Tara to process that. 'So…you were the secret source? I see. She never mentioned that.'

'As I say, she's a good person. She could easily have blamed me.'

Tara nodded. 'You know, I only recently heard about all that flat-earth nonsense. I've been out of the country for a long time, and I completely missed it at the time. The first I knew of it was when my daughter's boyfriend told me about it. I gather you were in the eye of the storm.'

'You could say that, yes. The charity was my baby. I founded it and grew it into a successful outfit. I was about to wind it up, because it had achieved all its stated aims, when it was hijacked by the unscrupulous man whom I'd unwisely made my deputy.'

'Who was also my ex-husband,' said a voice behind Tara.

'For my sins.'

Tara turned to see a curly-haired young man of around thirty-five, with heavy bags under his eyes and a gold cross on a chain around his neck.

'I hope you don't mind, Tara, but I asked Craig to join us,' said Mel. 'He works over the road, and when I mentioned I was meeting you here, he said he'd really like to meet you if we could time it for the end of his shift.'

Only now did Tara notice that Mel had a spare glass in front of her, into which she now poured wine for the newcomer.

'Not at all,' she said, as Craig pulled up a stool and took the glass from Mel. 'What work do you do, Craig?'

'I'm a doctor, at Guy's. Orthopaedics.'

'Oh I see.' That explained the bags under the eyes.

Mel resumed her story. 'In the end, I was able to regain control of Orange Peel and shut it down properly, before it could do any more damage. But I could never have done so without Craig. He was the hero of the hour, and he sacrificed his own marriage to save the world from lunacy.'

'It was on the rocks already, to be fair,' said Craig, taking a large mouthful of wine. He looked as though he needed it. 'I'm sorry to read about everything that's happened to you, Tara. Obviously it's a different issue, but on the other hand it all feels alarmingly similar.'

Mel nodded. 'It really does feel like we've been here before. That's why we're more than happy to join forces. To give you the benefit of our experience, for what it's worth.'

'That's what I wanted to ask you about, Mel,' said Tara. 'And you, Craig, now you're here. Ever since this issue first arose, people have mentioned what happened to you. Obviously I can see that there's a similarity, but do you think they're actually connected?'

'It's a very good question,' said Mel. 'The flat-earth insanity came from one very specific place, which was why we were ultimately able to shut it down. From my understanding of all this Young Earth malarkey, it has emerged rather more organically, from a generation of guilty North Americans who are desperate to exonerate themselves of the crimes of their forebears by finding other people to denounce. But the madness seems to manifest itself in a very similar way: spread by social media, thriving on the persecution of heretics, and spreading along much the same tribal lines. Once people like that appalling man-child from *The Guardian*... What's his name?'

'Leon Smith,' said Craig.

'How could I forget? I read somewhere that his parents were Trots and they named him in their hero's honour. When someone like Leon Smith starts to drive the bandwagon, all his faithful followers take note that this is the latest issue they need to care about. Then they need some nice hate figures – preferably women, because we're easier to bully, and if they're a centrist Labour politician like Rita Denby, all the better – and they can all pile in and get recreationally furious. It's like football for people who don't like football, only without the terrace humour, the athletic prowess and the meaty thighs.'

'If only,' said Craig. 'Have you seen Leon Smith's gym selfies on Twitter? Chicken thighs, more like.'

'You are naughty,' said Mel, twinkling.

'One of the things I don't understand is whether they actually believe it themselves,' said Tara. 'I mean, I get that they're sincere in not wanting to offend these minority communities – even if, as a member of a minority community myself, I find the whole business deeply patronising. But going beyond that, have they really convinced themselves the world is only ten thousand years old, the dinosaurs are a hoax and the Big Bang never happened? Or are they just pretending to think this in order to impress the rest of their tribe?'

'Again, a very good question,' said Mel. 'We had similar conversations when these same people suddenly decided the earth was flat and denounced anyone who thought otherwise as an evil globularist. Did they actually mean it, or were they just saying it for self-advancement? I'm sure it varies from person to person, and I imagine it also changes over time. Personally, I think there's a useful analogy in North Korea. From an outsider's perspective, no one in their right mind would think Kim Jong-un is a wonderful guy. But if you live in North Korea, you have to *pretend* you think he's a wonderful guy, otherwise you'll die in a labour camp. And since you have to pretend to think it, wouldn't it save a lot of effort if you *actually* believed it? To me, that explains why that whole country was in floods of tears when Kim's father and grandfather died. When we in the West see those scenes, our immediate assumption is that everyone must be faking it, because those men were evil tyrants. But what if you've chosen to believe they're not evil tyrants, simply for self-preservation? Then the tears become sincere.'

'Hopefully it's not that bad in this country yet,' said Tara.

'I know. Of course not. Nobody's dying over this stuff. What I mean is, the process of compelled belief is very familiar in totalitarian societies. We're not used to these things in our own liberal democracy but, increasingly, the same kind of process is going on. The great irony is that it's pushed and enabled not by individual dictators but by the ultimate liberals, all those young men from Silicon Valley who go to work on skateboards and have ended up running the world.'

'I'd never thought of it like that,' said Tara. 'You know, it's funny you should mention Silicon Valley, because my boss was on her way to Palo Alto when this whole argument over geology blew up. I'd been really pleased for her, hoping the trip would go well and wishing her luck in all the funding meetings. I wish I'd saved my breath.'

Craig looked up. 'Palo Alto? Who was she meeting?'

'The…er…' For a moment, Tara couldn't recall the name. 'It begins with a T… The Talavera Foundation, that was it.'

The effect on her companions was extraordinary. They looked at each other in alarm and Craig demanded: 'Did they meet Joey? Is he the one who told her to promote Young Earth ideas?'

Tara was taken aback by his vehemence. 'I don't think so. I think they met his wife. And no, I don't think that's where this stuff is coming from. If it is, nobody ever mentioned it. Besides, Rowan complained about the supposedly offensive language in my report before she left for California. Why do you ask? Does it matter?'

'Does it matter!' Craig's eyes blazed.

'Gently,' said Mel, flashing him a look of admonition. To Tara, she said: 'Actually, it may. We can't go into detail, for reasons I won't bore you with, but Joey Talavera was a major player in this palaver last time round. If he's up to the same tricks all over again, we need to know.'

'I reckon we should do some digging,' said Craig. 'I can put out a feeler to Krystal.'

Tara had no idea what they were talking about, but that last name rang a bell. 'Krystal…as in Talavera?'

Craig nodded. 'I kind of...know her.'

Her mouth twitching with private amusement, Mel explained: 'Craig has actually stayed with Joey and Krystal on their estate. As their house guest. He has the kind of access for which your old boss Rowan would sell her granny. Including Krystal's personal phone number.' She mouthed the final two words, as if she were divulging a great secret.

Craig reddened. 'I went there with Shane, my ex. Krystal and I happened to hit it off, and between us we managed to kill the flat-earth nonsense once and for all. I can't believe Joey would knowingly be involved in something like this, but it would be good to sound her out.'

Mel looked unconvinced. 'There's no harm in asking the question, but I fear the answer this time is both simpler and harder to hear: the world is just getting progressively madder. To be honest, I think Tara's got the right approach. Tackle it head on in the courts, to draw a line in the sand.'

Tara left the pair of them after an hour. They were in the process of ordering another bottle, but Tara had promised to go home via Bexleyheath, which was a simple train ride from London Bridge, to hear more from Zoya about what the judicial process was likely to involve.

As it turned out, the ride wasn't as simple as it ought to have been. A couple of services were cancelled and the train she finally boarded was hot and overcrowded. She was tired, thirsty and sticky by the time she arrived at her solicitor's office.

'There will only be one question under consideration at this hearing,' Zoya said, once Tara had downed a glass of cold water and the two of them were ensconced on opposite sides of her solicitor's desk. 'The employment judge will seek to establish whether your view that the earth is billions of years old is protected as a philosophical belief, under section 10 of the Equality Act.'

Tara protested. 'It's not a belief. It's a fact, just like it's a fact that rain is wet.'

Zoya wagged a stubby finger. 'Not so fast. It's true that some beliefs are better founded than others. For instance, I believe the sun will rise behind the clock tower on Bexleyheath Broadway tomorrow morning, and that it will set behind the leisure centre in the evening. My belief is informed by centuries of daily observation by generations of people, as well as by scientific measurement of the earth's twenty-four-hour rotation, but that doesn't make it any less of a belief. Other people may believe something else, for example that the sun will set for the final time tonight and never come up again. You and I hope they're wrong, and we'll know for sure tomorrow morning, but until then it's all a matter of belief.'

Tara opened her mouth to object but her solicitor continued: 'Look, I get why you're annoyed. You think your belief in the age of the earth is so basic that it's an outrage to have to defend it. I would too, in your position. But in the circumstances, it's actually to our advantage to call it a belief. Section 10 of the Equality Act identifies a number of characteristics that are protected under the law. They include age, disability, race, sex and so on, but also religion or belief. If we can show that your particular belief in an earth formed billions of years ago is one of those protected ones, then we have a strong foundation. After that, we just need to demonstrate that you really were discriminated against because of that belief. Then it will be clear the IWA acted unlawfully towards you.'

'I see…I think,' said Tara. 'And how does the tribunal determine whether or not this particular belief is protected? Is it up to the judge to rule one way or the other?'

'Yes it is, but that won't happen in an arbitrary way. The judge refers to case law. Previous rulings, in other words. In this instance, the tribunal will assess your belief against a set of conditions called the Grainger criteria, which are named after the case in which this area of the law was first tested. There are five of those conditions. The belief must be genuinely held; it must relate to a weighty and substantial aspect of human life and behaviour; it must attain a certain level of cogency, seriousness and cohesion; and so on.'

Tara brightened. 'That sounds encouraging. My *belief* – she made sarcastic air-quotes – 'certainly ticks all those boxes, doesn't it? So we've got a cast-iron case, no?'

'Let's not count our chickens. I've worked in the law long enough to know there are no certainties in court. But I do think we have a very strong argument at this stage. After that, when it comes to proving they withdrew the job offer because of your belief, we've already unearthed some very damaging material in discovery.'

'Smoking emails, you mean? *Tara Farrier's an evil Yerf and we can't have her on staff*, that kind of thing?'

Zoya smiled. 'They haven't put it in quite those terms, but yes, that's the gist of it. It's all in the bundle I'll give you to take away and read.'

'How weird to be pleased to hear they wrote nasty messages about me behind my back,' said Tara.

'I know. Reading the bundle is going to be brutal, I'm afraid, precisely for that reason. Normally, most of us don't want to know what other people say about us when we're not in the room, because it isn't always flattering. But in this process, we actively seek out the most unflattering comments we can find. It's all rather perverse and you need a thick skin. Do you think you've got one?'

'A few months ago, I'd have said no, not at all. But perhaps I'm growing one. Thick*er*, anyway.'

'That's good to hear. And hopefully it will all be worthwhile in the end. If everything goes to plan, you'll get a decent settlement for yourself, as well as making sure this can't happen to anyone else.'

Tara nodded. 'Let's hope so. I've raised money from an awful lot of very kind and generous people. I don't want to let them down.'

'I'm sure you won't do that,' said Zoya. 'In the meantime, you need to finish drafting your witness statement, and we'll need to prepare you for cross-examination. But your ordeal will be over soon enough, and then I hope you'll be able to move on with your life.'

'Hear hear to that,' said Tara.

Notoriety had been an interesting novelty so far, but a return to uncontroversial obscurity would be very welcome.

19

The offices of the Central London Employment Tribunal were just round the corner from Lincoln's Inn, the traditional home of the legal profession. But Tara was surprised to learn that she wouldn't need to travel any further than Bexleyheath to give her evidence.

'They do a lot of these sessions online nowadays,' Zoya explained over the phone, with a week to go before the preliminary hearing. 'It started during Covid, when everyone realised the technology worked quite well and it was often a lot more convenient operating that way, so they carried on doing them like that. Particularly in cases like this, where the respondent's witness is based in New York.'

'Really?' said Tara. 'They're not putting up Rowan to speak for them?'

'No, it's Josh Hardy.'

'Who?'

'He's the vice-president for human resources.'

'Never heard of him.'

'It makes sense for them to field their head of HR. They're making him justify what's no doubt an immense salary.'

'I guess so.' Tara was disappointed. She had come to dread her own appearance as the date drew closer, and she'd consoled herself that at least she was inflicting the same torment on her nemesis in the London office.

'So if you come here on the days the tribunal sits, we'll have a webcam rigged up in our conference room,' Zoya continued.

It was news to Tara that such a facility existed at her solicitor's cramped premises, but she kept that to herself.

'And Den usually does the same from his own home,' Zoya added.

'Den?'

'Den Hooper, your barrister. Nobody calls him Denton.'

'Ah yes, of course.'

'Speaking of whom, he's asked me to set up a video call for the three of us. Obviously he's read all the papers, but he'd like to say hello before we start, as well as to give you some guidance on answering the questions from the other side.'

That was of course the part Tara feared the most. From what Zoya had already explained, Tara wouldn't be required to tell the judge her whole story from scratch. She had already done that in her lengthy written witness statement, which would be distributed to all parties before the session began. All her own counsel would do was ask a few friendly questions designed to highlight the key sections of her statement. This comparatively gentle experience would be the lull before the storm of cross-examination. The prospect of a hostile onslaught from the IWA's lawyers made her feel physically sick.

That was what she most wanted to discuss when, a couple of days later, she and Zoya met Den Hooper on a Zype call.

'How are you feeling, Tara?' her barrister asked.

'To put it bluntly, I'm crapping myself,' she said.

'That's quite normal,' said Hooper. 'To be honest, I'd be worried if you weren't crapping yourself. That would be a sign of complacency.'

He had sandy hair combed over a receding forehead, and a luxuriant beard in flaming red, almost long enough to qualify him as a hipster. He looked tall, Tara decided, even though the screen offered no real way of assessing his height, and she felt certain he was gay. He had a light voice that exuded breezy, expensively educated confidence and put her immediately at her ease.

'I'd love to tell you it'll be a piece of cake,' he continued. 'But you wouldn't expect me to give the IWA's witness an easy ride, and my opposite number will be looking to trip you up and find holes in your story. The formal purpose of cross-examination is to test the reliability of what you've said in your statement but, in plain English, they're trying to catch you out. My best and simplest advice is to tell the truth. Human beings have a natural tendency to exaggerate, embellish and misremember. But if you don't tell the complete truth, my opposite number is very likely to find you out, and then you'll look bad, which is precisely what they're aiming for. That's why it's important to be rigorously honest in your witness statement. Do please read it again. If there are any parts of it where you have the slightest niggling doubt – maybe you've added your own spin to your recall of a conversation, or you're over-egging a particular claim – then do say so, because it's not too late to amend it. I can't emphasise enough that honesty is your best friend in this process, even if you think that telling the truth on a certain point will put you in a bad light. An honest witness is a credible one. Conversely, if you lose your credibility with the judge, it can be very difficult to get it back.'

Tara nodded. She didn't think she'd exaggerated anything in her statement, but she would certainly re-read it to double-check.

Hooper continued: 'It's also important to listen carefully to the question you're being asked. If you don't hear or understand it properly, ask counsel to repeat or rephrase it. Again, this relates to credibility. If you answer a question that you've misheard or misunderstood, you may give inaccurate evidence that will later unravel and be used to make you look dishonest. Once that's happened, saying you didn't hear the original question will sound like a flimsy excuse and no one will believe you.'

Again, Tara nodded. She was beginning to feel nauseous.

He added: 'Moving on, if they're questioning you on something in a document, don't be afraid to ask to look at the reference, so you can refresh your memory. And always think before you answer. When we're under pressure, we often give the first response that comes into our head. But there's no hurry. Take a moment to think before you reply. Finally, don't try and second-guess the direction in which you think the questioning is going. In other words, answer the question you've been asked, not the one you think you're going to be asked in two or three questions' time. Even if you're right, you'll simply irritate the judge, who wants to hear you answer the present question.'

'I think I've got all that,' said Tara, wondering if she ought to have taken notes.

As if anticipating the thought, Hooper said: 'Don't worry if that felt like a lot to remember. I've got some bullet points written out, based on what I've just said. I'll email them over to you. The important thing is to try and relax. I know that may sound like a tall order, but if you follow the most important golden rule of all and tell the truth at all times, everything else should fall into place.'

Zoya raised her hand. 'Can I add a couple of points, Den?'

'Of course,' he said. 'By my guest.'

'Right. Now, Tara, I don't want to contradict Den, but there is one golden rule that's even more important than telling the truth.'

Hooper frowned.

'What's that?' said Tara, bemused. Shouldn't her legal team both be on the same page?

'Go to the toilet before your evidence starts,' said Zoya.

Hooper laughed, clearly relieved to find that this wasn't a more serious challenge to his authority.

'Fortunately, you'll be at my offices so I'll frog-march you there before the tribunal begins,' Zoya continued. 'Now, once the cross-examination gets going, it may feel really unpleasant. In fact, there's no two ways about it, it *will* be unpleasant. But it's vital not to get angry. If you like, we can burn an effigy of Den's opposite number – her name's Robertson, by the way – once the Zype feed is switched off, but while you're on screen, don't let any anger show. It may feel like you're under personal attack but, remember, they're deliberately trying to get under your skin. Your best way of fighting back is not to let them. Also, bear in mind it's not really personal. They're just doing their job, like Den will be doing his.'

Tara could not imagine any universe in which she wouldn't hate the IWA's counsel, but she nodded along.

'Another thing,' her solicitor continued. 'They may receive your answer in silence, like they're waiting for you to say more. It's a classic lawyer's trick, in the hope you'll start babbling and say something rash. Don't fall for it. When you've given your answer, stop and wait for the next question. By the same token, don't let them interrupt you. If you haven't finished your answer, say so. And finally, don't expect Den to shout "objection!" if things get tough for you. That only happens in American TV dramas.'

Hooper laughed again. 'It's true, I'm afraid. If I did that in real life, it would send a signal to the other side that I think you're in trouble, which would make them go in all the harder.'

Tara was pleased they both found everything so amusing. Maybe she would do so too, eventually, once all this was over. For the moment, she just felt more queasy than ever.

20

Although everyone had advised her to get an early night, Tara stayed up late the night before the tribunal was due to start, re-reading her witness statement and generally stressing about the day ahead. When she did sleep, technicolour scenes from her forthcoming ordeal dominated her dreams. Then nerves jolted her awake at five, and the same scenes played out in her waking mind, putting paid to any hope of getting back to sleep. Eventually she got up and went out for a walk. Although the fields were still parched after the long, hot summer, the Kent countryside had an early morning freshness that raised her spirits. This part of the tribunal would be over soon, she told herself.

When she got back home and checked her phone, there were messages from both Laila and Rob wishing her luck, as well as from Rita, Helen and Mel. There was nothing from

Sammy, but she told herself how busy he was with work, and that he had always been terrible with dates. Even if Sorrel was one of Helen's persecutors, that didn't mean she had turned Sammy against his mother. Today of all days, Tara needed to focus on the positives and not dwell on anything that might undermine her confidence, least of all some imaginary slight from a son who had simply forgotten what day it was.

As she prepared to leave the house, she picked up a simple tin lapel badge from the table beside the front door. She'd received it in the previous day's mail from Mel. In green letters on a purple background, the badge bore the words HERETICAL GLOBULARIST. The attached note had read: 'One of our supporters made these when we were fighting the flat-earthers. They were a way of showing defiance and solidarity. I thought you might like to pin it somewhere, even if it's not very visible, by way of a good luck charm.' Wearing it visibly at the hearing might be provocative. Instead, Tara pinned it to the lining of her bag.

She had allowed herself an hour and a half for the drive, in case of roadworks or other delays, but traffic was relatively light on the M2, with barely any hold-ups until the last few miles through the fringes of outer London. She found a space to park in Broadway Square and arrived with more than three-quarters of an hour to spare.

'How are you feeling? Confident? Calm?' beamed Zoya, in what was clearly meant to be encouragement.

'I wish,' said Tara.

'You'll be fine,' her lawyer said. 'Just don't forget the golden rule.'

'I know, I went before I left the house, but I'll go again before we're due to start.'

Zara laughed. 'Well done, but not that golden rule. I meant the other one: tell the truth at all times, because an honest witness is a credible witness.'

'Ah yes. Don't worry, I got that message loud and clear from Den.'

'And did you have another chance to read your witness statement?'

Tara nodded. There was no need for Zoya to know how late she had stayed up doing so.

'Good. In that case, it sounds like we're all set. Let me take you through to the conference room and give you a chance to get settled.'

The room was bare, cheerless and stuffy. Any conference it hosted would need to cap attendance at four people, because that was how many chairs were squeezed around a tired-looking office table. It was at the back of the building, facing away from the Broadway, so there was less traffic noise. On the downside, it faced south; the room would be sweltering once the sun climbed higher. A freestanding webcam stood on a pile of legal text books, pointing at the chair in which Tara was to sit. Next to it, a laptop screen showed the live feed from the court. At the moment, all Tara could see was a high-backed swivel chair, with a plaque of the royal coat of arms on the wall behind. In front of the chair was a microphone. The chair itself was empty.

She picked up her phone to kill some time.

Zoya, who had gone in search of water, arrived back with a plastic bottle. 'I'll take that, if you don't mind,' she said, snatching the phone from Tara's hand.

'Hey, what are you doing? I was looking at that.'

'And what precisely were you looking at?' Her solicitor

stared down at her from her full five-feet-two, hands on hips.

'I was going to just go on Twitter to see what my supporters have written.'

'Oh yeah, because Twitter consists of nothing but messages of support?'

It was true that, for every public declaration of solidarity, there were always three or four poisonously abusive comments. But Tara was reluctant to admit defeat. She pleaded: 'I'm not going to look at the negative stuff.'

Zoya raised a sceptical eyebrow. 'And how, precisely, are you going to screen the hatey messages out?'

Tara sighed, thwarted. She knew her solicitor was right, but was still not quite ready to say so to her face.

'You can have your phone back when you've given your evidence,' Zoya said.

'There's no need to treat me like a naughty teenager.'

Zoya laughed, breaking the tension. 'Then don't behave like one.'

Not quite ready to abandon her sulk, Tara was on the point of protesting that she had nothing to distract her while she waited for the session to start, when she noticed movement on the screen in front of her. A fiftyish man in a dark business suit, with heavy-rimmed glasses and close-cropped steel-grey hair, had slipped into the swivel chair and was adjusting the microphone for height.

'It looks like we're about to start,' said Zoya. 'Here, have a boiled sweet. It'll help calm your nerves.'

Disgusting as Zoya's menthol sweets were, Tara's mouth had gone completely dry, so she took one. The fumes trailed up into her sinuses, which offered a distraction of sorts.

The judge began to run through the preliminaries, asking if

the barristers for both sides were present, giving permission to the clerk in charge to open the video feed to those members of the public – including many of Tara's supporters – who had been given passcodes to watch the proceedings online, and warning that anyone posting opinionated material in the chatroom sidebar would immediately be asked to leave. Then he invited Den Hooper to present the claimant's case.

'Off we go,' whispered Zoya.

Tara's barrister appeared on the screen. He seemed to be in his own private living room. There was a mantelpiece to his left, with a large abstract canvas above it, while a floor-to-ceiling window on the opposite wall looked onto a garden. From his height relative to the fireplace, it was clear that Den was on his feet. Tara approved of that. If there was to be any passionate oratory, it would come much better from a standing position.

Not that there was any swagger or emotion in Den's opening remarks. His tone was businesslike rather than declamatory. Aside from the fact that he addressed the judge as 'sir', they might have been colleagues at a meeting, as Den solicitously pointed him to a particular page in the bundle, waited for him to find the reference and made friendly remarks about his opposite number.

Once he'd completed the preliminaries, Tara's barrister began to summarise her case. He provided a potted history of her involvement with the IWA, including the way it had come to an end, and emphasised his sole intention in the present hearing: to establish that his client's belief that the earth was billions of years old was protected under the Equality Act of 2010. Tara wondered if he would add that this 'belief' was shared by most people on the planet, including the overwhelming majority of the population of the UK, but he didn't. Frustrating as this was, she could see that it made it a certain kind of sense. If she was the victim of discrimination, it helped her case for the court to collude in the fiction that her views were somehow minority or niche, and therefore in need of greater legal protection.

And then, before she knew it, she was being sworn in: solemnly, sincerely and truly affirming that the evidence she was about to give would be the truth, the whole truth and nothing but the truth. *I get it, honesty is my best friend*, she wanted to say. As she repeated the words, she saw herself on the screen. Without having left her seat, she was in the witness box.

'Good morning, Ms Farrier,' Den began.

This would sound forced if they were in a real courtroom, where everyone would know they'd been talking to each a few moments earlier, but today it was genuinely the first time they had greeted each other.

'Good morning, Mr Hooper,' said Tara. Her voice sounded croaky, and she reached for her water glass.

'The court has read your witness statement and I don't propose to take you through all of it,' Den said. 'What I would like to do is focus on the particular matter of belief. Could you begin by telling us in what capacity you joined the Institute for Worldwide Advancement?'

Tara cleared her throat and considered her response for a moment, as Den himself had told her to do. 'I was invited to join the IWA as a research fellow,' she said. 'Specifically, they asked me to write a report on the civil war in Yemen.'

'Why did they ask you to write it? Couldn't one of their existing staff have done it?'

'I can't speak for the background of their staff, but I have some degree of expertise, as a journalist, an academic and most recently living in the country itself.'

'And what was the intended purpose of the report you were asked to write?'

'The IWA hoped to use it to help alert politicians on both sides of the Atlantic to the major humanitarian consequences of the civil war.'

'Did you agree with them that such a report might be helpful?'

'Yes, very much. The war is causing great suffering to millions of people, but it's very low on most politicians' list of priorities, even though the US and the UK have provided many of the weapons that are being used to attack civilians. The political roots of the conflict are complicated, so it's easy for people in the West to say Yemen is too difficult to understand. We all hoped my report might demystify the situation and spell out the key information that everyone ought to know, namely that huge numbers of people are facing death, starvation or disease as a result of this totally unnecessary war.'

'Thank you. And can you explain why you felt the need to refer to the age of the earth in your report?'

'Yemen is a distant country about which most people in the West know very little. If any of them got as far as looking at a map, they'd see it's at the southwestern end of the Arabian peninsula, adjoining Saudi Arabia, and they might assume it was just more of the same, with lots of empty desert space, not many people and limitless amounts of oil. In reality, Yemen isn't at all like that. It's a very poor country, one of the poorest in the world, because it doesn't have the vast mineral wealth of its richer neighbours. What it does have is agriculture. It's remarkably green, because it's mountainous, and in biblical times it was known as Arabia Felix, or 'happy Arabia', because it had the best climate in the region and the most fertile soil. It was also remarkably self-contained, because it's surrounded by mountains. Before the age of aviation, those mountains were very difficult to cross. I thought the best and most striking way to explain the topography would be to refer to the tectonic movements that created those mountains in the first place.'

'So you wrote about certain geological events that occurred, in your opinion, millions of years ago?'

'Yes. I'm no expert on that kind of thing, by any means, and to be honest I can't quite remember how many millions of years ago those events took place, or what precisely the tectonic movements involved. It was one of those things where you google it and remember the answer for as long as it takes to write it down. But I thought it got my desired message across very effectively.'

'Did you intend it to be controversial?'

'No, of course not. I had no idea at that stage that anyone would have a problem with it.'

'And when Rowan Walker told you some people might have a problem with this language, how did you react?'

Tara paused, conscious that it was important to get this right. 'At first, with utter bafflement. I had no idea what Rowan was talking about. In her email to me, she referred to "current sensitivities", clearly assuming I'd know what she was talking about, but I didn't have a clue. I'd been out of the country for a long time and I could see I might have missed something, so I asked my son and daughter if they knew what

Rowan was talking about. They didn't, but my son's girlfriend was eventually able to tell me, correctly, what she thought the problem was. At that stage, I was astonished. It seemed to me absolutely absurd not to be able to refer to the scientifically accepted age of the earth because it might hurt the feelings of people who don't believe in science.'

'Thank you. Given that you felt so strongly, may we infer that you refused to remove the references to tectonic movement from your report?'

'No, not at all. I made clear my view that it was ridiculous to pander to these so-called sensitivities, but I also said that my short passage about the formation of mountain ranges in Yemen wasn't vital to the report itself, so Rowan could remove it if she wanted. I wouldn't be especially happy about it, because I thought the reasons were ludicrous, but neither would I stand in the way of doing so.'

'Thank you. Now, if I may, I'd like to explore some of your other beliefs. Could you explain your own personal connection to the Middle East?'

'My mother was a Palestinian, born in Jerusalem, who ended up as a refugee in Jordan after the 1948 war. When she married my father, who was English, she moved to this country and spent the rest of her life here.'

'And what was her religion?'

'She was a Christian.'

'And your father... Forgive me: is he still alive?'

'No.'

Den nodded understanding. 'Was he a Christian too?'

'Yes. He was Anglican, whereas my mother's family were Byzantine Catholics.'

'And would you also describe yourself as a Christian?'

'In heritage, yes, but not in belief. I'm an atheist.'

'Is Yemen a Christian country?'

'No, very much not. It's an overwhelmingly Muslim country.'

'Remind us, how long did you live in Yemen?'

'Seven years.'

'Did your own Christian heritage present any kind of problem for you, or for anyone else, in all that time there?'

'It certainly didn't for me, and I'm not aware of it doing so for anyone else.'

'What about your atheism? Did that create any ill-feeling or other difficulty for you?'

'No, but that's because I rarely mentioned it. In my experience of living in the Middle East, there's a widespread understanding and acceptance that some people are born into different religions, but the idea of not believing in God at all is very alien. While some of my Yemeni friends were more secular than others, I don't think any of them would describe themselves as atheists. I always found it simpler to call myself a Christian – which was culturally true – because it saved a lot of difficult explanation. And of course, I wasn't there to proselytise about my beliefs.'

Whatever that rag Earth News *may write*, she wanted to add.

'Thank you, Ms Farrier. I believe you mentioned some biblical characters in your draft report for the IWA. Is that correct?'

'Yes.'

'Could you tell us more about those references?'

'According to legend, the city of Aden was founded by Cain and Abel, the sons of Adam and Eve. It's also said that Noah's Ark came to rest on the top of a mountain in Yemen when the waters of the great flood subsided, and that Noah's son Shem founded the capital city, Sana'a. I referred to all three of those stories in my report.'

'Do you believe in the literal truth of those stories?'

'No, because I don't believe the entire human population of the earth descends from one man and one woman in the Garden of Eden. Nor do I believe that God flooded the world to get rid of corruption and violence, saving a small number of humans and animals in a single ship.'

'In other words, you don't believe that Cain, Abel, Noah or Shem ever existed?'

'I'm not a biblical scholar. It's possible Noah was based on a figure who really existed. But for me, those names are characters from myths, not real historical personages.'

'In that case, why did you refer to them in your report?'

'I wanted to make the point that Yemen has played a part in the stories that we in the West tell ourselves about the history of the world. I thought it would make this faraway country more relatable for people in the US and the UK if I associated it with names from our own creation myths.'

'Thank you, Ms Farrier. No further questions.'

Tara reached for another sip of water.

'Well done,' whispered Zoya, holding her thumbs up. 'Really, really good.'

'Thank you,' Tara mouthed back. 'But that was the easy part.'

21

There was barely time to breathe, let alone relax, before the judge was back on screen.

'Ms Robertson, your witness,' he said.

The opposing barrister appeared. Unlike Den, she seemed to be in a formal office. Dressed in a neat black jacket and a cream blouse, she had ringleted blonde hair styled back from her forehead and tumbling to her shoulders, and her skin was pale and freckled. She must be a breath of fresh air in her chambers, among all those men in suits. For a moment, Tara wondered if she might get an easier than expected ride from this person who looked like a perfectly nice woman. But she pushed the thought out of her mind, telling herself not to be so naive.

'Good morning, Ms Farrier,' her adversary began.

'Good morning.' Tara smiled, part of her still hoping she

could win this woman over with friendliness.

'Ms Farrier, in reply to one of Mr Hooper's questions earlier, about whether you were prepared to remove the sensitive passage from your report, you said you had no objection to Dr Walker removing it. Is that correct?'

'Yes.'

'But you didn't offer to remove it yourself?'

'No, I don't think I did.'

'I can confirm that you didn't, Ms Farrier. If you look at the message you posted on Clack on the subject… You'll find it on page 123 of your bundle.'

Tara fumbled through the pages, conscious of the webcam pointing at her.

'Can you see it? If you can't find the place, perhaps Ms Parveen can assist you.'

'It's all right, I've got it now.'

'Oh good. As you'll see, you actually said, "I'm quite content for Rowan to remove from my report the references to the mesozoic era and so on, if they're genuinely likely to cause problems." You conspicuously didn't volunteer to cut those words yourself, did you?'

'No.'

'Why not?'

'Because I thought, and still think, the instruction to remove them was ridiculous. If Rowan – Dr Walker – wanted to remove that passage, it wouldn't make any difference to the substance of the report, which was designed to highlight the current human tragedy in Yemen. So if she really wanted to take it out, it wouldn't do any harm. But I didn't see why I should do so, because there was absolutely nothing wrong with those references.'

'And because you thought, perhaps, it would compromise your own personal integrity if you complied with Dr Walker's request?'

'A little, perhaps.'

'Sorry, Ms Farrier…was that yes or no?'

So much for friendliness. Tara reminded herself of Zoya's instruction not to let her irritation show, and kept her expression as neutral as she could. 'Yes.'

'Would you say your integrity is very important to you?'

'No more than for anyone else, I shouldn't think.'

'But this argument mattered to you, didn't it? Enough for you to try and engage colleagues in discussion about what had hitherto been a private exchange between yourself and Dr Walker?'

'Yes, I posted something on Clack because Dr Walker had assured me when I joined the organisation that staff were encouraged to have debates on any issue that interested or concerned them. She said the ethos was *share, discuss, don't hold back*, and she told me Clack was the place for such discussions. I made clear, in the line you've just quoted, that I wasn't fighting a battle about the words in the report, and that it wasn't my intention to criticise Dr Walker. I was genuinely interested to know whether my colleagues agreed with her on this subject.'

'But in effect, you were publicly criticising her decision, weren't you?'

'That wasn't my intention, as I hope I made clear. If that wasn't obvious from what I wrote, then with hindsight perhaps I didn't emphasise it enough. But I thought at the time I had done so. I was simply curious as to whether everyone else thought it was offensive to mention indisputable scientific facts about the age and formation of the earth.'

'And how many of your colleagues responded?'

'None.'

'Did that not suggest to you that your own position was making your colleagues uncomfortable?'

'No, it didn't. It suggested to me that I'd broken some kind of taboo by raising the matter. I found that very odd, particularly in light of Dr Walker's insistence that the organisation was so strongly in favour of lively debate.'

'Would you say you were frustrated by the lack of response?'

'As I say, I was primarily surprised. When I posted my question, I expected I might get some disagreement, some pushback, particularly if it related to an issue that had become current in the West while I was living in the Middle East. Maybe someone would tell me what I was missing, some angle I wasn't seeing. I didn't expect total silence. That was disconcerting.'

'It threw you?'

'Yes.'

'But after you'd got over your initial surprise, it also frustrated you, didn't it, Ms Farrier?'

'Yes, it did. I barely knew my colleagues, having met just a few of them in person on no more than two occasions, and having had almost no online interaction with them. But as far as I was aware, they were intelligent, highly motivated, well-meaning people. It was of course frustrating to see them accepting censorship, both in terms of what I was allowed to write in my report, and when it came to what was appropriate for any of us to discuss on Clack.'

'So at that point you aired some of your frustrations on Twitter, didn't you?'

'I went on Twitter, as I'd been encouraged to do by both Dr Walker and Matthew Tree in New York, to see if I could find any further discussion of this issue. I remained flabbergasted that factual remarks about the history and formation of the earth were now regarded as politically controversial.'

'You commented on the case of Professor Helen Kottsack, did you not?'

'Yes.'

Robertson waited, expecting her to continue, but Tara remembered her own solicitor's warning that this was a classic trick. She folded her hands on the table in front of her, making it clear she had nothing to add.

The barrister continued: 'Professor Kottsack is at the centre of a long-running protest on her campus, is she not?'

'I don't know how long it's been going on, but she's been the target of protests, yes.'

'Would you agree that the issue at stake in Professor Kottsack's case is broadly the same as the one Dr Walker raised with you, regarding the wording of your own report?'

'I'd say it's exactly the same. Helen Kottsack teaches earth sciences, and she has been vilified for stating the clear fact that the earth is billions of years old.'

'But there are other points of view on that, aren't there, Ms Farrier?'

'There are other points of view on everything.'

'In this particular case, isn't it true that a number of students maintain that Professor Kottsack has shown insensitivity to beliefs held by certain marginalised minorities?'

'As far as I'm aware, I don't know any of the students picketing Professor Kottsack's lectures, so I'll have to take your word for that.' *As far as I'm aware.* That would cover her if – heaven forbid – Sorrel did turn out to be one of the protestors.

'Yet you tweeted about those very students, didn't you, Ms Farrier? Would you mind reading out what you wrote? I can give you the reference. You'll find it on page 154 of the bundle. The third tweet down.'

Tara's heart pounded as she thumbed through the bundle, looking for the page. Was Robertson allowed to humiliate her like this?

'Can you see it, Ms Farrier?' the barrister prodded.

This was one of those moments where Tara really did want Den to jump in and cry 'objection'. She reminded herself it wasn't going to happen.

'Do you have it, Ms Farrier? The third and final tweet.'

'Yes, I can see it.'

'Please read it for us.'

Tara took a deep breath and read in a deadpan voice, very different from the tone in which she'd written it: '"So can we please call this what it is? It's a bunch of students with mummy issues who have found a great way of shouting at a middle-aged woman and claiming progressive points for doing so. I'm sorry, but it won't wash."'

'And do you stand by those words, Ms Farrier?'

Tara faltered. Did she? It would be easy to tell the court she was upset when she wrote the tweet, which was certainly true, and that she had expressed herself in an intemperate way which she now regretted. But Den's words came back to her. *Honesty is your best friend in this process, even if you think telling the truth on a certain point will put you in a bad light. An honest witness is a credible one.*

'Yes I do,' she said. 'There are male teachers in the same

department as Professor Kottsack who haven't faced any protest at all. If these students' primary concern was the supposed issue itself, they would surely harangue anyone in public life who mentioned dinosaurs or volcanoes. But they don't do that. They focus all their fury on one middle-aged woman. That's why I make no apology for calling it an ugly display of misogyny and ageism, dressed up as a so-called progressive issue.'

'I see. You also said, did you not, that these students, or "aggressors", as you called them, were protesting on behalf of – I quote – a "nebulous group of people" who are – I'm quoting again – "supposedly indigenous"?'

'If you say so.'

'It's on the page in front of you, Ms Farrier. Those words are contained in your first and second tweet, are they not?'

'Erm…' Tara stared miserably at page 154.

'Yes or no, Ms Farrier?'

Don't let the irritation show. 'Yes.'

'Can you explain why you put the word "indigenous" in inverted commas?'

'Because I was quoting the most common description of the people who are supposedly offended.'

'Supposedly? Don't you believe they're offended?'

'I'll believe it when a student on Professor Kottsack's campus comes forward to say they attend her lectures as part of their course and that they come from a First Nation community, on whatever continent, that worships the potter goddess Ctat…' – inevitably she stumbled over the name – 'Ctatpeshirahi. But I've never met anyone who meets those conditions and, as far as I'm aware, Professor Kottsack hasn't either. So to answer your question, no, I don't believe the offence is genuine. I believe it's confected. Performative, in fact. That's probably the best word.'

'Thank you, Ms Farrier. That's very revealing.'

Tara inwardly groaned. Had she made everything worse by expressing herself so candidly? But no, it could simply be another barrister's trick, designed to sap her confidence by suggesting she was playing into her opponents' hands.

Robertson continued: 'I'd like to clarify something else you said in your evidence to Mr Hooper earlier this morning, if I may. You told him you were an atheist, did you not?'

'Yes, that's right.'

'How long have you been an atheist, Ms Farrier?'

Tara tried to remember. 'Since my early teens, I think, but I don't recall any specific decision to call myself that. I don't think I ever took the notion of God very seriously. I always saw him as a make-believe concept, along the lines of Father Christmas or the Tooth Fairy, and I was surprised when I realised lots of other people took the idea so literally.' She didn't know where Robertson was going with this and she realised she was rambling, so she brought herself to a halt.

'But you also said you misled your friends and neighbours in Yemen, hiding your atheism from them, did you not?'

'I explained my reasons for that to Mr Hooper.'

'Sorry, just to be clear, Ms Farrier: was that yes or no?'

'Yes.'

'Thank you. As for the explanation you offered to Mr Hooper, I confess to a certain confusion. You've brought this action against my clients as – I'm quoting one of your tweets – "a vital test case about freedom of belief". And yet you spent seven years, on your own admission, hiding one of your own beliefs. Isn't that rather a striking contradiction? Doesn't it make you a hypocrite?'

'I don't think it's a contradiction, and no it doesn't. I chose not to speak about my atheism because I thought it would drive an unnecessary wedge between myself and the people I was living alongside. I'm a strong advocate of freedom of belief, but that doesn't mean I have to proclaim all my beliefs to everyone I meet.'

'But you wanted to have your cake and eat it?'

'No. As a temporary resident in a volatile and highly religious country, I chose to be private about my own lack of religious belief, for my own comfort and that of those around me, and perhaps also my safety. I was once kidnapped in Yemen, so I think I'm aware of the risks. Quite separately, having now returned to my own country, I'm asserting the right not to lose my livelihood just because I believe in the established scientific fact that the earth is billions of years old. Those two positions are perfectly consistent.'

'That's very interesting. Thank you for your frankness. Finally, Ms Farrier, before we perhaps break for lunch, can I ask about something you wrote in your message on the Clack message board? You said your personal motto – again, I'm quoting – was that "people deserve respect but ideas don't", did you not?'

'That's correct.'

'Can you explain how that works?'

'In what sense?'

'For example, if you met a First Nation follower of the goddess Ctat…'

As Robertson consulted her notes, Tara offered: 'Ctatpeshirahi?'

The barrister gave her a wintry smile. 'Thank you, Ms

Farrier. If you met such a person, would you tell them their ideas don't deserve respect?'

'No, of course not, just as I don't tell practising Catholics on first meeting that I think it's ridiculous to believe a piece of rice paper is the literal body of Christ.'

'But if pressed… If, for example, you embarked on a discussion of theology, you would express that view, would you not?'

'Yes I would, but hopefully not in a pugnacious way. The aim would be to remain friends, because we might agree on all sorts of other things. Even if we didn't, you can respect someone even if you disagree with their ideas. That's the point of my motto.'

'So you don't believe that ideas *per se* are worthy of respect, but you're bringing this case against my clients because they didn't respect your ideas. Isn't that another contradiction?'

'No, not at all. I'm not demanding respect for my ideas, even for ideas that happen to be indisputable scientific facts. For the purposes of this tribunal, I'm simply asking not to be discriminated against for holding them.'

'Thank you, Ms Farrier.' Addressing the judge, Robertson continued: 'Sir, I have a little more ground to cover with in cross-examination this afternoon, but this is probably a good place to pause.'

'Very well, Ms Robertson,' said the judge. 'We'll break for an hour, resuming at two o'clock. Ms Farrier, can I remind you that you're still on oath, so you mustn't discuss your evidence with anyone during the break, including your solicitor.'

This seemed a bizarre condition, but Tara nodded assent. Then, to her immense relief, the screen went dead and the red light on the webcam blinked off. She took a gulp of water then leaned back in her chair. She realised she was trembling.

'As the judge said, I'm not allowed to discuss anything with you,' said Zoya, but she held both thumbs up and mouthed, *You're doing really well.*

'Really?' said Tara. 'It doesn't feel like it.'

Really, her solicitor mimed, then said aloud: 'Now, what would you like to do for lunch? I can send out for some sandwiches, or would you prefer to go out yourself, to clear your head?'

'Actually I think I would like to go out. I feel like I've been punched in the head about twenty times, so I'm not sure I'll be able to stand up straight, but I should probably try.'

'Good choice.'

'Can I have my phone now?'

Zoya shook her head gravely. 'Sorry, but I really don't think it's a good idea. You're bound to look on Twitter, where I suspect you'll find a load of notifications from a bunch of seriously nasty people all trying to undermine your confidence by saying horrible things. I can't stop you looking on there at the end of the afternoon, but it's really not a good idea while you're in the middle of your evidence.'

Tara could see the sense in that. In any case, she was too drained to argue. She got to her feet, stretched, and squeezed out of the conference room, then made her way down the stairs into the glare of Bexleyheath Broadway. It was weird to see ordinary life going on as normal, when all she wanted was for the entire world to stop, tell her she'd done a better job than she feared and give her a big hug. She glanced down into her open bag and saw the badge Mel had given her. She brushed her fingers against this good luck charm, drawing solace from it. Catching herself, she shook her head and laughed softly. She really must be feeling needy, to be seeking comfort from a flimsy piece of tin.

Robertson's cross-examination in the afternoon seemed to go on on forever. Tara was glad she'd been advised not to try to second-guess the direction of the questions, because these ones hopped around all over the place. If there was any grand plan, any master narrative that the respondent's counsel was building, Tara couldn't see it.

Perhaps the real purpose, she realised after her ordeal eventually finished, was to exhaust her, so she would drop her guard and say something rash. By the end, she was past knowing – and almost even caring – whether she had done so or not. But Zoya, who was now allowed to talk to her without restriction, assured her she'd done nothing of the kind. Tara assumed her solicitor always told clients they had done well, however abysmal their performance; but she needed the kindness, so she chose to go along with it, sincere or not.

The drive home, on a motorway clogged with rush-hour traffic leaving London, was hideous. She had barely had time to kick off her shoes and pour herself a tall glass of iced water from the fridge when there was a knock on the door.

She sighed. She wasn't in the mood for cold-callers.

When she opened the door she saw, to her relief, the towering figure of Helen, holding a home-made Victoria sponge on a china plate.

'Helen! How wonderful to see you,' she said, and meant it.

'I imagine you're desperate for a stiff drink but I didn't want you to be hungover for tomorrow's proceedings, so I thought sugar was the next best thing,' said her friend, following Tara indoors and setting the cake down in the kitchen. 'But I also wanted to say congratulations. You did an amazing job. I don't think I could have stayed that cool in this weather, let alone under that kind of pressure.'

'Thank you for the cake. It looks amazing,' said Tara, taking two plates down from the crockery cupboard. 'And thank you for saying that. Did you watch the whole thing? I had no idea who was online.'

'I had it on in the background all day, so yes, I saw the whole thing. I know Rita was watching too, and Ginny. We all thought you were fantastic. They've both sent you messages, I think.'

'Oh, my phone! I've been so dazed since my cross-examination ended, I haven't even looked at it.' She pulled the phone out of her bag and saw a string of WhatsApp notifications and text messages, as well as private messages on Twitter and Facebook. 'Oh wow. There's dozens and dozens. From my daughter and her boyfriend, and Rita and Ginny, and Mel and Craig, and God knows who else…' Still nothing from Sammy, but she was determined not to read anything into that.

'Sorry, would you like me to leave you in peace so you can look through them all?' said Helen.

'No, not at all. It's really lovely to see you. I'd far rather have actual human company than disappear down the usual digital rabbit-hole.' She admired the cake. 'This looks wonderful. It really is exactly what I needed. And you're quite right about avoiding a hangover, but I do think we should have one decent-sized gin and tonic. If not now, when?'

Helen laughed. 'I'm game if you are.'

'Good.' Tara fetched a bottle of Gordon's from the fridge and poured two large measures.

'Call me old-fashioned, but shouldn't you leave some room for the tonic?' said Helen. 'Apart from anything else, I've got to drive home.'

'Spoilsport!' Tara suddenly felt lighter than she had for weeks. She chopped slices of lemon, knocked ice cubes out of a tray and finished assembling the drinks.

'Here you are,' she said. 'It really is lovely to see you, and I'm so grateful for the support.'

'Nonsense. What are friends for?' Helen raised her glass. 'Here's to you, for getting through today's ordeal so brilliantly. How many more days to go?'

'Tomorrow it's the IWA's turn in the witness box – their head of HR, a guy from the New York office – and then that's it. After that, we have to wait for the preliminary ruling. I'm not sure how long it will take. And then, in the best-case scenario' – she groaned aloud at the prospect – 'we move to the full tribunal and I have to go through the same ordeal all over again.'

'Don't think about that today,' Helen said. 'Let's just celebrate your performance today – and look forward to your barrister giving their man hell tomorrow.'

They clinked glasses. It was indeed an exciting prospect.

By the end of the glass, Tara was willing to concede she had overdone the measures, so they moved on to coffee and cake.

'Aren't you worried about not sleeping?' Helen wanted to know, as Tara stirred the pot on the stove.

Tara shook her head. 'Not because of the coffee, anyway. It really doesn't seem to affect me like that. Maybe that's a warning sign, that I drink too much of the damn stuff.'

'Perhaps, but I guess now isn't the time to give up. You've got more important things on your plate.'

'Tell me about it.' Tara poured the coffee and cut generous slices of cake, which they both chewed contentedly in silence for a few moments. 'This is delicious, by the way,' said Tara, when she'd emptied her mouth. 'It's every bit as good as it looked. I'm so impressed you have the time to bake.'

Helen shrugged. 'I find it therapeutic. A complete break from the stresses and strains of the day.'

'I can imagine. How is your fan club these days? No let-up?'

'Unfortunately not. Sometimes one or other of the little darlings loses their voice, having over-exerted it by screaming insults about me, but there always seems to be another of them ready to take their place. Speaking of which, I meant to tell you: I think I've spotted that girl you were asking about, the one with the pink and purple hair.'

Tara froze. 'Sorrel?'

'Yes, if that's her name. Didn't you say she had a bird's nest of coloured dreadlocks? I happened to be looking out of my window at them the other day, and I saw one of them take her baseball cap off to adjust it, when she thought no one was watching. She matched your description exactly. Who is she? How do you know her?'

22

Even though she was beginning to consider Helen a close friend, Tara couldn't bear to tell her who Sorrel really was. Alongside the feeling that she'd been kicked in the stomach, she experienced an overwhelming sense of shame that someone who was effectively part of her own family was still actively persecuting the beleaguered academic. She'd become used to people praising her bravery but, for the moment, she didn't have the courage to tell Helen that the girl with the multi-coloured dreadlocks was Sammy's girlfriend.

So she fobbed Helen off with a misleading half-truth – 'I've actually only met Sorrel once, so she's someone I barely know really' – then apologised and said she needed an early night, because she had another long day ahead. Having enjoyed the surprise visit until now, she suddenly wanted more than anything else to be alone. Helen said she of course understood, and left Tara in peace shortly afterwards.

It was dark outside by now, but Tara didn't have the will to draw the curtains or switch on a lamp. Instead she sat in the gloom of her living room, trying not to let her mind run away with itself; but it was a losing battle.

First there was her anger at Sorrel herself: this poised, confident young woman who had seemed so smart and grown up, but was behaving like a silly, bratty child, with no thought for other people's feelings. Tara's first instinct was to ban the girl from the house, because how could she possibly be polite to her, knowing what she now knew, and behave as if nothing was amiss? But then she saw that a hasty emotional reaction might well backfire on her, because Sammy would doubtless take his girlfriend's side, so Tara was in danger of losing her son.

And then, with horror, she realised that this was something that might have happened already, and banning Sorrel would be an empty gesture because neither of them had any intention of coming anywhere near Willow Tree Cottage. She constantly excused Sammy's absences by citing the pressures of his work, but what if he knew exactly what he was doing when he'd failed to wish her luck that morning? Could he really be that cruel? That wasn't the Sammy she recognised, but kids changed, so what if he had now embarked upon a journey that would end up in complete estrangement? It was too horrific to contemplate, and she knew she oughtn't to dwell on it. But how could she not?

She eventually forced herself to get out of her chair and go to bed, but she knew she wouldn't sleep. In the ensuing hours, as she shifted from this wakeful position to that, she went over and over the possibilities in her head. Could she bear a breach with her son? If not, should she pull out of the court action? Was that even possible at this stage? She imagined trying to explain such a decision to her supporters, to all those people who had parted with ten or fifteen pounds to help her challenge the IWA and its deranged policy. They were depending on her. Her head spun as she acted out the various possibilities in her imagination...

She must eventually have fallen asleep, as her brain got tired of the subject and decided to have mercy on her. When her alarm went off in the morning, her first reaction was relief, because that meant she must have slept for a while, at least. But then the cause of the previous night's anguish came flooding back, and she felt gut-kicked once more.

After completing her evidence the day before, she'd told Zoya that she didn't see why she couldn't just log on and watch the rest of the tribunal from home. But her solicitor had said she ought to come to Bexleyheath, and Tara was grateful for that instruction now, because the need to get going was the only thing that could have hauled her out of bed. Following her night of anguish, she was at least certain of one thing: she was not going to give this action up. Too much was riding on it, and she couldn't let all her supporters down. She could only hope and pray, to a god she didn't believe in, that her relationship with Sammy would survive the strain.

She resolved not to mention this new crisis to Zoya. Yesterday, the two of them had rubbed their hands together at the prospect of watching Den cross-examining Josh Hardy. Tara would not permit a spoiled little girl like Sorrel to take that away now, she told herself as she got behind the wheel of her Renault and started her journey to the London suburbs. She would put a brave face on it and behave as if nothing was amiss: that would be her task for the day.

An hour or so later, as they settled down in the oppressively hot conference room to view the proceedings, Tara saw that Hardy was a preppy-looking man of about forty, his hair trimmed close at the sides and quirkily parted on top. His teeth were slightly too large for his mouth, an impression accentuated by their inevitable gleaming whiteness, the obvious hallmark of an affluent American.

Like Tara the previous day, he was given a gentle ride at first, with a series of easy questions from Robertson… Was Ms Farrier an employee? No, she had simply been asked to write a report, on a freelance basis, in her capacity as an acknowledged country expert… Did the IWA make any commitment to put Ms Farrier on staff once she had written her report? No, no such binding commitment was made… Did Ms Farrier's beliefs play any part in the decision not to put her on staff? Since she was simply a freelance consultant, there was no such decision; but the IWA would never discriminate against anyone for their beliefs, provided those beliefs didn't expose their colleagues or associates to discomfort or harm… Thank you, Mr Hardy. No further questions.

Although the webcam light was on in Zoya's conference room, which meant Tara and her solicitor were potentially visible if the tribunal administrator chose to show their screen, their microphone was muted, so they could talk to one another. Tara didn't entirely trust the technology, not least because the administrator could unmute them remotely, so she confined herself to whispering. During Hardy's examination, however, she struggled to contain her outrage. *Of course* they had promised Tara a contract. She had it in writing. And *how dare* this puffed-up young man, who had never met or interacted with Tara in any way, suggest she had exposed anyone to harm?

Zoya did her best to talk her client down. 'Don't worry, that's what cross-examination is for. The more dishonest the witness is under examination by his own counsel, the better it is for our case, because Den will be able to expose the inconsistencies.'

'*Inconsistencies*?! Lies, more like!'

'Lies then. Call them what you wish. Trust me. Den will shine a light on them.'

Tara certainly hoped so, but she had started the day in a foul mood, and she wouldn't be satisfied until she had seen Hardy eviscerated. Metaphorically, at the very least.

Now Den appeared on screen, beside his fireplace with the abstract painting above it. 'Good morning, Mr Hardy,' he began.

Hardy bestowed a toothsome smile on him. 'Good morning, sir.'

'Thank you, but "Mr Hooper" will do. In these proceedings, the judge is "sir".'

'I see. I'm sorry sir…I mean, Mr Hooper.'

'So Mr Hardy, you told Ms Robertson a little earlier that you would never discriminate against someone for their beliefs, yes?'

'Yes. Provided those beliefs don't expose their colleagues or associates to discomfort or harm.'

'Can you provide an example of the kind of belief that might expose colleagues to discomfort or harm?'

'I guess…strident racist beliefs. Or homophobia.'

'I see. So you vet your prospective staff regarding their views on race, homosexuality and so on?'

'No, we don't do that.'

'In that case, how can you guard against colleagues being exposed to their harmful views?'

'The IWA's position is that no views should be expressed in a work space that are incompatible with our corporate values.'

'So it's the expression of the views that matters, not the belief? In other words, you're allowed to hold them as long as you don't say them out loud?'

'Yes, if you want to put it like that.'

'Yes or no will suffice, Mr Hardy.'

Hardy sighed audibly. 'Yes.'

'And when you refer to work spaces, that includes digital ones, yes?'

'Yes.'

'To the best of your knowledge, did Ms Farrier express racist views in any physical or digital space belonging to the IWA?'

'Not that I'm aware.'

'As I say, to the best of your knowledge. Yes or no, please, Mr Hardy.'

'No.'

'Did she express views that were incompatible with your corporate values?'

'She wrote something on Clack that caused consternation among some associates.'

'Are you referring to the post reproduced on page 230 of the bundle? You should have the bundle in front of you.'

'Yes I do.' There was a pause as Hardy thumbed through the document. Having been in the same position herself, Tara was pretty sure he was playing for time: every second would be a refuge from having to answer the question.

'I don't want to rush you, Mr Hardy, but can you see the post?'

'Er…yes, I can.'

'And is that the post you referred to, which you say contained views incompatible with your corporate values?'

There was a further pause as Hardy made a point of reading through the whole passage. 'Yes, it is.'

'In it, Ms Farrier expresses surprise at having been told it was offensive to North American ears to say the earth is billions of years old, because this contradicts certain Indigenous creation myths, yes?'

'Y…yes.'

'Is that the part that's incompatible with your values?'

Hardy continued to pore over the text.

'Mr Hardy? Is her expression of surprise incompatible with your corporate values?'

Hardy seemed to come to a decision. 'No, the surprise is not the issue.'

'Thank you. Is it the part where Ms Farrier refers to herself as indigenous, because her mother was Palestinian?'

Hardy seemed more certain on this point. 'No. The IWA's corporate position is to affirm people however they choose to identify.'

'Ms Farrier also says she has no objection to Dr Walker deleting the words that had caused controversy, yes?'

'Yes.'

'Surely this willingness to co-operate isn't incompatible with your values?'

'Not my values. The IWA's values.'

'Yes, thank you for clarifying that, Mr Hardy. The distinction is important. I will rephrase: surely this willingness to co-operate isn't incompatible with the IWA's values?'

'No, it isn't.'

'In that case, Mr Hardy, which part of this short passage – less than three hundred words – caused the consternation you mentioned?'

'It was…it was the penultimate sentence. Where she says her personal motto is that people deserve respect, not ideas.'

'That caused consternation, you say?'

'Yes.'

'Why should it do that?'

'There was a feeling, expressed to me by various staff via email, that some people might be offended by it.'

'By the notion that people deserve respect?'

'No, by the notion that ideas don't deserve respect.'

'I see. Do you respect all ideas, Mr Hardy?'

'My opinion is irrelevant. I'm here to give evidence on the IWA's corporate position.'

'Very true. You've pointed that out already. So, once again, let me rephrase for the sake of complete clarity: does the IWA respect all ideas?'

'Erm…'

'Perhaps I can make it easier for you, Mr Hardy, with a few examples. According to one idea that once had a certain popularity, there is a genetic correlation between race and intelligence? Does the IWA respect that idea?'

'No, of course it doesn't, because…'

Den held his hand up. 'Thank you, Mr Hardy. There's no need to explain why. I'm simply interested in knowing whether there are any ideas that the IWA doesn't respect. Let's take another one. What about the idea that mental exertion could jeopardise women's reproductive health, therefore they shouldn't be allowed to vote? Does the IWA respect that?'

'No.'

'And what about the idea that global warming is a hoax created by the Chinese in order to make manufacturing in your own country, the United States, uncompetitive? Does the IWA respect that?'

'No.'

'So it's not the position of the IWA that all ideas deserve respect, is it?'

Hardy's gleaming smile was a distant memory now. 'No.'

'In that case, can you explain why Ms Farrier's statement was so problematic?'

'Because she…she said no ideas deserved respect.'

'I see. In your estimation, does Ms Farrier reject all ideas?'

'I can't speak for Ms Farrier, but I doubt it.'

'In your estimation. Yes or no, Mr Hardy.'

'No.'

'Why not?'

'Because Ms Farrier has ideas of her own. We all do. It would make no sense to reject all ideas.'

'Sorry, the feed crackled at my end just as you answered. Did you say it would make no sense to reject all ideas?'

Tara glanced at Zoya, who was smiling to herself. Neither of them believed Den's line had crackled.

'Yes,' said Hardy.

'Thank you. So we can conclude that Ms Farrier was making a slightly different point, yes?'

'Yes.'

'And what did you take that point to be?'

'She made the remark as part of her complaint at being

asked to respect the religious sensitivities of a marginalised community.'

'Her complaint? Can you point to the phrase that suggests she was complaining?'

Hardy frowned over the document in front of him. 'She… she was challenging Dr Walker's judgement.'

'Really? Could you read out the phrase in which she challenges Dr Walker's judgement?'

Hardy consulted the text once more. 'She says, "I just wanted to throw the question out there".'

'That's not the whole sentence, is it, Mr Hardy?'

'N…no.'

'Could you read the rest of the sentence, please?'

Hardy's earlier confidence had completely withered, and misery was now etched on his face. '"…Because I'm genuinely interested in what other people think."'

'Thank you, Mr Hardy.'

Tara almost felt sorry for the guy as the cross–examination wore on and Den corralled him into ever narrower logical traps. But she reminded herself that these rarefied semantic arguments all related to the IWA's attempted assassination of her own character. Hardy deserved no sympathy.

'Can we now turn, Mr Hardy, to the question of Ms Farrier's employment status? You told Ms Robertson earlier that no commitment was made to put Ms Farrier on staff once she had written her report. Yes?'

'No binding commitment, no.'

'You use the qualification "binding". Are you suggesting some other kind of commitment was made?'

'Not by my department.'

'Was any commitment made by any other department?'

'I can't say for certain, but if it were, it wouldn't have been binding.'

'Because it didn't come from your department?'

'Yes.'

'Mr Hardy, could you turn to page 279 of the bundle? You'll find an email to Ms Farrier from Matthew Tree, your co-director of development finance. Can you see it? Good. Would you mind reading out the last paragraph?'

With a murderous look, Hardy begin to read. '"I'm excited to hear how your meeting with Ms Denby goes. In any case, there's of course going to be a role for you here at the IWA. Don't worry on that score. I just need to make time to get the contract drawn up. My apologies for not doing so until now."'

'Thank you, Mr Hardy. Would you say that email constituted a commitment to give Ms Farrier a permanent position?'

'Not a binding one.'

'Was it a commitment, Mr Hardy?'

Hardy paused. 'Yes.'

'And having received that email, was Ms Farrier justified in believing that the IWA intended to give her a permanent position?'

'She was justified in believing that Mr Tree intended to give her a permanent position.'

'But not the IWA?'

'No.'

'Why not?'

'Because the…er…commitment, if you will, was made by Mr Tree and not by my own department.'

'I see. Can you remind us who invited Ms Farrier to return from Aden to London and to join the IWA as a research fellow, initially tasked with writing a country on Yemen?'

Hardy hesitated.

'Mr Hardy?' pressed Den. 'Who made that offer?'

'That would be Mr Tree.'

'Thank you, Mr Hardy.'

Tara, her mood improving, flashed a smile at Zoya. Her solicitor winked and popped another menthol sweet into her mouth. As an afterthought, she offered the packet to Tara, who wagged her finger to decline.

Den continued: 'Can we now return, Mr Hardy, to the second paragraph of Ms Farrier's controversial Clack statement? If you need to refer to it again, you'll find it on page 230 of the bundle. Have you found it? Good. In the second paragraph, Ms Farrier says she's been told it's offensive to North American ears to say the earth is billions of years old. In your own experience as a North American, is that true?'

'There are more than half a billion North Americans. I can't speak for them.'

'We all appreciate that, Mr Hardy. But is it offensive to you?'

'As I've said, Mr Hooper, I'm here to speak about the IWA's corporate position rather than my own views.'

'I know, Mr Hardy. You've made that very clear a number of times. But you're our only North American witness, so the court has a legitimate interest in your view on this question. Do you believe the earth is billions of years old, or only ten thousand?'

'I'm not an earth scientist.'

'Neither am I, Mr Hardy, but I have an opinion on the matter. Don't you?'

'I repeat, I'm not an expert.'

'So you're saying you'd need to be an earth scientist even to take a stab at how old the earth is?'

Tara was sure she saw Hooper gulp. He seemed to have noticed, too late, that he was painting himself into a corner.

'That might be...one of the...one of the qualifications, yes.'

'I see. Can I draw your attention to the series of four tweets you'll find on page 119? These were posted by Ms Farrier a few hours after she put her remarks on Clack. In the first of those tweets, she mentions someone called Helen Kottsack. Do you know who that is, Mr Hardy?'

'I didn't at the time, but I do now.'

'Can you tell me what she does for a living?'

'I believe she's a university lecturer.'

'In what subject?'

'I'm not certain.'

'Are you sure about that? There are some annotations in the bundle which may help.'

Hardy bit his upper lip but didn't look down at the document. 'I think it may be earth sciences.'

'Thank you. She is indeed a professor of earth sciences. And in her series of tweets, Ms Farrier explains that Professor Kottsack works at the university where she herself also once worked, yes?'

'Yes.'

'She refers to protests outside Professor Kottsack's lectures, yes?'

Tara closed her eyes. In the cut-and-thrust of the cross-examination, she had allowed herself to forget about the shock of Sorrel's betrayal, but now she fought back a new wave of nausea as the memory returned.

The witness nodded. 'Yes.'

'And Professor Kottsack's supposed offence is to teach the science that you just said was a qualification for knowing the age of the earth, yes?'

'I said it was one of the qualifications.'

'Yes or no, Mr Hardy.'

'Yes.'

'Could you now turn to the email exchange of the following day between yourself and Dr Walker? You'll find that on page 120.'

As Hardy consulted his bundle, Tara inwardly cheered. This email exchange was the smoking gun unearthed in disclosure.

'Have you found it, Mr Hardy?'

'Yes.'

'There's an email from you to Dr Walker, in which you say a cohort of associate staff approached you that morning to voice concerns that Tara Farrier was expressing offensive viewpoints on Twitter, and that her profile listed her as a research fellow at the IWA. Yes?'

'Yes.'

'You suggested to Dr Walker that she should ask Ms Farrier to remove that mention of the IWA from her profile and she should make it clear her tweets were solely her own opinions. Yes?'

'Yes.'

'Did Dr Walker make that request?'

'I believe she did.'

'And did Ms Farrier comply?'

'Yes.'

'If you look below that email, Mr Hardy, you'll see a second one from Dr Walker to yourself, in which she says, and I'm quoting, "OMG, this is going to hell in a handbasket". Could you tell me what this email referred to?'

Hardy consulted the document in front of him. 'This was after Ms Farrier liked an offensive tweet.'

'Could you read out the tweet she liked? It's the one from a user called Dr Ross Geller, in brackets Palaeontologist, and you'll find it on page 121.' To the judge, he added: 'Sir, this account has an obviously facetious name, referring as it does to a character from the sitcom *Friends*, but I will refer to the tweeter as Dr Geller for simplicity.'

'Thank you for the explanation, Mr Hooper,' said the judge. His tone was dry at the best of times and it was impossible to tell if he was being sarcastic or expressing genuine gratitude.

'Have you found it, Mr Hardy? Do please read the tweet aloud.'

With visible reluctance, Hardy read: '"I see the Young Earth cultists are having a completely normal one today."'

'And could you read the subject line of Dr Walker's email?'

'It's just three letters. U-G-H.'

'Spelling an exclamation of disgust, yes?'

'Dr Walker wrote it, so you'd have to ask her.'

'But you took it as such?'

'I can't remember how I took it. I may not have noticed.'

'Were you aware of the exchange to which Dr Geller was referring when he tweeted that the Young Earth cultists were having, I quote, "a completely normal one"?'

'If I was, I don't recall.'

'You were unaware that a number of Twitter users had been issuing death threats against other users whom they described as "Yerf scum"?'

'I didn't know that.'

'Do you know what "Yerf" means?'

'I didn't at the time, but I do now.'

'It's a pejorative term for people like Ms Farrier who believe the earth is billions of years old, yes?'

'So I understand.'

'So you understand now, although you didn't at the time?'

'Yes.'

'To be clear, then: you didn't know the context for the tweet that Ms Farrier liked, yet you were happy to accept Dr Walker's expression of disgust at her behaviour? You certainly didn't challenge it, did you?'

'As I say, I may not even have noticed the subject line.'

'Do you often open emails without reading the subject line, Mr Hardy?'

After a long pause, Hardy muttered: 'No.'

'Sorry, Mr Hardy. I didn't catch that.'

'No.'

'Thank you Mr Hardy. No further questions.'

Tara's mood had steadily improved during those final exchanges. Although she could not completely banish her family worries from her mind, Den's performance had been a powerful tonic, and her eyes were shining as she turned to Zoya. 'Den is amazing!'

Her solicitor grinned. 'What did I tell you?'

'That last bit was a complete thrill-ride. He massacred the guy.'

'Don't start feeling sorry for the witness. Apart from anything else, he's very well rewarded for his trouble.'

The pair turned back to the screen, where the two barristers now had the chance to make their concluding statements. That took another hour but, as far as Tara was concerned, Den had nailed it already. Eventually the judge wrapped up proceedings, announcing that he would aim to make his preliminary ruling as soon as possible, but he couldn't say precisely when. The webcam light went off, and the preliminary tribunal was over.

'How do you think it's gone?' said Tara. Having seen what a shambolic bunch her former bosses really were, she was more determined to win than ever. She would do it for everyone who had backed her – and as one in the eye for bloody Sorrel.

Zoya shrugged. 'As I've said before, I've worked in the law for long enough to know there are no certainties when it comes to judges' rulings. But we've made a very strong case.'

Tara wasn't really listening. 'Oh to be a fly on the wall of the IWA's HR department at this moment! They must know they've lost this round, mustn't they? How could any judge in his right mind rule against us at this stage?'

23

The judge ruled against them.

He took three months to reach this conclusion, and the heatwave seemed a distant memory, amid the wettest October for years, when Tara received the call from Zoya.

She had been struggling not to let her worries about Sammy, and the possible consequences of his relationship with Sorrel, bring her mood down. She had seen Sammy only once, when he came over for lunch on his own, and she had deliberately steered clear of the subject, which made the whole encounter fraught with tension, as far as Tara was concerned. But they continued to exchange WhatsApp messages every week or so, and she tried to fend off her deepest fear, that her son would end up turning against her.

Whenever she felt herself dipping into a depression, she made the effort of will to focus on the one thing that was certainly going in the right direction: her legal team had wiped the floor with the IWA in the first round of the tribunal.

When she saw therefore that it was Zoya calling, on the day the ruling came through, she answered the phone brightly, because it remained unthinkable that the news would be anything but good.

As soon as she heard her solicitor's tone, she knew something was wrong.

'What is it?' she demanded, suddenly panic-stricken.

'Can you come into the office, Tara? I'm afraid it's not something I can explain over the phone.'

'Really? Why, what's happened? Is it bad news? And why can't you tell me over the phone?'

She heard her solicitor take a deep breath. 'Tara, when the draft judgement is ready, we're granted sight of it in advance, so we can read it and correct any factual errors. Mainly typos, that kind of thing. We're permitted to show you the draft, but we can't let it out of the office.'

'So it's arrived today? Is that what you're saying?'

'Yes.'

'And it sounds like it isn't good news? Is that also what you're saying?'

'As I say, I can't make any comment over the phone. But…'

'What?'

'Well…I wouldn't get your hopes up.'

She set out on the drive to London in a daze and arrived in an utter state, in a shorter time than the journey ought to take if she'd obeyed the speed limit. As she parked the car, denial crept in and she wondered if perhaps she had misunderstood Zoya on the phone, and the situation wasn't as bad as she feared. But that illusion was dispelled as soon as she saw her solicitor's face.

'I'm so sorry,' Zoya said, ushering Tara into her office and gesturing for her to sit. 'I'm afraid the judge decided you failed to meet one of the Grainger criteria.'

For a moment, Tara thought she might actually bring up her breakfast. 'What? How? Which one?'

'Number five.'

'Sorry, you'll have to remind me what that was.'

'That your belief must be worthy of respect in a democratic society, not be incompatible with human dignity and not conflict with the fundamental rights of others.'

'And mine isn't? Seriously, is this a joke? Believing the earth is billions of years old isn't worthy of respect in a democratic society? Has the judge lost his mind?' She was shouting, but she didn't care.

'It's certainly hard to believe that anyone in their right mind could consider all the evidence and reach that conclusion.'

'But that's just one of the criteria, right? I fulfil all the others?'

'Yes, but I'm afraid the point of the Grainger criteria is that all five must be met.'

'Why? Who says?'

'The law says. More precisely the case law, but that amounts to the same thing.'

'That's ridiculous. This isn't justice. It's the very opposite. Can't we challenge it?'

'We can't challenge the law, but we can appeal against the judgement.'

'Yes, that's what I meant.' The room was beginning to spin.

'Look, why don't you go through to the conference room and read the ruling for yourself. Then you'll have a clearer idea of what we're up against. I'll get you a cup of tea while you make a start.'

As Tara entered the familiar room, effectively the witness box for her ordeal under cross-examination, she remembered the last time she'd been there: that sweltering day when the awful discovery about Sorrel had been alleviated, at least in part, by her own certainty that she had won this round. That delusion now seemed like something from another life.

Sitting at the conference table with a mug of milky tea at her elbow, she forced herself to concentrate on the judgement. The judge's problem, it seemed, was Tara's 'absolutist' stance. 'Ms Farrier's position,' he wrote, 'is that if she meets an Indigenous colleague who tells her they sincerely believe the earth is no more than ten thousand years old, she will refuse to countenance that idea. Such an attitude cannot be said to be worthy of respect in a democratic society. Even paying due regard to the qualified right to freedom of expression, people cannot expect to be protected if their core belief involves violating others' dignity and creating an intimidating, hostile, degrading, humiliating or offensive environment for them.'

Tara read the paragraph twice over, in growing disbelief. This was the exact opposite of what she had said! She had patiently explained that disagreement with a belief was no bar to respecting someone. That was the whole point of her supposedly notorious personal motto. How could the judge – the judge! – misrepresent her so grotesquely? The guy hadn't appeared senile to her, and he seemed to be awake the whole time. So what the hell was his problem?

'The bastard! How can he do this?' she said, when she had read the whole judgement and rejoined Zoya in her office.

Her solicitor shook her head. 'I know. I need to re-read and digest it properly, and I'll seek advice from Den. We can either request that the tribunal reconsider the judgement, or we can appeal it on the grounds that this decision is perverse, but then we'd have to go back to court and put our arguments to a different judge. In the meantime, there's a more immediate ordeal to go through. They've given us early sight of this ruling but it will be public knowledge in a few days' time. Then you'll face an onslaught from your opponents, I'm afraid. *Earth News* will be cock-a-hoop.'

'Bastard, bastard, bastard! How dare he? Not worthy of respect in a democratic society! How can anyone say that?'

'I'm so sorry,' said Zoya. 'Look, I suggest you go home. Scream out loud on the motorway, if it helps get the anger out of your system. But try not to kill anyone on the road.'

'Can I tell anyone else about this?'

'You're not meant to. But of course if there's someone you can trust to keep their mouth shut, I can't stop you telling them.'

Tara nodded. 'Message received.'

'And we'll need to agree a statement, so we're ready to give our reaction as soon as the media receives the ruling.'

On her way home, Tara considered who best to choose as her confidant. She would of course tell Laila, but for the moment she felt the need of an older, wiser shoulder on which to cry. She had seen less of Helen lately, because she still felt guilty about Sorrel's involvement in the picket, and now was not the time to address that. The person in whom she actually hankered to confide, although they had only met once, was Mel. The Orange Peel founder had been through this kind of ordeal herself, or a version of it, and emerged relatively unscathed. She also exuded an air of easy authority, giving the impression she was the person most likely to be the adult in any given room. No doubt that simply came with private education and smart breeding, but no matter: Mel was the kind of person Tara needed right now. Someone who would tell her, however unlikely it might seem at the present moment, that everything would be all right in the end. That was the role parents played when you were small and sometimes, however old you were, you still needed people like that. This was one of those times.

Hoping she didn't sound too needy – she would hate Mel to know she had placed her *in loco parentis* – she texted as soon as she got in.

Hi Mel. It's Tara. I'm sorry to burden you with this, but I've just had some devastating news. Officially I'm not meant to share it with anyone yet, but my solicitor has indicated it's OK to do so very discreetly. Would you mind very much if I gave you a call?

She filled a pot of water for coffee but Mel texted back before she had even put it on the stove.

Of course. Call. M

Putting the coffee on to boil, Tara hit dial. When Mel answered, Tara dispensed with polite preliminaries and went straight to the story of the judge's ruling, pouring it all out without interruption.

'The guy sounds like an utter pillock,' Mel said, when she had finished. 'Surely there are grounds to challenge the ruling, if he's attributing views to you that directly contradict what you yourself said under cross-examination? What do your lawyers say?'

'You'd think so wouldn't you? They haven't had a chance to discuss it properly yet. Zoya said she's going to re-read it and then talk to Den once she's digested it. Apparently we can either ask the tribunal to reconsider the ruling, or appeal the whole thing and do it all over–'

She didn't finish the sentence, as she struggled to maintain her composure. She had held it together through the humiliation of being told the IWA no longer wanted her, and the trauma of the cross-examination, but her strength had its limits.

'Are you all right?' said Mel.

'Just give me a moment,' said Tara.

'Take your time. Breathe.'

'I know. Thanks.'

As Tara tried to regulate her breathing to calm herself, Mel made all the right noises at the other end, somehow managing to be both soothing and vengeful. It was a blend that struck Tara, even in her distress, as remarkably astute.

Over the next couple of days, she and Mel spoke often over WhatsApp. Together they worked out a form of words they could issue as a statement. When they were both satisfied with it, Tara emailed the text to Zoya, who came back with a couple of minor adjustments. By Friday lunchtime, they knew the tribunal would make the ruling public the following Monday. It was due out at noon, whereupon Zoya's office would issue a statement saying her client was considering her options. At the same time, Tara would tweet: 'This judgement removes the right to freedom of belief and speech. It gives judicial licence for women and men who speak up for objective truth and clear debate to be subject to aggression, bullying, no platforming and economic punishment.'

Noon on the Monday arrived. Within seconds, Zoya was proved right about the aggression and bullying, as a torrent of triumphant and abusive messages surged into Tara's feed. Most were variations on a limited number of themes: she was a bigot, she was a bitch, she had got what she deserved. Some of the messages consisted entirely of the crying-laughing emoji, repeated as many times as the character limit would allow. Those were more wounding than the outright abuse. That total strangers should derive such enjoyment from her own unjust treatment was a horrible thought.

It was Leon Smith, with sadistic precision, who first focused on the most withering line of the judgement, declaring that Tara herself was 'not worthy of respect in a democratic society'. In its own instant news story on the judgement, *Earth News* took the same approach, headlining its piece 'Court finds anti-Indigenous lobbyist Tara Farrier "not worthy of respect in a democratic society"'. Within an hour, the mocking hashtag *#NotWorthyOfRespectInADemocraticSociety* was trending.

Once again, Tara couldn't have got through that day without Mel's presence at the other end of the phone. In the late afternoon, Laila – by now completely in the loop – arrived to offer moral support in person, having left work half an hour early to be with her mother.

She took a tough line on Tara's mobile phone access and confiscated the handset. Tara of course saw the sense of it: all these hateful people were trying to upset her, and by viewing the material they tweeted, she was allowing them to succeed. But perhaps there were also supportive messages that might make her feel better…?

Rather than return the phone to her mother, Laila took it upon herself to read from her own device the messages she thought Tara would like to hear. There were heartfelt good wishes – and tirades against the judge – from all the usual stalwarts: Rita, Helen, Ginny, as well as various other commentators who had taken her side since her case had become a *cause célèbre*. In addition, a number of friendly lawyers offered their thoughts on whether or not there were grounds to challenge the judgement. The consensus was yes: if the key element of the ruling rested on a fundamental distortion of Tara's consistently expressed views, not least under cross-examination, there was clear cause. There was less agreement on whether or not this required a full re-run of the hearing before a different judge, or if it was simply a matter of making the existing judge see sense.

There was no word from Sammy, but Tara tried as ever not to dwell on that. Emotionally battered as she was, some survival instinct deep within her recognised there was only so much hurt she could process in one day. She still hadn't told Laila about the confirmed sighting of Sorrel at the campus picket. Laila herself either hadn't noticed Sammy's lack of support or, for whatever reason, chose not to talk about it. That raised a further series of questions for Tara about how much Laila knew that she wasn't telling her mother, but there would be time for all that some other day, her tired brain told her.

Later, while Laila made an omelette for their supper, Tara was allowed her phone back to call Zoya, so they could discuss the options for contesting the ruling.

'Obviously it would be simpler and cheaper just to get them to look again at the ruling,' her solicitor said. 'We'd simply point out the obvious gap between the views the judge attributes to you and what you actually said under cross-examination. On the other hand–'

Tara cut in. 'If he didn't understand that the first time, what prospect is there of him understanding it now?'

'Well, exactly. Either way, from conversations I've been having with colleagues all day, I'm confident we can challenge this. I know it's devastating to have this initial setback, but this isn't over, by any stretch of the imagination. And I imagine it will galvanise support for you. The judge has effectively told 99.9 percent of the population that their beliefs aren't worthy of respect in a democratic society. I don't think he has any idea how angry that's going to make people once they learn about it.'

'I hope you're right,' said Tara. 'I worry the reverse will happen, and people will be even more nervous of speaking out—'

'Oh my God!' Laila stood in the doorway, staring at her phone screen.

'Sorry, Zoya. Hold on.' Tara glared in Laila's direction. Having her daughter around in these dark hours was a priceless boon, but she did need to talk to her solicitor uninterrupted.

Laila was impervious to the facial rebuke. 'This is unbelievable! Mum, you've got to see it!' Her eyes were shining.

'Just wait till I've finished my call. I'm talking to Zoya.'

'Yes, I know you are. But Zoya needs to hear this too.'

Tara sighed, the emotional exhaustion really beginning to kick in. 'What is it?'

'Put Zoya on speaker and I'll read it out.'

Reluctantly, Tara did as her daughter asked. Did everything really have to come to a halt because Laila had found something on the internet?

'Listen to this,' Laila said, raising her voice so that Zoya could also hear. 'It's a tweet.'

'Who from?' said Tara.

'Just listen, all right? It goes: "Pray to whoever you please. Believe whatever you like. Embrace whichever cultural heritage appeals to you. Live your best life in peace and security. But force women out of their jobs for stating that geology is real?" That's where the main text of the tweet ends – it's, like, a rhetorical question – but it's followed by a couple of hashtags: *#IStandWithTara* and *#ThisIsNotADrill*.'

'That's nice,' said Tara. 'Very powerful and supportive but…what am I missing? Why did we have to interrupt our conversation for this?'

'Who's it from?' came Zoya's disembodied voice.

Laila pointed to the phone in Tara's hand and nodded approvingly, as to congratulate Zoya for asking the right question. She looked as if she were about to burst with glee.

'Well?' said Tara irritably. 'Who tweeted it?'

Laila grinned silently for a couple of seconds more, then delivered the bombshell she was so clearly dying to drop.

'It was only Emily. Actual. Zola!'

24

Emily Zola had fourteen million followers on Twitter. By the end of the evening, more than a hundred thousand of them had liked her tweet in support of Tara.

Ginny was the first of Tara's crew to call. 'Are you on Twitter?' she asked breathlessly. 'Sorry, that may be a silly question. But I just wanted to alert you, in case you hadn't seen it.'

'Oh, we've seen it,' said Tara. Laila had given up trying to police her mother's screen time, and Tara had now regained control of her own phone.

'Isn't it amazing? I'm just sitting here watching the numbers go up before my eyes. Who knew that could be so entertaining?'

Tara laughed, and realised it was the first time she had done so for a fortnight. 'If you fancy a change of entertainment, you could always watch my follower count clicking up.' She and Laila had been watching the total surge up by tens and twenties every couple of minutes. 'I'm finally beginning to grasp just how influential Emily Zola is.'

'Have you heard from her directly?' asked Ginny. She sounded like a star-struck adolescent.

'I sent her a direct message thanking her for the support, and she sent me back a heart emoji. My daughter was very jealous of that.'

'Sammy will be too, when I tell him,' called Laila from across the room.

Mention of her son made Tara's heart leap. The situation couldn't be quite as bad as she had feared, then. Otherwise Laila would never have brought up his name.

'I'm glad to hear you sounding more cheerful,' said Ginny. 'I know from Mel how hard it's been for you, these past couple of weeks. Let's hope Emily Zola's support is the beginning of your fightback. I bet it will work wonders for your crowd-funder.'

'Here's hoping.'

Within the hour, *#IStandWithTara* was trending. Helen called to commiserate on Tara's loss but to congratulate her on this exciting social media development, and barely had they ended the call when it was Mel's turn.

'Craig tells me you're trending,' she said. 'I don't really know what that means, but I gather it's a good thing.'

Tara had learned that Mel enjoyed playing the fogey who lived on too elevated a level to understand new-fangled fads such as the internet.

'It is, in this case,' said Tara.

'I'm delighted for you. Really I am. Perhaps it will give

those swine at the IWA pause for thought. They may have won the first skirmish, but they haven't won the battle, let alone the war.'

'I hope so. Let's not get too carried away, but it's certainly cheered me up.'

'Good. You deserve it.'

When Tara had hung up with Mel, Laila got to her feet and said she had to get home. 'You know, I really can't wait to tell Sammy about Emily Zola,' she said. 'He's not that bothered about the age of the earth, but he'll be well impressed by your famous fan.'

All Tara's previous good intentions about not getting into this today fell away. If this was not the time to raise the subject, then when? 'Even if Sorrel is one of the fanatics spreading hatred about me?'

Laila blinked in bewilderment. 'What are you talking about, Mum? You don't still think she's one of the lunatics picketing your friend Helen?'

'I don't think it. I know it.' Tara trembled with fury – directed at Sorrel, at Sammy, even at Laila: at anyone not privy to her own agonies of the past three months.

'What? How? And why didn't you tell me?'

'Helen saw her. She told me on the first day of the tribunal.'

Laila's mouth fell open. 'And she thought that was a good time to mention it?'

'Don't blame Helen. It's not her fault. She has no idea who Sorrel is. I asked her ages ago if she'd seen a girl on the picket with purple and pink dreadlocks, and she hadn't. But recently she did, and she told me at the first opportunity. She doesn't know it's Sammy's girlfriend.'

'And you didn't tell her?'

'How could I?' In her distress, Tara was shouting. 'I was too ashamed.'

'But why didn't you tell *me*, for God's sake?'

'Because…I don't know.' Her anger began to subside, replaced by relief that she was finally sharing this torment with Laila. 'I was scared of putting it into words. It felt like that would somehow make it worse, forcing you to take sides between me and Sammy.'

'Between you and Sammy? You're not seriously trying to tell me he's one of those loonies too? Because if he is, I'll rip out his stupid hipster beard with my bare hands…'

'You see? That's what I was afraid of! More rifts, more hatred… Haven't I had enough to deal with?'

'I know but…' Laila paused and took a breath. 'Is he really one of them? He honestly hasn't said a word about it to me.'

Tara shrugged. 'I can't help noticing that your brother has been much less supportive than you. I know he's got his own life to lead and I don't have any automatic right to his support. But he didn't wish me luck on the first day of the tribunal and I haven't heard a word from him since finding out I lost. Can you blame me for assuming the worst?'

'He may not even know you lost. Have you told him?'

'Well…no. I was so nervous…'

'Mum! You used to live in a war zone. When you got kidnapped, you thought it was a great laugh. And you're allowing a stupid spoilt brat like Spinach to terrorise you? Sammy is your son. Text him now to say you lost the tribunal. I bet he has no idea. It's not like he spends his whole life on social media. Like you say, he's always really busy with his job.'

'All right, but I'm not doing it with you standing over me. I'll message him as soon as you've gone. I promise.'

'Promise also that you'll let me know what he says. Even if it's nothing and he blanks you. Although I don't for a moment believe he will.'

Tara nodded. 'I promise.'

'Come here,' said Laila.

Tara allowed her daughter to pull her into an embrace. 'But promise me something in return,' she said.

'What's that?'

'I won't have you two falling out over me. If Sammy has been snared by this idiotic cult, I don't want you taking sides with me and falling out with him. This is my battle, not yours.'

'Let's cross that bridge when we come to it, shall we?'

'That didn't sound like a promise.'

Laila sighed theatrically. 'All right. I promise I won't pull his stupid hipster beard out with my bare hands until you've had the chance to do it first.' Ignoring her mother's frown, she looked at her watch. 'Sorry, I really have to get going now. I've got an early start tomorrow.'

'Thanks for everything, *habibti*. Seriously.'

After she had gone, Tara sat down to WhatsApp Sammy, as she had promised. After a couple of false starts, she settled on: *Hi* habibi. *I don't know whether you've heard by now, but I lost the first round of my tribunal. It's all been pretty devastating but my lawyers say we have good grounds for appeal and I've had fantastic support, including an amazing tweet from Emily Zola, no less. So I'm down but not out. Love you xxx.*

Sammy must have just finished his shift because the reply came straight back. *No, I hadn't heard. Very sorry to hear that. But Emily Zola! Amazing! x.*

Tara stared at the words, trying to interpret them. He didn't exactly sound devastated for her, where the tribunal was concerned. But it was a friendly, prompt reply, and it was signed with an 'x'.

Since her phone was still in her hand, Tara checked her follower count on Twitter. It had now passed fifty thousand. That was extraordinary, and an amazing boost to her confidence. Laila was right she couldn't let an enlightened little madam like Sorrel put her off her stride. She had chosen her path and there was no going back now. Particularly not with Emily Zola and a hundred thousand of her fans cheering her on.

25

Next morning she woke to the backlash.

The first thing she saw when she logged onto Twitter – which she now did over breakfast every morning, even before reading the news sites – was a video of something burning. She didn't pay much attention at first, but it was being shared here, there and everywhere, so she eventually clicked on it to see what was going on. The short clip consisted of a young woman with dyed blue hair standing in front of a brazier, screaming something unintelligible as she tipped a pile of books into the flames. Tara watched this on loop two or three times before she realised that the girl was incinerating her entire *Sandy Snaith* collection.

Emily Zola had, it seemed, simply by expressing support for Tara, appalled those of her devoted young readers who had now become politically conscious twenty-somethings. In their eyes, the author had not only trashed her own reputation by coming out as a Yerf bigot. She had also betrayed them, and they were determined to take it personally.

A day or so later Danielle Cardiff, the young *Sandy Snaith* star about whom Laila had teased Rob, issued a statement to the media. 'Indigenous people have the right to believe what they like,' she said. 'Any statement to the contrary erases their identity and dignity, reinforcing the trauma of colonialism. I'm very sorry that Em can't see this.'

Zola's supporters responded to the diminutive actress by patiently pointing out that her supposedly offending tweet had specifically said that everyone was free to believe whatever they wanted. Cardiff was therefore denouncing her for saying the exact opposite of what she had actually said. But this cut no ice with Emily's detractors. For them, the once-saintly author was a turncoat whose sole aim in life was the eradication not just of followers of the potter goddess, but of every Indigenous person in North America, and no doubt on every other continent too.

Lateefa Latif, who was apparently an actress, although none of Tara's friends could name anything she'd been in, issued a public appeal to Zola on Twitter. 'Please follow more Indigenous people, please read about their experiences in this world and know you are contributing to their erasure, abuse and suffering by supporting those who deny their identity/ existence. Please wield your immense power to protect those most at risk,' she wrote. Ridiculous and misleading as it was, her tweet received nearly a million likes.

As the days passed, however, Zola showed no sign of making the public climbdown demanded of her. Having pledged themselves to the cause of destroying her, her attackers had no choice but to step up the hyperbole. Without Emily herself needing to say anything further, her reported crimes became steadily graver: she had tweeted obsessively about Indigenous people, it was confidently asserted; her books were revealed to be a hitherto unnoticed sewer of colonialist supremacy, evidenced by the total lack of First Nation characters within their covers; she would not be happy until she had whipped up a further genocide that would finally eradicate all original inhabitants from the continent of North America.

Two weeks in, the vitriol continued to surge through social media, and BBC journalists began routinely to describe Zola as 'controversial' whenever they mentioned her, without ever explaining the roots of the controversy, or that it had been confected by people telling outright lies.

On the front page of *The Guardian*, three young writers whose names had never troubled the bestseller lists announced they were defecting from their literary agency, because it happened also to represent Zola. 'We cannot in good conscience remain on the books of a company that is happy to profit from the eradication of Indigenous people,' they said in a joint statement.

'Absolute hypocritical bastards!' fumed Ginny to Tara over WhatsApp. She had just looked up the rest of the agency's list, and discovered that it also represented Bruno Rage, a boxer notorious for his tirades against women, gays and Jews. 'It never offended their consciences to share an agent with him,' she railed.

'Write a letter to *The Guardian* about it,' suggested Tara.

'Nah, they'd never publish it. Don't worry, I'll place an article somewhere about these opportunist toerags.'

She was as good as her word, publishing a piece in *The Critic*.

But *Earth News* – all of whose birthdays and Christmases had come at once with the Zola furore – couldn't resist getting its own dig in. 'Controversial "journalist" Ginny Pugh stirs up culture war with unprovoked rant at principled pro-Indigenous writers,' read its headline.

While the bulk of the attacks were directed at Emily, they also targeted Tara. As she discovered to her cost the first and only time she tried it, googling herself was a deeply unwise move. Badmouthing her had become a shorthand way for people of a certain mindset to assert their political and cultural values. The more angry and intemperate their outburst, the more virtuous they imagined themselves to appear.

This applied not just to ordinary members of the public but also, it seemed, to prominent personages. Tara was actually more bewildered than hurt to find herself under attack by a former soap star who had somehow ended up as a Labour peer. Another grandstanding hater was a barrister who had become a national joke after boasting on social media about clubbing a hedgehog to death with a hockey stick while dressed in a sarong. He was understandably keen to salvage his reputation and seemed to think that trashing Tara was the way to do it. The depressing thing, Tara realised, was that he might be right.

She was even mentioned on the floor of the House of Commons. That was Rita's doing, and it was intended as a supportive gesture: her MP friend took the opportunity of a debate on freedom of speech to make a contribution that mentioned both Helen and Tara. She ended by quoting Emily Zola: 'Force women out of their jobs for stating that geology is real? I hope the House will agree with me that this is completely unacceptable.'

Rita's speech might have gone unnoticed had she not been loudly heckled by a fellow Labour MP called Lloyd Kruger-Dunning. This angry firebrand leapt to his feet as soon as Rita had finished, clearly incensed that anyone should speak up for such heretics. Jabbing his finger at Rita, and creating a cloud of spittle that was visible in the TV clips, he roared: 'The idea of supporting anti-Indigenous racists like Emily Zola and Tara Farrier is disgusting and you should be ashamed!' The Speaker stood up and told him to moderate his tone, but Kruger-Dunning swatted this warning away and raged on, puce in the face, until he suddenly collapsed, having ruptured a blood vessel. He had to be stretchered out of the chamber, thereby guaranteeing himself a slot on all the evening news channels.

On social media, *#SackRitaDenby* trended for two days, with some of the more outspoken anonymous accounts accusing her of not being content with trying to eradicate Indigenous people from Canterbury and the wider world, but of deliberately endangering her colleague's life. Meanwhile, the excitement caused by the episode gave the story a few days' traction in the Westminster village. Political journalists who had until now ducked the Yerf conflict – officially because it was a fringe issue, but unofficially, Tara suspected, because they didn't want their prematurely politicised teenage kids to hate them – finally acknowledged there was news value in it after all.

Amid the furore, Labour's leader, Sir Mark Terries, offered a public apology in a BBC interview. Unfortunately this was directed not to Tara and Emily, but to any followers of the goddess Ctatpeshirahi (he had clearly been rehearsing) who might have been offended by Rita's speech.

Furious on Rita's behalf as well as her own, Tara called her MP friend on FaceTime. 'I'm so sorry that you've been dragged into this,' she said. 'I can't believe Terries is blaming you for it. He's throwing you to the wolves and making you look like you've done something shameful. Honestly, I don't know which is worse, his cowardice or his stupidity. If his own core voters knew that our crime was actually just to believe what virtually everyone in the country believes anyway…' She trailed off, knowing she was preaching to the converted.

Rita had dark patches under her eyes and looked exhausted, as if she hadn't slept, but she merely shrugged. 'Welcome to my world. But Tara, listen to me: there are many, many people who owe me apologies, and you are not one of them. Neither of us chose this fight, but now we're in it, we're in it together.'

Tara knew she was right, but she was also impressed by Rita's steely refusal to capitulate to the haters within her own party. Tara herself could hide away in the safety of her cottage, knowing that all her neighbours in the village were on her side. Rita, by contrast, ran a gauntlet of malice every time she took her seat among her colleagues in the parliamentary chamber.

The government, which had been tanking in the opinion polls, couldn't believe its luck. The Tory prime minister brought the issue up in his next clash with Terries, asking if Labour would ban the daily prayers that began each parliamentary session, for fear of offending any creationist followers of a previously unknown potter goddess in Alaska or the frozen north of Canada. This made his own benches roar with laughter, Conservative members waving their order papers in derision as the opposition squirmed, but Labour's supporters in the media came back fighting. *The Guardian* declared the PM's jibe beyond the pale; he had made a minority religious community a political football in what had clearly become an open culture war, an editorial concluded, while taking care not to explain any of the roots of the argument to its readers. For all those readers were aware, Emily, Tara and Rita really might be campaigning for genocide.

Since the 'sensitivities' around the history of the planet had now been dubbed a culture war, it should have come as no surprise, in the ensuing months, when the row began to affect the arts.

All twelve seasons of *The Big Bang Theory* were removed from every major TV streaming service, and the US Film Academy announced it was dropping *Ice Age* from its list of top ten animation movies of all time. Closer to home, a group of Oxbridge-educated children's authors whipped up a campaign against Coleen Coogan, a writer of humbler origins, whose crime was to have created *Danny the Dinosaur*, a primary-age picture book. Dinosaurs, as 'progressives' of the world now recognised, were a notorious anti-Indigenous dog-whistle. Not only was the book withdrawn from most bookshops and libraries, but Coogan was also told she was no longer welcome to read to children in schools.

Coleen was still reeling when Tara, who had now become a *de facto* leader of Britain's growing band of Yerfs, made contact by phone.

'I just don't know how this happened,' Coogan told her. 'I wrote about dinosaurs, for God's sake, and that now makes me a genocidal racist? And you know the worst of it? When

I try to explain to my friends and family what has happened to me – like, to normal people who don't spend all their time on Twitter and have no idea what crackpot ideas are being dreamed up in the name of social justice – none of them believe me. They assume I must have done something wrong, and I've left it out of the story. I don't blame them. I wouldn't believe me either!'

In that respect, at least, the National History Museum did Coogan a favour when it announced the closure of its world-renowned dinosaur gallery. Suddenly, millions more people became aware that something seriously mad was happening in the name of cultural sensitivity. Protestors in inflatable T-Rex costumes highlighted the issue by picketing the museum with signs saying HANDS OFF SCIENCE, WE WON'T BE EXTINGUISHED TWICE and THIS IS NOT A DRILL. An array of prominent Indigenous figures in North America – from the vast Nunavut territory in Canada to the Nahua homelands in Mexico – wrote to the director, stressing their own conviction that dinosaurs had once roamed the earth and imploring him not to carry out such swingeing anti-scientific vandalism in their name. Featuring prominently in the conservative press, the letter was ignored by the BBC and *The Guardian*.

During all this time, Tara's only contact with Sammy had been via WhatsApp. At Laila's urging, however, she organised a family dinner one Tuesday night, when Sammy would be free. Rob had agreed not to come, to make it less awkward not to include Sorrel, so it was just the three of them.

Sammy was the first to arrive. Tara stood aside on the doorstep to let him pass, nervous that he might shy away if she attempted to hug him. The rebuff would be unbearable, so it was self-protection that held her back. He seemed wrong-footed by the unexpected formality, but he embraced her nonetheless, and the awkwardness eased.

She asked him about the café.

'It's mad, as ever. I'm permanently shattered.'

He looked it, too. The bags under his eyes were darker than when she had last seen him.

'And...Sorrel?' The awkwardness flared again, as she tried and failed to adopt a casual tone.'

'She's fine,' he said.

Tara wondered if he might add 'and she sends her love' or 'says hi', but he didn't, and seemed unwilling to linger on the subject. For the first time, Tara wondered if the relationship might have suffered under the strain.

'More importantly, how are you?' he said. 'That was a real bummer, with the tribunal. But you're appealing, right?'

'Yes, I am,' she said, looking him straight in the eye.

'Good for you,' he said. 'I'm proud of you, whatever... Well, I'm proud of you.'

It had sounded as if he was going to say 'whatever anyone else says', and suddenly she saw how tough it might be for him, attempting to put family loyalty over cultural peer pressure. She was about to say as much when they heard the crunch of tyres on the drive, announcing Laila's arrival, and the moment passed.

The date they'd arranged happened to be when the Natural History Museum row was still at its height. Laila wanted to talk about the controversy, and how crazed it made Tara's opponents look. Before they sat down to eat, she made them gather around her phone to watch a viral clip of Terries being interviewed that morning on Nick Ferrari's breakfast show.

Tara pulled a face at her daughter behind Sammy's back, nervous that this might be too provocative, but Laila just smiled, exuding confidence that all would be well.

Tara had no option but to watch as Ferrari asked: 'Sir Mark, can you tell us whether dinosaurs existed, or were simply a gigantic imperialist hoax?'

Sammy leaned in closer, open-mouthed, as the leader of the opposition visibly squirmed:

Terries: Nick I'm not... I don't think we can conduct this debate with...you know...I mean, we need more...

Ferrari: We need more what?

Terries: Well, sensitivity.

Ferrari: Very well, let me ask you again, with sensitivity. *[in a mockingly gentle voice]* Sir Mark, did the dinosaurs exist?

Terries *[sighing]*: I don't think discussing this issue in this way helps anyone in the long run. I do find that too many people hold a position that is intolerant of others. I don't like intolerance. I like open discussion.

Ferrari: So do I. That's the whole point of this programme, to discuss things. So if it's not too much trouble, Sir Mark, I'll ask you again: do you personally believe that dinosaurs really existed?

Terries *[looking like he wished he could sink through the floor]*: No no no it's just...No no no I just...

Ferrari: So dinosaurs are a hoax?

Terries: I didn't say that. *[testily]* With the greatest respect, Nick, please don't put words in my mouth.

Ferrari: So dinosaurs aren't a hoax?

Terries: Nick, there are many more pressing issues that I'm sure your listeners want to hear about, so can we please move on?

Ferrari: Actually, Sir Mark, we had a lot of emails when we told our listeners you were coming on the programme, all raising questions they want me to ask you. By far the most popular was about the Natural History Museum. So I'll ask you for the fourth time. Or maybe it's the fifth – I'm afraid I've lost count. Did the dinosaurs exist or were they a racist hoax?

Terries: I don't know. I'm not a palaeontologist.

Ferrari: I'm not a palaeontologist either, but I still have an opinion.

Terries: Well, I don't.

Ferrari: That's your last word? Cross your heart and hope to die, Sir Mark Terries, leader of His Majesty's Opposition, you have no idea whether dinosaurs existed or not?

Terries: Correct. I just don't know.

By the end, it was clear that Tara had fretted needlessly. Laila had to play the clip another twice because all three of them were laughing too much to hear it properly.

'This is seriously crazy, Mum,' she said, when they had all eventually heard enough. 'The people at the top have gone nuts. That's why they hate people like you. You're shining a light on the insanity. You mustn't stop now, whatever you do.'

'I'll drink to that,' said Sammy.

'Really, *habibi*?' said Tara, frightened almost to believe her own ears.

'Really,' he said. 'You've got to fight this. For everyone's sake. To be honest, when this was all about volcanoes and tectonic plates, I found it hard to get too excited. But now they're coming for the dinosaurs, I'm mad as hell. I loved that gallery when you took us there as kids. If Laila or I have children, we won't be able to do that. That's not OK.'

'Oh Sammy.' Tara pulled her son into a hug. The relief was indescribable. Whatever other damage this awful battle might do, it was not going to rip her own family apart.

Emily Zola √ @EmilyZolaOfficial
Pray to whoever you please.
Believe whatever you like.
Embrace whichever cultural heritage appeals to you.
Live your best life in peace and security.
But force women out of their jobs for stating that geology is real? *#IStandWithTara #ThisIsNotADrill*
RT 98.4 L 234.7K

Goddess Ctat @young_earth_matters
Replying to @EmilyZolaOfficial
DIE YERF DIE YERF DIE YERF DIE YERF DIE YERF DIE
YERF DIE YERF DIE YERF DIE YERF DIE YERF DIE YERF
DIE YERF DIE YERF DIE YERF DIE YERF DIE YERF DIE
YERF DIE YERF DIE YERF DIE YERF DIE YERF DIE YERF
DIE YERF DIE YERF DIE YERF DIE YERF DIE YERF DIE
YERF DIE YERF DIE YERF DIE YERF
RT 756 L 1.9K

Nessa Pollock √ @FirstMinister
I think it's important in terms of public confidence that we perhaps have a bit less heat and a bit more light on these matters. It's time to dial down the toxic rhetoric on both sides
RT 194 L 1.2K

Jan Lewis @blablaricecakes
As an author, I'm sickened by the death threats issued to @EmilyZolaOfficial simply for expressing support for @tara_for_now. I hope the @Assoc_of_Writers and its chair @Donnanougat will unequivocally condemn the appalling language used by @young_earth_matters and others
RT 1.2K L 4.6K

Donna Blitzen ✓ @Donnanougat
Replying to @blablaricecakes
Power is loud. Money is loud. Influence is loud. People with power, money and influence do not experience the same effect from online abuse as those with less power. That doesn't mean we should approve of abuse. But 'silencing' a person in power doesn't actually silence anything
RT 21 L 183

Coleen Coogan @CooganColeen
Replying to @Donnanougat
I have no power, money or influence, yet serious attempts were made to silence me for the same reason as they tried to silence someone with power and money. I can give examples if you wish to see them
RT 5 L 27

Donna Blitzen ✓ @Donnanougat
Replying to @CooganColeen
If my tweet doesn't describe you, then it wasn't about you
RT 6 L 56

Donna Blitzen ✓ @Donnanougat
Fellow authors, a question: have you ever received a death threat (credible or otherwise)? RT for best results
1. Yes
2. Hell, yes
3. No, never
4. Show me, dammit
RT 1.2K L 10.9K

Jan Lewis @blablaricecakes
Replying to @Donnanougat
Seriously? You think the death threats against @EmilyZolaOfficial are a joke? That poll would be sick if you were just an individual author. But coming from the chair of the @Assoc_of_Writers, it's in staggeringly bad taste
RT 693 L 3.5K

Donna Blitzen √ @Donnanougat
Replying to @blablaricecakes
Who said anything about Emily Zola? I never mentioned her.
My poll on death threats to authors had nothing to do with
Emily Zola
RT 651 L 5.5K

Jan Lewis @blablaricecakes
Replying to @Donnanougat
Pull the other one, Donna. It's got bells on
RT 257 L 1.2K

Donna Blitzen √ blocked **Jan Lewis**

Lord Walford @michaeldoughertyE20
I've just watched @NickFerrariLBC's hectoring 'interview'
with @mark_terries. This disgusting prejudiced performance
was an insult to the Indigenous people of the world. I'm
glad to have a party leader who wouldn't stoop to the
questioner's level
RT 954 L 1.9K

Coleen Coogan @CooganColeen
Replying to @michaeldoughertyE20
Mate, it was a car crash
RT 346 L 1.5K

Lord Walford blocked **Coleen Coogan**

Lord Walford @michaeldoughertyE20
I've never been so happy to block someone
RT 24 L 298

Ginny Pugh √ @GinnyPugh

Replying to @michaeldoughertyE20

Hi Michael. Lunatics are trying to erase science in the name of a racial minority that never asked to be patronised like this. People are being cancelled for saying dinosaurs existed. @mark_terries' refusal to address the issue was embarrassing

RT 62 L 1.1K

Sally Jenkinson @saljenk07342

Replying to @GinnyPugh

STFU Yerf

RT 15 L 263

Lord Walford blocked **Ginny Pugh** √

Lord Walford @michaeldoughertyE20

I've never been so happy to block someone

RT 15 L 116

Tara Farrier @tara_for_now

Replying to @michaeldoughertyE20

Sir Mark Terries could be our prime minister in a couple of years' time. Don't you think the public has the right to know whether or not he's signed up to a deranged cult that's trying to impose creationism on us all?

RT 209 L 4.3K

Lord Walford blocked **Tara Farrier**

Lord Walford @michaeldoughertyE20

I've never been so happy to block someone

RT 23 L 346

Tarquin Waugh KC √ @TarquinWaugh
Replying to @michaeldoughertyE20
Solidarity, Michael. We selfless allies are often reviled because of our sympathy and support for marginalised minorities. That is the cross we must bear for our decency. We must stick together
RT 17 L 128

Yerfosaurus Rex @YerfosaurusRex
Replying to @TarquinWaugh
What marginalised minorities? Hedgehogs?
RT 283 L 1.4K

Tarquin Waugh KC √ blocked **Yerfosaurus Rex**

Lord Walford blocked **Yerfosaurus Rex**

Leon Smith √ @LeonSmith84
This site is a hate-filled cesspit. Down with vile Yerf scum. Everyone despises you. You will die sad and lonely
RT 1.3L L 5.6K

Tara Farrier @tara_for_now
Replying to @LeonSmith84
Every teacher you've ever had was a Yerf, Leon
RT 263 L 904

Leon Smith √ blocked **Tara Farrier**

Ginny Pugh √ @GinnyPugh
Can anyone tell me which First Nation people worship the goddess Ctatpeshirahi? Has anyone ever met one of her Indigenous followers? This is not a gotcha. I'm asking genuinely for information
RT 58 L 476

Ricky Singleton @RickyTheEditor
Replying to @GinnyPugh
Ugh. I mean, really. Ugh
RT 476 L 3.1K

Olli Watts @FW10926
Replying to @GinnyPugh
LMFAO. Educate yourself, Yerf bitch
RT 231 L 860

Ginny Pugh √ @GinnyPugh
Er, I'm trying to. But no one will give me an answer. Don't
worry, I'll carry on asking the question until they do, no
matter how much misogynistic abuse I get
RT 46 L 205

Olli Watts blocked **Ginny Pugh** √

Jeremy Vine √ @theJeremyVine
Sorry to ask but what exactly is going on here?
RT 1 L 23

26

The appeal took place the following spring, almost exactly a year after Tara had first arrived back in England. A new judge delivered a fresh ruling a couple of months later. For once, she thoroughly enjoyed the *Earth News* coverage.

Indigenous hurt and anger as race-row lobbyist Tara Farrier wins tribunal appeal

by Nic Vickers, *Earth News* staff writer

Controversial political lobbyist Tara Farrier, whose legal action against a charitable think tank was dismissed by an employment tribunal last summer, has won her appeal, in a move that has sent shock waves through Indigenous communities around the world.

Farrier, whose case has been supported by Emily Zola, leading to worldwide condemnation of the multimillionaire *Sandy Snaith* author, launched legal action last year against the New York-based Institute for Worldwide Advancement.

The former Christian missionary, who lives near Canterbury, worked for the IWA in a freelance capacity, but was dropped after her bigoted views upset large numbers of staff. Smearing Indigenous people as 'a nebulous group' and referring to pro-Indigenous protestors as 'a bunch of students with mummy issues', she refused to respect First Nation sensitivities in her work.

She claimed the IWA's move contravened her freedom of belief under the Equality Act, but the Central London Employment Tribunal threw her case out at a preliminary stage, saying her views were unworthy of respect in a civilised society.

In shock news today, however, the appeal tribunal overturned that judgement, paving the way for Farrier to bring her full case for employment discrimination. Farrier's supporters were immediately triumphant. As soon as the judgement was announced, Zola tweeted: '*Brava*, Tara. I'm delighted the tribunal has seen sense and agreed that a belief in basic science is worthy of respect in a civilised society. Embrace whichever cultural heritage appeals to you. But don't force women out of their jobs for stating that geology is real. #WORIADS.'

Both the court's judgement and the crowing reaction to it by the wealthy author, who has been blamed for starting a culture war, triggered worldwide condemnation.

Tweeting in the United States, 'Goddess Ctat' said: 'This is sadly typical of Yerf Island. First a judge rules that Tara Farrier's anti-Indigenous bigotry is worthy of respect, and five minutes later Emily Zola reignites her genocidal campaign. We could have told y'all this would happen.'

Tarquin Waugh KC, the campaigning pro-Indigenous barrister, tweeted: 'Litigation is about whether you pass certain defined legal thresholds. In my view the original judge was right that Tara Farrier didn't do so. But while enemies of progressive causes may jubilate now, I'm confident that justice will ultimately prevail.'

And the British-born actress Lateefa Latif, now based in Hollywood, added: 'I am sending LOVE to all my Indigenous and First Nation friends in this terrible hour for them. Evil people are trying to exterminate you but I LOVE YOU and WE WILL SAVE YOU from this bigotry xxx.'

It is not yet known when the full tribunal will take place.

27

The celebrations following Tara's appeal victory were a blast. With a growing number of supporters, many of whom had generously supported her crowdfunder, she was able to announce the name of a pub – the Half Moon, just round the corner from Holborn tube – and convene an instant party. Earlier, a gaggle of dinosaur-costumed Yerfs had wandered around Covent Garden with placards reading simply 'WORIADS'.

Amid the general air of triumph, it was easy to forget that this was still only a preliminary hurdle. There was now even more cash to raise and the tribunal proper to fight. In any case, there was no shortage of people trying to burst Tara's bubble. At the IWA, nearly ninety of her former colleagues – most of whose names she didn't even recognise – wrote a letter to Alessandra Bianchi, their executive vice-president, expressing disappointment at the overturning of the ruling and urging her to appeal the appeal.

'We believe the original verdict was correct when it found that this type of offensive and exclusionary language causes harm and therefore could not be protected under the Equality Act,' they wrote. 'This is a moment where we need to live our values and show that we mean them.'

Their letter was leaked to *Earth News*, which reported its contents in slavish detail. The website had invested its entire credibility, such as it was, in this issue, and was clearly in no mood to ease off on its rhetoric.

'So what happens now?' said Laila, on the phone to her mother a week or so after the appeal ruling. 'Is it just a matter of waiting for a tribunal date?'

'If only,' said Tara. 'There's a whole case to prepare and a huge amount more money to raise. The full tribunal will last longer, which means it will cost a lot more. On the upside, I've got loads more followers than I used to have, so the pool of support is much wider.'

'All thanks to Emily.'

'She's certainly made a huge difference.'

Zola continued to offer Tara outspoken public support, generating more fury from the Young Earthers every time she did so. After the various victories they had won so far, the cultists had become used to getting their way, and could generally rely on an immediate grovelling apology from any celebrity who blundered into any of the new taboo areas. In that context, Zola's refusal to give the slightest ground perplexed and wrong-footed them. Nevertheless, they carried on exerting their pressure on those parts of the media that were prepared to submit to their will. *The Guardian* obliged by dropping Zola from its celebrity birthdays list, giving her spot to the Labour MP for St Helens. This was not 'cancel culture', her adversaries insisted; it merely showed that bigoted actions had consequences. When sales of the next *Sandy Snaith* adventure actually increased, hitting record levels even by the standards of a series that had already broken all of them, they said this further proved that cancel culture was a myth. Then they redoubled their efforts to cancel her, never quite realising that she was too big to destroy.

Tara had yet to meet Emily, but they had exchanged messages. Although Tara knew she herself couldn't be held personally responsible for the avalanche of hatred that had crashed onto her famous supporter, she still felt guilty about it, because Emily would never have had to put up with all this if she hadn't intervened in Tara's case. Nevertheless, the writer seemed resolutely upbeat. It seemed that, despite all the abuse, she was enjoying being able to speak her mind.

It also pained Tara that the legal battle had diverted her own energy from the plight of Yemen, where war continued unabated. In that context, she was deeply moved when Emily announced she would personally match donations, up to a limit of £1 million, in support of Yemeni children. The author also donated a massive sum to ease conditions in that country's largest displacement camp, home to thousands of people who had fled the capital. Naturally, neither of these generous acts appeased the zealots who insisted that Zola was a genocidal monster; but what really impressed Tara was that the author didn't care. She hadn't made these commitments to improve her public image; she had donated because she cared about the cause itself.

Meanwhile the insanity continued, with the contagion

of Young Earth censorship spreading beyond the internet and into real-world settings. Its hold on public institutions seemed to tighten every day. Schools and colleges were now too scared to talk not just about geological history, but also the theory of evolution. One of the casualties was Helen, who decided life was too short to face a barrage of abuse every day and resigned from her job at the university, citing constructive dismissal. Meanwhile local museums, taking their lead from the curators in South Kensington, removed their fossil collections. Climatologists erased all reference to the Ice Age from their textbooks. Student protestors in Cambridge marched on Darwin College, demanding it change its name to something more First Nation-friendly; Tara suspected the only reason they hadn't proposed renaming it after Ctatpeshirahi was that none of them would be able to pronounce it. As she watched the lunacy spread, she was more certain than ever that she had been right to challenge it in the courts, whatever the personal toll.

Not even the world of science was immune to the contagion. To fend off the obvious charge that they were anti-science, the fanatics needed some science of their own, and the more pliant parts of the scientific establishment stepped up to provide it. Under the headline 'Stop Using Phony Science to Justify Anti-Indigenous Bigotry', an opinion piece in *Scientific American* insisted that 'actual research shows the age of the earth is anything but settled'. The article itself, written by a doctoral candidate whose name had never previously appeared in the magazine, rested heavily on the observation that no human had ever seen a living dinosaur, and that all supposed knowledge of these creatures was based on the fossil record, which was subject to misinterpretation and wishful thinking. It also noted that those who put the age of the earth at 4.6 billion years admitted a margin of error of 50 million years either way, and were therefore in no position to sneer at anyone else's estimate.

The logical leaps were dizzying, but the paper was written in sufficiently opaque language that few of the people who triumphantly cited it had actually tried to read it. For them, the headline and the authority conferred by the publication's title were all that mattered. As the article became ubiquitous on the internet, a new generation of university-educated social justice warriors basked in the conviction that 'progressive' scientists had accurately carbon-dated the entire planet to within a century or two of the desired ten thousand years. Anyone who tried to reason with them, no matter how patiently, was liable to be told to *STFU and read a book, dumbass*.

One weekday morning in May, while Tara was doing some basic tidying in the garden, she heard a car turn in at the gate. She dropped her secateurs and walked around to the front of the house, wondering who this unexpected visitor could be. To her delight, she saw Sammy's little scarlet Fiat pulling up. But her heart sank when she realised her son was not alone. Sorrel was in the passenger seat.

The sight threw Tara off kilter. She had grown used to the idea that Sammy was now on her side, but had that changed? Was this some kind of deputation? She had been feeling stronger lately, having learned how to tune out most of the public battering, but a family confrontation was another matter. She wasn't sure she was up to it.

Unfortunately, it didn't look as if she had much choice. She adopted her best welcoming smile as the pair of them got out of the car.

'Hello, you two. This is a nice surprise. And Sorrel! It's been such a long time. I'd almost forgotten what you looked like.' As if. Nobody forgot that gaudy bird's nest of dreadlocks.

'Hi Mum.' Sammy kissed her on both cheeks but his smile was weak and unconvincing. He seemed unwilling to look her in the eye, which did nothing to allay Tara's fears. Everything had seemed fine that evening, when he had pledged his troth in defence of the dinosaur. What had happened to upset that?

'Hi Tara.' Sorrel also looked grave. Subdued – that was the best way of putting it. Although Tara hardly knew the girl, that wasn't a state she would normally associate with her.

'Mum, sorry to drop in unannounced, but can we come in for a moment? Sorrel has something she wants to say to you.'

'Oh dear, that sounds ominous. Should I be worried? But yes of course, do come in. You surely don't need to ask?' Tara carried on talking as she led them in through the kitchen door, in an attempt to mask her own nerves. 'Would you both like coffee before Sorrel says her piece, whatever it is?'

'Maybe afterwards, Mum.' Sammy dropped his voice, taking advantage of the fact that Sorrel had hung back before following them inside. 'Don't worry. This will be much harder for her than it will be for you.'

Relief coursed through Tara's body. Whatever was coming, it might not be as bad as she had initially feared. 'As you prefer. Shall we all at least sit down?'

They each pulled out a battered wooden chair – bought at auction, years ago – from around the kitchen table. Sammy folded his hands and stared down at them, while Sorrel looked like she wanted to sink through the floor. Tara realised they were waiting for her to kickstart this showdown, if that was what it was, but in a moment of defiance she resolved that she wouldn't make any effort to ease their discomfort. They had brought this awkwardness into her home; let them stew in it.

Understanding that Tara and Sammy were waiting for her to begin, Sorrel cleared her throat. 'This is quite difficult, so bear with me, Tara, if you can. I have a confession to make.'

'Really?' said Tara. She tried to keep her voice neutral: too censorious would indicate that she knew what Sorrel had done, while too surprised would involve a degree of play-acting that she wasn't confident she could pull off.

'I'm afraid so. I need to tell you something.'

Tara composed her face in what she hoped was a similarly neutral way. 'I'm listening.' Under his beard, she noticed, Sammy was blushing hard.

'Well, you know when you first asked me about the campaign against Professor Kottsack? And I said I had some friends who were involved?'

'Yes, I remember.'

'I wasn't entirely honest about that. I mean, I did have friends who were involved, but I was...well, I was one of them. I was part of the picket. I didn't go very often. I only went, like four or five times. But I was there.'

If she had only been four or five times, it seemed bad luck that Ginny had photographed her on of those occasions and Helen had clocked her on another. But Tara sensed that this was not the time for that. 'I see,' she said.

Sorrel continued: 'I'm not proud of it, and I know she's a good friend of yours. All I can say in my defence is that I thought it was the right thing to do at the time.'

This time it took a major effort for Tara to keep her voice

calm. 'And…you don't any more?'

'No, I don't. I have to admit, when you first became involved in all this, and you were treated so badly by the people you worked for, I felt very awkward. I knew you were upset by it, but I was on the other side of the argument and it was…well…difficult. That's why you didn't see much of me.'

'I did wonder.'

'I knew you would. I told Sam you were bound to suspect.'

Sammy's nostrils flared in annoyance. This had evidently been a bone of contention between them.

Tara attempted to nudge the narrative back in a more constructive direction. 'So you're saying…you think differently nowadays?'

For the first time, Sorrel looked her directly in the eye. 'Yes I do.' She swallowed, still clearly in discomfort, but she held Tara's gaze.

Tara realised the ball was back in her court. It was entirely up to her how she responded: with the anger and bitterness she instinctively felt, or with the kindness and indulgence that women of her age were meant to show to errant members of their children's generation. She found herself torn. On the one hand, Sorrel really ought to know how much hurt and anguish she had caused, to Tara herself as much as to Helen. On the other, Tara could see that this unexpected turn of events was a far better outcome than any of the scenarios she had imagined in the worst of her tormented, sleepless nights.

She opted for polite but cool. 'I see. That's good to hear. Can I ask… What changed your mind?'

To her surprise, Sorrel's face dissolved into a smile.

'I hope this doesn't sound too corny, but it was actually a film.'

'A film?'

'You remember the first time I came round here, and we talked about *Inherit the Wind*?'

'Of course I do. The film version of the Scopes Monkey Trial, with Spencer Tracy and Fredric March. You told me all the ways the film-makers had distorted the real trial.'

'In far too much detail, probably. I tend to go on about it too much.'

'No, it was interesting. To be honest, I can't recall much of what you said, but I remember finding it fascinating.'

'Anyway, that film is massively important to me. As you probably also remember, it's the subject of my PhD, but it was kind of in a separate compartment of my life, you know? Then, on one of those days when I was on the picket outside Kottsa...sorry, Professor Kottsack's office, I drew the connection. It suddenly hit me: if the Monkey Trial happened again today, I'd be one of the mad creationists saying you can't talk about evolution. Because we evolved from apes much longer ago than ten thousand years, right? So I realised I was on the wrong side. It was a massive moment of revelation. Like, I could see everything clearly for the first time, and I couldn't understand why it hadn't been obvious before. You know? After that, I swear I withdrew from the protests. I haven't hung out with those friends since then and I just want... Well, I wanted to tell you how sorry I am for getting it so wrong. Like, really, really sorry. And I'm hoping you can forgive me, but I'll understand if you can't.'

Tara said nothing for a moment as she digested this. There were many things she'd like to say. *So you only realised you were on the wrong side because of a black-and-white Hollywood film?* Or: *There was nothing about banning mention of dinosaurs and volcanoes that might previously have alerted you to the fact that you were in a crackpot cult?* But what would that achieve, especially with Sammy sitting watching? He seemed more nervous than ever now, waiting for her verdict. So she said: 'Thank you for saying that, Sorrel. I'm so glad to have your support. For Sammy's sake, as well as mine. I'd have hated him to face a conflict of loyalties.'

Her son blushed more deeply than ever.

'Anyway, I'm sorry for not seeing you were right, and for my bad choice of friends, and for not being here for you earlier,' said Sorrel. 'I'd like to make up for that now, if you'll let me.'

Despite herself, Tara was impressed. The girl had been an idiot, but her apology sounded heartfelt and she had delivered it with considerable aplomb. 'Thank you,' she said. She stood up, intending to draw a line under the scene and make some coffee, but so did Sorrel, and Tara realised the other woman was expecting a hug – a gesture that would put a physical seal on her absolution. So Tara had fallen into the indulgent maternal role after all, she thought, offering the embrace. But as she relaxed into it, Tara felt better for the gesture too. In this present battle, she was in no position to be fussy about her supporters, and she could never have too many hugs.

'One thing, though,' she said, when they had released each other. 'It would mean a lot to Helen if you apologised to her too. She may not work at the university any more, but she's deeply scarred by what happened. I know from personal experience how horrible it is to be on the receiving end of personal abuse. I also know how welcome it is if someone is big enough to admit they were wrong, as you've just done to me.'

Sorrel bit her lip, thinking it over. 'I know I should.' Then she nodded. 'You're right. I will. Do I need to go and see her, or…?'

'No, don't do that,' said Tara hastily. She shuddered to imagine Helen's reaction if one of her former persecutors appeared on her doorstep. 'I can't share her contact details, for reasons you can probably imagine. But perhaps if you write me an email? Then I can forward it to Helen, and she can reply to you directly if she wants.'

Sorrel looked relieved at not having to face Helen in person. She smiled. 'I'll do that, I promise. And thank you so much for being so nice about all this. I was nervous you might not be, but you've been amazing.'

Tara gave herself a mental pat on the back for not speaking her mind a few minutes earlier. 'Don't worry about it, *habibti*. I'm just glad we're all on the same side now.'

'Just one other thing, Tara. Please don't blame Sam for any of this. He fought your corner really hard the whole time, and we were on the rocks for a while because of it. I had to come grovelling back when I came to my senses.' She looked at her boyfriend. 'Didn't I?'

He confined himself to a brusque nod, embarrassed either by the praise, or by having the details of the relationship exposed to his mother.

But Tara was grateful to Sorrel for saying it. She had naturally worried, in the course of this confession, how much Sammy had known of his girlfriend's activism. It was a great relief to learn that he'd been so loyal to his mother.

As the atmosphere in the kitchen relaxed, the visitors drank their coffee but declined Tara's invitation to stay for lunch.

When they were leaving, Sammy let Sorrel go ahead and

took his mother aside. 'Thanks for going so easy on her, Mum. Easier than she deserved, if I'm honest. It's been eating me up, ever since I found out she was involved in that crap. I was so angry with her. I wanted to tell you, but I didn't know how.'

'Don't worry, *habibi*. None of this is your fault. And thank you for sticking up for me.'

For a moment, she contemplated telling him that she had known about Sorrel's behaviour anyway, and that very little of this had come as a surprise. But she decided to keep that to herself.

28

Five months later, as Tara prepared to enter the fray for what she hoped would be the last time, she received a card in the post from Sorrel and Sammy.

It was the original poster for *Inherit the Wind*, with colour pictures of Spencer Tracy, Fredric March and Gene Kelly beneath a large sepia photograph of a chimpanzee wearing spectacles, and the slogan 'It's All About The Famous Monkey Trial That Rocked America!' On the back, Sorrel had written: 'Did you realise it's nearly a century since the original trial in Dayton, Tennessee? Good luck in the tribunal. We hope you make monkeys of them!! xxx'

Tara was touched by the gesture. She'd been thinking about the Monkey Trial too, wondering what her mother, who had so loved *Inherit the Wind*, would think if she knew her own daughter was now at the centre of a farcical re-run of the same debate. Although perhaps it was best not to dwell on the parallels. After all, the creationists won the Monkey Trial.

She felt an inevitable sense of *déjà vu* as she got in the car to drive to Bexleyheath. The routine now felt familiar, almost second nature, and she didn't feel any of the terror she had experienced when first confronted with the prospect of cross-examination. She had spoken often about her ordeal these past couple of years, always following her lawyers' instruction to stick rigorously to the truth. Their advice worked just as well in the outside world as in the courtroom: with nothing to hide, she had become fluent in her own story. Opposing counsel would of course try to exhaust, rile and goad her into saying something intemperate that would show her in a bad light, so complacency was unwise. Nevertheless, she was looking forward to the days ahead.

The way Den had explained it when last they spoke, the case was strong. Having established that Tara's 'belief' – she still bridled at the word – was protected under UK law, they now had to prove discrimination.

'We know they disapproved of your views,' he had said in a conference call with Tara and Zoya, a week before the tribunal was due to start. 'They made that very clear at the time, and many of their staff have made it even clearer since then by writing a joint letter letter about your case, which then received further media publicity. We need to establish that this disapproval from within the organisation directly influenced the decision to withdraw the offer of a permanent role. As you know, our request for all their internal communications about you has turned up plenty of material to suggest that was the case. The other side knows it doesn't look good for them. So they will argue, as we can already see from the witness statements in the bundle, that it wasn't your beliefs they objected to, so much as the way you expressed them.'

'You're joking?' Tara had seen enough lawyers arguing about angels dancing on the heads of pins to know Den was dead serious. Nevertheless, were there no depths of sophistry to which these people wouldn't sink?

'I'm afraid not,' he confirmed. 'I know it's frustrating, but that's how these things work. To be fair, I'd do exactly the same in their position. And we can counter it. We simply have to show there's no meaningful distinction between your belief and your expression of it, as far as their disapproval was concerned.'

'Do you think you can do that?'

Zoya intervened. 'That's what you're paying him for. The problem with finicky little philosophical arguments like this is that the lawyers themselves may be able to bluster their way through them, but making their clients understand the finer points is much harder. Den can tie their witnesses in knots under cross-examination.'

Den allowed himself a half-smile. 'Let's not count our chickens. But as Zoya rightly says, if a barrister presents a particularly abstruse argument, there's a serious risk that their witnesses won't be on board with the nuances. That presents an opportunity in cross-examination for me to undermine my opponent's case.'

Tara nodded. There was reassurance in this, but she remained stunned by the nerve of these people she was up against.

'Our opponents' case is stronger when it comes to the job offer itself,' Den continued. 'As you know, the IWA argues that you were only ever a freelancer and they had no contractual obligation to employ you. We will argue in return that they had every intention of giving you a job, as they said on a number of occasions. We're not disputing their right to change their mind if circumstances changed, for instance if they no longer had the budget to employ you permanently, or your work on the Yemen report was disappointing. What they don't have the right to do is change their minds purely on the basis of your protected belief. That would be discrimination. We'll also argue that you were victimised by their actions, which has led to ongoing suffering, reputation damage and loss of earnings. And as you also know' – he smiled more fully this time – 'we're also hoping to put some icing on the cake, if we can get what we need in time. Speaking of which, do either of you have any news?'

After trying to dig it up for more than a year, they were hoping to present killer evidence that would, if all went to plan, make headlines around the world. There was only one snag, namely that the evidence was not yet completely in the bag. For weeks, they had been waiting for the thumbs-up that their star witness was prepared to appear.

Zoya shook her head. 'Still nothing. It's very frustrating. Should we consider asking for an adjournment?'

'The last I heard, the chances were good,' said Tara. 'That was a couple of days ago.'

'All right,' said Den. 'Let's go with that for the moment. If we still haven't got the witness pinned down as we enter the second week, let's consider asking for an adjournment at that point.'

The proceedings were currently scheduled to take place over ten working days, with the possibility of nudging into a third week if business overran. The first day was for opening arguments. After that there would be two reading days, in which the judge would attempt to get through the enormous bundle the two legal teams had prepared, including Tara's own statement. Then the examination of witnesses would begin.

And now that first day had arrived.

'How are you feeling?' said Zoya, when Tara reached her office. 'All set?'

'I think so,' said Tara.

'Good. You're becoming an old hand at this now.'

'Yes, aren't I? No offence, but I hope these are the last two weeks I have to spend in your offices.'

Zoya laughed. 'None taken. As you know, I don't like to count chickens, but we have a strong case.' She checked her watch. 'Anyway, it's nearly time. Let's go through to the conference room.'

They squeezed into the cramped space where the webcam and screen were set up in their usual places. Tara remembered how hot it had been during the first tribunal. This summer had been just as scorching, but autumn had set in now, so the room was comfortable in respect of temperature, if nothing else.

Back in that first round, Tara had hung on the clerk's every word as he went through the various bits of business that participants and spectators needed to know: conduct during the proceedings, acceptable behaviour in the chatroom and so on. Now, having heard all this stuff so many times, she was able to tune out, like the regular flyer who already knew every possible way to inflate an emergency life-jacket. Most of the judge's introductory patter also fell into this category, and Tara only began to pay full attention once Den, in his usual position beside the fireplace in his living room, began his opening remarks.

'Madam, we've now established that Ms Farrier's belief that the earth is billions of years old, rather than ten thousand, is protected under the Equality Act. This belief put her at odds with the respondent, which made clear its official displeasure when Ms Farrier was asked to remove her IWA affiliation from her Twitter biography if she wanted to continue expressing that belief in public. Moreover, even when it was established at this tribunal that her belief was protected under the law, a large number of Ms Farrier's former colleagues signed a letter condemning that belief. In doing so, they made it clear they thought someone holding such a belief should have no place in their organisation. And I draw the court's attention to the response of IWA management to that letter. Far from reprimanding their staff for disrespecting a protected belief, the IWA's director of communications told *Earth News*, and I quote: "Our president and executive vice-president were grateful to receive the letter, which they felt was thoughtfully framed, considerate and in the best spirit of the IWA's culture." That's to say, the institute's official spokesperson explicitly confirmed that the illegal condemnation of Tara Farrier's protected belief was in the best spirit of IWA culture. No wonder, madam, they couldn't wait to get rid of her, to cancel the offer of a permanent job that they had made on several occasions, and to vilify her in public.'

He paused for a sip of water, then continued: 'That vilification has been profoundly damaging, in ways that I will detail. I will also address the nature of the offence that Ms Farrier is alleged to have caused. I will do that by exploring the claim that her beliefs were somehow hurtful or damaging to marginalised people. To this end, madam, I'd like to ask permission to introduce some evidence that isn't contained in the bundle. My apologies for this. We've been trying to secure a witness statement, which has been difficult to achieve because the person in question is a US citizen, based in California, and is also a figure of some prominence, which has created certain logistical complications.'

'This is highly irregular, madam,' cut in Robertson, who had not spoken until now.

'Thank you, Ms Robertson,' said the judge. 'It is indeed irregular, Mr Hooper. Who is your witness?'

'It's Mr José Talavera, madam. Better known as Joey Talavera.'

Had this been a real courtroom, rather than a glorified conference call, there would surely have been an outburst of excited muttering from the spectators, whereupon the judge would have had to call for order. Tara had to make do with imagining the reaction among her supporters and opponents, not to mention the watching press.

The judge herself, a woman with short hair and round tortoiseshell glasses, was unreadable. 'And who is this Mr Talavera?'

'He's a tech entrepreneur in Silicon Valley, madam. He runs a large commercial corporation as well as a charitable foundation.'

'But you don't yet have a witness statement from him?'

'That's correct, madam. A member of my team is still trying to obtain it. If he's successful, I hope Mr Talavera will be available for examination at the end of next week. As I say, I'm very sorry for the inconvenience, but the witness is a man with many other commitments.'

Robertson interrupted: 'Madam, I reiterate that this is highly irregular. Mr Hooper has had more than a year to prepare his case. If he wants to introduce new evidence at this stage, we need proper time to consider it.'

'Thank you, Ms Robertson,' said the judge. 'I understood your point the first time. Mr Hooper, this process depends on proper consideration of relevant evidence, not theatrics. I certainly can't agree that a piece of evidence is relevant if you're not in a position to tell me what it is.'

'Yes, madam, I fully appreciate that and I can only repeat my apologies. The logistics have been, as I say, complex. Suffice to say, I'm confident the evidence will be highly relevant when it comes to the nature of the offence that Ms Farrier's beliefs are alleged to have caused. I hope that will be apparent once we're in a position to submit the written statement. And I'd be more than happy to agree to an adjournment if the court wants more time to consider it.'

'Very well,' said the judge. 'If your witness can deliver a statement by the end of this week, I'll consider its relevance. But there are limits to my indulgence, Mr Hooper, and that's the longest delay I'll permit.'

'Thank you, madam,' said Den.

Checking their microphone was muted, Tara turned to Zoya. 'We've got to make them understand how urgent this is. If Joey won't testify, we need to line up someone else who can present the same evidence.'

Zoya was tapping at her phone. 'I know. I'm messaging them now.'

'And what about the other guy?' This was the other surprise they had up their sleeves.

'Who, the teacher? He's ready and waiting. But Den doesn't want to introduce his evidence until we've had Joey; otherwise it won't make sense.'

'The judge won't like that.'

'Den says he'll cross that bridge when he comes to it. He's relying on the fact that a fair judge will admit relevant evidence, even if he gets a slapped wrist for it. And we've got a decent judge here, despite that grouchy exterior.'

When Den's introductory remarks eventually came to an end, it was Robertson's turn.

'We accept the ruling of the appeal court that Ms Farrier's belief is protected under the Equality Act,' she began, 'even though Mr Hooper will do his best to convince you that we don't. But there's a difference between holding a belief and expressing it in a way that causes offence or harm to others. I will show that Ms Farrier did precisely that. I will also demonstrate that her only relationship with the IWA was a verbal agreement to write a country report based on her expertise in the field, on a purely freelance basis, and my client was under no obligation, and certainly not a legal one, to offer her a permanent position. Therefore...'

The barrister carried on in similar vein at what seemed like interminable length, essentially confirming everything Den had said about her likely strategy.

However familiar Tara had become with the process, the smears didn't get any easier to hear. She listened to herself characterised as an outspoken bigot, shouting her opinions into other people's faces and brooking no dissent. She wanted to unmute her microphone and interrupt: 'Too right, I brooked no dissent, because we're not talking about random beliefs chosen from the shelf of some belief superstore, where each one is as valid as the next. We're talking about scientific fact versus medieval ignorance, which you would reject as strongly as I do if it came in the form of fundamentalist Christianity, Islam or Judaism. It's the gap between knowledge and ignorance, where some opinions are objectively more correct than others. Why can't I assert that?'

But she couldn't do that, and not just because the judge would tell her off for speaking out of turn; it would upset their whole case, which was that she had never been aggressive. And that was the line she would take in cross-examination: of course she *wanted* to be assertive, because she knew she was right, but in practice she never was, and had been scrupulously respectful of the person, if not the idea.

What a truly preposterous situation, she thought, as she tried to focus on Robertson's words, and not on how much she loathed this woman for acting as the enforcer for the cultish insanity that was taking over the world.

However lonely and exposed she felt in her current position, it was always useful to remind herself that people near and far were watching this tribunal and relying on her to lead the fightback for sanity.

29

As the claimant, Tara was the first to give evidence, which at least meant her cross-examination would be over early in the week.

Much as she had expected, Robertson tried hard to find weaknesses in her story and to provoke her into saying something intemperate or 'absolutist', as the original judge might have put it. But she survived the experience by sticking to the mantra of telling only the truth, and by the end she felt pummelled but not defeated.

'You really are getting better at this,' said Zoya afterwards, which had the ring of truth, Tara thought, even if it undermined her solicitor's gushing assessment of her earlier performances.

With her own contribution out of the way, she could now focus on Den's cross-examination of witnesses, most notably of Alessandra Bianchi, the IWA's executive vice-president.

Speaking from New York, Bianchi was called into the virtual witness box on the Friday afternoon of the first week. She was an elegant woman in her forties with a neat bob of blonde hair framing a sharp-featured face. She replied to Robertson's tame questions in an accent that suggested Italian origins but many years in the United States.

'Good afternoon, Dr Bianchi,' Den began, once his opposite number had finished her examination. 'Or good morning, your time.'

'Good morning, Mr Hooper. Or good afternoon.' She smiled, and Tara recognised – from being in the same position herself – an attempt to win over hostile counsel with charm. Good luck with that, she thought.

'I'd like to begin, if I may, Dr Bianchi, with the appeal court ruling. It found that Ms Farrier's belief about the age of the earth, namely that it's billions of years old, is protected under United Kingdom law. Yes?'

'That's correct.'

'Do you accept that ruling?'

'Yes, I do.'

'If I can break that down, do you simply accept that the belief is protected under UK law, or do you accept Ms Farrier's right to hold it?'

'Both.'

'Thank you. Just to clarify, you're saying that even if the court hadn't ruled that the belief was protected under UK law, you would still have accepted Ms Farrier's right to hold it.'

'Correct.'

'So when the preliminary tribunal initially ruled the

opposite, namely that Ms Farrier's belief was unworthy of respect in a democratic society, you must have disagreed. Yes?'

Bianchi faltered for a moment. 'No. The court ruled on a matter of UK law, and the appeal court disagreed on the same matter. Since I'm neither a lawyer nor a UK citizen or resident, I don't presume to have an opinion one way or the other on that question.'

'I see. But the fact that you respect Ms Farrier's right to hold that belief means you think it's worthy of respect in a democratic society. Yes?'

Bianchi paused and narrowed her eyes, as if trying to work out what she was getting herself into. 'Yes,' she said, cautiously.

'Are you certain about that?'

She nodded and repeatedly more confidently: 'Yes.'

'And once more, just to be clear, did you always think that, or did you change your mind once you read the appeal ruling?'

Bianchi hesitated. 'Pardon me? Could you repeat the question?' She either hadn't been concentrating or she was stalling.

'Did you always think her belief in the age of the earth was worthy of respect in a democratic society?

Another falter. 'Yes.'

'Yes?'

'Yes.'

Robertson interrupted. 'Dr Bianchi has answered the question.'

'Mr Hooper, if the witness has answered the question already, there's no need to ask it again,' said the judge.

'Yes, madam. Understood. Dr Bianchi, may I draw your attention to the letter addressed to yourself and another senior colleague, and signed by eighty-seven members of the IWA's staff? You'll find it on page 347 of your bundle.'

Another pause ensued as Bianchi thumbed through the hefty document to find the right place. 'Yes,' she said, when she got there.

'The letter says, in the middle paragraph – and I quote – "we believe the original verdict was correct when it found that this type of offensive and exclusionary language causes harm and therefore could not be protected under the Equality Act". Yes?'

'Yes.'

'You've already said you accept the appeal court's ruling that Ms Farrier's belief was protected under the Equality Act, so it follows that you disagree with your staff members. Yes?'

Bianchi stared at the text. 'This letter isn't talking about a belief,' she said at length. 'It refers to offensive and exclusionary language.'

'Oh I see, thank you. So there's a distinction between the belief and the language in which it's expressed?'

'Yes.' Bianchi showed the trace of a smile, as if she was pleased to have made him understand the nuance. But Tara could see the trap ahead, even if the witness couldn't.

'So whereas you wouldn't presume to have an opinion on whether a belief is or isn't protected by UK equality law, you do have a clear opinion when it comes to the kind of language the Equality Act prohibits?'

'Um…'

'Even though the part of the Act that refers to belief doesn't say anything about the language in which those beliefs may or may not be expressed?'

'Well…um… I think it's important to emphasise that I'm

not responsible for the wording of a letter that was addressed to me.'

With her mouth full of boiled sweet, Zoya whispered to Tara: 'That's what we in the legal profession call a reverse ferret.'

Den continued: 'Very true, Dr Bianchi. I never suggested you wrote those words. With that in mind, can we move on to a comment given to *Earth News* by your director of communications, Mr Dabrowski? You'll find it on page 348. Mr Dabrowski is quoted as saying, "Our president and executive vice-president were grateful to receive the letter, which they felt was thoughtfully framed, considerate and in the best spirit of the IWA's culture." To the best of your knowledge, is that an accurate representation of his statement, Dr Bianchi?'

'I didn't make the statement myself. You'd have to ask Mr Dabrowski.'

'I appreciate that you personally didn't give the statement to *Earth News*. But it was designed to convey your own reaction to the joint letter, so you must have approved the statement before it went out. Yes?'

'Yes, I imagine I did. But I can't remember the precise wording, so I can't tell you if this version of it is exactly the one I approved. It was more than a year ago.'

'Let me put it another way, Dr Bianchi. When that statement appeared in *Earth News*, saying you thought the joint letter was thoughtfully framed, considerate and in the best spirit of the IWA's culture, did you have any reason to complain to that website, or to upbraid Mr Dabrowski for issuing a misleading statement?'

'No, not that I recall.'

'Thank you, Dr Bianchi. So, to recap, a large number of your staff expressed the collective view that Ms Farrier's language was offensive and exclusionary, that it caused harm, and that it could not be protected under United Kingdom law. Even though you've just told me you don't have any opinion on UK law, you authorised your director of communications to issue a statement praising your staff for their letter. Yes?'

There was a long pause.

'Dr Bianchi?'

'Yes, but—'

'Do you now regret authorising that statement?'

Bianchi paused again, weighing her options. 'I regret giving the impression that I took a view on UK law. That's not my business.'

'You didn't just give the impression that you took a view, did you, Dr Bianchi? You clearly did take a view. No?'

'I can't honestly remember what was in my mind at the time.'

'Irrespective of what was or wasn't in your mind at the time, can we agree that you no longer wish to express a view about UK law?'

'Yes.'

'So let's return to your statement endorsing the letter from your staff. Do you still believe Ms Farrier's language was offensive and exclusionary, and that it caused harm?'

'Yes.'

In their conference room, Zoya's phone pinged. She picked up the device, read the message and hissed: '*Yes!*'

Tara looked at her expectantly. 'Well? Have we got Joey?' she whispered.

Zoya winked at her.

On the screen, Den continued: 'You've just said you still believe Ms Farrier's language was offensive and exclusionary. Could you give me an example of her offensive language?'

Bianchi had her answer ready, having anticipated the question. 'She said ideas don't deserve respect.'

'I see. Whom does that offend?'

'The holders of those ideas.'

'People, in other words. Yes?'

Bianchi frowned slightly, as if it were a stupid question. 'Yes.'

'So when Ms Farrier actually said "people deserve respect, not ideas", what makes you think she doesn't respect the people who hold ideas?'

The witness cleared her throat. 'The implication is that she wouldn't respect people whose ideas she didn't respect.'

'But since she says she doesn't respect any ideas, and all people hold ideas, your interpretation would mean she doesn't respect anyone. But she actually said the opposite, didn't she?'

Bianchi pushed a strand of hair away from her face. 'That's not how I read it.'

'In that case, I put it to you that you misread it.'

'No.'

'Thank you, Dr Bianchi.'

Seeing her opportunity, Zoya reached forward to unmute their microphone. 'Apologies for the interruption, madam, but I've just had an urgent message regarding our proposed witness, Mr Talavera. I think my counsel will want to know about it immediately, and I know it will be of relevance to the tribunal, given your own instructions about the introduction of this witness.'

'Go ahead, Ms Parveen,' said the judge.

'Thank you, madam. I'm happy to confirm that we do have a witness statement from Mr Joey Talavera, which will be added to the bundle over the weekend. He's willing to submit himself for examination on the afternoon of next Wednesday, Thursday or Friday, as the tribunal pleases. Please note that he'd prefer an afternoon slot because of the time difference between the UK and California.'

'Thank you, Ms Parveen,' said Den. 'I hope that's acceptable, madam.'

'It is, Mr Hooper, subject to my confirmation that the witness statement itself, when we all receive it, is as relevant as you claim. For the moment, I suggest you resume your cross-examination of Dr Bianchi, since time is getting on.'

Zoya muted the microphone once more and sat back with a look of deep satisfaction on her face. For someone who didn't believe in counting chickens, Tara thought to herself, her solicitor looked pretty pleased.

Den continued: 'Very well, madam. Dr Bianchi, we were talking about your approval of the statement that Ms Farrier's language was offensive and exclusionary, and that it caused harm. We've dealt with the first part, but can we turn to the question of harm and exclusion? Whom did Ms Farrier's words exclude and whom did she harm?'

'Anyone who believes in the goddess Ctat...Ctatpe...' She stumbled.

'Ctatpeshirahi?' offered Den.

'Yes.'

'Have you ever met such a person, Dr Bianchi?'

'That's not the point.'

'Please answer the question. Have you ever met such a person?'

'I don't ask the religious affiliation of everyone I meet, so I can't possibly know.'

'Has anyone ever told you they're a believer in the goddess Ctatpeshirahi?'

'No.'

'Thank you, Dr Bianchi. Finally, I'd like to explore some of the beliefs you think should or should not be expressed. Ms Farrier was told she couldn't mention a geological event that took place between 50 and 35 million years ago because that might offend people who think the earth was created ten thousand years ago. Yes?'

'Yes.'

'It follows that referring to anything that happened more than ten thousand years ago would risk causing similar offence, yes?'

'To anything that *allegedly* happened more than ten thousand years ago,' corrected Bianchi. 'Yes.'

'Therefore no mention of dinosaurs?'

'There was no need to mention dinosaurs in a report about the civil war in Yemen.'

'But if there had been? If, say, an important dinosaur fossil had been found in disputed territory? Would it have been offensive to mention that?'

'I'd have advised against it.'

'Very well. What about evolution? If, for example, Ms Farrier had made a similar prehistoric reference in her report to our human origins as apes?'

'I don't see how that's relevant.'

'Nor do I, madam,' interrupted Robertson.

'It's relevant, madam, because the genus *homo* evolved, according to molecular evidence, around three million years ago. I'd like to know if expressing a belief in the Darwinian theory of evolution would have constituted offensive, exclusionary and harmful language, in Dr Bianchi's eyes.'

'Very well,' said the judge. 'Dr Bianchi, you must answer that question.'

Bianchi pushed her hair back again. 'Once more, I'd have advised against it.'

'For fear of causing offence?'

'Yes.'

'To hypothetical people you'd never met?'

'It's quite normal to moderate our language to avoid giving offence to strangers. That's what it means to live in a civilised society.'

'Isn't it another hallmark of civilised society to be curious about our origins?'

'I don't know. It's not...something I've ever considered.'

'You've never considered the origins of the human species?'

'I'm not a biologist.'

'Nor am I, Dr Bianchi, but I'm aware of the theory of evolution. Are you seriously telling me you've never even thought about that question?'

Robertson cut in. 'The witness has answered the question. She said it's not something she has ever considered.'

Den shrugged theatrically. 'Very well. I just wanted to be sure. Thank you for your time, Dr Bianchi. No further questions.'

30

At the end of the first day's session, when the video feeds and microphones were turned off, Tara set off for home, leaving Zoya to hit the phone and arrange to take Joey's witness statement.

In the event, this involved a long Zype interview conducted later that evening, which Zoya's secretary converted into written form using transcription software, and which Zoya herself then edited into shape. After that, the text had to go back to California for approval, but somehow it was all finished by Saturday afternoon, when Zoya submitted it to the tribunal clerk to add to the evidence bundle.

Tara herself had the chance to read it on Sunday. Much of it was heavy-going: Joey hadn't skimped on technical detail and had no great talent for rendering geek-speak into intelligible English. When she fast-forwarded to the end, however, the conclusions could hardly be clearer. Even to Tara, who had come to think she was immune to shock at the lunacies of this affair, they were jaw-dropping.

By Monday morning, the journalists covering the case had also found the new addition to the bundle. No doubt they had also struggled with the geeky jargon, but they too had reached the end and understood the thrust of the story. Ginny Pugh's piece in *The Times* was broadly representative of the coverage, with its headline:

Tech billionaire Talavera claims 'First Nation' potter goddess in Farrier case is 12-year-old hoax with roots in south London

It was going to be a dramatic week, once Den had a chance to explain the new developments to the tribunal.

'Good morning, madam,' he said to the judge. 'Thank you for allowing us to add Mr Talavera's witness statement, which is now in the bundle and has been widely reported in the news media this morning. I hope the relevance of this evidence is clear: it speaks to the offence and harm that Ms Farrier has been publicly accused of causing to marginalised people. As Mr Talavera's statement shows, that damaging allegation can't possibly be true.'

Robertson interrupted. 'Madam, this is one man's claim. It hasn't been proved and the evidence needs to be tested.'

'That's very true, madam,' Den acknowledged. 'To that end, Mr Talavera has agreed to make himself available for cross-examination on Wednesday afternoon, which I hope will be acceptable to both you and Ms Robertson. But I also have another late witness statement to offer. Once again, I apologise for not being able to lodge this evidence sooner, but it comes from Mr Elias Vasiliou, whose role in this story has only just come to light thanks to Mr Talavera's evidence.'

'Madam, this is not—' began Robertson.

But the judge cut her off. 'Who is Mr Vasiliou, Mr Hooper?'

'He is the original source of the Ctatpeshirahi story. Mr Talavera refers to him in his witness statement, although not by name. We've managed to track him down. He will confirm that Mr Talavera's account is accurate, and he can elaborate on it. That will help unravel the mystery that the papers are talking about this morning.'

'It's not the job of this tribunal to unravel interesting media mysteries, Mr Hooper, as you well know. It is purely to establish the merits of your client's case. However, I agree with you that this is relevant to the harm and offence that Ms Farrier's language is alleged to have caused, so I'll allow the evidence, provided you add the witness statement to the bundle today or tomorrow.'

'It's bring prepared at this very moment, madam.'

Tara knew this was true; as she watched the proceedings from the conference room, Zoya was in her office next door, interviewing Vasiliou, a soft-spoken British Cypriot with sad eyes and greying temples.

There was more testimony over the next two or three days from IWA management, including Matt Tree. Tara ground her teeth as she listened to them all repeat the familiar baseless slurs about her and attempt to maintain the same flimsy distinction as Alessandra Bianchi between holding a belief and expressing it in an inappropriate way. But was it her imagination, or had they become less certain in their condemnation since the Talavera story had broken? The US media had yet to mention it, but the New York bigwigs must have seen the British coverage. How long could they maintain their outrage without looking utterly ridiculous?

Finally, Wednesday afternoon arrived and Joey Talavera was sworn in.

At first, Tara thought the tech mogul was using the kind of Zype filter that allowed you to pretend you were in some exotic outdoor location rather than a dull bedroom or office. But as she looked closer, she realised Talavera really was sitting on a Californian terrace, under a perfect azure sky, with a swimming pool behind him.

Joey himself looked craggier than in the pictures she had seen, but that was only to be expected since the online shots were all red-carpet affairs or magazine photo-shoots in which he was impeccably groomed for the cameras and then airbrushed for public consumption. Despite that, he was still strikingly handsome, with his mane of black hair, his deep Californian tan and the extravagant biceps visible under the short sleeves of his t-shirt.

'Good morning, Mr Talavera,' Den began, adjusting his greeting to Joey's time zone. 'Thank you for joining us. We all appreciate you're a very busy man.'

'No problem,' said Joey. 'Happy to help in any way I can.'

'Mr Talavera, you've already provided an extensive witness statement, but some of it was necessarily in technical language. I'd be grateful if you could summarise the content of that statement.'

'Yeah, sure.'

'Before you do that, is it correct that you set out to search for the origins of the goddess Ctatpeshirahi?'

'Yeah, that's right.'

'Could you start by explaining why you did so?'

'Well, your client, Ms…er…'

'Ms Farrier?'

'Yeah. Ms Farrier is a friend of a friend of my wife, so I heard about her case. As it happens, we also had the guys from the IWA out here a couple years ago, at my foundation. So I was interested. And I got to wondering, why had I never heard of this goddess Ctat…whatever she's called… So I started searching for her, and I discovered something very interesting.'

'What was that?'

'I found a lot of references to her online, but all except one of them were no more than five years old.'

'And just to be clear, Mr Talavera, when you say you searched online, you're talking about a more sophisticated search than most of us would undertake? You don't just mean Google, do you?'

'There's nothing wrong with Google. For every search, you need a search engine. But there are ways of making your search more sophisticated, more than just typing a name into a search bar. Also I have a lot of smart people working for me, so I put some of them onto the job. They scraped the internet for me.'

'And what did they conclude?'

'Have you heard of XAnon?'

'Let's assume I haven't. Could you explain?'

'It's like QAnon, which is better known. As you probably know already, QAnon was a giant conspiracy theory about this big bunch of Satanist paedophiles…' He made air quotes as he said that phrase.

This prompted the judge to intervene. 'Sorry to interrupt your flow, Mr Talavera, but do bear in mind that we need a transcript of your evidence, and any hand gestures won't be recorded on it. Do you mean you don't think these people really were Satanist paedophiles?'

'Yes, your honour. That's correct, I don't.'

'Thank you, Mr Talavera. And "madam" will do, not "your honour". Do continue.'

Joey floundered, having lost his thread.

Den came to his rescue. 'You were telling us about QAnon, Mr Talavera.'

'Right. Like I said, it's a giant conspiracy theory featuring this bunch of people who were *meant to be* Satanist paedophiles and *were supposed to be* taking over the world.' He emphasised his verbal alternatives to the air quotes with hammy theatricality. 'All the information about it came from a shadowy character called Q, who sent messages out into the world from a bulletin board, and his followers all thought he was a major guru who knew everything and could see into the future. In reality it was just some dude making it all up. Like, messing with people's heads for the hell of it, because he could.'

'Thank you. And XAnon?'

'It's another bunch of guys, or maybe the same ones, but with XAnon they're targeting a different audience. QAnon was for Republicans who'll believe anything about Democrats worshipping Satan and stealing elections. XAnon targets liberals, to try and make them look dumb. They push out stuff they call Fashionably Irrational Beliefs, just to see how far they'll go.'

'Fashionably Irrational Beliefs? So that would be Fibs for short?'

'Yeah, I guess. Crazy shit…sorry, ma'am…I mean crazy stuff that no one in their right mind would believe in normal circumstances. But once they think it's politically correct to believe it, they go along with it and try to punish anyone who doesn't.'

'And you're saying this XAnon outfit invented the goddess Ctatpeshirahi?'

'No. I'm saying that, with one notable exception, there was no reference anywhere in the digital world to that goddess until five years ago, when suddenly there was a spate of posts about her, all traceable to the XAnon message board. Then a lot of accounts started tweeting out her story, but you can see those accounts are all based in the same location, in Bangladesh. It looks like a co-ordinated bot campaign.'

'And what was that one exception?'

'It was in 2012. A library in London posted a story written by a student on a creative writing class. It was the creation myth of the potter goddess.'

'The goddess Ctatpeshirahi?'

'Yes.'

'And it was explicitly billed as a piece of creative fiction?'

'Yeah.'

'Was it signed?'

'No, it was anonymous, and it was uploaded by the professor in charge of the class.'

'Thank you, Mr Talavera. No further questions.'

Tara's heart raced. This extraordinary witness statement hadn't just devastated the IWA's case, it had also made the whole organisation look like a bunch of buffoons. Zoya had just picked up her phone to take a call, so Tara couldn't swap reactions with her. Instead she texted Mel, who had told her she would be watching online.

Did you see Joey's evidence?

The response came straight back. *Yes! Amazing!*

One of these days you and Craig will tell me what you've got on Joey, to make him do that!

Ha! was all Mel replied.

On the screen, Robertson was about to begin her cross-examination.

'Good morning, Mr Talavera,' she said.

'Good morning.'

With no further preamble, the IWA's barrister began pugnaciously. 'Do you believe it's possible for something to exist if it has never been mentioned on the internet?'

A frown creased Joey's handsome brow. 'Yes, sure.'

'Can you remind us when the internet was invented?'

'It goes all the way back to the sixties and seventies, but the internet in its present form really only dates from the nineties.'

'The First Nation people who worship Ctatpeshirahi' – Robertson had clearly been practising too – 'come from a society that traces its history back many hundreds of years, don't they?'

'I can't say. I've found no evidence they exist.'

Robertson glared at him. 'Indulge me, Mr Talavera. Let's say a marginalised First Nation people do worship that goddess. If that's the case, we can say they've been doing it since long before the invention of the internet, can't we?'

'Hypothetically, I guess.'

'And do you know what proportion of First Nation people

have access to the internet, Mr Talavera?'

'I don't.'

'Well, in Canada, for example, it's 24 percent of Indigenous households, compared with 94 percent of all Canadians.'

'Is there a question for Mr Talavera, madam?' interrupted Den.

Before the judge could reply, Robertson continued: 'Here's my question, Mr Talavera. Do you agree it's possible that a First Nation people could worship a particular goddess for hundreds of years without that goddess ever finding her way onto the internet?'

'Yes, that's possible.'

'Do you also agree that your inability to find any reference to Ctatpeshirahi before 2012, only about fifteen years into the life of the internet proper, is not proof that she's a work of a fiction?'

'Yes, but the proof–'

She cut him off. 'Yes or no will do, Mr Talavera. Moving on, I'm curious about your involvement. You say Ms Farrier is the friend of a friend of your wife. What's the name of that friend?'

'Craig.' He pronounced it the American way, *Cregg*.

'Second name?'

'I don't know. He's my wife's friend, not mine.'

'Yet you went to considerable trouble for him?'

'I did that because my wife asked me to. She's a very persuasive woman.'

Tara wished, once again, they were in an actual courtroom. That line would surely have raised a laugh from the spectators.

'I think you mentioned you met a delegation from the IWA. Did that include Dr Rowan Walker, the person with whom Ms Farrier had her initial falling out?'

Den butted in again. 'There was no falling out, madam. As you can see from the correspondence in the bundle, Ms Farrier's communications were entirely amicable.'

'I'll rephrase, madam. Mr Talavera, did that delegation include Dr Walker, who originally asked Ms Farrier to remove sensitive language from her report?'

'I didn't say I met them, ma'am,' said Joey.

'You may call me Ms Robertson. Only address the judge as madam.'

'Sorry, Ms Robertson. I didn't say I met them. The delegation came to the foundation and my team looked after them. And maybe also my wife met them.'

'Did the delegation include Dr Walker?'

'I don't know. I'd have to check with my team and circle back to you on that.'

Robertson permitted herself a smirk. 'Thank you, Mr Talavera. What I'm driving at is this: is your intervention in this case motivated by some kind of animosity, either on your part or your wife's, towards the IWA in general or Dr Walker in particular?'

'No. My foundation gave them money.'

'But in the last few days you've suspended that funding, haven't you Mr Talavera?'

'We haven't suspended it, but we've said there won't be any more unless the situation with Ms, um, Farrier, is resolved.'

'Again, why do you care so much, Mr Talavera? Help me understand.'

Tara could see what Robertson was doing – trying to hint at some kind of impropriety that had caused Krystal Talavera to despise Rowan.

But Joey was having none of it. 'There's been an injustice here,' he said. 'And I'm not a fan of injustice.'

'Thank you, Mr Talavera. No further questions.'

The afternoon was drawing on, and the judge asked Den if he would prefer to reschedule the next witness, Elias Vasiliou, for the next day.

'Thank you, madam, but Mr Vasiliou has made himself available today. I won't need very long with him. If Ms Robertson needs longer, we can see if he's available for cross-examination tomorrow.'

'Very well, Mr Hooper. Go ahead.'

Vasiliou was sworn in and smiled broadly, waiting for the questioning to start. It was an odd expression, in the circumstances, and Tara wondered if it was a cover for nerves.

Den began: 'Mr Vasiliou, thank you for being with us at short notice. Could you tell me what work you were doing in 2012? That was the year of the London Olympics, if that makes it easier to remember.'

Vasiliou nodded. 'I was doing a number of things, including teaching a creative writing class at East Greenwich library in south London.'

'And who were your students?'

'A mixture of ages, occupations and talents. Almost all women, I think. They paid a small fee for a six-month course. It was designed to be affordable, so as not to exclude people on low incomes, as the bigger creative writing courses often tend to do.'

'And did you on one occasion give your class an assignment to devise a creation myth?'

'I did.'

'This was specifically fiction, yes? It wasn't some kind of

research assignment into little-known religions?'

'It was a creative writing exercise. Pure fiction.'

'And how did your students rise to the task?'

'The quality was mixed. That's normal in this kind of class.'

'Did any one piece stand out?'

'Yes it did.'

'Could you tell us about it?'

'It was about a potter goddess with a long and peculiar name, who sculpted the earth out of clay and then used parts of her own body and her bodily fluids to make first women, and then men.'

'Did the story mention when these events were supposed to have happened?'

'Yes. It said it happened nine thousand, nine hundred and ninety-nine years ago.'

'And was the goddess called Ctatpeshirahi?'

'Yes.'

'Do you remember the author's name?'

'I do. But she was very anxious to remain anonymous. She suggested she had strong reasons to keep her name off the internet.'

'You're under oath to reply to the best of your ability, Mr Vasiliou. We can redact the name from the court transcript, if necessary, as we've done with your statement in the bundle.'

After a moment's hesitation, Vasiliou said: 'It was Polly. Polly Lennox. I asked her if I could put her piece online, thinking she'd be pleased, but she wasn't. And after that she never came back.'

'And was Polly Lennox by any chance First Nation or Indigenous?'

Vasiliou's smile took on a bewildered air. 'Sorry, I don't

understand what you mean.'

'Was she Native American? Or Inuit, perhaps?'

Even with this explanation, the witness still looked as if he thought the question was absurd. 'No, not at all. Actually, I think she was the only white British woman in the class.'

'Did she mention why she chose the name Ctatpeshirahi for her goddess?'

'Not that I recall.'

'Do you read *The Times,* Mr Vasiliou?'

'No. Normally just *The Guardian* online.'

'So you won't have seen a letter in this morning's paper from a Mr William Frobisher of Stourbourne in Kent. May I read it, madam? It's very short.'

'Mr Hooper…' growled the judge.

'I assure you it's relevant.'

The judge sighed. 'Very well.'

'Thank you, madam. The letter reads as follows:

Sir,

As a friend and neighbour of Tara Farrier, I've been reading your coverage of her employment tribunal with interest.

In particular, I'm intrigued by the peculiar and unpronounceable name of the goddess Ctatpeshirahi, who may be completely made up, according to the latest reports.

As an avid crossword solver, may I point out that the name is an obvious anagram of 'I hate this crap'?

Yours etc.'

Den paused.

'Is there a question, Mr Hooper?'

'Only this, madam. Mr Vasiliou, from what you remember of Polly Lewis and her attitude to her own story, do you think the name of the goddess might have been an intentional anagram of that phrase?'

Vasiliou smiled more broadly than ever, and this time it seemed genuine. 'Yes, Mr Hooper. I think it may well have been.'

31

The expression on Robertson's face, as she saw the case collapsing before her eyes, was an absolute picture. Looking back on it afterwards, Tara couldn't quite believe they'd managed to pull off those *coups de grâce* from Joey and Elias.

It was Ginny who had pushed hardest, for many months, to probe the origins of the Ctatpeshirahi story. On Twitter, no matter how much abuse she attracted, she asked week in, week out if anyone had ever met an Indigenous worshipper of the potter goddess. The query became known as 'the Pugh question'.

'It's not as if I haven't tried to look it up,' she had explained one evening, in a Zype call with Tara, Mel and Zoya. 'One of the difficulties is that North America is absolutely huge – nearly three times the size of Europe – and it was home to a vast array of different peoples before the Europeans invaded.

That means there was a huge variety of religious traditions, not just from nation to nation but from tribe to tribe. Some believed in one god, others believed in several, but there were also animists and shamanists. I've done my best to look into every possible Indigenous group. It takes forever, because there are so many of them, but I can't find Ctatpewotsit anywhere.'

Tara had always struggled to see the point of this obsession. 'Sorry, Ginny. I don't want to sound negative, but I don't understand why you're so bothered,' she said. 'I really don't care who worships her. I just object to being told I have to pretend to believe in her too.'

Zoya raised her hand to speak – a formality she always observed in these situations, even when no one else did. 'Correct me if I'm wrong, but I think Ginny's suggesting that Ctatpewotsit may not actually exist. Aren't you Ginny?'

Ginny nodded. 'There are times when certainly I'm tempted to say that, but of course it's hard to prove a negative with any certainty. There's always the possibility that I just haven't looked in the right place.'

Tara's couldn't stop her frustration bubbling over. 'I'm sorry, but the whole thrust of this inquiry makes me uncomfortable. So what if you do somehow manage to prove the goddess is made up? You're implying it would be acceptable to police speech that contradicts the teaching of creationist religions that really do exist.'

Ginny nodded. 'I hear what you say, and of course I don't mean to imply that. You're right, it's ridiculous to deny science for the sake of any religion, full stop. I promise you, I have no intention of losing sight of that. But I do think it's fascinating that this goddess appeared out of nowhere and that I can't find any reference to her before the Young Earth

356

crowd latched onto her.'

So far, Mel hadn't spoken. 'Can I make a suggestion?' she said. 'I think we can all see Tara's point. What has happened to her, and what's happening in schools, colleges, museums, universities and so on, is utterly appalling. Science is being censored to pander to religion, which is wrong whether it's a global faith like Christianity or Islam or something very obscure that's known only to a tiny tribe in Alaska or Mexico.'

They all nodded agreement, including Ginny.

'That being said,' Mel continued, 'Ginny does seem to have stumbled upon something intriguing. No matter how many times she asks the Pugh question...it must be hundreds...?'

'At least,' said Ginny.

'Right. No matter how many times she asks the question, no one can answer. That certainly sparks my curiosity. Obviously we don't want to base our case on it, not least because any decent lawyer only asks a question in court to which they know the answer already.'

'Very true,' confirmed Zoya.

'Nevertheless, if we had the means to investigate, wouldn't it make sense to look into it? Just to see what we can dig up?'

'Do we have the means to investigate?' said Tara.

Mel's mouth twitched in one of her private half-smiles. 'I think we may.'

She was talking, of course, about Craig and his relationship with the Talaveras, which Tara still didn't understand, and Mel refused to explain, because she said she and Craig were both sworn to secrecy.* It was plain that everyone else thought this was worth pursuing, so Tara decided not to stand in the way.

* I'm not. You can read the whole story in *The End of the World is Flat*. Simon Edge

Since Craig was the one with Krystal Talavera's private number, it was agreed from the outset that any approach to Joey needed to come from him. But Craig was a busy hospital consultant, not a legal investigator, so whatever persuasion he used, he had to apply it in his limited windows of free time.

Having resolved not to interfere, Tara let him get on with it at his own pace. The process took months, but eventually the message came back that Krystal had agreed to help. That was of course only the first step. They then had to wait for Joey to conduct his investigation, with the date for the final tribunal steadily creeping up on them, and no guarantee that the digital search would turn up the result they wanted. But then it did, and Tara could see that it really did blow the IWA's case out of the water. Ginny had been right all along to pursue the angle.

Even then, they had to persuade Joey to make a witness statement and agree to be examined by the tribunal, and they needed to do that before the proceedings opened. When they missed that deadline, the new hurdle was persuading the judge to allow a late addition to the evidence bundle, not to mention tracking down Elias and allowing his testimony too. Somehow, miraculously, it had all come together, making all the effort and stress worthwhile.

Now they just had to wait for the ruling.

A month after the end of the proceedings, Tara was sitting in her living room with her feet up, reading the news sites on her iPad, when Zoya called.

This time, there was a smile in her voice. 'Morning, Tara. We've heard from the tribunal. You know the routine. Perhaps you'd like to come into the office?'

Tara had learned to be cautious, however good things looked. 'Sure. I can set out now. Erm…is it my imagination, or do you sound happy?'

Her solicitor laughed. 'You know I'm not allowed to tell you anything over the phone. But I will admit there's a spring in my step, and not just because I put an extra sugar in my tea.'

Tara spent the whole drive telling herself not to get her hopes up, because even with good news, there was bound to be a catch of some kind. But when she reached Zoya's office, she finally allowed herself to believe it.

'We won!!!' her solicitor cried as soon as she saw Tara, pulling her into an uncharacteristic hug.

Tara found that she was laughing and crying at the same time. 'Really? No catches? No downsides?'

'We won on every count. The judge ruled that the IWA discriminated against you and victimised you on the basis of your protected belief. After everything you've been through, you really have won!'

'Oh wow. I don't know how to thank you. And Den. And…' She blinked, trying to let it sink in properly. 'Am I allowed to tell anyone? And what about damages? Do we know how much I get?'

'The judgement says remedies – which is legal-speak for how much they have to cough up – are to be arranged at a later date. As for telling people, I'm afraid the normal rules apply. This is confidential for the moment. I can't stop you telling the people closest to you, but you have to swear them to secrecy.'

Having read the judgement in the conference room, Tara made her calls from the car on the way home. Laila let out a whoop, and Tara had to shush her, because even though Laila had her father's surname of Palmer, her colleagues surely knew she was Tara Farrier's daughter and they would be capable of putting two and two together.

Gina was exuberant too, cheering at the other end of the phone. Mel was more restrained, because frenzied joy was not her style, but Tara was pretty sure she could hear her friend taking a moment to steady her emotions on the other end of the line. That reaction moved her, because it was so out of character.

When she reached home, Tara also sent a message to Emily Zola, thanking her for everything, because she would never have managed to raise the funds without her. Emily messaged her straight back with a string of heart emojis.

Having sworn all four of them to secrecy, she spent an agonising week not being able to telegraph the result far and wide. There was so much she wanted to do and say, but she had to wait. Pretty much all she could do was book the back room of the Half Moon for the day the ruling was due to be made public, and even then she had to do it in the name of Laila Palmer, to save the news slipping out.

Once more, the ruling was made public at noon on the appointed day. At one minute past twelve, Tara tweeted: 'I won my case! The tribunal found that @i_w_a discriminated against me and victimised me for my belief that the earth is billions of years old. I want to thank my brilliant legal team and everyone who supported me in this long ordeal. Believe what you like. But geology is real.'

Since she had a couple of characters left, she added the party popper emoji. Then she logged off Twitter. There would be lots of messages of support, but they would be balanced by more smears and abuse, and she didn't want to see any of that today.

Someone had ordered champagne and the victory party at the Half Moon was in full swing. Zoya and Den were there, as well as Mel and Craig, plus Rita, Helen and Ginny, the Frobishers (Willie accepting champion's plaudits after the knockout punch of his *Times* letter) and a host of newer friends and supporters. A couple of them had come in inflatable dinosaur costume and kept tripping over bar stools and bumping into people, amid general hilarity.

Bizarrely, it was the first time Tara had met Den in the flesh. 'Thank you again for everything,' she shouted up at him. It was the umpteenth time she had expressed her gratitude; she could blame the champagne for that.

'We couldn't have done it without your fortitude,' he said. 'I know how tough this ordeal has been for you. But make no mistake, this is a landmark ruling. Other people in similar positions will be able to cite the Farrier judgement to show their beliefs are protected under the law.'

'That's wonderful. Although hopefully we've laid the potter goddess stuff to rest by showing it up for the nonsense it was.'

'Yes, but I wouldn't be too complacent. You heard that phrase Joey used – Fashionably Irrational Beliefs? We may have seen the last of this one, but there'll be something equally crazy along soon enough.'

'What a depressing thought.'

'Lunacy is the spirit of the age, I'm afraid. But don't think about that now. Today is all about celebration.'

'Did you know we were going to win?'

'Nothing's ever certain. We saw that when the preliminary

tribunal said your belief was unworthy of respect in a democratic society. But in this case I was pretty confident. There wasn't really any way back for them, after the double whammy of Joey and Elias. Also I've met that judge a few times before, and I knew she'd be fair and decent.'

'Joey was amazing,' said Tara. 'I'd never heard of him before I went to the IWA, but he's now very high on the list of my all-time favourite people.'

'I'm not surprised. Although I still don't know how Craig managed to get him on board.'

'Nor do I. Whenever I ask Mel about it, she's always very cagey.'

'Give her a few drinks, and maybe she'll tell you tonight.'

'Maybe I will,' Tara laughed.

She could see Mel and Craig at the end of the bar. Leaving Den talking to Zoya, she went over to join them.

'Congratulations once more,' said Mel, clinking glasses.

'I couldn't have done it without you two. Thank you again, from the bottom of my heart.'

'Our pleasure,' said Mel.

Tara paused, wondering if this was the right moment, then took the plunge. 'So are you going to tell me, Craig, what hold you've got over Joey Talavera? There is something, isn't there? He's one of the biggest players in Silicon Valley, yet somehow you had him running at your beck and call.'

Craig grinned. 'We're sworn to secrecy, I'm afraid. In any case, it's not really a matter of having a hold over him. We didn't need that. He's keen to do the right thing because…'

He trailed off, as if doubting whether he should continue.

Mel picked up the thread for him. 'Put it this way, Tara. Joey himself has reason to be familiar with those Fashionably

Irrational Beliefs he was talking about. Without giving too much away, he has a strong need to redeem himself, to demonstrate he's the nice guy he always wanted to be. By putting the resources of his corporation at your disposal, he's more than demonstrated that.'

'I see,' said Tara, although she didn't really. 'Anyway, I obviously love the guy to bits, and I would do even if he weren't so easy on the eye, but of course that helps. Did you know he's told the IWA they have to give me a job as a condition of further funding from his foundation?'

'Really? That's marvellous,' said Mel. 'But could you bear going back there, after they way they treated you?'

'Not if I had to go into the office, when I'd always be wondering which of them signed that horrible letter about me. But if I could carry on working from home, it might be possible. It would mean I could get back to focusing on Yemen, which was the whole point of working there in the first place.'

Mel shrugged. 'Rather you than me. Although I'd love to be a fly on the wall when they have to offer you your job back. Talk about humble pie.'

'You see? I think it may be worth doing just for that.'

Craig changed the subject. 'Have you heard anything from Emily Zola?'

'We've been in touch a few times in the past couple of weeks. The last message I had from her was yesterday.' Tara looked around the bar. 'She said she'd try and be here.'

'I do hope she comes,' said Mel. 'Even if we're all a bit old to be *Sandy Snaith* fans.'

'Speak for yourself,' said Craig.

'Really?'

He swelled with pride. 'I've read them all. I like kids' books. They're great escapism. Trust me, you need that if you work in the NHS.'

'I haven't read any of them but I'm starstruck,' said Tara. 'Someone that famous and successful never needed to put herself out for me.'

Mel nodded. 'She's like her great-grandfather. If there's an injustice, she can't look the other way, even if half her readers hate her for it.'

'Does that make me the Captain Dreyfus of our times?' said Tara.

'Well, aren't you?' said Mel.

'At least you didn't have to spend five years on Devil's Island,' said Craig.

'There is that. Let's be thankful for small mercies,' said Tara.

She felt a hand on her arm. She turned to see Helen at her elbow.

'Sorry to interrupt, Tara. There's someone in the front bar asking for you. She says she doesn't want to come back here.'

'Who is it?'

'I don't know. I'm just passing the message on. Don't worry, I think she's friendly. She doesn't look like a loon at any rate. But I'll come with you if you want back-up.'

'Thanks for the offer, but how bad can she be? I can always call the pub's security stand if she turns out to be hostile.'

Wondering who this mystery woman could be, Tara made her way forward into the front bar. It occurred to her, amid her champagne euphoria, that this might be an elaborate ruse to introduce her to the great Emily Zola, amid more popping corks and cries of 'surprise!'. But when she reached the front of the pub, there was no sign of the author's distinctive blonde ponytail. Neither was there anyone else she recognised. But her own face had become well known, so she would have to wait until this new stranger made herself known. Sure enough, a small woman of about her own age, with tired eyes and close-cropped greying hair, stepped forward. Dressed in an anorak zipped up to the chin, this person looked badly out of place in a West End bar full of young men in suits.

'Tara?' she said nervously.

'Yes, I'm Tara.'

'Thanks for coming out of your party. I didn't want to go back there, because I didn't know if I'd be welcome. But I wanted to meet you, and when Elias said you'd be here…'

The penny began to drop. 'Wait, are you…?'

'I'm Polly Lennox.'

'Oh wow. The origin of the origin story. How amazing to meet you.'

'I am so sorry. I honestly had no idea about any of this. I literally didn't have a clue that my stupid goddess had acquired a life of her own till I saw it on *Have I Got News For You*, during your tribunal. If I had known, maybe I could have done something about it sooner.'

'It's honestly not your fault that some crazy hackers found your story and put it out in the world as a hoax religion. It's not your fault a bunch of dumb, virtue-signalling white people – no offence – pounced on it to demonstrate their anti-racist credentials. And it's certainly not your fault that my former employers joined the cult and victimised anyone who wouldn't play along.'

Polly visibly relaxed. 'Thank you for saying that. I was scared you might hate me.'

'Don't be silly. Why would I hate you?' said Tara.

Polly shrugged. 'Thanks for being so nice. You needn't have been.'

'Don't be daft. Thank you for coming. Is Elias coming too? I think my solicitor said she'd invited him.'

'He sends his apologies. He's working.'

'I hope he knows how grateful I am to him.'

'I think he does, but I'll pass that on.'

Tara frowned as she thought back to Elias' evidence. 'At the tribunal, he said he hadn't seen you since you left the course.'

'Yes, that's right. When I saw that stupid anagram name of the goddess on TV, I googled it, and I couldn't believe the results. She was everywhere. But I also found the news reports of Elias' testimony. He wasn't hard to find, because he's still running evening classes in my borough. So I met up with him and he filled me in on everything I'd missed. I wanted to contact you before now, but he suggested I wait till the judgement came out. He said it might be more diplomatic.'

'I'd have been happy to hear from you before now. But tell me, was he right when he said you were embarrassed by your story?'

'Yes. I really hate New Age crap – I said so in the anagram, didn't I – and I couldn't believe I was writing it myself.'

'So that's why you wanted to remain anonymous?'

'Yes. I'm quite a private person anyway, but it was no bigger deal than that. The news reports all said my name had been withheld for legal reasons, which sounded really dramatic, but there aren't any that I know of.'

'And are you still writing? Elias said you had a real talent.'

'No, I gave up. I got bored of not getting anywhere.'

'You inspired a crazy cult that spread all over the Western world. That's not my idea of not getting anywhere.'

'Don't!' Polly flushed with embarrassment.

'Look, come through to the party and have a drink. I'll introduce you to my friends. In fact, there may be another writer coming later, if she ever shows up. She may have some tips to help you get started again. And I know my legal team would love to meet you.' Seeing the other woman's look of panic, Tara added hastily: 'I mean, because you played such an interesting part in the story.'

Polly shook her head. 'Thanks, but I won't stop. It's not really my scene. I just wanted to say sorry for all the trouble I caused.'

'Honestly, don't think like that. It's lovely of you to apologise, but none of it was your responsibility.'

They kissed each other on the cheek and Tara watched her go, before making her way back to the private room full of her own crowd.

Helen saw her come back in and came to meet her. 'Who was it? Friend, I hope, not foe?'

'Definitely friend. Someone who wanted to apologise, even though there wasn't the slightest need.' She related her full encounter with Polly Lennox.

Helen was suitably enthralled by the story, but as Tara neared the end, her companion's face froze in horror. She grabbed Tara's wrist and said: 'Don't look now, but we do have an actual foe in our midst. That girl with the pink and purple dreadlocks. She's just walked in!'

Tara wheeled around to see Sorrel and Sammy picking their way through the crowd, on their way to the bar but also looking around for her. She shrank back, trying to stay out of their eye-line. In ordinary circumstances she'd have been delighted to see them, but she cursed her own stupidity for not warning Helen that she might encounter Sorrel – and indeed for not telling her any of that saga.

She placed a reassuring hand on her friend's arm.

'Don't worry,' she said. 'That's just Sorrel. She's… Well, I know her.'

Helen blinked in confusion. 'What?'

To Tara's disappointment, Sorrel had never written the promised email of apology to be forwarded to the professor, but Tara hadn't pushed it, and then she'd plunged back into the world of statements and evidence bundles as the tribunal approached, so she had never found a way of raising the subject with Helen.

'Oh dear,' she said now, wishing she had drunk slightly less, and stepping further sideways in the hope the newcomers wouldn't spot her yet. 'I'm so sorry, I should have warned you. I told you I barely knew her, which was true at the time, but it was only a half-truth. She's actually my son's girlfriend.'

Helen clapped her hand to her forehead. 'And I told you she was one of my loons on the first day of your tribunal! Oh Tara, that must have been devastating for you. I'm the one who should be sorry.'

'You weren't to know. I should have explained who she was, but I was mortified. Anyway, the important thing is, that's all water under the bridge now. Sorrel has broken with her friends on your picket and apologised for everything she did. I decided to forgive her because I'd been so terrified of losing my son and it made life so much easier. I did tell her she had to apologise to you too, but then I forgot to hold her to it, what with everything else.'

Helen bit her lip. 'Well, maybe she'll do it now. They've seen you and they're both coming over.'

'I honestly won't blame you if you don't want to speak to her. I can fend them off and make sure she stays away from you.'

'No, let's give the girl a chance and see—'

Dizzy with the sudden stress of this awkward encounter, Tara wheeled back round to find herself looking up at her son. '*Habibi*, I thought you were working tonight! How lovely to see you!'

'I managed to swap a shift. Congratulations, Mum.' Wine glass in hand, he bent to kiss her.

'I'm so glad you did. Thank you. And Sorrel! Thank you for coming.'

Also bearing a glass, Sorrel stepped forward to kiss Tara on both cheeks. 'Congratulations, Tara. I'm happy for you, truly I…' Her eyes widened and she trailed off as she did a sudden double-take and recognised Helen. 'Oh. Professor Kottsack. I didn't realise. Sorry, we're interrupting.' Her exuberance had left her and she backed away as if to flee.

Tara raised her voice amid the celebratory din. 'Don't go. Helen honestly won't bite. And now might be a good chance for you to tell her what you told me, don't you think?'

Sorrel inched back towards them. She looked pained, as if she might be physically sick. 'I'm sorry, Professor Kottsack. I'm sorry for taking part in the picket and I'm sorry for not saying sorry sooner.' Normally so poised, she sounded overwrought.

Helen spoke calmly. 'That's all right, Sorrel. We all make mistakes. And I appreciate your apology.'

'Thank you, Professor Kottsack.' It came out as a wail of relief.

'For the first time, Helen smiled at her. 'Honestly Sorrel, it's all right. And you can call me Helen.'

Tara stepped forward. 'Thank you,' she said. 'Both of you.

Sorrel for having the guts to apologise to Helen's face, and Helen for being a big enough person to accept your apology. Neither of those things are easy, and lots of people go through their whole lives without ever being able to do what both of you have just done. I don't want to get too sentimental or anything' – she sensed, through a happy blur of champagne, that she might have failed already on that score – 'but I'm very proud of my family and friends.'

'I'll drink to that,' said Helen, raising her glass.

Sammy and Sorrel raised theirs too, and they all looked each other in the eye as they clinked.

Tara wiped her eyes, which had suddenly become moist, with the back of her sleeve. 'Anyway, I'm glad I didn't get sentimental,' she said, laughing. At the same moment, the phone in the pocket of her suit jacket buzzed with a notification. She pulled the device out and opened a text message. It read: *Sorry, the traffic from Suffolk was horrific. Just round the corner from the Half Moon now. See you in five! Em xxx*

Beaming broadly, Tara looked up at her companions. 'And for my next trick,' she said, 'who wants to meet Emily actual Zola?'

The Guardian ✓ @Guardian
Just because Ctatpeshirahi doesn't exist doesn't mean Tara
Farrier wouldn't offend real Indigenous communities, writes
@LeonSmith84 in today's paper. Click on the link for the full
article
RT 56 L 294

Tara Farrier @tara_for_now
Replying to @Guardian
Seriously? Is it really that hard just to admit you were wrong?
RT 462 L 1.9K

Sally Jenkinson @saljenk07342
Replying to @ @tara_for_now
STFU Yerf
RT 16 L 87

Jeremy Vine ✓ @theJeremyVine
Replying to @ @tara_for_now
Sorry to ask but what exactly is going on here?
RT 1 L 16

AFTERWORD

When I wrote my fifth novel, *The End of the World is Flat*, I took pains to conclude the story with what I hoped was a satisfying and entertaining resolution. I'm always nervous of billing my work as comedy, because readers will be better judges than me of whether it's funny or not. But since the Greeks defined comedy as having a happy ending, I could at least supply one of those.

In doing so, I tied everything up too neatly for my own good. If a writer is planning a sequel, they leave loose ends – the sort of stuff that screams 'recommission me' on TV. In my case, I had no such plan: this was going to be my sole foray into this subject in fiction and then (as my late Italian husband would have said) *basta*. But as *The End of the World is Flat* made its way around the English-speaking world, in a word-of-mouth journey for which I'm truly grateful to my readers, it became clear that many of them wanted more.

How could I provide it? Having poked fun at the absurdities of gender ideology by recasting it as flat-earthery, I had then killed and buried anti-globularism, and I couldn't resurrect it. The only solution was to construct another allegorical vehicle. I needed a new Fashionably Irrational Belief (Fib) – something that was obviously daft, but no more daft than the public utterances of politicians, academics, civic leaders, charities and corporations in the service of the gender cult. (Incidentally, I'd love to claim the Fib coinage as my own, but credit goes to the blogger Ghurwinder Bhogal, who used it in his essay *Why Smart People Believe Stupid Things*.)

In this novel, the goddess Ctatpeshirahi (a deliberately difficult name that I still can't spell, even now resorting to cut and paste) is invented under pressure in a library in southeast London. The character who creates her does so unwillingly, and does not seek to attach her to any particular culture.

In my own mind, however, I was aware of some of the absurdities in parts of the English-speaking world, where people of obvious settler heritage yearn for worthier roots. This creates a landscape of gullibility, where well-meaning people fall for anything as long as it's dressed in a suitably Indigenous fashion. In Canada, the cumbersome 'LGBTQIA+' apparently isn't enough to describe the ever-expanding rainbow umbrella: the required version is '2SLGBTQIA+', where '2S' means 'two-spirit'. This ancient Indigenous rainbow identity dates all the way back to 1990.

To many readers, it won't come as a surprise that the legal drama at the heart of *In the Beginning* is inspired by the experience of Maya Forstater, whose hard-won victory established that UK employers who sack staff for wrongthink are breaking the law. For anyone who followed her story, the parallels aren't hard to spot. And I hope JK Rowling won't mind my adapting her celebrated tweet in support of Maya to fit Tara's case.

Equally clearly, the harassment of the anagrammatic Helen Kottsack is inspired by the parallel, real-world persecution of Professor Kathleen Stock. As regards a further obvious parallel, I set my story in Kent for reasons too boring to go into; it was only once I got started that I realised this offered a serendipitous opportunity for Tara to make friends with Canterbury's Labour MP, viciously persecuted by her own party for daring to believe that volcanoes and dinosaurs existed. Rita Denby, meet Rosie Duffield.

All that being said, the characters inspired by these real-life figures aren't meant to be them. I don't know Maya, Kathleen or Rosie well enough to know how they or their families reacted privately to their ordeals; the behaviour of Tara, Helen and Rita comes entirely from my own imagination. The same applies to the entirely fictitious executives of the equally fictitious Institute for Worldwide Advancement.

All novelists put themselves into their characters and there's plenty of my biography in Tara's. I began my journalistic career running the Yemen desk (among others) at *Middle East Economic Digest*. I even wrote a book called *Yemen: Arabian Enigma*, but I wouldn't recommend it, even if you can find a copy in print. If you want to know more about that stunning country, you'd be much better off with Daniel McLaughlin's excellent Bradt guide, which I used to refresh my memory. I was never kidnapped in Yemen but I vividly remember the reports of some of the people who were; several of them enjoyed it just as much as Tara.

Everything I know about the Scopes Monkey Trial comes from Edward J. Larson's *Summer for the Gods*, a detailed, readable and endlessly surprising book which won the Pulitzer Prize for History in 1998.

For my knowledge of the three tribunals in the case of *Maya Forstater v CGD Europe & Anor*, I relied heavily on the incredible work of the volunteer collective Open Justice with Tribunal Tweets, whose live reporting of a number of important legal challenges now stands as a great archive resource.

When it came to creating my fictitious version, I discovered that writing courtroom drama is way harder than it looks. Not only do you have to make your legal counsel walk, talk and be vaguely entertaining; you also have to make them construct coherent cases, and not score goals for the other side. There's also a yawning gap between the order in which witnesses appear in a real-life case and the order a writer wants them to appear for the sake of drama. I'm full of admiration for those people who write this stuff all the time. I'm very grateful to m'learned friends Liz, Deb and David – as well as to Lightning Books' proper legal crime writer Abi Silver – for helping with endless boring technical queries.

My thanks also to the MPs Neale Harvey and James Cartlidge (who really is a former member of the All-Party Parliamentary Committee on Yemen, as well as my own member of parliament); to Gavin McGillivray, Barbara Segall, and Arty Morty; and to Anya Palmer, a key member of Maya's legal team, who drew me into the gender farrago in the first place. Tara's married name is an intentional hat-tip.

At Lightning Books, thank you as ever to Clio Mitchell for copyediting and typesetting, to Ifan Bates for another fantastic cover, to Dan Hiscocks for his endless support (allowing me to venture into territory from which less courageous publishers would shy away) and above all to my friend Jane Harris, an editor of tireless diligence and immense insight, who has helped me shape *In the Beginning* into the novel I wanted it to be.

It does have a happy ending, which I hope will eventually be reflected in the real world. Maya won her case but, at the time of writing, is still waiting for her former employers to agree a financial settlement; she recently had to crowdfund once again to try to achieve a resolution. As for the wider madness, the pitfalls of Fashionably Irrational Beliefs are becoming better understood by some of the decision-makers who have led the rush to adopt and impose them. The fate of the Scottish National Party – which currently seems to be on the verge of dinosaur-scale extinction – may prove a salutary lesson to others.

But it's a crazy, unpredictable world. Who knows what will have happened by the time you read this?

Simon Edge
April 2023

By the same author

The End of the World is Flat

Mel Winterbourne's modest map-making charity, the Orange Peel Foundation, has achieved all its aims and she's ready to shut it down. But glamorous tech billionaire Joey Talavera has other ideas. He hijacks the foundation for his own purpose: to convince the world that the earth is flat.

Using the dark arts of social media at his new master's behest, Mel's ruthless young successor, Shane Foxley, turns science on its head. He persuades gullible online zealots that old-style 'globularism' is hateful. Teachers and airline pilots face ruin if they reject the new 'True Earth' orthodoxy.

Can Mel and her fellow heretics – vilified as 'True-Earth Rejecting Globularists' (Tergs) – thwart Orange Peel before insanity takes over? Might the solution to the problem lie in the 15th century?

Using his trademark mix of history and satire to poke fun at modern foibles, Simon Edge is at his razor-sharp best in a caper that may be more relevant than you think.

A satire of Swiftian ferocity
Matthew Parris, The Times

A bracingly sharp satire on the sleep of reason and the tyranny of twaddle
Francis Wheen

I laughed so hard I nearly fell in my cauldron. A masterpiece
Julie Bindel

The Hopkins Conundrum

Tim Cleverley inherits a failing pub in Wales, which he plans to rescue by enlisting an American pulp novelist to concoct an entirely fabricated 'mystery' about the poet Gerard Manley Hopkins, who wrote his masterpiece *The Wreck of the Deutschland* nearby.

Blending the real stories of Hopkins and five shipwrecked nuns with a contemporary love story, while casting a wry eye on the *Da Vinci Code* industry, *The Hopkins Conundrum* is a highly original mix of fiction, literary biography and satirical commentary.

A splendid mix of literary detection, historical description and contemporary romance which will appeal equally to fans and detractors of Dan Brown
Michael Arditti

Thoroughly enjoyable hokum. Edge wears his Hopkins learning lightly, avoiding didacticism or handholding... A merry page-turner
The Spectator

A deft fusion of genuinely funny writing and deeply poignant drama
Daily Express

A funny, genre-fusing page-turner
Attitude

A witty satire... By turns gripping and laugh-out-loud funny
Press Association

I love this novel. It pulls off the three-card trick of being entertaining, genuinely touching and a fascinating insight into Gerald Manley Hopkins' poetry
Harriett Gilbert

The Hurtle of Hell

Gay, pleasure-seeking Stefano Cartwright is almost killed by a wave on a holiday beach. His journey up a tunnel of light convinces him that God exists after all, and he may need to change his ways if he is not to end up in hell.

When God happens to look down his celestial telescope and see Stefano, he is obliged to pay unprecedented attention to an obscure planet in a distant galaxy, and ends up on the greatest adventure of his multi-aeon existence.

The Hurtle of Hell combines a tender, human story of rejection and reconnection with an utterly original and often very funny theological thought-experiment. It is an entrancing fable that is both mischievous and big-hearted.

A clever and enchanting fable
The Lady

Simon Edge has given us a creator for our times, hilariously at the mercy of forces beyond even his control
Tony Peake

An interesting and funny theological thought-experiment
Attitude

Edge delivers a warm-hearted narrative of redemption that's never judgemental but is inclusive, funny and undoubtedly heretical. Read it or burn it, depending on your sense of humour
Gscene

Wonderful... frequently hilarious... this thought-provoking exploration of homosexuality, atheism and God with a telescope is a delight
NB magazine

A Right Royal Face-Off

It is 1777, and England's second-greatest portrait artist, Thomas Gainsborough, is locked in rivalry with Sir Joshua Reynolds, the top dog of British portraiture.

Gainsborough loathes pandering to grand sitters, but he changes his tune when he is commissioned to paint King George III and his family. So who will be chosen as court painter, Tom or Sir Joshua?

Two and a half centuries later, a badly damaged painting turns up on a downmarket TV antiques show being filmed in Suffolk. Could the monstrosity really be, as its owner claims, a Gainsborough? If so, who is the sitter? And why does he have donkey's ears?

Mixing ancient and modern as he did in his acclaimed debut *The Hopkins Conundrum*, Simon Edge takes aim at fakery and pretension in this highly original celebration of one of our greatest artists.

One part mystery, one part history, one part satire, and wholly entertaining. A glorious comedy of painting and pretension
Ryan O'Neill

A laugh-out-loud contemporary satire skewering today's tired reality TV formats married with a tale of vicious rivalry
Liz Trenow

I enjoyed this beguiling book very much. Beautifully managed and brilliantly resolved
Hugh Belsey

The more of Simon Edge you read, the more you realise that every element of his stories is hand-selected and glued to the bigger picture – it's whimsical, farce-like…scrapbooky, in the best possible way
Buzz Magazine

Anyone for Edmund?

Under tennis courts in the ruins of a great abbey, archaeologists find the remains of St Edmund, once venerated as England's patron saint, but lost for half a millennium.

Culture Secretary Marina Spencer, adored by those who have never met her, scents an opportunity. She promotes Edmund as a new patron saint for the UK, playing up his Scottish, Welsh and Irish credentials. Unfortunately these are pure fiction, invented by Mark Price, her downtrodden aide, in a moment of panic.

The only person who can see through the deception is Mark's cousin Hannah, a member of the dig team. Will she blow the whistle or help him out? And what of St Edmund himself, watching through the prism of a very different age?

Simon Edge pokes fun at Westminster culture and celebrates the cult of a medieval saint in another beguiling and utterly original comedy.

I loved this smart and divinely wry book. What a terrific eye and ear is at work here!
Elinor Lipman

A sharp-edged political comedy guaranteed to make you laugh out loud
The i Paper

Hilarious and painfully believable
The Lady

A dose of history with flawless comedic timing and pacing
Foreword Reviews

The perfect pick-me-up. Funny and uplifting
Waitrose Weekend

If you have enjoyed *In the Beginning*, do please help us spread the word – by putting a review online; by posting something on social media; or in the old-fashioned way by simply telling your friends or family about it.

Book publishing is a very competitive business these days, in a saturated market, and small independent publishers such as ourselves are often crowded out by the big houses. Support from readers like you can make all the difference to a book's success.

Many thanks.

Dan Hiscocks
Publisher
Lightning Books